KILL KARMA

KELLY L. MARSH

Published by Jellyrum Press
www.jellyrumpress.com

This book is a work of fiction. Names, characters, businesses, organizations, places, events, and incidents are either products of the author's imagination or, if real, are used fictitiously. All the characters in this book are fictitious, and any resemblance to actual persons, living or dead, is entirely coincidental.

KILL KARMA
Copyright © 2021 by Kelly L. Marsh.

All rights reserved. No part of this book may be used or reproduced in any manner without the publisher's written permission, except in the case of brief quotations embodied in critical articles or reviews.

Cover designed by MiblArt

ISBN: 979-8-9850331-1-3 (Ebook)
ISBN: 979-8-9850331-0-6 (Paperback)

Printed in the United States of America.
First edition: October 2021

*For my mom and
best friend, Ellen.*

*Thank you for always believing in me,
even when I didn't, and teaching me
that the sky's not the limit.*

CHAPTER 1

O n the perimeter of a dilapidated marina and directly behind a NO TRESPASSING AFTER DARK sign, the branches of a honeysuckle bush rustled as Pepper crouched down further and scooted back as far as she possibly could within the unchecked flora.

One more inch back, and she'd be knocked out of hiding, exposed, her bum firmly planted on the creaky wooden planks of a pier. Scant feet behind her and the row of hedge bushes providing her shelter, the foul-smelling water of the Naples Bay lapped at the seawall, the murky water as black as the night sky above.

While impatiently waiting in her hiding spot, Pepper triple-checked her surroundings to make sure the area was indeed vacant before anchoring her eyes on a lone bench, drenched in darkness, that resided outside the doors of Tin City. A thriving fish-processing plant in the Roaring Twenties, Tin City, over time, morphed into a waterfront marketplace filled with local mom-and-pop shops. Come nightfall, Tin City closed its doors for the night, making it the Goldilocks of dead drop spots.

When Pepper's phone buzzed unexpectedly from the back

pocket of her black pants, she nearly jumped, her nerves beyond frayed. Her fingers couldn't answer the call fast enough.

"Hey, sleepyhead. Sorry to disturb your slumber going on, oh, three hours now. You mind calling Kimball and telling him to stop *exploding up* my phone?"

"It's *blowing up* my phone, Pops—Wait, why is Kimball calling you?" Pepper whispered, confused.

"Beats me. Said he's been trying to call you, and you won't pick up. I told him you're exhausted, have finals fatigue, and have been sleeping most of the evening away. Then he insisted I check on you—"

"N-n-no need for that, Pops. I'm"—Pepper faux yawned—"I'm getting up. I promise. Was up all last night studying and then all the tests today—"

"I know, I know, kiddo, which is why I haven't bothered you. But the night isn't getting any younger, and we have to get up at the crack of dawn for that final appointment with your probation officer before I leave for Miami. After tomorrow, we can finally put this whole horrible year behind us and start a new chapter. *That* is cause *enough* for celebration, but the window for celebrating is narrowing by the minute, so get your tush out of bed already."

"Fine. I'll be out in a few minutes. Just let me wake up and de-crankify."

Headlights sliced through the inky-black night, their trajectory creeping ever closer to Pepper's stakeout location. Panicking, she balanced the phone on her shoulder, her ear pressed against the hot screen, as her trembling hands excavated night-vision binoculars from inside her satchel.

The moment the vehicle came into focus, her jaw clenched as pure fear took hold. *Oh, no-no-no! This can't be happening!*

"Pepper, you there?"

"Uh-huh," she replied, her voice shaky.

"One more thing before you hang up. Kimball asked me to tell you to say hello to Savannah for him. Who's Savannah?"

A chill washed over Pepper, which was at odds with the beads of sweat on her skin from the sticky ninety-degree weather outside. In hindsight, wearing a mask and long sleeve pants and top in oppressive Southwest Florida heat probably wasn't the wisest of decisions, but she couldn't chance being spotted.

"No clue. He's probably drunk. Gotta go." Her shaky fingers ended the call and promptly powered off the phone.

Ever so slowly, the squad car stalked towards the marina and purred by the thicket of honeysuckle bushes.

Terrifying thoughts ran on a loop through her mind: *What if Kimball ratted me out? What if I get arrested for breaking curfew?* The judge had delivered a stern warning that should he see Pepper Bell's face in court again, he wouldn't be so lenient the third time around.

After lowering the car's windows, the cop swiveled his Maglight back and forth. The cone of light swept Pepper's way and halted on her hiding spot. She held her breath and didn't dare move a muscle.

An escape plan hatched in her mind. She could jump in the bay and swim to the other side, to Kelly's Fish House. The distance was five minutes by bike from the marina and over Tin City Bridge to the restaurant. But could she hold her breath long enough underwater to avoid detection? Either that or juvie. She could already hear the gavel slamming down, same as the bars on her jail cell.

Now or never! On the count of three. One, two—

From inside the cruiser, Pepper heard a communications officer dispatch the cop to a domestic disturbance. He goosed the squad car's engine, tires spitting gravel, and then disappeared down a side street. Breathing a sigh of relief, Pepper shucked off the sweat-logged ski mask. The brine-laced trade winds went to work blow-drying her damp face.

As per the PGP-encrypted communiqués between Pepper and her karma-for-hire client and classmate, at precisely eight-thirty (ten minutes ago!) Savannah was to retrieve the heisted item from underneath the west-facing bench outside the doors of Tin City.

Gravel crunched as the wheels of a Volvo skulked into the vacant lot. Savannah's flaxen locks billowed in the breeze as she made her way westward to the dead drop. While mock tying her shoelaces, Savannah's free hand deftly swiped the heisted flash drive taped underneath the bench.

A smile tugged at the corner of Savannah's lips while perusing the note attached. No doubt she silently celebrated the fact that, thanks to Pepper, she was finally in possession of a key piece of evidence that would help prove her father's innocence in his ongoing criminal trial.

Once Savannah's Volvo was out of sight, and the coast was clear, Pepper jumped on her beach cruiser and hightailed it home, pedaling faster than the bike could handle. Her impatient dad would only ignore the DO NOT DISTURB sign dangling from her doorknob for so long.

Pepper's blunt bangs caked to her forehead as a stream of sweat coursed over her brown skin. A quick swipe with her forearm and she flicked the perspiration away. In Pepper's neck of the woods, the dog days of summer were in full swing, the salt-laced air sticky and humid.

After breezing past the 7-Eleven, the only convenience store for miles, and its perennially sand-drenched terrazzo floors, courtesy of beach bums and surfers galore, Pepper was welcomed home by Aqualane Shores. The quaint community, located a stone's throw from the pristine beach, mimicked the shape of splayed fingers. Occupying the negative spaces were canals that provided direct access to the Gulf of Mexico. In other words, a boat lover's dreamscape.

After veering onto her street, flanked by shady pongam trees that provided shelter to a chorus of cicadas, Pepper bicycled into her next-door neighbor's driveway and secreted the beach cruiser in a row of Surinam cherry bushes that served as a barrier between the two properties. Before sprinting to safety, Pepper scouted the area for police, her pops, anyone.

Ample buttery light choked the inside of the charming mid-century modern rambler Pepper called home, which was one of a handful of relics left standing, echoes of 1950s Olde Naples. Newly constructed mansions bookended the dwelling or derivative monstrosities, as Pepper's pops called them.

Pepper's five-foot-seven frame tiptoed along the fringe of the horseshoe-shaped driveway, past the retro porte cochère to her left, which cradled an absurdly adored, wood-paneled 80s station wagon named Lola. Her dad's pride and joy was quite the gas-guzzling eyesore.

Pepper stole inside her bedroom window, practically hugging the deep-water canal. The sailboat currently occupying the rental space danced on the balmy current. A gentle, rhythmic clanging sounded as her hull gently *tap-tap-tapped* the sea wall, her halyards tickling the masts.

Right as Pepper popped the screen back into place, her head mechanically craned upward as if sensing she was being watched. Her downturned eyes locked onto her next-door neighbor, Kimball Garcia, who caught her red-handed, breaking court-ordered curfew and violating the terms of her probation. Limned in an eerie blue glow, he lorded over her from his balcony, his lips forming a dash, one eyebrow cocked.

Pepper cast a "mind your own business!" glare his way, then snapped her blinds shut. Still, Kimball always got the last word. He didn't drop a dime on her to the cops, or her pops, which meant he wasn't done with her yet. Well, she'd worry about that later.

She shrugged out of her ninja get-up, threw on the standard Naples wear—flip-flops, spaghetti-strapped tank, and short shorts —then opened the door slowly and peeked down the hallway and into the living room. Everything appeared to be copacetic. Her pops, Larry, was parked on the sofa, with his paramour du jour draped over him like a beach blanket; both were glued to the TV, waiting for late-breaking updates on the sensational murder trial that had been one of the most closely watched cases in Collier County history.

Shoes flip-flopped along the pearly-white tile as Pepper bypassed a bathroom, then the wall of Bell family photos. Umpteen framed pictures of the ebony-maned teenager and her dad devoured the length of the wall. Pepper and Larry picnicking at the beach. Pepper posing with a freshly caught snook from one of their many fishing excursions. The Bells at their favorite gun range. Yearly father-daughter trips to Disney World.

Pepper halted behind her dad and Penny, anxious to hear the updates herself.

The nightly news correspondent said: "WBBS is on the scene at the Collier County Courthouse complex, where residents and case followers alike have been picketing for hours and vocalizing their sheer outrage over the verdict delivered a short time ago. In a shocking twist, a grand jury found first-degree murder suspect Miles Leagan not guilty. The victims' loved ones are beside themselves with abject grief and dismay. They've bemoaned the injustices over how the trial played out, some even referring to the trial as a three-ring circus where the magician placed the rule of law into his top hat. An abracadabra later, justice vanished without a trace."

The news replayed a snippet of Miles as he exited the courthouse with his attorneys. The female correspondent, her cameraman right on her heels, followed Miles to an SUV idling curbside. She thrust a microphone into Miles Leagan's cadaverous, pockmarked face, thwarting his attempt at jumping into the backseat. "Any comment, Mr. Leagan?"

Staring right into the camera, Miles Leagan said, "Karma is dead," his lips pulling back in a sneer. Chuckling, he dove inside the vehicle, and the SUV sped away.

That cryptic statement caused goosebumps to hatch along Pepper's arms. A beat later, an electrical twinge zapped through her wrist. On autopilot, her other hand wrapped around her aching wrist, and her thumb got to work massaging the area. The pain vanished just as quickly as it had appeared.

Lobbing curses at the verdict, Larry slammed his thumb on the remote to mute the TV. "I tell ya, Penny, Lady Justice must be on an extended furlough. That man was the very definition of guilty. They caught him red-handed at the scene of the crime, for cryin' out loud. Literally. His hands were blood-soaked, the dead bodies were next to him, and yet the jury, clearly comprised of oxygen thieves, found him not guilty? Are you kidding me? I tell ya, the world's gone to pot." Her dad was onto something. *That* Pepper couldn't deny.

Larry depressed the mute button on the TV, and the nightly anchor continued reporting: "... five females between the ages of nineteen and twenty-five have disappeared within the last week from Collier County. Police are searching for the latest missing female." A picture of a white-skinned girl with lavender hair, the Naples Pier in the background, filled the screen. "Leslie Conway, a student at Edison Community College, was last seen leaving the Coastland Center Mall on Thursday around five in the evening. Anyone with any information on Leslie's whereabouts is urged to call the Collier County Sheriff's Office hotline."

"I've had it. That's enough news for the night!" With that, Larry turned off the TV.

Banners festooned the wall of glass sliders that opened up onto the expansive screened lanai: HAPPY BIRTHDAY and CONGRATULATIONS, they screamed. Pepper's heart melted when she eyed a cake lording over the dining room table to her right. A carrot cake mantled in cream cheese frosting, her absolute favorite and from her favorite restaurant, too—Truffles. *Soon you'll be reduced to crumbles, cake!*

When Pepper cleared her throat, Larry jumped to his feet, and said, "'Bout time. I was *this close* to getting you out of bed? You certainly slept late enough. Y'know, when I was your age, I had two jobs. Mowed lawns, delivered papers ..."

By rote, Pepper lip-synced her pop's meaningful diatribe. If he only knew how his daughter made serious coin. "Yeah, yeah, well, I'm a teenager. Sleeping every available minute, it's what we do."

Larry sprinted into the kitchen and grabbed matches off the bar. Candles were no sooner flickering. Larry, Penny, and Pepper gathered around the oblong table, bracketed by the living room and kitchen. "… happy birthday, dear Pepper, happy birthday to you." The fifty-something male with a rather pronounced gut sharply inhaled, then continued on crooning. "… for she's a jolly good fe-ell-loooow, which nobody can deny!"

"My birthday, well, technically tomorrow, high school graduation, last day of probation—it's like the hat trick of awesome!" Pepper whipped her long ebony mane into a messy bun before blowing out all seventeen candles.

Two loping steps later, Larry was in the living room. His thick limbs ambled across the beige carpet to an entertainment center that spanned the length of the far wall. Once the needle on the retro turntable licked the surface of one of Larry's vast collection of vinyls (those newfangled iThingies were way too complicated for him) a soulful rendition of *You Are My Sunshine* filled the airwaves. This was their song since she was a little girl when she'd stand on her daddy's feet as he twirled them around the living room and serenaded (off-key) the light of his life.

Larry extended his hand to his daughter. "Do me the honor?"

Head cocked, Pepper side-eyed Penny and sighed. Dancing was their thing, not a performance for her dad's latest girlfriend.

Realizing her pops wasn't about to budge, she eventually gave in. She kicked off her flip-flops and twirled into her father's loving arms. Crooning along to the song, Larry leading, they waltzed about the truncated space to the countrified ballad, artfully avoiding two sofas, a coffee table, and a recliner abutting the wall-to-wall sliding glass doors.

He dipped a laughing Pepper. The crow lines grafted about his hazel eyes crinkled as he smiled, then pulled her upright before landing a kiss on her forehead. "My little girl, a graduate, and a year early at that. Probation aside, I'm so very proud of you, kiddo. So proud."

After wiping away tears with his red bandana, Larry ran it across his forehead, then shoved it back into the pocket of his khaki cargo shorts. His brow had been cruelly flogged by the sun until it accordion'd from the pressure, his lips always thirsty for lip balm. A constellation of muted freckles dotted his ruddy complexion and splashed across his bulbous nose that Pepper *so* did not inherit, hers more of the button variety.

Another thing Pepper didn't inherit were her pop's eyes and hair color. His eyes were hazel to Pepper's brown, his dark blond hair shot through with gray, while Pepper's was black. As for Pepper's dimple, that wasn't a paternal trait either. Unarguably, Pepper favored her Filipina mother, who sadly passed away from cancer shortly after Pepper was born, or so the story went.

According to Pops, theirs was a whirlwind love affair, a ship romance. Though when pressed for specifics, Larry would clam up and act confused. Scratch his head. Then wind up flustered. Eventually, Pepper read between the lines. Their affair was more of the one-night stand variety that ended with a child. Regardless, Pepper rarely pondered the past, life being short and all. Besides, her mind was too preoccupied with all manner of vengeance. Between that and taking care of a father who was flirting with diabetes, her teenaged hands were rather full.

"Pops, what's with that dopey grin of yours?"

"Seems like yesterday you were crawling." His eyes lit up with joy. "You've turned into a beautiful young lady."

"Even though I'm a criminal?"

"Even though you're a criminal. Makes you well-rounded. Gives you the street crad."

"Cred, Pops. Street cred."

"Would you be a darling and grab us some bubbly before you open presents?" Penny interrupted as she ran her fingers along Larry's chest, playing with his exposed gray hairs and then his gold necklace.

"Sure," Pepper replied, her teeth clenched. She wanted for nothing but to smack away Penny's greedy hands and fully button her father's fish-printed shirt.

Three months and two days—that's how long it had been since Penny disembarked a cruise ship in Fort Lauderdale. Pepper waited with bated breath for D-day (tomorrow!), aka Penny's departure. And like all the other uber-rich women Larry "befriended" on cruise ships and brought back with him like a souvenir (though Pepper would've preferred a magnet), they, and Penny included, never overstayed their welcome, and would never become permanent fixtures. Because the free birds they were would inevitably answer the call of freedom. When the next world cruise hoisted its anchor, they too would spread their wings and sail away with it, right into the sunset. Bon voyage!

Pepper exited through the sliding glass doors and into the lanai. Square-footage-wise, the screened-in patio dwarfed the main abode. It housed not only a waterfront, kidney-shaped pool but a separate pool bath and sun-worshipping spot complete with chaise lounges. Then she ambled to the far corner of the screened lanai and landed in the art-cum-laundry room—a cabana detached from the main house. The air was redolent with creativity, that sadly went to waste, and commingled with the acrid odor of oils and acrylics and turpentine left behind by the owner of the house—Ms. Wilhelmina Davidson (Willa for short), an octogenarian who claimed domicile in Carmel-by-the-sea, California.

To keep rent on the cheap side, Larry served as a live-in home watch when he wasn't hosting on cruise ships. Hosting was how the pair, Larry and Willa, made their acquaintance and how Larry paid the bills and supported his daughter.

From time to time, Pepper sent Willa care packages laden with homemade cuisine and vitamins galore. Frankly, Pepper's gifts weren't wholly altruistic, if at all; it was imperative to keep the woman's ticker ticking so that a roof remained over the Bells' collective heads.

Besides, Pepper, quite the foodie, had a penchant for cheffing and what better way than to try out her recipes on Willa? Like lumpia. Willa specially requested that fried pick-me-up. Then nothing. Feedback on cheffing creations and lumpia demands stopped abruptly.

No news *was* good news, and the rent checks were still being cashed. Plus, Pepper couldn't dwell on trivial matters, not when she had bigger lumpia to fry, like dealing with an unfortunate arrest and court-ordered housebound-ness and other unpleasantries.

Pepper inspected the refrigerator reserved for beverages and yearned for alcohol of any kind—it had been quite the day. But the final drug and alcohol test tomorrow, the last time she'd have to report to her probation officer, squelched any desire she had of taking the edge off; failing equaled a stint in the clinker. So soda it was. After grabbing bubbly for those not monitored by a probation officer, Pepper meandered back to the celebration.

The group shuffled into the living room, then unceremoniously fell into plush sofas, their bellies bloated with carrot cake. As Larry unfastened the top button of his shorts, Pepper wasted no time in ripping open a galaxy of gifts. Clothes, more clothes, oh look, shorts, to gift cards galore were sprawled at her feet.

The pièce de résistance—from his index finger, Larry dangled a set of car keys. "Now Lola is officially yours till I get back. Please shower the wagon with love. Y'know, I hate having to leave you, Pepper, but the money's real good, and we have your college to think about, so—"

"Pops, stop nursing the guilt already. A few months is nothing. Seriously. I'll be fine. I've done it before. Not a big deal." Besides, Pepper already had tuition covered, thanks to her karma-for-hire business, a salient point unknown to Larry.

"It is a big deal. I'm missing your birthday tomorrow and—"

Pepper crossed her arms over her chest and raised an eyebrow.

"Okay, fine. Listen, I ran into Bunny Garcia earlier today and briefly mentioned I'd be leaving town and left it at that. She didn't ask where I was going, only said she'd definitely watch you, 'like a gargoyle' were her words, I believe. Between you and me, I think Bunny's self-medicating again. She was definitely off. Hope I'm wrong. Maybe *that's* why Kimball was trying to call you earlier. Anywho, should you need Bunny, she was emphatic that she wasn't planning on going anywhere, was here to stay. So, tomorrow before I leave ..." He continued to go over the forget-me-nots.

After closing her bedroom door, Pepper hotfooted it to her laptop to check on her funds. Savannah had deposited bitcoins into Pepper's wallet, the final karma-for-hire payment. Not too shabby. Larry might've had his jobs, but Pepper had her karma-for-hire business, which was a veritable cash cow.

The Chatnow app chimed on her computer. Against her better judgment, she accepted the video call. Her next-door neighbor's obnoxious mug hijacked the screen. "What do you want, Kimball?"

"We need to talk. So come over. Now."

"No!"

He waggled a ski mask, *Pepper's* ski mask, then played time-stamped video footage of her sneaking out of her house tonight and the night before and the night before that, and so on. To kick the intimidation up a notch, he played a recording of himself composing an email to Pepper's probation officer, and included the incriminating evidence within its body. All that remained was for him to press SEND.

Pepper's blood chilled. "I'll be right over."

CHAPTER 2

Pepper traipsed onto the Garcia's immaculately groomed property and scoffed the moment she eyed Kimball's newest toy—a cherry-red Ferrari 488 Spider.

Long, long ago, when Pepper and her next-door neighbor, Sheldon Kimball Garcia II, met for the first time when they were single-digits, they got on like a dream and, in no time flat, forged an inseparable bond. At least until the harsh mistress middle school drove a wedge between them.

Middle school, aka the institution where civility and compassion go to die. Sixth grade crushed Pepper's spirit, and it also marked the beginning of the eating of her emotions. Pepper had a lot of emotions to contend with. Couple that with a penchant for cheffing and, well, she practically lived in the kitchen.

Pepper's knuckles rapped on the glass front door of the Garcia's multistory modern monstrosity.

"Be right there," the matriarch of the manor, Bunny Garcia, growled.

In times past, Bunny took on a maternal role when Pepper needed it the most. So Pepper hoped her dad was wrong, that Bunny hadn't fallen off the wagon and returned to pill-popping and boozing.

Oh, dear Lord! Pepper's eyes pained at the horrific sight beyond the glass door of Bunny prowling along the marbled floor. Whatever ailment Bunny was in the throes of was far worse than Pepper and her dad had imagined.

Tonight, thirty-something Bunny wore not her usual body-hugging dresses that showed off her lean physique and breast implants, accentuated with high heels, but the standard-issue wardrobe of senior citizens found throughout Naples: clam diggers, a pastel-hued, too-big T-shirt, and bejeweled thongs. Her normally artificially tanned skin was looking rather pasty. As for the Southern belle's hair, usually held up by a can of hairspray—and that much closer to Heaven—well, tonight her locks were downright wretched and closer to Hell.

Perhaps this abrupt change in style was Bunny's Mayday call. There wasn't an occasion Bunny wouldn't dress up for, including a trip to the mailbox at the end of her driveway. Either way, Larry had called it; Bunny's days of sobriety were over all right. Pepper's heart hurt.

The door spun ninety degrees on its axis, granting Pepper passage. "Pepper Bell. Neighbor." As her head canted, bunny's tone was stiff like an automaton. In fact, Bunny spoke as if recalling a memorized dossier.

As Pepper stood in the foyer, Mrs. Garcia eye-groped and sniffed her as if Pepper were the main course and Bunny wanted nothing more than to devour her whole.

"Uh, Mrs. Garcia, hi, I'm just here to have a word with Kimby, so—Ow!" What felt like razor burn on top of a wicked sunburn erupted on Pepper's wrist, the same wrist that had hurt earlier. Only this time, massaging her wrist didn't chase away the agony.

Bored already, Bunny directed her attention elsewhere and spun on her heel, scurrying and disappearing into the dark kitchen.

Just like that, the agonizing pain stopped, leaving a few electrical twinges in its wake. While breathing a sigh of relief, Pepper said loud enough for Bunny to hear, "O-kay, I'll just show myself to Kimball's bedroom, then."

The Garcia residence wasn't so much a home where one could kick up her feet and relax so much as a showcase for modern wares, like a museum. Pepper always envisioned a DO NOT TOUCH sign looming near all furnishings.

Rabid art collectors, the Garcias had rather eclectic tastes. Soviet agitprop artwork dominated the limestone walls. Pepper never failed to go all goosey, feeling as if the cold and austere renderings of the iconic hammer and sickle spied her every move, waiting for the slightest of missteps, then off to the gulag she'd go. The Garcia chateau—strike that. The Garcia's palace was fit for a Bolshevik.

Paradoxically, the patriarch and first-generation American Sheldon "Shelly" Kimball Garcia I wasn't Russian but of Cuban descent, whose mother escaped Castro's dictatorial regime and built from the ground up a lucrative real-estate empire, which she bequeathed to her first-born son upon her untimely death.

On the second floor, the catwalk, lording over the great room, carried Pepper to Kimball's wing of the palace. Before she could knock, the door whipped open. Kimball, reeking of Johnnie Walker upon first breath, ushered her inside. "Hurry up!" Those bloodshot, dung-colored eyes of his appeared to be teetering on the event horizon, contemplating jumping out of their collective sockets. "Watch out for the salt!" Pepper jumped over the threshold before he whipped his head left and right.

After gingerly securing the door behind him, Kimball poured the contents of a tube of table salt along the threshold, repairing what Pepper had disturbed when she'd crossed it. Then he rested his weary body against the frame for a beat and said, "Phew! That was a close call."

On the far side of his majestic two-story lair, he plopped down in an office chair and got busy rolling what was most likely not the first joint of the night. The room, mantled in reds, blacks, and greys, was awash in an eerie blue hue that spilled forth from several large computer monitors—monitors focused on all manner of Bunny.

After shoving myriad dirty clothes aside, Pepper sat down on the ripe-smelling bed. A miasma of incense, marijuana, candle wax, ripe BO, and alcohol suffocated the airwaves and assaulted Pepper's senses.

"You in the midst of a bender? Because that would be the only logical explanation for the creepy paranoia."

Empty liquor bottles peppered the shag carpet. A dusting of residual white powder marred a nightstand. Kimball, too, was in disarray. His curly, sunflower-hued locks with black roots shining through were an ungoverned, righteous mess. Peachy fuzz colonized his jaw. His eyes direly needed de-puffing.

"What do you want, Kimby?" Pepper barked, her patience running on empty.

"For starters, holster the judgy tude," Kimball snapped.

Pepper shuffled to the door in a huff.

"If you walk out that door, I'll click send."

Pepper's hand froze on the door's latch.

"Bell, I'm not bluffing."

Pepper sighed, pivoted on her heel, and walked toward Kimball.

Scads of photos incriminating Pepper flickered on the computer screen, proof positive that she'd violated probation. "Exhibit A. With Savannah's case alone tonight, you've racked up quite the impressive amount of criminal offenses, all felonies, I might add. B and E, cell phone pilfering, breaking court-ordered curfew, grand larceny. Need I go on?"

Pepper's heart rattled against her rib cage, like a prisoner trying to escape its cell. A foreshadowing of her future should Kimball rat her out to her PO.

"Well, your silence speaks volumes." He wrapped his lips around a bottle and drained the dregs of amber-hued liquid within. "Finally, I come face-to-face with the storied Alonzo Steele," Kimball said, his slurring becoming more pronounced.

"What, was your 'blackmailing' me, and that's not an admittance of any wrongdoing, by the way, some elaborate ploy to get me to come over to your room because you can't bear to party alone?"

"Don't flatter yourself, Bell. Clearly, I'm fine all by my lonesome." His heavy-lidded eyes sailed lazily across the space, then back to Pepper, where they adventured downward, appreciating her from head to toe. "My, my, it appears as if the constructive criticism I plied you with over the years has paid off royally. You've lost a shit-ton of pudge. Your dimple is more pronounced, too. Though you could stand to lose ten more pounds. If so, I'd totally salt your pepper. Y'know, if I didn't already know you. And you're welcome."

"Stay classy, asshole." Though Pepper fancied her average build, she took umbrage with his backhanded compliment and could feel her face screw up with revulsion.

Middle school was the whetstone to Kimball's blunt-edged tongue. Those three years enabled him to hone his innate ability to inflict razor-sharp cruelty to perfection, Pepper his target practice.

But he wasn't the only one honing a skill during those three long years. What began within Pepper as a savage hunger for vengeance only worsened with time, the why a mystery. Did Kimball's bullying serve as the catalyst for her unchecked urge for revenge? If not for Kimball and the other kids and their cruel remarks lobbed at Pepper, would she have discovered and tapped into her innate ability to exact vengeance on behalf of victims to restore balance to the Scales of Justice?

What started as harmless acts of karma, where Pepper would find clever ways to get even with bullies on behalf of her victimized classmates while sating her hunger for vengeance, organically transitioned into a lucrative enterprise. It turned out that sleepy Naples, Florida, was rife with the afflicted. So, a few years ago, around the age of fourteen, she started a karma-for-hire business online, her identity cloaked in secrecy.

Between that and word of mouth, soon business was booming. *Ka-ching!* Pepper's jonesing was under control and her clients-slash-satisfied customers, forsaken by the criminal justice system, reveled in watching acts of karma play out in real-time: their smug oppressors enjoyed freedom one day and were thoroughly decimated the next. Still, something felt off, was missing, like a phantom limb, there but not. If only Pepper could grab it and tap into it to round out her avenging skill set.

"Moving on. Moments ago, Naples High School's resident volleyball phenom, Savannah, posted a bevy of confiscated texts, pics, and emails proving her father's innocence, all the while incriminating the so-called victim, who is quite the mythomaniac, as it turns out. Consequently, a WikiLeaks-ish scandal's brewing on Naples Teen Scene dot com and every message board and social media site from here to Estero has blown up. Students are all atwitter. Tip of the hat to you, Bell." He pantomimed doffing an imaginary cap. "Or should I call you by your nom de guerre, Alonzo? That name alone is bandied about, spread around like an STD. Yet never discussed openly, only in whispers."

Savannah, like so many kids before her, had stumbled across the storied Alonzo Steele and "his" business listing on the virtual pinboard of Naples Teen Scene—a website set up to foster the development of entrepreneurship for young adults. Buried beneath the vloggers, crafters, writers, budding chefs, and artists, et cetera, et cetera, was an advertisement for AN EYE FOR AN EYE. For a fee, Alonzo Steele vowed to mete out justice, right the wrongs, rebalance Lady Justice's scales, play the role of karma.

After sniff-testing his clothes, Kimball shimmied into a bright yellow top, then clicked the mouse to snuff out the screen saver to reveal Pepper's e-store hidden discreetly within the Naples Teen Scene website. "As per the mission statement, Alonzo Steele will perform feats of derring-do, enter the line of fire, scale rafters, or parachute off tall buildings while escaping danger; nothing is off limits when it comes to vindicating his clients' honor. He vows to tirelessly toil the nights away until he serves the foe their just deserts. Tell me, Bell, what type of feats does one do while derring?"

"It's more of a colorful selling point, really."

"After emerging from his shadowy lair, Alonzo rights all the horrible injustices meted out to the citizenry … for a hefty fee. Not very altruistic of you, if you ask me."

"Well, nobody asked you! Besides, it's supply and demand in action. Dishing out karma's expensive. Between the countless hours spent strategizing, and the equipment needed, I—"

Pepper abruptly stopped yakking and mentally flogged herself for nearly exposing the proprietary methods of her enterprise. Pepper gathered all incriminating evidence on a perp and delivered it to her client, granting them the unique opportunity to act on the intel supplied.

"What I find curious is why you never went after the guys who treated you like a footnote. And there's been *a lot*, so checking off your unrequited love list should keep you busy for quite a while."

Breathing constricted, heart ticking fast, Pepper clenched her fists by her side. She harkened back to her dad's advice whenever she'd cry over a boy: *Do you think he frets over you nightly, Pepper? Cries himself to sleep? Or even wastes one minute thinking about you? No! So don't you waste one more minute of your life obsessing over him.* Though his words came off as harsh, Band-Aid ripping was what Pepper needed to salve her wounded heart and help her move on. Until another boy caught her attention.

"Because there's no penal code for the crime of unreciprocated feelings. So me going after them wouldn't befit Lady Justice," she replied.

"Fair enough. To think that none other than wallflower Pepper was behind the mask this whole time. Tsk-tsk, surely the Naples High geek squad will clutch their pearls and shake their fists at the Heavens—*why, God, why?*—when I shatter the image they hold so dear of their superhero vigilante, saving one pathetic life of theirs at a time." His index finger and thumb rubbed his chin.

"One click of the mouse is all it'll take for me to expose Alonzo's identity."

"I hate you!" Years' worth of tamped-down anger surged to the surface. "I worked my butt off to graduate early, and happily, after tonight, I'll never, ever be forced to look at your *ugly face* again. Mark my words, Kimby, karma might be sparing you her wrath, your elitist juiceboxer friends included, for the hell you've inflicted on your peers, but the same can't be said for me."

"C'mon now. You know damn well I'm far from ugly." A smirk touched his lips.

Pepper could feel an inferno igniting within—a vise clenching around her pounding heart. Myopically focused on harming Kimball, she plucked the first item within her reach and lobbed the empty whiskey bottle at his head. Kimball ducked and fell out of the office chair.

His bottle slipped from his grasp and landed on his chest, spilling its contents over his Polo. "The hell, Bell!"

Another empty bottle at the ready, Pepper raised it above her head.

"Stop, vile demon! Don't come any closer." He extracted a flask marked with a cross and lobbed its aqueous contents at Pepper.

"Holy water? Really?" Pepper wiped the moisture off her face with her hand.

"Nothing happened." Perplexity froze on Kimball's face. "You're acting kinda rage-y, so I figured the holy water would've burned you or something."

"While the idea of hurting you is alluring, I'll table it. For now! Explain to me why I'm here already." She'd laugh at his dramatics if not for the boiling anger.

Once his shoulders collapsed, he shrugged out of his shirt, chiseled chest on full display, then hooked a few strands of his hair behind his red-tipped ears. Pepper stared at him in disgust. His mane wasn't oh so lustrous like all the girls at Naples High seemed to think, but a cloud of chaotic tendrils, much like Shirley Temple in her prime, only messier.

He took a few calming breaths. "Your proclivity for violence is *so* not normal."

"That's debatable. It's not like I physically harm the perps, only because I can't. The law has my hands tied. Hello! But if I could with impunity, oh happy day. If you'd step out of your drug haze, you'd notice all is not well in the world. Every day, mainstream media showcases stories about the guilty getting away with murder. Naples is merely a microcosm of just that. Hello! Serial killer Miles Leagan, free as a raptor! I'm just doing my part to rebalance Lady Justice's askew scales. Besides, what can I say, Kimball? I'm just not a turn-the-other-cheek kind of girl."

Pepper figured that Kimball had already exposed the skeletons in her closet, so she hoped that by explaining her motives, perhaps Kimball would shelve whatever scheme he had up his sleeve and let her go home.

His corded soccer legs carried him past his ginormous en-suite bathroom and into the kitchenette, commandeering the opposite side of the bedroom, to grab a bottle of water. "Tell me, Bell. How are you any better than the abusers? Yeah, yeah, you give them a taste of their own medicine with your karma delivery service. I get it, but aren't you stooping to their level?"

"I've never purported to be better than them. Nor has that ever been my intention. People must pay the piper. And if I have to inflict pain and misery and take away that which means the world to them for that to happen, then so be it. But I have a set of tenets that I live by. I never strike first. And I only mete out punishments to the responsible party." There was a steely edge to her timbre, her demeanor bitterly cold.

"Dayum, Bell, what the hell happened to you? I mean, your dad's actually a nice guy who truly loves you, worships the ground you walk on." Bitterness tinged his voice with that last statement. "So, you have *that* to be thankful for. So, where does the rage originate from? I mean, it far exceeds the allotted amount of teen angst."

"Don't know, don't care. What do you want, Kimby, besides company? I'm tired, and it's been a long ass day." Fatigue strained her vocal cords.

"Fine. Even though house arrest has ended, I know that technically you're still on probation. And if you were caught violating said probation because of the felonious nature of the crimes you committed, i.e., grand larceny, along with the drugs that were found on your person at the time of your arrest—Oopsy, the onus of blame is on me for the latter. Anywho, as I was saying, as per the judge, should you violate said probation, he will immediately send you to juvie. No motions for continuance, gavel banged, case closed." He massaged his chin like a cartoon villain. "I'm willing to destroy the passel of evidence I've compiled against you, but on one condition. I need to hire you for an important job, where discretion is key. Only you'll take it on as pro bono."

"So, you're blackmailing me."

"Semantics. Will you help me with a dire matter or not? You know I possess not a quark of compassion, or so you've claimed. A borderline sociopath, I believe you've called me time and time again, so it should come as no surprise that I could press send on this email addressed to your probation officer and not bat an eye." The incriminating letter on the laptop glared menacingly at Pepper.

"Obviously, I'm here, aren't I?" Pepper's patience was threadbare.

Kimball scampered up the steps of a vertical ladder leading to a loft.

"Y'know, your mom's behavior earlier—"

"That thing *is not* my mother!" Looming above Pepper, Kimball's eyes glinted with fury beneath his beetled brow. Box in hand, he slid down to the ground.

Pepper was taken aback when she saw his bloodshot orbs

swimming in tears because, to date, she had never experienced Kimball channeling any emotions save jackholery.

Spinning on his bare heel, he wiped away the trace of humanity he had shed, then pivoted back. Graveness seized his features, and his body tensed with fright. "Tell me, Bell, do you believe in demons? In things that go bump in the night? Demonic possessions?"

"Wait! You're not seriously blaming demonic possession for your mom's … setback, are you?"

"That *thing* downstairs, it looks like her, but it's not. Don't believe me, watch this." Kimball replayed footage recorded earlier in the day of Bunny hovering outside his bedroom, her tongue flicking in and out, lips snarling, her body jerking.

Pepper was rendered speechless, her mouth agape. *The CCTV cameras outside the door of his bedroom and elsewhere made sense,* she thought.

In a graveyard tone, he stated, "I'm gonna need your unique flavor of expertise in proving that my father killed my mother and summoned a demon to hijack her body. Once you complete that task, you must avenge my mother's death."

CHAPTER 3

"*Y*ou expect little old *me* to go up against your titan father, *the* Sheldon Kimball Garcia the first, the number one ranked real estate agent and developer in Florida and third in the United States, who has more money and influence than God? The same Sheldon Kimball Garcia, who runs in the same circles as the Bonovese crime family, who have staked their claim in Miami, which is a short drive away, I might add?" After catching her breath, Pepper finished with, "You *are* on a bender."

Kimball ignored Pepper and continued on. "Or Shelly hired someone to do the murderous deed. Regardless, your unique expertise can aid in bringing my father down once and for all. My mom, she cared about you, Bell, and you her. You can't deny that. As for me, I've been nothing but a constant disappointment to her." He paused for a beat. "She loved me, in her own special way, I think, at least when Shelly's philandering didn't blunt her attention. When she wasn't turning a blind eye to that pain by popping pills. Turning to vodka to chase away the tears. Yet, she's all I have. Had. I don't even know anymore." His eyes reflected sadness, and for a moment, he resembled a lost little boy. "So, what say you? Will you help me find out what happened to her? Help me find *her*?"

"You really believe she's possessed? By a demon?" This bomb-shell was too much for Pepper to handle.

"Not just believe. I have proof. And, Bell, it's not just my mom. Coby's mom, Mrs. Olsen, she's morphed into a demonic Stepford-bot as well. So has Chad's dad"—he ticked off names with his fingers—"and Stephen's mom. Valerie's dad. Tracy's stepmom. Basically, my whole squad has at least one parent that's in need of an exorcism."

"In other words, most of the spouses of your father's business associates?"

"Yes! See, that's why I hired you!" He sported a wicked grin.

"You mean blackmailed." Pepper sighed, realizing Kimball would admit to no such thing and that he essentially had boxed her into a corner, her choices obvious: either she comply or go to jail. So, she reluctantly put on her karma-for-hire hat and got to work. "What I'm wondering is if these so-called possessions go beyond your dad's inner circle."

"Not sure. But I'll tell you this much. Demons have possessed The Real Housewives of Naples. Evil's afoot in our backyard, setting up shop, preparing, but for what? Bell, I'm freakin' out. Too scared to leave my bedroom, the better to remain one of the living. I mean, look at me." He pointed to his body. "What demon *wouldn't* want to occupy this Adonis-like vessel?"

Pepper's emotions were a tangle of confusion, fright, shock, disgust. "You mentioned having proof. When did you notice a change in Bunny? I mean, even I noticed your mom wasn't exactly herself tonight, but why go straight to demonic possession and not, say, drugs?"

"She's not abusing drugs!" he growled. "As for the proof. A few days ago, me and Coby, the entire gang, went boating. Before I left, Mom was in a cheery mood, was up and about, getting her hair did, applying warpaint. I overheard my father gifting her with a 'you deserve it' cruise around Marco Island aboard a char-tered yacht for her and her closest friends. The guest list amounted to the moms and dads of my friends I just mentioned and Coby's mom—she's the wife of Jeremiah Olsen, Shelly's real estate attorney and business partner. You've met her before."

Pepper nodded and made a hand gesture to get to the point.

"Okay. Jeez. Details matter here, Bell. So, it's like you said earlier. Everyone who went on the cruise has one thing in common: their spouses all work with my dad in some capacity. Coincidence, much? To further whet Mom's appetite, the menu for the VIP excursion consisted of massages on Keewaydin Island, followed by a five-course meal on the beach, yadda yadda yadda. Shelly's a pro at carrot dangling. But I digress. After sunset and dropping off the guys, I docked my boat and got to rinsing it off. Mom was already home from her all-day excursion, and, well, she stood on the edge of the seawall and gazed at everything like she had once been blind and was gifted with sight. It's a miracle! At first, I figured she had started popping pills again. Happened before. Who can forget my eleventh birthday party?"

Pepper visibly cringed, remembering the embarrassing spectacle that had caused her pops to usher a drunk and very high Bunny away from the kids.

"Yeah, that wasn't the case this time. Her eyes were vacant and soulless like all the other times, but they weren't my mother's eyes. There's not a life inside her, Bell, at least not human. And whatever is inside her, the way it looked at me … gives new meaning to the saying 'if looks could kill.' So, after taking a shower, I went to grab a bite to eat in the kitchen and, oh God—" Kimball dry heaved.

"What?"

"She was slurping blood from a raw flank steak. She, *it*, just about unhinged its maw like a boa constrictor before devouring the raw beef whole." Kimball got all goosey and retched again from the memory. "I felt sick and had to turn away, and that's when I briefly glimpsed her reflection in the glass door of the fridge, and she, it … shifted. Not sure what else to call it. Bell, I eyed an entity shifting in and out of her body, like it was adjusting itself, wedging deeper, getting comfortable. On the sly, I exited the kitchen and ran to my bedroom, then vomited. Later, Coby called me in a panic. Said his mother tried to kill their dog."

Pepper recalled the idle gossip she had overheard at school about her former classmate and Kimball's friend earlier in the day. "What about Slade? You didn't mention him or his dad, Erik. And what is Erik's connection to your dad?"

Kimball's sun-kissed face grimaced. "You must have heard." When Pepper nodded quickly, he cleared his throat and continued. "Slade's other dad, Kyle, is Shelly's wealth manager. And no, Kyle's husband, Erik, didn't make the charter guest list."

Kimball validated the gossip Pepper had heard and filled in some missing pieces. A few days ago, in the meat department at Publix, Erik had attacked an employee.

"Slade witnessed the whole thing. I saw the footage myself. He filmed his dad go from swallowing fistfuls of raw meat to snarling and jumping on an employee stocking shelves in the canned goods aisle. Bell, Slade's dad tore out a chunk of flesh on the dude's bicep and neck, fingernails ripping into him. And the aftermath ... oof. Like a clean-up-on-aisle-4-now mess. Blood spatter everywhere." Kimball then divulged the most chilling part. "The cell phone footage disappeared right as Slade and I were viewing it. Poof! Like it never happened."

In response to Pepper asking if someone else had witnessed the attack and where were the police, Kimball said, "Obviously, the victim did, and I'm sure there were other witnesses, but their minds have been erased, like the footage. As for cops, they never showed up at the scene. No crime, no cops, I guess."

Pepper countered with a slightly raised eyebrow and a head tilt.

"I'm serious! Go into our Publix, Bell, and see for yourself. It's weird. Like, *Invasion of the Body Snatchers* meets *Rosemary's Baby* weird."

From inside the box Kimball had procured from upstairs, filled with candles and creepy whatsits, he extracted a tome titled *Black Arts & Magic Casting for Quarterwits*. "The things you can find on the Internet. Anyway, I recited an incantation within this bad boy right after I caught a glimpse of the demon possessing my mother." He tapped the bloated grimoire. "I believe the protection spell for keeping demons at bay was written in a language called Laramaic. Thank God for phonetics. Neither here nor there. But the experience itself was about as creepy as you can imagine."

"Okay, playing along here. Let's say a demon's possessed your mother. Why hasn't she gone all *grrr* and demon-y like Publix Shopper Erik and, I don't know, killed you?"

"Oh gee, I don't know, probably because it CAN'T GET INSIDE MY ROOM! The spell, remember? Try to keep up, Bell." He snapped his fingers thrice. "This isn't amateur hour. I'm lit and am more alert than you, just sayin'. *Obviously,* I tested the spell out. Called that *thing*"—he vocalized the word like it was an expletive—"up to my pad and guess what? The spell worked! She, it, refused to cross the threshold. Wouldn't even open the door. Just stood there and glared into the security camera, vengeful wrath reflecting in its soulless eyes. Or maybe the spell was hogwash, and the salt's the key. No matter."

Kimball took a much-needed breath.

"I swear, Bell, that thing could see me through the lens. Its dead eyes met mine and wouldn't let go. Even narrowed its eyes when I blew raspberries at it. Had my father not've walked through the front door when he did, well, I shudder to think what would've happened. I mean, how long can I stay holed up in this bedroom? Spoiler alert: not much longer."

Pepper pinched the bridge of her button nose, trying to wrap her head around what Kimball had divulged. "Wait. Back up for a sec. Has your dad mentioned your mom's odd behavior to you? Said anything about it at all?"

"You mean during one of our nonexistent family dinners?" he harrumphed. "Whatever, Bell. We coexist, and that's about the extent of it."

Pepper realized that nothing had changed, that her relationship with her dad had remained night and day to Kimball's. "Why do you think your father summoned an evil entity and offered up Bunny's body for possession purposes? What's his motive? I mean, it's not like he got rid of her, per se."

"When Daddy-O closes a very lucrative deal, he sports this shit-eating grin. Well, he's exhibiting the same reaction now. Trust me. He's behind the demon summoning. As for motive, well, that's where you come in. Or I should say your special skills in all manner of revenge. I need you to put them to the test and prove Shelly's behind my mother's disappearance and the demon infestation menacing Naples. Bell, if anyone deserves karma's wrath, it's him. So, do you believe me?" His pathetic red-rimmed eyes beseeched Pepper to say "yes."

Pepper sighed. "I totally agree that's not your mother downstairs. But where would I even start?"

"Boat Captain Walt, aka the last man to see Bunny Garcia alive. I have a friend reconning his marina as we speak, so by tomorrow, I should have garnered more intel, like the best way for you to break inside and do some sleuthing."

"Understand this, Kimball. I'm not helping because of you or your unscrupulous tactics that strong-armed me over here tonight. I'm doing it for your mother." And avoiding time in juvie, if she was being honest.

To avoid being devoured by a blood-thirsty demon, Pepper decided it best to leave by way of pongam tree, a flash from the past when the duo were friends. Its foliage canopied the side of Kimball's balcony; not even a moonbeam could slip through and breach its leafy fortifications. Propping his five-foot-nine frame against the wide-open sliding glass door, Kimball stifled laughs while Pepper awkwardly attempted to gain purchase on a sturdy bough.

Pepper lobbed an eye roll his way while suppressing a laugh of her own. For a moment, she caught a glimpse of the Kimball she had once known, her childhood best friend, fragile and innocent. A blink later, that boy vanished, a broken shell all that remained.

"Hey, Kimby, in the future, when in need of a helping hand, sometimes a simple 'can you help me?' will suffice."

CHAPTER 4

"How does it feel to be freed from the manacles of the law?" Larry asked, reveling in the sight of his daughter grinning and giggling as they headed to Lola, resting in the parking lot outside the Collier County Probation Offices.

With that, the father-daughter duo had concluded their two errands for the day, the first being more delicious: newly minted seventeen-year-old Pepper getting her driver's license! So now she could legally drive. Her charge of Driving Without a License, stemming from her first arrest, on its way to being sealed. And fingers crossed, the felonious infractions would follow suit.

"Looks like your ride to PortMiami's here." A silver pickup truck pulled up next to them. "Try to have fun, Pops, will ya? Make new friends, but don't bring any home. Take lots of pics. Oh, before I forget"—Pepper swiveled on her heel and reached inside the backseat of the station wagon—"I packed a vitamin organizer and included explicit instructions for what to take and when."

Larry pecked his daughter on the head. "I promise to take all my vitamins if you do me a favor." He had Pepper's attention. "New season of *Gone Squatchin'* starts tonight. All I ask is you don't delete them from the DVR to free up space for your cooking shows."

"I won't. Promise. I'll even take it a step further and wait to watch until you return."

Larry smiled. "TV binge weekends with you are the best." He wrapped his arms around Pepper and delivered a fierce papa-bear hug. "I love you to the moon, to the stars, and to infinite galaxies and back, kiddo."

With her head buried in her pop's chest, Pepper replied with, "Ditto, and then some!"

"Should be back right after All Hallows' Eve, so stay out of trouble, will ya?" Larry opened the passenger door of the truck. "And one more thing. Wouldja mail the rent check? It's on the backseat. The rest's junk mail."

Pepper aye-aye-captain'd her dad and wished him a bon voyage. Out of her pop's eyeshot, she wiped away leaky tears.

After mailing the rent check at the post office, Pepper returned to Lola and fired up the engine. Her foot halted on the accelerator when phantom, incoherent murmurings commingled with the synthesized beats of the roaring radio. Pepper put the car in park and silenced the tunes.

The susurration continued beckoning her. "Open me," the disembodied voices whispered, as if trapped in an echo chamber.

Goose pimples erupted along her arms as she homed in on the whispers and then scooped up the pile of junk mail that Larry had tossed on the backseat. As she thumbed through the sheaf of envelopes and fliers, the whisperings increased several decibels. Warm. Warmer. Hot!

The loquacious culprit was none other than a curious butter-milk-hued envelope addressed to the Bell residence with no return address. On tenterhooks, Pepper examined the correspon-dence, flipping it back and forth, then held it near her ear as if it were a seashell. When the letter kindly demanded, albeit softly, that she opened it already, that time was a-wasting, Pepper lurched, her heart beating something fierce. She plucked the letter from its papery nest lest it become angry at her hesitation and clams up altogether.

An emblem in the shape of a broken infinity materialized at the top of the letter and floated above the parchment. The infinity symbol was intact, for the most part, until the line on the bottom left-side loop broke off, made a hairpin turn, and traveled in a forward linear direction. Unable to help herself, Pepper ran her hand through the space between the emblem and the paper and felt a tiny shock of electricity as the broken infinity tumbled, then righted itself.

Pepper's eyes nearly barreled out of their sockets. Squaring her shoulders, she barely wrangled calmness as she read on.

Dear [name redacted],

Greetings, Initiate! Destiny has called upon you to answer an unparalleled calling to become an Agent of Karma—a sisterhood of assassins, who, since time immemorial, have worked under the auspices of Goddess Karma, their primary duty to assassinate those who pervert justice, the cruelest of the cruel.

We've been observing you for some time now, ever since your innate ability to engage in karmic acts of retribution was brought to our attention. So impressed by your skills and the palpable vengeance residing in your heart, we have been greatly anticipating today, your seventeenth year. And by now, you should have undergone your Awakening.

Goddess Karma and the Nine invite you to attend Karma Academy, where the elite in the field will train you in the art of vengeance, assassination, martial arts, deception, dark sorcery, necromancy, memory manipulation, spells and magic gems, and poison craft.

But, as with anything in life, the choice is ultimately yours to make. Should you decide to pass on the offer, may the grace of Goddess Seren be with you always in all your inter-dimensional pursuits and otherwise. Now, if this invitation to attend Karma Academy has at all piqued your interest, then continue perusing for further instructions.

Instructions: First, create a chaosgate. Chalk in hand, trace the outline of a door on a flat surface; a wall is most beneficial. Don't forget the knob or skeleton lock. To the best of your ability, render the Karma

Academy emblem in the exact spot where the door's lintel would be. (A way-sign is most imperative when chaosnauting, for, without a directional, Initiate, you could wind up lost in Witherwhere.) Next, color in the chaosgate's lock with your blood, for it is the only key that will unlock the portal. Once that's done, arrange the candles in a circle, then light the wicks in a counterclockwise fashion. By this point, the Initiate should be fenced within a fiery nimbus. At twenty-one hundred, not a minute before nor a minute later, chant the below incantation. Go-bag at the ready, sit and wait for your rukba to arrive.

Incantation:

I firmly believe that life isn't fair, and scores of injustices are too hard to bear. When envisioning oppressors bathing in the blood of the dead, my eyes drown in a sea of furious red. Nightly I dream of righting man's wrongs and delight in catching whispers of their erelong death songs. For born from the rage coursing within me is a manacled magic that yearns to be free. Alas, Karma, 'tis only thee who holds the key. I [insert name here] solemnly swear that my will is free, and all the above applies to me. With that said, Karma, I call out to thee.

Supplies needed: chalk, nine candles, matches (apologies for the obvious nature of what it takes to set a candle aflame, our meticulousness is to blame), a vessel of blood (a fair amount should do the trick, but not too much to trigger swooning), a sterile instrument for skin breaking purposes, e.g., boiled needle or athame as most mages already have one on their person.

On behalf of Karma Academy, we do look forward to making your acquaintance.

May Seren be with you always,

[name redacted]

Mouth agape, eyelids incapable of blinking, Pepper couldn't muster a thought or formulate a word, let alone string a cohesive sentence together.

After that spell of gobsmackery abated, her mind stilled, well, somewhat, and she whipped around, believing she wasn't alone. Kimball, the reigning lord of jackholes far and wide, had to've cobbled together this elaborate ploy to gaslight Pepper. So, was

Bunny in on the joke, too? Pepper spotted no one suspicious milling about the parking lot, just errand-runners. Then who else could have punked her? A former victim of hers?

Though a part of Pepper thought herself bat-guano crazy, a greater part resonated with the contents of the invitation. Decision made. Come nine o'clock tonight, Pepper was bound and determined to meet her destiny head-on. What was the worst that could happen? But first, she had to go see about a Captain Walt.

CHAPTER 5

W hips of lightning lit up the night sky, and cracks of thunder trumpeted the stay-inside advisory. Between the buckets of rain crashing down and the fierce swishing back and forth of the wagon's windshield wipers, Pepper could barely discern, even at idle speed, the twisting skinny roads.

She placed a prattling Kimball on speaker before resting the cell on her lap, both hands free to grip the wagon's wheel.

"According to my source, Walt has been on a fishing expedition all day, and Kurt, that's Walt's first mate, is currently a sozzled mess and singing karaoke at the Drunken Manatee. Even though the bar's within walking distance from the marina—scratch that. I guess everything's technically in walking distance within the borders of the redneck-choked neighborhoods. Point being, Bell, Kurt's not going anywhere, especially in this weather." Kimball sounded overly confident from the comfort of his bedroom.

Pepper was fully entrenched in Isles of Capri, a sleepy little community. In fact, the neighborhood was easy to bypass, as there was nary a sign welcoming visitors and strangers alike. Shoehorned within a pocket of the ever-sprawling Collier County, then shoved down even further into the out-of-reach areas, where it forever remained out of sight and mind, gathering lint. Which, truth be told, was probably a selling point to its denizens, who rather enjoyed the isolated hideaway encircled by bays and planned to keep it as such; further driving that latter point home was the absence of Big Business. Mom-and-pops dominated this community, scant though they were.

"If Walt's involved in the demonic possessions, there's sure to be some type of evidence left behind," Kimball stated.

"What, like an altar with blood and guts strewn about?" Walt's multistory dry stack marina rested on a tiny peninsula in the boondocks of Isles of Capri, at a dead end and perfectly isolated, surrounded by predator-infested canals and a tangle of mangroves, all the better for getting away with murder. Pepper's bowels gurgled something fierce. "I'm here. Only there's a light on inside, second floor." Panic strangled her vocal cords.

"Probably a security light. Nothing to worry about."

"Says the boy, who's safe and dry in the comfort of his bedroom suite."

"Less feck and more grit. Channel that inner moxie and make it peal, Bell—"

"Huh? Would you shut up already? I'll call you when I'm back in the car."

Pepper killed the engine at the boat-less wet slips, then crept to the destination, bypassing an overflowing canal, murky turbulent waters climbing onto the soil, ebbing and flowing. She sought shelter under an awning that ran the length of the towering complex. A deluge of rainfall pelted down on the corrugated metal roof, then tumbled to the briny soil.

Trapped between a curtain of water on one side and a windowless tin wall on the other, Pepper shuffled sideways along the makeshift trail. Blotted by rust, many sections of the oxidized tin structure were beyond repair, the brine-laced wind pilfering bits at a time, leaving behind bullet-sized holes.

She rounded the side of the building and spotted her way inside. Stormy winds battered and violently lashed out their fury on the door, its chains rattling in revolt. Pepper glided her average build through the cramped space between the door and frame. Once inside, she was greeted by a blast of cold air.

The dry marina was cast in an eerie glow, shadows crawling about every which way. Pepper surveyed the space, seeking a place to begin her investigation. It was more of a catacomb for boats, some suspended and stacked ceiling-high.

To her left and high above rested a glass wall, the perfect spot for a manager to oversee his domain. Before taking another step, she scanned the area for the stairs and spotted them off yonder.

Her sneakers squished along the cement flooring, so she rose to her tippy-toes. Right as Pepper placed her foot on the treads of the staircase, the unmistakable sound of a gun being cocked aborted her forward momentum.

CHAPTER 6

"Don't move a muscle," a man growled.

Pepper's body stiffened.

"Hands where I can see 'em."

Lips quivering, hands up in surrender, Pepper said, "There, there must be some type of mistake." Ever so slowly, Pepper pivoted to make eye contact with the gunman. "Kurt, he told me to meet him here. Y'know, for some midnight delight. We were just at the Drunken Manatee." *C'mon, buy the lie, whoever you are.*

"Nice try. You're not exactly Kurt's type. He doesn't fancy lady parts." He gruffly patted Pepper down, fishing her phone from her back pocket in the process, then pocketed it, her only lifeline, before jerking her one-eighty. "Head forward and don't turn back 'round again. Now walk."

"Walt, listen." She took a wild stab in the dark at the name of her captor.

He shoved the cold muzzle against Pepper's neck. "I said walk!"

At the landing, light spilled from the office. "Inside, go on. GO, I said!" He shoved the firearm against her back, applying ample pressure, prodding her like cattle. "The safe, over there, put the rest of the money in the duffel."

Pepper gave the office a cursory search in the hope that her break-glass-in-emergency would show itself. To the right of the rectangular space was the glass wall she had eyed downstairs. On the left was a safe, bookended by file cabinets, and a large duffel bag nearby. An antique-style desk fit for a gumshoe resided in the back, attached drawers on both sides, a kneehole in the center, though the back partition wasn't flush with the floor but contained a slit perfect for feet to jut out. Directly over the desk, a pendant dome light dangled from an exposed pipe on the ceiling.

No computer, which meant no VoIPing for help. But there was a landline, which meant she could dial Kimball. Then what? Her only option was to squeeze through the row of narrow windows up high on the wall and directly behind the desk—her sole ticket to freedom—but first, she'd have to distract this desperate man and then open a window in record time.

Pepper's heart panged with the realization that she was screwed! If only she were Alonzo Steele, a derring-do master. If only her mission statement wasn't jam-packed with creative lies.

"On the ground. Start emptying the safe. NOW!"

Pepper did as commanded and crouched down in front of the floor safe. Her shaky hands plucked up stacks upon stacks of money and placed them next to the duffel. An acrid odor assailed her the millisecond she unzipped the bag; distinct notes activated in succession, first orange, then java, and rotten eggs trailed behind. The scents amalgamated, then dissipated altogether.

"I told your boss no more. She said fine, just had to complete one more mission." Walt was frantic, talking a mile a minute. He swiped the gun against his scorched, sweat-beaded brow, a feral look painted about his mug. "That was supposed to be the last time. My stomach can't handle anymore. Yet the bitch sends you. What, to finish the job? Yeah, well, I beat you to the punch, now didn't I?"

He caught Pepper eyeing the rotary phone desk-side. "Don't get any funny ideas." After producing a utility knife from his jeans pocket, his portly body carried him to the desk, where he sliced the cord. His lips curled back in a sneer, remnants of tobacco chew coating his yellow teeth.

Pepper's blood chilled. "I have a curfew and parent who's waiting for me as we speak. You'll never get away with whatever you have up your sleeve."

"Darlin', these waters are bulging with alligators and bull sharks. Swimming around, chomping at the bit for the mother lode like you. They'd devour you whole, gristle, and bones and all. Then what? No body, no proof, no evidence, case closed. Besides, I'm currently stranded at sea. See, the motor died, and the storm dragged me further out, and what with no cell phone signal—alibi locked and loaded."

He acted as if his plan was foolproof, and it had been until Pepper came along. She was a loose end, and everyone knows what happens to loose ends—*Dear God!* And just like that, the pain in her wrist returned with a vengeance.

Pepper slowed down her pace to buy herself precious time. Because once the bag was filled, then what would become of her? Shark chum?

While trying to breathe through the throbbing pain in her wrist, she eyed a business card wedged in the corner. A blank card at that. Curious, she plucked it up, deftly slid it into her top, and nestled it within the confines of her padded bra.

Walt's frenzy mushroomed, which prompted him to commence a one-sided conversation. "Didn't want any more blood on my hands. So I bowed out. Just a few more times, *she* said, flashing more Benjamins, and I agreed. Couldn't say no to the money." His eyes glimmered with greed. "It was good. *Real* good. Paid off debts accrued, kept my business afloat, collectors at bay. Kept the missus off my back, shut her pie hole. The job itself was easy, at least in the beginning. Pickups were discreet. I'd track down the targets. Slip them a mickey here and there. Never an eyewitness to pin me. But I lived up to my end of the bargain. Followed my orders. So, how did it come to this? To her sending you to kill me?"

"What? Uh, that's not why I'm here! Wait, you have to hear me out!" Pepper panicked.

Howling winds sounded from the bowels of the marina. A beat later, the door creaked open. A phantom zephyr slithered in the room, gently tossing back Pepper's bangs.

Walt jerked his head toward the door. He hesitantly approached, stopping at the threshold. Gun at the ready, Walt peeked out into the blackness. Glancing back at Pepper, he barked, "Stay put, or I'll pull the trigger. Darlin', I've nothing left to lose, so that is not an idle threat," then walked onto the landing.

In a snap, the violent throbbing in her wrist stilled. Then, from inside her mind, a strange voice not-Pepper's demanded she follow his lead. *If you want to live, do not fight me.*

Her body rose of its own accord, a sensation akin to that of being immersed in a virtual reality world like she was merely a spectator smack dab in the middle of a battle scene. She felt her body being directed across the room, taking determined strides, and then squatted down within the kneehole of the desk on the grungy concrete floor and peered through a hole in the center meant for cords.

Get ready, the voice warned eerily.

Pepper replied with a gulp.

Walt about-faced and snapped, "Where did you go, girlie?"

A gun fired. But it wasn't Walt's. No, it belonged to whomever, whatever, the winds had delivered.

A pistol was trained on Walt, but only the arms of the one calling the shots were visible; darkness cloaked the rest. Stepping into the wan light was none other than a teenaged girl. A porcelain beauty with a utilitarian ponytail of ashen hair, hot-iron pressed, cascading down the back of her raven catsuit.

This girl didn't just possess a hint of menace; it was full-blown, like that of a seasoned killer. To give even more credence to her "you mess with me, you die" vibe, she was armed to the teeth, her body serving as an ambulant armory of sorts: sword strapped to her back, an empty holster on her hip, and another twined around her thigh, which held a skinny tube-like object. A blowpipe?

Icy blue eyes shimmering with homicidal intentions bore into Walt, and the message they channeled was received loud and clear. The missed shot moments ago was merely saber-rattling on her part, a warning for Walt to stand still and obey, or else.

But the not-so-jolly Kris Kringle doppelgänger refused to acquiesce and pulled his revolver's trigger. *Boom-boom-boom!* Bullets whizzed in the blonde's direction. She weaved her way effortlessly past every slug—left, right, falling to the ground and tumbling, every movement lithesome, supernatural. Kicking up to her feet, she crouched in a defensive position, ready to pounce.

Pepper's breath caught in her throat when she spotted the Karma Academy emblem stitched over the heart on the femme fatale's catsuit—the broken infinity symbol. Painted a neon violet, it crackled with energy, almost sentient, electrified even, like the thunderbolts outside tonight, whipping the darkened sky into submission.

Perhaps Pepper's break-glass-in-emergency had appeared, after all. A fellow sister-in-arms was here to rescue her. Ensure Pepper made it home with enough time to spare to recite the incantation necessary for transportation to Karma Academy. How very thoughtful, this ashen-haired agent.

But the mysterious voice within Pepper disagreed vehemently. *Tread lightly with this one. It's kill or be killed.*

The ashen blonde fired her Sig Sauer, and the bullet ricocheted off Walt's one and only line of defense, expelling it right from his grasp. Behind Pepper, the plate-glass windows shattered, a gaping maw of jagged teeth remaining. As Walt's gun skittered Pepper's way, she quickly snatched the weapon.

Planning her escape—and how to do just that without being seen?—Pepper figured it was now or never. Best to capitalize on those two fighting to the death.

The girl kicked the door shut and stood in front of it. "Ye know what happens to rats? They get eaten by cats. *Meow!*" The girl's posh British accent, coated in the finest of honey, belied the murderous psychopath within.

"I didn't tell a soul! I swear!" Walt already saw the writing on the wall.

The English Rose clucked her tongue as she extracted the blowpipe, wrapped her matte-red lips around it, then blew. A dart careened right into Walt's jugular. Bullseye!

While swatting his neck, clawing for whatever had pricked him, he crashed into one of the filing cabinets and held on for dear life to a flung-out drawer.

"Listen up, Walt. That nearly imperceptible needle-like dart possesses a pinprick of poison."

Eventually, his legs gave out, and he crumpled to the floor, bringing the cabinet along for the ride. Flat on his back, Walt clutched at his throat, eyes bulging.

"Poison, that'll constrict yer throat within a minute. Tick-tock. Tick-tock." As she strode Walt's way, the heels of her boots harmonized with her mimicking a clock. "Like a fish out of water, ye'll swallow air. Gulping like a clot. Oh, look, I do believe ye've reached that stage. Yay!" She demurely clapped her hands as if in attendance of an operatic performance. "Sloppy, sloppy, ye blubbery sod. Yer antics could've ruined everything." In a snap, her tone soured as she reproached Walt. "Mate, consider yourself a loose end. Snip-snip!" She pantomimed scissors cutting. "Couldn't wait for All Hallows' Eve, could ye?" Blondie clucked her tongue.

Walt had lost the fight and was under the blonde's designer jackboot as she loomed over his writhing corpse, a fact from which she derived great pleasure. "The fun part's right around the bend. Just a prelude to the full-body paralysis. Blood'll stop flowing any second now." Even her threats of murder had a dignified air to them, what with that prim-and-proper accent of hers.

"Eventually, the heart'll stop its beating. And ye might or might not be alive when yer bowels're voided, 'cause that's also a side effect of the poison, an inevitability. So, ye have that to look forward to, or not."

She placed the kitten heel of her boot on his Adam's apple and applied pressure. Walt choked in response.

"Now, now, Walt, I hear ye. Karma's a bitch. *I* should know; she's my boss. Now, now. Shh, shh. Stop writhing and let death take ye already. But not before I deliver a message from Boss Lady. 'Should've kept your goddamn mouth closed, and ye'd be home eating dinner with the fam right about now-oh-clock.' Walt, Walt, Walt. Did you really think ye could hide? C'mon now."

Walt's head lolled to the side, bulging bloodshot eyes latched onto Pepper's. Blondie toed his body to check for signs of life.

A puddle of urine pooled, and Blondie lurched backward. "Not on the Jimmy Choos! That was rude, Walt."

Pepper felt immobilized by the blonde's ninja-assassin prowess. Yet all the same, Pepper waffled with whether or not to tell her she was an Initiate, a would-be Agent of Karma.

But then the internal voice returned. *She's not here to rescue you, Pepper! One false step and you'll be wearing a Colombian necktie! Can't make that any clearer.* Was the voice's tone actually tinged with exasperation?

Decision made. Pepper would obviously wait it out. Wait for Blondie to vacate the premises.

The kitten heels of her boots slapped the concrete as she strode in Pepper's direction. Each step measured evenly, like the steady ticking of a metronome. Pepper's heart raced. Was there something on the desk that she wanted? A pen? Paper? *Oh, please let there be something and not someone.* As Pepper's mind whirled with scenarios, the blonde dipped down and peeked her cherubic face into Pepper's hidey-hole.

"What are ye doing down there, poppet? Upsy-daisy."

Play along, the voice ordered.

Pepper slipped the firearm in the waistband of her jeans and beneath her tank top, then scrabbled out from the kneehole. Keeping her back to the windowed wall, Pepper waited for further instructions from her keeper. *Now would be most wonderful, el capitan.*

"For what it's worth, I only destroy despicable ruddy blighters. Well, for the most part. And Walt fits the bill. Isn't that right, Walt?" Blondie looked Walt's way for a split second, then returned her attention to Pepper. "Guess he won't be answering." She tee-heed. "Poppet looks sad. Walt your lover?"

Pepper's face screwed up with abject disgust, seeing as Walt was a fifty-something countrified Santa Claus.

Pepper noted that the Karma Academy emblem was neither electrified nor dyed a fluorescent shade at the moment, but the faintest of black, almost like the storm had blown over, or perhaps Pepper was trapped in the eye and the worst was yet to come.

"Not lover, then. Dad? Uncle?" Her eyes demanded an explanation.

"I don't know the dead dude from Adam. And he was *this close* to whacking me, had you not've shown up." Pepper figured she could affect an air of toughness that smacked of, "Hey, I see death every day, no biggie," to walk the great divide from potential death—which was where she was currently hovering—to sisters-in-arms, aka precious life. And possibly toy with blondie's sympathies, if she possessed any to begin with.

"That so?" She canted her head slightly, a smirk splitting her face. "Say, what's your name?"

"Pepper"—she stalled for a beat—"Li." A sprinkling of truth ensured that Pepper's facial expressions remained neutral. Li was her middle name, after all. What if Blondie was a walking lie detector? Besides, giving out her last name would link Pepper to her dad, which could—*would*—put him in harm's way.

Her smirk straightened to a line. Recognition and confusion mixed in Blondie's eyes as she studied Pepper, a warmth ghosting over her otherwise icy demeanor. But a beat later, the assassin was back, scanning Pepper's being like a robot, determining foe or friend. Brows beetled as Blondie struggled internally with her verdict. "When ye hang out with rubbish, eventually ye begin to reek. And ye, poppet, stink to high Heaven. So, I'll ask ye one more time, Pepper, what is yer connection to Walt?"

"Do you recall what became of the curious cat?" *Pepper, one day that biting tongue of yours will come across the wrong person,* Larry had warned. Still, Pepper couldn't help it, couldn't suppress her sass. Potential danger be damned!

While waiting for a response, Pepper noted Blondie's eyes and how they mirrored Bunny's, as far as far-off-ness was concerned, save for the parasitic-ness; there wasn't a trace of that anywhere on Blondie.

The girl's matte-red lips twitched, a lopsided grin forming. "'Tis a pity, really. I rather fancy ye, but die ye must."

The emblem crackled to life, the broken infinity throbbing violet.

Blondie quickly drew her firearm at champion gunslinger speed and fired. As if time had slowed down to a crawl, the bullet careening through liquid, Pepper's body soared through the air. The internal pilot at the wheel of Pepper's mind had returned, Pepper's body the ship. Avoiding every blasted bullet, ducking, feinting left and right, Pepper somersaulted on the cement to break her fall, then jumped to her feet.

The feats of derring-do on Pepper's behalf sent Blondie in a fit of gobsmackery. For half a beat, she figuratively scratched her head and reassessed the target. "You sneaky minx. A mage, are you? Pocketing magic gems? What's poppet gonna do when those marbles run outta juice? No matter, the fun's been amped up." She bit her bottom lip and tossed a cheeky wink Pepper's way.

Pepper fast drew her revolver and made the last bullet count. She, or the pilot, leveled the gun on Blondie's Sig and fired. The busted gun was flung out of Blondie's hands, then tore out the room and *crash-bang-clang*-ed down the stairs.

Capitalizing on Blondie's smarting hand, scant blood dripping to the concrete, Pepper used the desk as a pommel horse, springing atop the metal surface, then sprung off. Soaring through the air, and directly above Blondie's head, and while airborne,

Pepper snatched the katana from Blondie's back, then unsheathed the gleaming blade in one fluid motion. Pepper's body tucked into somersault formation, to prepare for landing, and then whipped around. Once on her feet, her back to Blondie, Pepper twirled ninety degrees, brandishing the sword, ready for battle.

Blondie flicked her wrist and cast Chinese stars at Pepper. The take-no-prisoners sliced through the air.

The katana a bat, Pepper whacked the death-dealing devices and sent them barreling across the room where they wedged deeply into the ticky-tacky walls.

The blonde was PO'd. Like a bull, she charged at Pepper, emitting a creepy-as-hell battle cry. Turning the katana on its side, Pepper used the new position to thwart and deflect Blondie's swinging appendages.

But the blonde grabbed the serrated blade, her hands slicing, blood gushing from her wounds. The searing pain she must have felt didn't deter Blondie one iota, and she continued to struggle for control of the weapon. Eventually, she kneed the weapon out from Pepper's steely grip and sent it clanging to the cement.

Like greased lightning, Pepper sprang onto the felled filing cabinet, leaped to the exposed piping above. Then swung from pipe to pipe, monkey-like.

From below, Blondie fought to grab Pepper's sneakers, but to no avail. Pepper held on like a skilled trapeze artist, the pipe her swing, and kicked Blondie in the head. That did it! Untold fury seized Blondie's face.

Pepper flipped down on the desk, then wasted no time in swiping the coiled phone cord before pommeling off the desk and winging into the air once again. Mid-flight, Pepper dove over Blondie, wrapped the cord around Blondie's neck right as she passed over her, then cinched the cord tighter as she dropped to the floor.

Now facing Blondie's writhing back, she tugged the cord backward and held on for dear life. Blondie struggled, her movements enacting a deathly waltz; the Agents of Karma twirled and snapped around every which way, but Pepper got a good enough hold on the blonde and began to squeeze and squeeze, the blonde clawing the cord, choking.

Kill or be killed, the voice continuously warned.

Pepper's heart raced as she fought the compulsion to let Blondie live. In that split second hesitation, Blondie's willowy legs climbed the wall, then thrust her form over Pepper's, freeing herself from the coiled strangler. In a flash, the cord dematerialized. An act that rooted Pepper in place.

That misstep of Pepper's allowed a beet-red Blondie to gain the upper hand. She delivered a formidable swift kick right into Pepper's solar plexus, forcing a storm of air from Pepper's lungs.

Keeled over, Pepper struggled to breathe as Blondie stomped toward her. The blonde nearly upon her, Pepper connected an open hand right into Blondie's nose. Blood spurted, pouring down her catsuit.

"Oh shit!" Pepper's eyes widened in horror as the blonde's blood-soaked pillowy lips suctioned around the blowpipe of death. Pepper swung her leg in an arc and kicked the device right out of the blonde's mouth.

Both females were now weaponless. The stench of death and cordite choked the hushed air—air that was pregnant with the terrifying notion that only one of them would walk out of the dry marina alive.

Blondie was clearly bent on being the victor; the corners of her mouth turned up into a sinister smile, and her lambent eyes reflected a raging inferno. And that wasn't metaphorical. Flames literally licked her pupils.

In unison, their chests rose rapidly and fell as they sized each other up and contemplated making their next move.

Whatever, whoever had Pepper under compulsion didn't cotton to surrendering but employed a never-say-die attitude. Pepper caught Blondie's eyes latch onto the blowgun inches from the safe before averting them away just as quickly.

They both dove for the weapon. Meeting in the middle,

Blondie clotheslined Pepper, and Pepper fell to her knees. A move that allowed Blondie to put Pepper in a chokehold. Pepper kicked her in the shin and karate kicked the legs out from under her, sweeping her off her feet.

Blondie got right back up and flew into the air. She drop-kicked Pepper in the back, sending her flying into the wall.

Head smarting like a mother, Pepper blinked away afterimages, light occluding her corneas. Body revolting, every joint screamed in agony.

Get up and keep moving, the pilot barked. *There is no other option!*

Fear pummeled Pepper. She tried to squelch it, to suspend it, at least for the moment. But everything boiled down to this. Pepper wasn't ready to shuffle off the mortal coil. Sure, she might've been nearly knocked off and was hanging by its metal tip, but she was gonna climb that sucker to its very peak.

Blondie levitated shards of glass from the cement, then hurled them at her enemy. Pepper darted out of the way until one came within a hairsbreadth of her sweat-soaked face.

Her internal pilot fashioned a barrier, then willed the glassy instruments of death to do his bidding. *Change trajectory, change trajectory*, the voice willed the twenty-odd inanimate objects.

Acquiescing, the turncoat shards of doom boomeranged back to their creator. But Blondie's catsuit repelled them, and try as they might, they couldn't impale her. When she ducked, the remaining shards crashed into the pendant lamp, causing it to swing above the desk. The lightbulb exploded, and bursts of sparks rained down, wires now exposed. The acrid smell of electrical fire further suffocated the air.

Out of nowhere, the door next to Pepper's position slammed into the wall. An action that seized both girls' attention.

"Ooh, company," Blondie said through a bloodied lip. Pepper crabbed backward.

The interloper, a male sporting a jet-black leather hoodie and a menacing weapon strapped to his back, halted for a beat as his eyes surveyed the scene. The gleam of metal winked from inside his jacket, most likely belonging to a sidearm.

Just great! Blondie's well-armed backup had arrived. Wisely, Pepper stayed put, all the while awaiting marching orders from her internal captain.

The interloper, looming above Pepper, gave her a cursory glance, the firelight reflecting on the mirrored frames of his aviator sunglasses.

Blondie lobbed a litany of vitriolic expletives the interloper's way as she summoned the glass shards to rise and attack. Only her magic was spent, the broken infinity emblem flickering to off, violet-hued no longer, and the summoned shards tumbled to the ground.

They clearly weren't playing for the same team. So, who the hell did this guy work for?

Don't wait around to find out, the pilot snapped. *Could be an Agent of Death, for all we know.* That ominous statement got Pepper to her feet.

Expending every last drop of strength remaining, in short order, Pepper sailed to the felled filing cabinet, grabbed the abandoned blowgun, and tucked it into her waistband where it joined Walt's gun. "I'll be taking this back, dickwad!" She removed her phone from Walt's corpse.

From the top of the filing cabinet, Pepper leaped to the pipes, then climbed across them as if they were monkey bars, her movements swift and preternatural. Once she was close enough to the bank of windows, she made a leap for it and soared through the narrow, jagged-toothed maw.

On the corrugated roof, lightning whipping, rain pouring, she hazarded a glance back, a small part of her hoping that Blondie would emerge victorious. The stranger, haloed by the raging inferno, removed his shades, his eyes forged from every shade of green and blue found in the ocean's offing, met Pepper's. He removed a weapon that eerily resembled a scythe and raised it to its zenith.

At that moment, Pepper pegged him as Death incarnate. And when the voice within didn't beg to differ, her heart shuddered. Had she really escaped Death's clutches? Once Death had Pepper's undivided attention, he about-faced to Blondie and was moments from delivering the coup de grâce.

"Cheerio, poppet," Pepper said under her breath as she hitched a ride with the rain that surged down the slanted tin roof, then shimmied down a pipe and legged it to Lola.

JHI MADE no attempts to stop Sawyer when she bolted to her feet and elbowed Jhi out of the way, then scampered down the stairs like a cockroach. And just in time, too, for her catsuit's emblem fashioned from magic gem dust was out of juice.

Thank you, Sawyer, Jhi thought. A new lead just dropped in Jhi's lap—the ebony-maned girl with the whiskey-hued eyes, the girl he let escape.

Jhi extracted a vial from his jeans pocket. Once uncorked, a misty vapor escaped and hovered. After a few jerks and tweaks and twitches, the amorphous entity appeared as if it was being poured into a human-shaped mold, adult-sized. First, a set of legs materialized, then a torso, a neck, and head. The jinn resembled a human male, a few inches shorter than Jhi, about five-nine or so.

"Friday, shadow the girl. Read her. Find me an in. Then report to me. Go!" Jhi ordered his partner. The jinn saluted right before dematerializing.

Right as Pepper goosed the engine, Friday stole into the station wagon, sight unseen. From the backseat, he wrapped his ghostly arms around her head. Let the reading begin!

CHAPTER 7

Pepper thundered through the front doors of her home and glanced at her cell phone. 8:54. Luckily, she had culled the requisite supplies for tonight's sorcery. T-minus six minutes till showtime!

The phone chimed angrily for the umpteenth time, and Pepper clicked the F-you button for the umpteenth time. Talking with Kimball, the very Kimball who got her into this hellacious mess, was not on the agenda. Moreover, Pepper couldn't focus, couldn't muster the energy needed to explain what the hell had gone down at the marina. And she was still unpacking the occult-like happenings.

Fear, discombobulation, shock, adrenalin, this teenager was a tangle of emotions. Emotions that wrapped around her tighter by the second, constricting her, intricate knots forming. The only one who could unravel her was Karma.

Pepper desperately needed to explain the colossal misunderstanding to the goddess. Get her to call off the sisterhood of crazed assassins who were ostensibly on the warpath to kill Pepper. What, with Pepper trying to kill one of their own.

Karma Academy missive in hand, she perused the instructions for portal summoning, then paused with a niggling thought.

What if she was blindly walking into a deathtrap set by Karma? Blondie delivered a proxy message from her "boss lady" to Walt about how he should've kept his mouth closed. So, Walt, at one time, worked for Boss Lady. Blondie later admitted to dying Walt that Karma was her boss. QED, Karma and Boss Lady are one and the same.

Begged the question, why would Blondie stop at nothing to slay Pepper at the behest of Karma? The very Karma who hand-picked Pepper to attend her eponymous academy, to join the sisterhood of assassins? But then again, Blondie had been touched by crazy, or so it had appeared, deriving delicious pleasure from maiming, so perhaps her word wasn't the most credible. And where did Kimball's mother and father fit into all of this? Or demonic possession, for that matter?

A deluge of urgency to contact Karma ASAP assailed Pepper; her life depended on it. More agents could be on the way. Or that guy with the eyes resembling sea glass. Demons in search of fleshy vessels. With that, Pepper swift-kicked that pesky caution of a looming deathtrap awaiting her at Karma Academy to the wind.

Step one: trace the outline of a door, preferably on a wall. Her trembling hands struggled to hold on to the chalk, dropping it a few times. The end result wasn't exactly ruler-straight but a riot of wobbly lines—ditto for the Karma Academy emblem rendering and the knob. Hell, by this point, a three-year-old doodler would have put Pepper's artwork to shame.

All that remained was the universal skeleton lock symbol—a circle joining a long triangle; at least, that's what Pepper hoped the mystifying instructions had suggested. The finished product wasn't a masterpiece, per se, but it would certainly pass muster.

8:58

Next up was filling in the lock with her blood. Pepper winced as she sliced her flesh with the blade. Once she colored in the skeleton keyhole, her blood the medium, she sat on folded limbs in the center of her bedroom.

8:59

After striking a match, Pepper lit the cobbled-together circle of candles—votives, rotund bouquet-scented ones, bearded tapers—with the flame, all the while moving in a counterclockwise direction.

9:00

"… I, Pepper Li Bell, solemnly swear that my will is free, and all the above applies to me. With that said, Karma, I call out to thee."

Encompassed by a fiery nimbus, Pepper, wrought with anticipation, breathlessly awaited the showstopping finale to begin, for her rukba to arrive, whatever that was.

9:04

What … a downer. Remnants of a spell unfulfilled glared Pepper's way. Wax stained her carpet. A blood-marred knife, front and center. A wall straight out of a creepy crime scene. Magic was real. Magic existed. Tonight Pepper witnessed those truths firsthand. So, why had the incantation for portal summoning fallen flat? After all, Pepper had followed the instructions to the letter.

Disillusionment superseded the fugitive elation Pepper had momentarily felt. Now that she'd missed the window for summoning Karma—from 9:00 P.M. to 9:01 P.M.—was that it? One shot was all the Academy had granted her, and in a snap, her destiny slipped through her fingers like sea foam? With a heavy heart, she extinguished the candles.

What if Pepper had narrowly dodged a bullet, and her gut had been right all along? That Karma Academy amounted to nothing more than a deathtrap? Yet, in the span of a day, she had eluded Death, not once but twice. So, was her lucky streak over? Surely, the Dark Angel would wise up and foil anymore free passes that came Pepper's way.

Shaken by the notion that her grasp on the land of the living was seemingly tenuous at best, Pepper resolved to be more mindful of her gut. She'd start by feeding it.

A *tap-tap-tap* on the windowpane interrupted visions of leftover carrot cake dancing through Pepper's head. Tossing her attention to the disruptive noise, she swallowed back fright. The muzzle of a gun tapped one final time before lowering.

As for the one who controlled the weapon—sea-glass eyes fixed on Pepper with their menacing glare, the boy's lips curling back in a sneer. Pepper had been outwitted, and it would take more than luck to extricate her from danger this time, for the Dark Angel had come home to roost and finish what he had started, once and for all.

"We need to talk."

My, my, what a sonorous tone Death has, Pepper thought.

"Your life's in danger, and we don't have much time! Let me inside!" His brows furrowed as he darted glances left and right.

"And by 'talk,' will that gun of yours be doing all the communicating?"

Pepper didn't wait around for a response. Instead, she sprang off the floor, then barreled out of her bedroom and down the hallway, her fingers fondling every switch. The goal was to flood the house with ample illumination to exorcise encroaching evil. Yet after buttery light bathed the house in toto, evil hadn't been in the least bit thwarted.

A rapping sounded on the front door, followed by a request to be granted entrance. Pepper's ticker paused from sheer fright, only to struggle to regulate its arrhythmic beat. Shuffling about the living room in a desultory fashion, nibbling on her nails, Pepper contemplated her next move and the items that would best be suited for banishing Death. But her mind drew a blank.

"Under no circumstances will I open that door." Pepper's tone mimicked that of a fearless warrior, yet she was anything but, her knees threatening to give out at any moment, her heart rolling in her chest.

"Right now, I'm your only hope of staying alive. So, let me in, and I promise to protect you." The chivalrous manner in which Death spoke possessed an air of magnetism, as if each word had been charged with sincerity. But what if it was all a veneer, and once demagnetized, his claims amounted to nothing more than an enchantment?

As if in a trance, Pepper walked directly to Death, proof positive that bewitchery was afoot. Curiosity occupied her mind to the exclusion of everything else, like safety and overall well-being. And curiosity was what compelled her hand to cup the knob and her eye to peer out the peephole. Her finger flicked the light switch to her immediate right to glimpse Death lurking under the porte cochère, leaning against the station wagon, his arms crossed.

Limned in a soft amber glow, Death had divested himself of his forbidding ensemble from earlier—the leather hoodie, the shade of midnight—and now donned a more aesthetically pleasing livery: jeans and T-shirt. He looked like a proper teenager; still, Pepper couldn't help but wonder if he, Death, had transmogrified himself into one, the better to beguile. *If so, checkmate, Death,* Pepper thought.

"Your antics are wasting time. Grant me entrance already." A devil-may-care forelock trickled down his prominent forehead to flirt with his eyelashes. Death mechanically swatted the wavy tendril to the side and tucked it behind his ear. He was cursed with a wicked cowlick, something Pepper could relate to.

His fathomless sea-glass eyes riveted on the peephole as he holstered his weapon—a sign of peace, perhaps?—then cheekily waved with his hand. His face betrayed no emotion, not even a hint of annoyance.

Pepper backed away from the door and took her confusion out on her already-battered fingernails. "You must think I'm stupid," she replied. Taking a gander once more through the peephole, she gasped and clutched her bosom. Death was gone.

Pepper caught a movement from out of the corner of her eye. The wall underwent a phase change—solid to undulating liquid, then back to solid in quicksilver fashion. An outline of a door was being drawn as if by the hands of a ghost.

Death had found a way inside.

CHAPTER 8

"Oh, I don't think so!" Pepper jumped to her feet, then bolted to the wall that housed a picture of a rambling Victorian mansion painted by her landlord. Half the outline of a door had already been drawn; one more side remained. She spat into her hands and used the saliva to erase the line as it was being drawn. But it was no use.

When a door popped into existence, and a knob followed suit, the painting nearly being knocked off the picture hanger, Pepper extracted Walt's handgun from the waistband of her jeans. The years of target practicing at the gun range with her pops were about to come in handy. With the slide pulled back, she leveled the weapon on the magical doorway and stared down its barrel, waiting.

The door yawned open, and out stepped Death. Clocking in at nearly six feet, he had to duck to not knock his head on the frame.

"Stop right there, or I'll shoot!" Pepper hadn't thought out her next move should Death blatantly disregard her stern warning. Still, Pepper's arms remained locked and extended, the gun trained on Death.

He shot his hands up in surrender. "I'm not here to harm you. Scout's duty."

Scout's duty?

When he attempted to toss the requisite hand sign—and majorly failed in that endeavor—Pepper had to stifle a torrent of laughter because that wouldn't exactly bolster her "one false move and I'll end your life" stance.

"You killed Blondie, and I'm supposed to believe that you just want to talk and not do the same to me? You've not only insulted my intelligence, but to add insult to injury, you broke inside my house after I explicitly stated you couldn't enter."

"I didn't kill Sawyer, so delete that false narrative from your mind. She escaped right after you left. And as far as breaking into your house, I asked nicely. Even recited the magic word. Look, I feel like we're getting off on that foot, that thing. What is that saying?" He upturned his head to the ceiling in an attempt to dislodge the proper expression.

"The wrong foot? And what's this 'magic word' you speak of?" And here Pepper thought only her pops butchered idioms and the like.

"*Please.* In your world, that's like an invocation and will enchant the individual in question to bend to your will," he recited by rote, at least that's how it sounded to Pepper as if he'd memorized it from a manual on how best to infiltrate human society. "But apparently, you're impervious and have fortified yourself against such charms."

"Oh, I'm impervious, all right." To boys and their silver-tongued ways. Especially ones who were arrestingly handsome, ridiculously so like Death here, but Pepper would keep that observation under wraps. "Wait, you're not joking?" Pepper snickered. A reaction that oiled her stiff arms and caused them to drop to her side. Her shoulders loosened significantly.

She de-cocked the gun and slid it into the waistband of her jeans, then fell onto the sofa. "You better not have anything up that sleeve of yours. I'm still watching you, buddy." She latched gimlet eyes on him. "I could pin you to the floor and slit your throat before you could even formulate a thought as to how to thwart my advances and be back on the couch in no time flat. So, keep that in mind." Did he buy her palpably absurd claim?

Head canted, he bit his lower lip while inspecting Pepper. As his cherry-red lips bowed into a smile, he relieved his tousled mane of a beanie and tucked it under his arm before extending his hand. "Name's Jhi." He slowly approached Pepper, and she lurched backward. "Jumpy, much? Just wanted to shake your hand."

Pepper dialed down her defenses a notch and sanctioned his greeting. My, what a firm grip Jhi had.

"Not for nothing, but if I wanted you dead, you'd be dead."

Unsure how to respond to such a statement, Pepper remained silent.

Jhi wheeled around and stalked to his previous position, his movements sleek and panther-like, then draped his leather jacket over the back of the recliner before taking a seat. Pepper couldn't stop herself from appreciating every ounce of his being. In the least, she hoped Jhi wouldn't notice.

Beneath a hooded brow, his deep-set eyes watched her watching him, to which he smirked. Not one to back down, Pepper continued on and admired the shade of his hair, or more like shades—a chestnut brown shot through with cinnamon. And how the thick unruly tendrils curved up at his neck, some jutting out at the sides willy-nilly. Stubborn were his locks, for they refused to be tamed by his fingers as they raked across and through.

His cheekbones were knocking on the pearly gates, perhaps wanting to return to their creator. A razor hadn't touched his square jaw in a few days, and the accumulated chestnut stubble only lent itself to the rakish air that this boy gave off. And the glistening naturally beige hue of his skin would have been unblemished if not for the tattoos that peeked out just barely from the three-quarter length sleeves of his T-shirt and the scaly tail of a creature coiled around one arm.

Jhi was built like a warrior—broad-shouldered, lean, and

corded muscles flexed with every move from underneath his clothes. He appeared to be young—could be a glamour—perhaps a mile or two north of Pepper's age. Damn, he was—

"Happy birthday."

"What?" His sentiments snapped Pepper to full alertness, which was probably a boon to maintaining her dignity, because her adventuring eyes weren't quite fatigued. "How'd you know?"

He jerked a thumb at the banners festooning the wall.

"Oh, right."

"Pivoting back to the urgency that brought me here tonight. There's a contract out on your life. And Sawyer won't stop until the deed's been completed."

Pepper wasn't computing. Her eyes stared blankly at Jhi, her body frozen as if time had paused.

So Jhi further elaborated. "Uh, a murder contract. You're the target. And Sawyer will be back to take care of unfinished business. Perhaps bring along an army for support. Which means you don't have much time left."

That sobering statement halted the fluttering in her belly. "Whoa, back up! A murder contract?" A nervous laugh escaped. "Seeing as how you know this Sawyer, perhaps you can have a come to Jesus moment or Lucifer, whatever's your jam, and tell her to stand down! That would be a good start."

"Why would Sawyer be bent on killing you if not for a contract?" Jhi wouldn't break eye contact with Pepper.

"Girlfriend went all psycho and charged at me, I suppose in part because I was an eyewitness to her whacking Walt. If anyone had a contract out on his life, it was Walt."

"That's what Sawyer told you? The reason she wanted you dead?" Jhi probed.

"Well, not exactly. It's not like Sawyer went over her nefarious plot in detail like a cartoon villain before trying to kill me. But my theory has a more melodious ring than yours—Wait, you don't have proof or know for certain that there's a contract out on my life? Do you? Oh God! Why aren't you answering?" With each question Pepper asked, her tone raised an octave. "And who would want *me* dead?"

"You must've made an enemy," Jhi answered matter-of-factly. "And this enemy summoned an Agent of Karma to exact revenge on his behalf."

In a flash, Pepper's eyebrows began their rapid rise to new heights, and her tired eyes were jolted awake. She couldn't chance Jhi noticing the apparent look of surprise taking form on her face from the mere mention of an Agent of Karma, so she feigned annoyance at a pretend dust particle stuck in her eye. She rapidly blinked and pulled her upper eyelid down to her lower lashes.

Pepper's ploy must have worked because Jhi started explaining how Agents of Karma—the little he knew of them— were an inexorable force, bent on fulfilling their contractual obligations, destroying their targets, obstacles notwithstanding.

"Which means Sawyer will return to finish the job once and for all," Jhi said. "Can't rest until the job is done, part of the summoning spell and karmic job she agreed to exact. I believe that's how it works." If Pepper wasn't mistaken, Jhi wasn't so much stating a fact as asking a question, because he appeared to be waiting for her confirmation.

She wasn't sure whether to cry or laugh or head to the kitchen and raid the pantry. She chose the latter. After shoving a fistful of potato chips in her mouth, she took a few centering breaths, then snatched two chilled bottles of old-fashioned root beer for her and Jhi.

"Do I have enemies you asked?" After twisting off the cap, she took a sip while settling back down on the couch. "Sure, I have 'em, racked up a few over the years, or actually more than a few, but whatever, everyone I wreaked vengeance on deserved it— Wait a second." Clarity paid Pepper a visit. "Your theory explains Walt's death. But I was an innocent bystander. Sawyer didn't even know my name." Pepper was convinced Jhi was dressing up facts, incredulity written all over her face.

"Jeez, what does a guy have to do to get you to trust him?" His index finger ever so lightly tapped on his thumb. "Have you, at any time, made a deal with the devil? An Underlord? A Princess or Prince of Hell? Summoned a demon? Sold your soul or magic? Signed an ever-binding contract in your blood? Communed with a ghost by way of a spirit board and vowed to help it escape from its prison? Offered your body as a vessel? Taken part in Light as a Feather, Stiff as a Board?" He spoke rapid-fire.

She would've voiced the word "no" to all the above had it not been purloined by fear-laced shock, so she shook her head.

"Then consider yourself blessed by Goddess Seren because I will not be dragging you off to Hell, kicking and screaming and biting. So, we good? Can we forever bury the subject of me being here to sunder your soul from your body and move on to more pertinent topics, like your life being in grave peril?"

"But you're Death personified. Isn't that what you do, ferry the souls of the dead to their final destination? So, forgive me if I'm having trouble parting with that nagging issue. Or fully trusting you."

"Why do you keep *saying* that? If I were Death, we wouldn't be having this charming tête-à-tête. By the way, Death isn't one being, but scores. And they're not exactly chatty. More like taxed and cantankerous bureaucrats who work behind a window and call out, 'Now serving, enter ridiculous number here,' while they count down the days till their next holi—"

The grandfather clock chimed.

"Enough about Death. We can't afford to waste any more time. So answer me this. Who are you? And why were you at the marina?"

"I could ask you the same thing." Pepper tossed a channel changer his way. "Tell you what. Whoever wields the almighty remote has the floor, household rules."

He tossed it back to her. "Ladies first."

Pepper appreciated the gesture. "If you didn't kill Sawyer, then what happened to her?"

"Correct me if I'm wrong, but you harbor more than a tinge of concern for someone who was bent on ending your life. I even sense a note of protection, like you'd defend Sawyer if need be." He rubbed the deep auburn hairs on his chin. "You felt a kinship?"

Pepper now held the channel changer. "Perhaps. Yet Sawyer clearly didn't share my sentiments."

Jhi shrugged in response.

"Though she did utter something I found rather peculiar." Pepper repeated the message Sawyer had relayed to Walt regarding Boss Lady, all the while acting as if the Karma she mentioned was a human boss lady and not a goddess.

"That doesn't smack of Goddess Karma." He harrumphed. "One of a handful of Universal Elects, the personification of Lady Justice, Hilqa to demons, would *never* make a deal with a lowlie. So, no, Karma's not Boss Lady."

The bottle of root beer "slipped" out of Pepper's hands and its contents dripped all over her clothes. She yelped, jumped off the couch, and rocketed into the kitchen. There was no way in hell Pepper could have wiped her face of all expression when it came to Goddess Karma. Still, Pepper had a sneaking suspicion that Jhi tossed out "Agents of Karma" and "Goddess Karma" as bait in the hopes she'd bite. If so, she wasn't sure how much longer she could continue with the charade.

"I'm still listening," she called out from the sink while wetting her clothes and calming her galloping heart with square breathing, a technique her pops had taught her. Pepper froze as she envisioned Karma as an actual deity. It's one thing to assume, but to have your theory confirmed—holy cosmic deliciousness!

"Are you going to tell me who you are?"

After splashing her face with water and ensuring her rattled nerves were somewhat tamed, Pepper returned to the living room. "Nobody important. Two days ago, I was a normal teenager, living my life. Strike normal. A teenager minding her own damn business. Okay, not so much with the minding my own business. Listen, all hell's broken loose in my hometown. There's a demon next door—"

Jhi's brow elevated, as if mentally noting that revelation.

Pepper tossed the channel changer his way. "Explain the brow raise."

"Demons? What about them?"

"The demon's holding my … Now, what is Kimby to me?" She tapped a finger to her blushed lips. "My neighbor's mother hostage."

Jhi almost imperceptibly tattooed his finger on the tip of his thumb. "Does this demon know it's been made?"

While Pepper shook her head no, she waited for Jhi to betray an emotion. Any at all would suffice. No such luck. Jhi's mask of impassiveness remained cemented to his face.

After catching the pretend microphone, Jhi leaned his back against the recliner. "Why were you at the marina?"

"Following a lead. You?"

"Same. It appears as if our respective mysteries have collided. Tell me, Pepper, why didn't you lob magic my way when I walked through the chaosgate?"

"Seeing as how I don't have my Supernatural to English dictionary handy, a chaosgate is that door thingamajig?" Pepper stalled by lying, not wanting to out the mysterious voice or her inability to cast magic, in case that was the only thing keeping her alive.

Jhi quirked his lips into a smile. "Earlier, I interrupted a spell casting session. But whatever you were trying to conjure failed to work. And you didn't lob magic at me because you can't. Am I right?"

"Before I answer. How can I be certain that everything you've told me so far isn't fiction of your own making?" Pepper *really* wanted to trust him. Moreover, she desperately needed an ally.

"You can't. But mutual trust must be forged if we're to help each other."

Pepper figured squeaking out a modicum of truth wouldn't

hurt. "Fine. I'm not a mage, but a virtual eunuch when it comes to magic. I know what you're thinking. Then how did I walk out of the marina alive? Beats me! Two days ago, I couldn't do a pull-up if my life depended on it. And you can forget knocking out fifteen push-ups. Maybe ten on a good day. Yet at the marina, I was swinging from rafters, committing supernatural acts of daredevilry."

"Well, you came out unscathed after coming face-to-face with an Agent of Karma bent on retribution. Not many humans can say that, and by 'not many,' I mean none. Which means you're not a lowlie"—he noted Pepper's cocked head and look of confusion—"er, a human without magical powers. Unless borrowed magic is at play. Got any magic gems on your person? But even if that were the case, then you'd still have been a mage at one time. At the end of the day, lowlies can't cast magic."

"Nope. Didn't borrow any magic. Your turn. Why were you shadowing Sawyer?"

"She's involved somehow in my friend's disappearance." Rising from the recliner, Jhi joined Pepper on the couch. "Tell me why you are acting as if you've never heard of Goddess Karma or her Agents?" Jhi plucked his root beer from the coffee table. "Just ensuring you don't *accidentally* knock it over."

Pepper remained mum but absently nibbled on the skin surrounding her thumb.

"Might want to work on suppressing that obvious giveaway." Jhi's eyes navigated to her chewed fingernails.

Pepper stifled a reply, jaw clenched. Her silence lasted all of a few beats before her tongue broke free from its harness. "Says the man who subtlety taps his fingers. Ha, didn't think I noticed."

He paused and studied Pepper. The corners of his mouth twitched, the beginnings of a smile. "I'd be willing to wager my soul, and yes, I have one, so you can stop with the nail chewing, that Goddess Seren led me to you. Which means you and I were meant to cross paths." Jhi crinkled his eyes with impish intentions. Or perhaps Pepper was merely projecting her own thoughts. "To aid me in finding JD, of course." His eyes probed Pepper's, waiting for a reaction, or more like recognition, of this person's name.

Who the hell was this JD, and what was his—or her?—relationship to Jhi? *Please let JD be a guy and a friend*, Pepper pleaded to the Universe.

"Unfortunately, you're no help to me in your current magicless state. Listen, your life is in danger, and your days are numbered. I can't make that any clearer. So, come clean already. Tell me where your powers have gone?" He spoke in a soft and unhurried tone.

While waiting for Pepper to respond, Jhi swilled more root beer. When he removed his lips from the rim of the bottle, she couldn't tear her eyes away from the remnants of foam left behind. Imaginings of tasting his full lips occupied her mind.

A screaming car alarm snapped her to full alertness, freeing her from what felt like a trance.

"I really want to help you," Jhi said. "But in order for me to do that"—his sea-glass eyes, alight with sincerity, affixed on Pepper's—"you must trust me. You can't cast magic, yet you were attempting to summon a chaosgate. Where were you going?"

Pepper bolted from the couch to squelch the blush creeping from neck to cheeks, then returned with the mysterious letter from Karma Academy and more liquid refreshments, only this time of the spiked variety. She hesitated for a beat, considering her next move. In the end, her desperate need for help trumped any reservations she might have had.

"Promise me this will stay between us." After Jhi did as asked, Pepper proffered the missive and explained how it came into her possession.

He gingerly held the missive as if it was THE archaeological find of the century, a relic worthy of reverence and preservation. "Fact, you would never have received this invite if you weren't a mage or were at one time." As if lost in memory, a dreamy look reflected in his eyes.

"Any idea what or who the Nine are referenced in the invite?" Pepper inquired.

"No clue." Jhi lavished all his attention on the invite. "I doubt anyone but an Initiate has ever laid eyes on something of this magnitude." His plush lips bowed into a wolfish grin. "From the paltry bits I've garnered, Agents of Karma walk amongst the shadows, as trained assassins are wont to do. To date, nobody's ever lived to tell the tale after encountering one. At least that's my working theory."

"Except for you, I take it? If Agents of Karma are so super-secret, then how have you acquired knowledge of their existence?"

"A client of mine angered the wrong person and said person summoned an Agent of Karma to exact revenge on his behalf." Jhi explained as much as was permitted.

Enter Sawyer Van Arsdale. She tried to kill Jhi's client but failed. The poisonous blowdart entered the target's skin, but was no sooner ejected. And for good reason. Jhi's client had already sold his soul. For as long as a soul-selling client treads the Earth, they are rendered essentially immortal, free to commit nefarious acts with impunity in order to luxuriate in their spoils with nary a concern. Until the day comes for soul-reaping. Jhi's anecdotes and speculations were seasoned with pauses as he investigated Pepper for a hint of recognition.

When Jhi gingerly broached the topic of Agents of Karma with Dominus—contextually speaking, Pepper deduced Dominus referred to Jhi's boss—Dominus cast a forget-me-now-and-always hex.

"Luckily, I'd already armed myself with wards for something —Not important." Jhi quickly moved on to the topic at hand. "Of note. Scores of armed guards were sprawled about my client's fortress—Sawyer's handiwork. Though none were dead, only KO'd. Probably had a splitting headache when they came to, but at least they were still drawing breath, which lent credence to my working theory that Agents of Karma try not to shed the blood of innocents. At least not intentionally. Yet Sawyer tried to assassinate you, and you're still alive." Jhi inspected Pepper for a telltale.

"Yet I'm still alive."

After hearing just how deadly and formidable Agents of Karma truly were, Pepper's survival was nothing short of a miracle. Or her inner pilot was even more formidable.

Still, the corners of her mouth twitched, and a ghost of a smile journeyed across her lips. For resonating bone-deep within Pepper was the realization that she wasn't a freak, that she had found her soul's purpose. Dishing out karma wasn't just an itch, but her bailiwick, her birthright. And now more than ever, Pepper yearned to meet her goddess, to meet her kith and kin, and to finally become the assassin she was fated to be. Too bad one of them wanted her dead, or all of them, if she were to believe Jhi.

"So, do with that anecdote what you will. But I must ask. You positive you didn't render your magic to a demon? Do you have any fragmented memories of doing just that? Because Agents of Karma are a sisterhood of formidable mages, and unless there was a mix-up, then Karma, along with whoever else works under her purview, is under the assumption that you're a mage. And you survived a brush with one of the goddess' Agents. How was that even possible? If I didn't know any better, I'd think you had sold your soul. But you'd certainly remember doing that."

She lobbed a stink-eye his way.

"Well, someone sure is looking out for you, then. Otherwise, you'd be dead." Jhi's tone had a menacing edge; he wasn't referring to a guardian angel but something far more sinister.

Pepper decided it was best to play ignorant. "My dad swears I was born under a lucky star. Well, except for one—two mishaps." Pepper's face screwed up in disgust at the memories of her arrests, the latest being the worst, but chose not to highlight that horrific event. "For the record, you have yet to divulge who you are and how you're so in the know," Pepper deflected to halt Jhi's probing, at least until her galloping heart regulated.

"Just a soul broker searching for a missing friend."

Pepper tried not to betray an emotion when Jhi said "just a soul broker" and failed.

"Buying souls is quite lucrative, seeing as how they, sundered souls, constitute a large percentage of our currency in Pandæmonia, among other things; that's the capital of Hell, in case you were wondering. In the market for selling yours?" He tossed a cheeky grin Pepper's way.

"NO! And if I were?"

"Then I'd talk you right out of it. Besides, there's nothing I could offer you that you don't already have."

"Oh yeah, what's that?"

She might've had a knack for exacting pain and misery, for bringing perps to their knees, exploiting their weaknesses, to say nothing of her felonious talents, such as breaking and entering with only a switchblade at her disposal, but if history had taught her anything, it was that when it came to the art of flirting, Pepper was most certainly *not* gifted. And when it came to garnering the attention and mutual affection of boys, she crushed on hard, that lucky star of hers sure lost its luster and burned out. Or maybe her luck with boys was finally changing.

"Besides beauty, well, you're witty, astute, wickedly intelligent, sweet as pixie pie." His sea-glass eyes journeyed up and down her frame. "And best of all, an Agent of Karma, an assassin who possesses unparalleled skills in all manner of revenge, or will be one day. But back to the topic at hand."

That was a relief because Pepper could feel a fire blazing on her face, which she put out with the sweaty bottle, swiping it back and forth.

"So, about us joining forces. Time being of the essence and all. What say you?"

"Why are you helping me? What could I and my magicless-ness possibly have to offer?" While Pepper hooked an errant strand of hair around her ear, she noted Jhi inspecting her wrist.

"Something's awry in Pandæmonia, and a girlfriend of mine was dangerously close to figuring out what exactly is stirring.

And now JD's been abducted, or worse, and the window of time I have left to track her down is closing fast. Then there's the imminent danger steamrolling your way. I can help you with that, keep you safe. It's not a coincidence that the goddess of good fortune, Seren, shepherded me to you. And since coincidences are a thing of fiction, this proves you're somehow involved in JD's disappearance, if not the linchpin. So, do we have a deal? We'll help each other? You must verbalize it to make it official."

And there it was, JD's relationship with Jhi revealed. Pepper's heart juddered, a sting of jealousy felt when Jhi's mask forged from stone slipped, betraying his feelings that he had so fiercely guarded up until now. Jhi deeply cared for JD. Love and concern reflected in his eyes and were etched on his face.

The thrill of infatuation struck again. Pepper felt silly and wanted nothing more than to cringe. Only she couldn't, not now, so imbibing more frothy nectar would have to suffice.

"Well, the trail of clues has run cold. So, I'm not sure how I can help you." Pepper filled Jhi in on the lack of physical evidence collected at the marina, save a blank business card. Along with why she'd paid a visit to Walt's in the first place.

"Hm, well, I wouldn't give up on the business card just yet. You've entered my world now, Pepper, and things aren't always what they seem, and navigating it is not for the faint of heart. I'm talking about a world populated by demons, Karma and other gods, mages, necromancers, vampires, and that's just the beginning. So, about that deal ..."

Don't expect me to stick around for the snogfest-y homecoming, though, she thought. She tamped down the jealousy and squeak out a smile—practice makes perfect, as they say, and she had had plenty of that.

"Deal!" They shook hands to seal the agreement, to which Jhi's eyes alighted on her wrist and lingered, as did his grip, which wasn't helping Pepper's strictly business attitude.

"Do you want me to call Kimby over, to hear all about his plight straight from the horse's mouth? He's intricately involved in this mystery, too." Pepper wriggled out of Jhi's grasp and busied her hands by reaching for her cell.

"Hold off on contacting him for a second." His brows drew together in concern, his tone grave. "Pepper, can I see your wrist?"

Grudgingly, Pepper allowed Jhi to cup her hand in his once more. He donned his aviator sunglasses and then traced his index finger over a sprinkle of freckles on the inside of her wrist.

"These aren't freckles." After lifting his glasses, Jhi stared straight into Pepper's whiskey-hued eyes. "The most fiendish of demons who stole your magic and, most likely, your memories has branded you, bedeviled you, marked you as his. Possessed you."

CHAPTER 9

Wildly scratching the branding, Pepper shot to her feet and writhed about as if she were in the throes of St. Vitus's Dance. "Get this off me!"

"Why are you squirming?"

"Hello, you just told me I'm possessed, that a demon is nesting in my body, which more than merits an epic freak out. Is it parasitic? Oh God, is it like what's possessed Bunny? GET IT OUT OF ME!"

Jhi unfolded from the couch and placed his hands on her shoulders, assuaging her fears. All will be fine. Even cupping her hand in his and ushering her back to the sofa.

He fished out a fountain pen from his jeans pocket. "Let me see your wrist." She couldn't halt clawing at her skin. "Dammit, woman, would you stop the scratching."

His calloused hands inspected the inside of her left wrist, his fingers gliding over the network of veins. A sensation that not only quelled the willies but caused tingles to ignite, their whispery fingers running along the downy hairs on her arms and neck.

"Exhibit A, the constellation of freckles on the inside of your wrist, or more like a suggestion thereof, so muted they mostly blend in with your skin." His voice was hypnotic, like the gentle breaking of waves on the beach and the slow ebbing away. "Think of the beauty marks as dots, and if I connect them just so"—he glided the pen along her dermis, tickling her in the process— "touch hellfire ink to skin, it'll trigger the demon's form to take shape, so we can narrow down the list of suspects."

The Hellfire ink spilling forth from the pen was tinted a charred orangey-red with notes of burning wood, reminiscent of Lapsang Souchong, her pop's tea of choice.

When freckle-connecting concluded, a rune-like sigil stared back: a reversed, rudimentary-shaped R—not a curved line but straight—shared the spine with what could pass as an F, its spindly branches raised slightly skyward. The lower part of the spine coiled into a tail.

Once Jhi connected the last dot, completing the constellation of freckles, the hellfire ink soaked into Pepper's skin. As the creature came to the forefront, her skin rippled like water. A one-dimensional monkey squirmed and somersaulted on Pepper's wrist like flip-book animation. The oddity itself erupted a firestorm of super-fine needle pricks to jab away at her wrist. A beat later, the ink dissolved, as did the animated image.

"Hm. Very strange."

"You gonna elaborate or—"

"Oh, sorry. You've definitely been branded by a demon, no question about it. But this animated marking is odd. I've never seen anything like this before." His brow furrowed as he continued to investigate her wrist, causing tingles to explode on her scalp and down the back of her neck.

In a moment of shock, Pepper, talking more to herself, let slip, "The voice ... its sorcery—" Before she could say "martial arts," her tongue tied yet again, the being inside Pepper preventing her from exposing its identity.

"A voice? What did this voice tell you?" Urgency coated Jhi's words.

Pepper snapped her mouth shut, her eyes widening with fright.

"Did this voice give you commands? Did the fixer appear to you, try to talk to you?" Frustrated at her silence, Jhi continued, "I can't help you if you don't tell me the truth. Is it controlling you now? Nod once if yes."

Shocked, in the throes of surreality, Pepper nodded slowly, an action that caused Jhi to avert his attention elsewhere, concern cementing on his face.

After a few gulps, Pepper regained her composure. "I didn't mean an *actual* voice, per se. Something took over control, like a pilot. Or more like possessed me."

That kernel of truth seemed to satisfy Jhi, as evidenced by a nod of his head. "That makes sense. You *were* in mortal danger, and the fixer has a stake in ensuring you remain alive. Don't for one second think its actions were altruistic. Helping you is nothing more than a contractual obligation."

"You keep saying that word—*fixer*."

"For good reason. The branding tells me you're still under contract. And it somewhat explains how you're still alive after running into Sawyer. But I don't see a fixer around." Jhi darted his head back and forth. "Unless there's something you're not telling me—"

"No! This is all so overwhelming. I just don't understand." She rubbed the heels of her palms over her eyes, pinpricks of stars occluding her vision.

"Fixers prey on the lost, the lonely, heartbroken, the fearful, the imperiled, those lost souls in Witherwhere—"

One needn't inquire what a fixer did; the occupation's name *was* tailor-made for idiots, after all. "I get it, fixers fix shit, but I wasn't broken. And that's not what I was asking originally. No, what I need to know is how did I come to be possessed"—Pepper gagged on the last word—"by a fixer without my say so?"

"You gave permission."

"No, I didn't."

"Yes, you did." Jhi silenced Pepper before a retort on the tip of her tongue let loose. "Listen, we can go round and round as much you'd like, but the fact will remain the same. A fixer took your magic some time ago, then tinkered with your memories, which is odd, seeing as how they would only do so with your permission. Even so, *you* summoned the fixer. And *you* willingly entered into a devil's contract, its fixing skills, in exchange for something priceless, in this case, your magic."

"There's no possible way I would have agreed to that."

"But you did. That's how the arrangement works. So, that leads me to believe you were in mortal danger; it was do-or-die, and you had no other recourse but to strike a deal with a demon. Perhaps an eleventh-hour rescue? Still, that doesn't explain why you would have handed over your memories to the fixer. Then again, if your life was at stake, desperation can render even the wisest a fool."

"The voice said 'it's kill or be killed.'" She immediately regretted divulging that truth.

"A voice talked to you? I thought you said it wasn't a voice."

This line of questioning made Pepper harken back to her time being interrogated by cops after her last arrest. "No. It wasn't a voice. Or it was, but it was robotic, synthesized, speaking programmed text. 'Kill'"—she imitated a robot, her movements jerky, speech monotone and staccato—"'or be killed.'" Pepper felt ridiculous and hoped he was buying this load of bullcrap.

He squinted his eyes, his brow knitted. "That's … different."

"The voice was referring to Sawyer. Like he could sense the danger. Not with Walt, though, which is odd now that I think about it. Walt was going to shoot me dead."

Realization dawned within Pepper. The voice might not have revealed itself with Walt, but her wrist had throbbed. Same with Bunny, now that she thought about it. Actually, the pain in her wrist all started with serial killer Miles Leagan when she first saw him on TV. Was the pain caused by the voice as a warning she was in—

"So, the robot is a *male*?" Jhi wore a look of incredulity.

Shit! "Um, no. I just said that. Ignore the sex. Robots are genderless. Jeez!" Pepper's internal temperature was rising.

"So, only when you were in mortal danger did this robotic voice, *not-male*, make itself known ...?" Jhi bit his lip, deep in thought. "Has this fixer ever spoken to you before?"

"No! Never. I would have mentioned it if so."

"I see. Just being thorough. I don't purport to know the ins and outs of how fixers operate, but what I do know is that they are solitary creatures who work alone, and right after striking a deal, they brand their clients. Think of it as collateral. Once the job's done, whatever that entails, the branding's removed. Everyone goes their separate ways. But you're still branded. Which means the job isn't done. It has been charged to protect you, but from what? And why take your memories? Without them, you have a target on your back."

Pepper's mouth opened wide, a realization ready to be shared. "Sawyer ... No." Her shoulders dropped. "That doesn't make sense. It can't be her. There's no way she could have known I'd be at the marina. Hell, I didn't even know until this morning. What if this invitation to attend Karma Academy is a ruse, and I wasn't a former mage? It's probably a good thing that I failed my first mission of opening a portal." She clucked her tongue. "Failed, even with the how-to spelled out. So pathetic."

"I believe Sawyer's gone rogue, if that makes you feel any better. So, I doubt she was referring to Karma when she mentioned Boss Lady. And stop beating yourself up about failing to open a chaosgate. You were missing a crucial ingredient—your magic."

"What makes you think I had magic to begin with?" Pepper direly needed reassurance.

"Well, fixers traffic in magic. It's their sole currency, their payment for services rendered. And they transfer the slivers of magical powers taken into gems. Sidebar, magic gems are a hot commodity in my world. Also, magic is needed to summon a fixer. And they don't waste their time with lowlies. Ergo, you had magical powers at one time."

"At least until the fixer drained me of my birthright, my first and last line of defense. In exchange for what though?"

"Only the fixer knows. Now, as for the robotic voice, I think it's part of a spell. There's probably a magical defense mechanism imbued within your branding that triggers a protection spell to manifest around you in the event mortal danger presents itself. So, the voice is programmed to evade death at all costs."

Pepper playacted by nodding her head in agreement and finished with: "Totally explains why I didn't die after running into Sawyer."

"So, returning to the topic at hand. You entered into a devil's contract. Why? Who or what was after you? And where have they disappeared to? If Sawyer was the nasty foe in question, the fixer would have parted ways and removed your branding, your contract fulfilled. But he hasn't. You're still bedeviled. So, that danger you were in before has mushroomed. There's something far more deadly than Sawyer after you. Chances are it's vectoring your location as we speak."

"We need to rehash." Outlining a thorny situation never failed to slow Pepper's whirling mind for the sake of clarity and anxiety taming. "Sawyer, a full-blown Agent of Karma, has gone rogue, or so you believe. She is also involved in your friend's disappearance. Sawyer, who is now out for my blood, me, an Agent of Karma Initiate. I bargained with a demonic fixer, the when and why unknown. He took my magic and memories in exchange for protection?"

"Not the memories. Fixers are self-serving, and memories have no value on the black market, so I'm not fully sold it was part of the payment."

"Still, who in their right mind would give away their memories anyway? Amnesia puts you in even more danger, rendering you a walking target."

"Unless the fixer put you under a cloaking spell. Would

explain why you're still alive." Jhi noted Pepper's furrowing brow. "Your memories, knowledge of who you are, your essence radiates into the aether, and that vibrational energy can be pinpointed during a locator spell. But if you didn't know who you really were, then it's as if you vanished. Cloaked from sight. In the least, this proves that whoever, or whatever, is after you is a part of my world, magically enhanced and a force to be reckoned with."

"Got it! Now, how long do I have until this unknown nemesis resurfaces and finds me?" Pepper craved potato chips, cake, or both simultaneously, whatever it took to stave off a panic attack.

"If you're under a cloaking spell, it isn't permanent—somewhat good news. Whatever job you hired this fixer for, it's still active. As for how long, not sure."

"And the bad news?"

"Whatever scared you enough that you had no choice but to sell your magic to a fixer in exchange for help is still out there. Looking for you as we speak. But this speculating isn't helping matters. We need solid answers. So, it's imperative we hunt down the fixer and pick his brain and retrieve your magic and memories."

"A fixer—is that enough of a solid lead to track it down?" Pepper instinctually knew the voice, her paladin, and the fixer were not one and the same. That the voice was not part of a magical defense spell. But she continued on with the ruse all the same.

"No. But the monkey branding is. In fact, I know a fixer who owes me a favor. Time for him to pony up. But before I leave, let's find out how your neighbor fits into the equation."

CHAPTER 10

K imball's voice quavered on the other end of the phone. "Her keening wails—they were ear-splitting. Bell, I tried so many times to call you, but you wouldn't pick up. I couldn't take the screaming any longer, so I left the safety of my room, and … they were inside Shelly's man cave, torturing the girl. And I just watched. I watched her die. The ones who partook in the slaying were laughing like they had no souls, so utterly cruel and depraved. After drinking her blood, Shelly was as high as a mother-effin' kite. He flew. Like, his feet left the ground. When the demon inside my mother spotted me, I ran, and it chased after me. And I've been trapped inside the pool bath ever since."

Before passing the phone to Jhi, Pepper briefly explained to Kimball how she ran into Jhi at the marina, leaving out the nearly dying parts. Then she firmly told him that if he wanted help, he'd have to shut up and listen.

"The girl, she was a mage," Jhi started. "Recall seeing any magic gems nearby? On her person? Your father's?" When Kimball paused in confusion, Jhi elaborated. "Magic gems, they resemble glass marbles, whorls and cat's eye, et cetera. Clueless humans collected them at one time."

Kimball replied with a hard "NO!"

"Then they ingested her magic directly. So, we're dealing with vampires," Jhi said, more to himself, perhaps reworking his attack strategy.

Kimball hyperventilated for a beat over the notion of vampires and swore up and down they weren't.

"If not vampires, Kimball, then how did they exsanguinate her without biting?" Jhi pressed. "Did they bite her, rip into her jugular?"

When Kimball confirmed canine teeth weren't involved in the bloodletting but creepily long serrated fingernails, Jhi explained that vampires weren't in his midst.

"If I didn't know any better, demon-bot Bunny's on a tight leash, as in her handler's thwarting her from ripping into me like I'm a porterhouse steak. But that's a big what-if. Dude, you gotta get me outta here." Kimball spoke in a staccato rhythm, each word separated by panicked breaths.

"If this demon-bot, as you call it, wanted to suck the marrow right out of your bones, it would've already," Jhi stated. "Guaranteed, its master hasn't sanctioned the demon to attack. Not yet. Now, as far as rescuing you, I can chaosnaut inside, but the magic involved to do that will cause a ripple effect in the energy, and the demon will know the house has been breached. Is your father still getting acquainted with the stolen magic coursing through his veins?"

"Uh-huh, and the more blood-infused alcohol they imbibe, the worse it gets."

"Perfect. The vibration created from chaosnauting will commingle with the already festering energy in the house, and they'll be none the wiser—"

"Wait! There's one more girl. I saw them grab her before I hid."

"Stay put. I'm on my way." Jhi slipped into his leather jacket and beanie as he strode to the wall from whence he had come. Pepper had been so distracted that she failed to note how the previous gateway had dematerialized.

Jhi unsheathed the sword he wore on his back. With the flick of a switch, the reflective blade retracted, emitting a sound like that of metal hitting metal, then folded in on itself like a walking stick. Moments later, a dagger had sprouted, its tip devoured by a viscous eggplant-hued matter. Essentially, the weapon Jhi had carried on his back was the equivalent of a Swiss Army knife, only larger, a mobile armory, if you will.

With the blade, he carved the outline of a door into the wall. Above the horizontal line of the chaosgate, Jhi dashed off *Kimball pool bathroom*. Pepper noted the lack of a keyhole, the lack of chalk, or Jhi's blood, for that matter. Or perhaps that was the substance on the blade. Either way, the door snicked open. And Jhi crossed the threshold into …

… BLACKNESS. A gush of dry arctic air engulfed him, then vast silence reigned. In a tunnel forged from chaos—formless matter fused into a chaosway courtesy of the eponymous god himself—artificial illumination, hellfire, or otherwise were snuffed out by nothingness. Should Jhi let loose a bloodcurdling scream, that, too, would be smothered.

Cloaked in Stygian darkness, Jhi could extend his arms outward and not touch a thing. Just how far did the boundaries reach? Jhi had yet to test the tunnel or chaosway's limits because even now, Jhi felt unnerved.

To assuage his trepidation, he'd walk in a straight line as if on a tightrope and count his steps—not that they made a sound. Experience taught Jhi that usually no more than fifteen steps would deliver him to his destination.

The flooring could be appropriately described as nonexistent. And walking on it felt akin to walking on air. Or, better yet, crowd surfing. Jhi imagined his weight was supported by a swarm of hands connected to the damned imprisoned in the fiery Pits of Tartarus, their arms extending upward, reaching, grasping for someone, anyone to extract them from their hellish eternal torment, their keening wails to be freed from the pain, the torture, the butchery squelched by the void. What if the bridge of hands buckled, disappeared, and Jhi was sent tumbling down into the bottomless void, or worse, falling into Witherwhere?

His mind ran rampant with theories of what his feet shuffled upon, what made up the innards of a chaosgate, because something held Jhi up, delivered him from point A to point B. If he thought too long about what exactly that something was, he'd fall off the tightrope and lose his way.

At least that was Jhi's greatest fear, not so much the chaosway itself, but being lost in Witherwhere. No one to hear his cries for help. Forever alone. A shudder rippled through his being.

Only Underlord Chaos knew what resided in the bowels of chaosways. For all Jhi knew, this was where raw, untapped magic had originated, where the Underlord had first come into his powers before dispensing his magic to other dimensions as a gesture of goodwill, at least according to lore.

Then again, hell-fireside tales tell another story entirely. At the dawn of time, Chaos stumbled upon reservoirs of primeval magic and kept the Serensend discovery under lock and key. For years, Chaos studied the curiosity and honed his skills at bending the laws of physics and manifesting somethings from nothing.

Corrupted by greed and drunk on power, Chaos never felt sated with his ill-gotten gains by way of magic, so he devised a way to manipulate space and time. Soon thereafter, he ravaged other dimensions in search of more ancient mysteries. Eventually, the Universal Elects caught up to Chaos, his crimes legion. They sentenced the Underlord to share his magic with nature, fellow demons, and other beings, including his clever chaosgates.

Jhi's earliest memories from childhood revolved around weapons training, martial combat, and schooling in arcane dark magics, so the fact he felt so profoundly unnerved within the confines of a chaosgate to where his blood chilled every time he walked through one was rather comical—even Jhi could grudgingly admit that to himself. He even convinced himself that he would always be fearful of what lurked in the darkness, regardless of age.

As it stood, Jhi was an adult, and his fears hadn't waned in the slightest; though his actual age was unknown, Mephistopheles, his dominus, estimated it to be around nineteen. Still, Jhi reminded himself as he walked, one foot in front of the other, that if he could convincingly play the undercover role of "soul broker" with aplomb, just another cog in the wheel, a low-level bureaucrat lost in the shuffle, then he could do the same with traversing a chaosway.

Jhi's meandering thoughts kept the lurking fear at bay, and when his steel-toed boots hit point B, he sighed with relief. He searched for the knob blindly, then nimbly torqued it clockwise and stepped into a dimly lit changing room; a rectangular pool visible beyond the glass door.

The air was thick with chlorine and fear. A riot of cement was splashed about. Very stark and very cold. Right as a severely terrified Kimball tiptoed out of a massive shower and tucked a cigarette behind his ear, the terrified cries of a female accompanied by shattered glass sounded in the background. Jhi placed his finger over his mouth. Formal introductions would have to wait.

As if sensing the question about to fly off Kimball's lips, Jhi said, "She's dead," his tone measured.

The hilt of Jhi's dagger sprouted into that of a quarterstaff, gleaming quicksilver. Brandishing the weapon as if ready for battle, Jhi sliced it through the air like a baton, tracing a lemniscate pattern, glyphs glowing green along its shaft. His movements were graceful yet fierce, his breath steady, as he harmonized his energy with the dim rays of light. Becoming a vibrational match was the goal. As the shadows bent to their summoner's will, Jhi and Kimball's silhouettes deserted them.

Kimball watched in rapt horror as his shadow merged with Jhi's and slithered along the ground, then up the wall, their combined length growing before they jumped into the center of the room and joined the dark cloud that cloaked the males. Even though they were shrouded in darkness, the boys could discern one another within their bubble.

Jhi instructed the wild-eyed chatterbox to keep chitchat to a minimum even though the shadows acted as a sound blocker for those cloaked and to cleave to Jhi's side no matter what; otherwise, the cloaking spell would be undone.

Jhi produced a stake dipped in silver and tendered the vampire-slaying weapon Kimball's way. "Just in case. Aim right for the heart. Seren willing, it won't come to that."

Kimball pocketed the stake, then gulped the whiskey dregs from his flask. Luckily for Kimball, his liquor-choked blood kept him from evacuating his bowels right there and then. The guy was a mess—quivering, sweaty palms, fevered eyes, hitched breaths. If not for the flask, Jhi would swear Kimball was going through withdrawal.

"Time to hunt the rabid Bunny," Kimball whispered, his voice shaky.

Gingerly, Kimball pushed the door open and began shepherding Jhi through his austere residence. Drunken laughter boomed in the distance, getting louder with each step.

They landed in the inner sanctum of the expansive kitchen, decked out with all the trimmings for a career chef. And off in the corner, gnawing on raw meat, sucking and slurping its viscous matter like a pro, was demon-bot Bunny, donning a bubble-gum pink tracksuit, blood smearing its chin and mouth, along with the ends of Bunny's blonde locks.

The demon froze as if sensing their presence. Head canted, it sniffed in all directions. After placing the rotting flesh on the counter, demon-bot Bunny padded in the boys' direction.

Had she felt Jhi chaosnaut inside?

Jhi stepped behind Kimball and held onto his quivering shoulders before waltzing him backward, then to the other side of an island, each orchestrated movement necessary to dodge the demonic Bunny.

Using the air, it sniffed as a guide, the demon-bot tailed them, its movements jerky. It jumped on the massive island and paused. Crouched on all fours, it jerked its head up and down, left and right. Sniffing, hunting, suspicious energy located. It vaulted to the other side, feet away from Jhi and Kimball, forcing the boys to backtrack.

Kimball gulped down air, his breathing staccato. Jhi could sense that Kimball was moments from fleeing, from letting loose a bloodcurdling scream. If need be, he was prepared to knock Kimball out. Even planned where he'd stash Kimball's unconscious body.

When the demon was within a whisker's length of the boys, Jhi opened his mouth and sucked in their scent, obliterating any sign of their presence.

The demon halted, its nostrils flaring. It jerked its head to the right, to the left, and flickered its tongue as if tasting the air. After a beat, demonic Bunny concluded the home hadn't been breached, and back to feasting, it went.

Jhi identified the demon possessing Bunny Garcia. After rifling through the file cabinet of his mind, through all collected intel regarding demons, Jhi then mentally thumbed through the folder dedicated to this particular species. Like a robot scrolling through downloaded intel, Jhi brushed up on this specific demon, and how to defeat it.

Kingdom: *Spiritus parasitus*

Genus: *Dæmon*

Species: *Dæmon peregrinus*

Common Name: Wanderer

Natural Habitat: Hell

Behavior: Extremely aggressive, guileful

Diet: Carnivore

Field Observations: When verifying if indeed a wanderer is in your midst, treat them no differently than you would a Gorgon; examine their eyes by way of a reflective surface. Discretion is paramount.

Jhi raised the quicksilver-mantled quarterstaff ever so slightly until the blade caught the demon's reflection. A silvery blue worm like that of a parasite ghosted over Bunny's chestnut irises. An action so fast that if you blinked, it would've escaped your notice.

Cautionary Advice: Forewarned is forearmed. Should you be in the presence of a wanderer, and eyed the shifting, and are not shadow-cloaked, don't move a muscle. Show no fear. Act normal. Because if a wanderer catches you surveilling them, identifying their presence, ten times out of ten, the observer is a dead man. Never forget—wanderers are the predator, and you're the prey, always and forever.

Empirical Evidence: Above all, wanderers hunger for a body to call their own. They'll taunt humans—a tactic that has proven to lower human defenses—spoil for a fight, do anything to steal inside a living, breathing form. The acquisition of a body occasions the onset of a killing spree, wherein no human in the general vicinity is safe.

What about a wanderer that hasn't attacked other humans nearby save for the individual whose body it heisted? Jhi added a mental note. Though he didn't have an answer, it was suspicious indeed.

Jhi jerked his head toward smashing plates and maniacal laughter, and they soon shuffled that way, following the raucous trail.

"… cheers to the snipping of loose ends. Hear, hear! And to Boat Captain Walt, you lily-livered coward, may you eternally burn in Hell."

Off the kitchen was a dining room fit for a Czar. A stone table that could seat upwards of thirty attendants tonight housed a meager three. All high on power, magic the drug. A Thanksgiving-esque feast and all the fixings sprawled about the dining room table. Bottles of wine poured their mind-numbing contents into perpetually draining goblets as if ghosts were waiters.

Jhi immediately posited that they weren't mages or demons or any other supernatural creature, but lowlies and magic-borrowers at that. This was clear by how they tested their limits like amateurs, like how adolescent mages, who had recently under-gone their unCloaking, came into their powers.

The patriarch of the Garcia household, who lorded over the head of the table, was mantled head-to-toe in a seersucker suit—a bespoke spring-y ensemble that lent itself to an uncanny vibe that, at any moment, Shelly'd doff a straw hat right before breaking out in an a cappella ditty, his barbershop quartet jumping in and harmonizing.

Mood lighting from the crystal chandelier above gleamed on the shellacked mane of the bottle-blond Shelly as he savagely ripped into turkey leg after leg, tossing bones over his shoulder, only taking breaks to swill blood-red vino. Dark brown eyes struggled to focus, his lips loosening with each sip, words slurring out of his mouth.

Shelly waved his hand in a flourish, conjuring more and more sustenance, but he seemed to run out of magical juice. Platters of food wavered into sight all right, but only a suggestion thereof, semi-incorporeal; eventually, the sustenance struggled for purchase with reality and won the fight, fully materializing.

His nose crinkled with annoyance, but not his forehead—that remained frozen with the help of Botox. With no glasslike marbles in sight, no gems imbued with magical essence handy to recharge his waning powers, Shelly's borrowed magic was on, well, borrowed time.

"If I were Gandalf for a day," Kimball barely whispered, "I'd find other uses for my wizardry besides food, and it would involve swimsuit models, just sayin'."

Jhi noted Kimball used sarcasm to deal with pain and fear.

Objects soared as if fixed on an elevated moving walkway, albeit invisible. Round and round they went, where they'd stop—

The boys ducked to avoid flying libations.

Jhi forced Kimball to the ground right as a knife whizzed over their heads, nearly giving their locks a trim, then landed in the bullseye of a pop-art Lenin poster lording over the far-right wall, right between the Bolshevik's eyes. The knife thrower tried to magically lob another dagger, but it dropped to the ground halfway on its trajectory. That severely angered the man.

"The ex-carney telekinetically showboating his knife throwing skills, and new biffle to my father, Shelly, is acquitted serial killer Miles Leagan. His trial was plastered all over the news for weeks. And the fatty stuffing his face over there is Jeremiah Olsen. His wife is also under demonic possession."

What about keeping the chitchat to a minimum did Kimball not understand? Jhi thought.

Jeremiah took the eating aspect of gastronomy to the extreme. With abandon, he poured libations into his Buddha belly like they were oblations, all the while exacerbating the patchwork of veins traversing about his bulbous nose and cheeks. Tears leaked out of his bloodshot eyes and commingled with a sheen of sweat.

No doubt about it, whatever occurred earlier in the evening had terrified Jeremiah. Perhaps he had even shat his pants. There was a waft of not only death but excrement in the air. Not enough cranberry sauce or spilled wine or pies galore could smother the stomach-churning odor that assailed Jhi.

Miles, donning a skinny sharkskin suit dripping in sheeny metallics, glided Jeremiah's way as if charioted by fire and brimstone, toes barely dusting the floor. He raked his fingers over his slicked-back hair, returning errant strands to their rightful positions. His vulpine sneer morphed into a rictus of disgust before yanking a turkey leg from Jeremiah's meaty hands.

"Ever hear of moderation?" Miles turned his attention to Shelly. "I say we bag us another mage-bitch and let the craven Jeremiah here draw the first blood, make up for him choking earlier." He returned his focus to Jeremiah. "Time to slay that cowardly lion holding up shop inside you before All Hallows' Eve. Gotta get as much practice in before then." The serial killer's teeth pulled back in a feral snarl that was most likely meant to be a grin.

Shelly flexed his index finger in a come-hither motion to an unknown object. Seeing as how nothing happened, his borrowed magic was on the fritz, nearly tapped out.

"How long"—hiccup—"will the magic last, next time? I mean, if we didn't have to share the bodies, because already my nails have whittled down to almost nothing. And right when I was getting the hang of the spell casting, too."

"The vampires didn't offer up details, strictly business those Russians," Miles offered.

Jhi had heard enough and gestured that it was time to move on.

Next up, the man cave that didn't at all resemble a cave but more like the gentlemen clubs in Miami Beach. Blue-neon ambient lighting? Check. Well-stocked bar? Check. The corpse of a lavender-haired mage draped over the edge of a pool table, blood spatter polka-dotting the walls? Another dead mage feet away, a female with a mop of black hair, drained of her life force, lying on a bed of glass shards?

As if he witnessed such savage sights daily, Jhi didn't bat an eye at the bloodshed. However, the same couldn't be said for Kimball because he was immersed in a battle, his will versus surging vomit. Due to the countless times he swallowed, he appeared to have won for the time being.

After noting all the pertinent details of the females, Jhi gave the man cave a final cursory glance before venturing to the pool bath.

"Nails growing at breakneck speed—that's a vampire trait," Jhi said. "Casting magic is not."

Jhi abruptly explained to a terrified Kimball that while vampires have preternatural speed and super strength, they are not magically inclined and cannot cast spells like mages, demons, or other beings.

"If someone signs an eternally binding soul contract, thereby transferring ownership of their soul to Lucifer, there wouldn't be a need to kill mages and drink their blood for a transfer of magical powers. Not if that's what they had asked for in return. Your father, who is *not* a mage," Jhi stressed, "and his cohorts *must* have sold their souls to have gained the ability to wield magic. Just have to prove it. But that would explain the sorcery. What I can't figure out is where vamps fit into the equation. Something's not adding up." Jhi shelved that conundrum for the time being.

After Jhi opened the chaosgate door, the bitter cold escaped. "I'm wagering that the wanderer possessing your mother's body is under contractual obligation, bound by the rules of Hell with the stipulation that under no circumstances is it to go on a murderous rampage until such a time permits. Perhaps that time is All Hallows' Eve. Regardless, staying here is the equivalent of navigating around a minefield. Your call."

"I'm not leaving without my mother." Kimball's voice quaked with suppressed emotion, plumes of his breath visible.

"Your mother's not here," Jhi said icily over his shoulder, his eyes twinning his tone.

"What does that mean? You're not insinuating that my mother's dead, are you?"

Jhi sighed and then said, "Earlier, you stated you witnessed the wanderer shifting in and out of your mom, like it was 'adjusting itself, getting comfortable.' Evidence that her soul and the wanderer were engaged in a battle of will, and Bunny was on the losing end. Only I didn't detect that tonight, so whether or not your mother's soul is still inside her body is anyone's guess. Odds are it's not, and she's gone."

Kimball inquired how a demon could hijack Bunny's body without express approval from Bunny. Jhi explained that it's possible only if the human was in a weakened state at the time. He used mind-altering drugs as an example. That divulgence must have convinced Kimball to get the hell outta Dodge because he was right on Jhi's heels.

"Maybe you should leave a note or some indicator that you've left. Don't want to raise any eyebrows."

"Shelly wouldn't notice my absence either way."

CHAPTER 11

Jhi joined Pepper in the art-cum-laundry room as she retrieved libations from the spare fridge.

Out of Kimball's earshot, Pepper whispered to Jhi, "I think we made a huge mistake bringing Kimball into the fold. You don't know him like I do. Him having ammo on me—I feel sick to my stomach." In Pepper's line of work, discretion was a cardinal rule of which she broke moments ago, right after Kimball and Jhi shared the occult happenings at the Garcia residence.

While Jhi plucked the ice-cold beers from Pepper's grasp, he said, "Understandable. But whether you like it or not, Kimball's an intricate link in our operation. He lives at ground zero, so we must reel him in. Keep him close at hand. Make him feel important. Use him until he's no longer valuable. Then we discard him," he said matter-of-factly. "You've got to give a little to get a little."

"Yeah, and I did just that. So why'd you go rogue and spill unnecessary intel to that selfish prick about my past without asking me first?" she whispered back, an edge of annoyance in her tone.

Pepper had cherry-picked the best parts to share with Kimball regarding her "encounter" with Sawyer, leaving out her "martial arts gifted" paladin and Karma, including the goddess' Academy. Not that Pepper could share the former, what with her tongue tying in knots when she dared to mention anything not approved by the being inside her. True to form, self-absorbed Kimball took the happenings at face value and returned to drinking and whining about his current predicament. To him, Sawyer was a thug and nothing more.

Jhi leaned in closer to Pepper, his breath hot on her ear, his stubble tickling her lobe. Those damn tingles erupted along her neck and head once again. "He agreed to be our eyes and ears on the ground, did he not? And it wasn't just *your* past I shared. I told him who *I* was, where *I* call home."

Pepper screwed her face in anger and pulled away from Jhi.

"Listen, chalk up my divulging your past to a fishing expedition. I needed to know what Kimball knows, or I should say his father. When not lost in self-absorption, Kimball doesn't exactly hide his emotions. Case in point, his shocked paralysis reaction upon finding out you were a mage at one time was genuine. And now, thanks to me, we have proof that *you're* not on the lips of Shelly Garcia or his cohorts, nor is Karma Academy. At least Kimball hasn't heard them breathe a word about you. Same goes for Sawyer. Kimball didn't flinch when you said her name. No, that was the first time he heard any mentioning of our rogue Agent of Karma."

As Pepper and Jhi returned to the living room, Kimball's mouth was drawn in a rictus of anguish but loosened when he spied a half-full bottle of microbrew beer on the coffee table; he drained its contents in record time. Head tilted, Kimball dangled the bottle over his gaping mouth, like a baby bird chirping to be fed. Jhi handed him a fresh beer, to which Kimball said, "You're becoming my favorite person."

"So, any theories on what's going down on All Hallows' Eve?" Pepper asked. "Because Sawyer mentioned that holiday to a dying Walt, and now Kimball's dad. Not a kawinkidink, as my pops likes to say."

"No clue just yet. But it proves that Sawyer's connected to whatever's going on next door," Jhi responded.

"I have a sneaking suspicion that whatever is planned for All Hallows' Eve is big, and it involves many players," Pepper said. "Each with their own tasks far removed from the others. Like a syndicate, complete with a hierarchy. Sawyer's the muscle and Boss Lady the queenpin."

It was terrible enough picturing Sawyer after Pepper, but a whole syndicate? What could she possibly have done to provoke their collective ire? Or maybe they weren't after Pepper. But then again, she's considered a loose end that must be dealt with sooner rather than later. Stressed, she nibbled the skin around her thumbnail.

"Can't we interrogate this Sawyer? She's the only viable lead we have to my mom's whereabouts." Kimball refused to entertain the notion that his mother's soul had already made the journey to the Great Beyond.

"While Sawyer's embroiled in whatever's going on, talking to her, or going anywhere near her, is absolutely out of the question." Jhi's tone was emphatic. "Besides, that could be exactly what she wants. To smoke Pepper out. Ever think of that?"

Defeat ghosted over Kimball's mug, and he further drowned his sorrows. Pepper pitied him for feeling the fool, for clutching onto the tail end of an evanescing hope. Was there even a glimmer of a chance that Bunny could come out of this ordeal unscathed and very much alive? Pepper tried to read Jhi to glean an answer, but he remained impassive.

Jhi canted his head and perked his ears as if receiving an alert from the cosmos. Shortly thereafter, a missive poofed into his waiting palm. He perused its contents, then said, "Duty calls." He shimmied into his soul-broker livery, sheathed his weapon, then slipped on his reflective aviator glasses. "I shouldn't be gone long. When I return, I will come bearing answers, hopefully." He paused before opening the chaosgate. "And Pepper, your house is the only safe place to be. But if you have to go out, do so during the day."

That sounded an awful lot like house arrest. *Been there, done that. No, thank you!* Pepper thought, her face reflecting as much.

"Listen, Sawyer doesn't leave loose ends, and seeing as how you're not dead … Kimball's father, who is very familiar with you, Pepper, is somehow involved in all this, but does he even know Sawyer? Probably not. But that safety net is a ticking time bomb. So, until I figure out what's going on next door, one thing is for certain. Vampires have infiltrated Naples and allied with your neighbor. They aren't friends of the sun or silver, are impossibly strong, and brutally savage—the myths are true, for the most part. They don't need an invite and can waltz right into your house. Where there's one, more will follow. You don't want to chance a swarm overpowering …" His piercing eyes bored the rest into her. *Overpowering a protective spell that kept her safe.*

Still, if a fight with a formidable opponent like Sawyer was dicey, what would happen with a gang of bloodthirsty vampires?

If Jhi was trying to put the fear of God into Pepper, he succeeded.

CHAPTER 12

"Bell, we've known each other for what, going on eleven years now? There was a point in our lives where we told each other everything. When we'd pretend to fight dragons and rescue fair maidens from wicked mages, not once did you show-case your supposed magical prowess. It was all pretend. So, I'm calling bullshit on you ever being a mage."

Kimball had a point. A demon might have tinkered with her memory, but not his. Or her pop's. But what if she was wrong? This mystery was getting more maddening by the minute.

"So"—Kimball extracted a lighter and began flicking it on and off, running his long fingers through the flames, testing his pain threshold, which amounted to zero—"what now?"

Pepper ignored him while she tidied up, gathering the empty bottles.

"Entertain me, Bell, before I pass out from sheer boredom."

"Maybe that's not such a bad idea, you passing out. Or how about you help me clean up this mess?"

"No, I'm good. I'll just sit back on this, er, not-so-comfy sofa, kick up my feet, and watch you play maid."

Why had Pepper agreed to provide shelter for Kimball again?

While Pepper putzed around the kitchen, Kimball asked over

the clangs and clinks ringing out from that general vicinity, "Where's the business card, the blank one you procured while PI-ing?"

Pepper extinguished all the light, secretly hoping Kimball would get the hint, retire to bed, and then she'd make her way back to the living room. Darkness reigned, save for the moonbeams that stole through the picturesque front window, drenching the carpet with its milkiness.

"Right here." She tendered the curious item Kimball's way, then folded herself onto the adjacent couch.

"Walt definitely had a hand in my mother's disappearance, and this's all you managed to uncover? A goddamn blank card?"

Noting Kimball deflating, a heaviness tugging at his eyes and mouth, Pepper shared, "Jhi said that in his world, which we're obviously a part of now, and saying that will never get old, things aren't always what they seem."

"That so?" With the aid of his cigarette lighter, Kimball inspected the card thoroughly before placing it on the coffee table.

The moment Kimball produced a cigarette from behind his ear, then wrapped his lips around it, the lighter casting an infernal glow about the dimly lit space, Pepper shot him a burning look and a stiff warning, "Not in my house!"

"Yes, Mommy." An errant spark refused to extinguish and lazily cascaded towards the coffee table, then alighted on the business card. One ember was all it took for flames to engulf the card.

Pepper flew off the sofa, grabbed a throw pillow, and frantically beat at the burning piece of evidence. But before she could fire off a fusillade of vituperative remarks Kimball's way, the funniest thing happened. The fire wasn't destroying the card, but breathing new life into it.

Tongue holstered, Pepper dropped the singed pillow. Luckily, the sofa caught her crashing bum. Side by side, the erstwhile motormouths sat in hushed silence, their jaws agape.

Burning, the naked business card curled in on itself, and when one spark remained, the embers shimmied, then exploded like a fireworks display, rendering a majestic bird of prey. As it soared around the room, flames danced along the creature's bloodred plumage and along its gold-tipped tail, a tail that resembled that of a peacock's. The firebird twirled and dipped, its movements divinely graceful. Up, then down it went, back-tracking even.

"It's writing something." The air, the paper, its body, the pen. Words materialized, resembling light graffiti: Красного люциана. "A message … Cyrillic. It's Russian." As for the fire-bird, well, once it had concluded its one job, it began to crackle and flicker. Then burst into embers that sifted down to the carpet.

The message drifted towards the area where Jhi had created a chaosgate. Right as the outline of the gate vanished, the message stopped and hovered in place. "A way-sign! Door! It's waiting for a door!" She barreled to the bedroom to grab the chalk.

Right as she finished rendering a chaosgate, the Красного люциана way-sign cascaded to the door as if drawn there by a magnetic wand. With an audible pop, a three-dimensional door hatched, knob and all, save for a rudimentary 1-D skeleton lock. Unfortunately, they did not know where the chaosgate would lead them because the directional dematerialized. Could lead them to Siberia for all they knew.

Arcane sigils ran the length of the chaosgate and angrily pulsed, casting an eerie glow about the darkened space. Pepper wasted no time in twisting the knob. But it was locked.

Kimball peeled his lazy ass off the couch. "Hold up! Some-thing evil could be lurking on the other side." He extracted a stake and brandished it like a knight. "Okay, now I'm ready."

"Door's locked. Where'd you get that weapon?"

"Your man crush, that's where."

After lobbing an eye roll, Pepper flicked through her recalled memory in all manners of chaosnauting, starting with the most recent in her quest to understand chaosgate unlocking. "Jhi didn't draw a lock on his way to your house. Why?"

"Well, I don't effing know!"

"I'm talking to myself, so silence or violence while I puzzle this out."

Jhi had known where he was heading, but what did that have to do with a lock? Karma Academy incorporated the rendering of a lock, but why? What was the underlying difference between Karma Academy's chaosgate and when Jhi opened one? Well, Karma Academy used a lock because it granted only VIPs entrance. "Blood! That's it!"

Pepper retrieved a knife in the kitchen, then grimaced before slicing her flesh. After she fed the skeleton keyhole with her blood, it failed to unlock.

"Wow, that was … something else." Kimball chased his snarky response with an eye roll.

"Revolver. Duh!" Palm throbbing, Pepper used her non-tortured hand to extract the gun from the waistband of her jeans. "Walt's blood coats the grip of the handgun, albeit dry. Don't you see? This chaosgate was tailor-made for Walt. Easy access, nary an eyewitness to his nefarious goings-on. Ergo, *his* blood is the key."

Once the gun was flush with the lock, Pepper gingerly scraped the crusty blood off the grip using the paring knife. The instant the flakes hit the lock's interior, they liquefied and pooled within the confines of the outline, and the chaosgate activated.

Pepper quickly retrieved a flashlight and Sawyer's blowpipe. Then, without further ado, Pepper went to cross the threshold, but Kimball threw his arm in front of her, halting her efforts. "Wait, you're seriously gonna walk through that door? Then what?"

"Yes, and I don't know. Sink or swim, Kimby. Wherever this chaosgate leads, your mom could be on the other end. If not, we're sure to find much-needed answers, in the least. C'mon, it'll be like old times." With that, Pepper stepped into the great unknown, a reluctant Kimball hot on her heels.

Years ago, Pepper and Kimball, in the throes of innocence, a few years shy of a decade, would spend countless hours adventuring about a fantastical world of their own design, a world that faced a terrifying evil unlike any seen before. Sir Kimball, always playing the role of a dashing knight in shining armor, would set out on a heroic mission to rescue Princess Pepper from Capital-E Evil's lair. Valiant, he'd wield his mighty (plastic) sword and defeat Evil once and for all, saving not only the princess but her kingdom as well, and they lived happily ever after!

The duo had finally reunited after quite a lengthy spell and were setting out on another quest to rescue a damsel in distress. Only this time, they were no longer playing a game of make-believe.

Between being cocooned in oppressive darkness and what felt like walking on the ocean floor, chaosnauting wasn't exactly the pink of fun. Should you need to call for help, you were out of luck. Your cries would be silenced, swallowed by the void.

After a few seconds inside the tunnel, profound loneliness and feelings of abandonment shrouded Pepper, their strength coiling around her heart like a noose. Not so much a voice, but a feeling, emanating from nowhere and everywhere, tried its damnedest to convince her that her dad was gone, her only family. There was no point in her existence. That she was insignificant. Nobody would miss Pepper, so just fall already. In response, her body listed to one side.

Pepper, listen to my voice only, her paladin demanded. *One foot in front of the other. Count your steps, if you must.*

Pepper pinched herself, the sting snapping her to the here and now, and mentally reminded herself that a location was scribbled above the lintel, albeit in Russian, that the tunnel will lead to a destination.

Speak of the devil, Pepper ran right into it. And Kimball into her. With quivering hands, she frantically quested for the knob. *Dear God, where is it?*

Once found, relief flooded her being, and she pushed Point B's ingress inward, as slow as could be, annihilating all door creaks before they had the chance to alarm anyone should they be within eye- or earshot on the other side.

Beyond the arctic-chilled barrier of the chaosgate, an empty room, swathed in moonlight, unfurled. Empty as far as bodies were concerned. Once Pepper gave the all-clear and stepped onto terra firma, a familiar odor assailed her senses. At first, an orange-java smell tickled her nosebuds, only to be chased away by pungent sulfur. "Do you smell that? Like rotten eggs."

"She who smelt it dealt it." Kimball snickered. "Bell … there was a voice inside that tunnel—"

"I know."

"It said my mom is dead. That she's waiting for me. And I could be with her if I just—Never mind." Kimball extracted a flask and gulped down liquid courage.

"Don't believe a word of whatever it said to you."

Flashlight in hand, Kimball gave a cursory search of the space, roughly the size of a studio apartment. One door. No, strike that. A chaosgate conquered the wall adjacent to the one they'd ventured through, ancient-looking sigils thundering and pulsating along its frame. But not a way-sign to be found. Perhaps answers to Bunny's whereabouts—her very soul—resided beyond the mysterious gateway. Then again, it could be a trap, and they could be unknowingly entering Evil's lair or Boss Lady's head-quarters.

Before taking the plunge, Pepper continued inspecting her surroundings. A bank of windows ran the length of another wall. Outside, herons roosted within the mangrove tree canopy. Teth-ered boats rocked at numerous docks. A fetid odor impregnated with fish guts and brine climbed up the steps of a stairwell off to the side.

"Wait, I know this place. The Red Snapper on Big Marco River." Kimball explained how his father was a private investor of the bayside seafood market-slash-grill on Marco Island—one of the Ten Thousand Islands, and a hop, skip, and a jump from Naples.

"Captain Walt could've simply delivered the day's catch here and nothing more, nothing nefarious afoot."

"Or not." Pepper jerked a thumb at the mysterious chaosgate.

"Yay, more suicidal ideations await." Kimball sighed.

"What is that?" Feet from the chaosgate, a translucent tentacle writhed on the floor in a pool of rust-colored matter. A beat later, familiar notes of an orangey java assaulted Pepper's nostrils, then finished with a deeply unpleasant sulfuric odor. Pepper crouched down and touched the substance. "It's fresh. Warm to the touch. Thick too."

"What is wrong with you? You are *so* not normal." Kimball screwed his face in disgust.

"You don't smell anything funky?" When Kimball shook his head, Pepper sighed and stood back up. "Point being"—she placed her hand on the wall as she felt woozy, her balance precarious—"is that whatever this is." Her body started folding, her heart slowing, and talking proved a challenge. "Whoever killed it … they were just here. We just missed them." She felt as if she were drifting off, carried on a wave, here but not.

"Or maybe they're going where we're going." Kimball eyed the one and only active chaosgate. "Pepper, can you hear me?" His voice was distant.

She bit back a cry of agony at what felt like razor blades tattooing her branded wrist.

"Holy shit, you're bleeding!"

Snapped back to full alertness, Pepper used her top to wipe away the blood on her wrist. "Okay, that was weird. What if that" —she pointed to the bloodied tentacle—"is what Walt was transporting? Before Sawyer whacked him, he said the job was easy. Pickups were discreet. And something about slipping his targets a mickey."

"It looks like a deep-sea creature's appendage, Bell, not some designer drug."

"True, but don't forget that we just walked through a dedicated chaosgate created solely for Captain Walt, his blood the key, so he definitely picked up his Mickey Finn here. Maybe his kill orders, too."

"Yeah, but how could whatever that thing is be connected to demonic possessions?"

"Cyanide." Right as Kimball began walking away in a huff, Pepper added, "Wait! Hear me out. Forty percent of the population cannot detect the telltale odor of the poison. I'm not imagining things, Kimby. I definitely pick up a strange scent from that weird alien-looking thing, but you don't. What if Bunny couldn't smell it either? A sip or two of a poisoned cocktail later and a demon waiting in the wings pounces on your mom's vulnerable body."

Kimball bit the inside of his cheek while considering her theory. "Shelly's always bitched about having to pay my mom alimony for life should they divorce, so what if he did the next best thing? Mom's technically out of the picture, and his coffers stay full. Ever the trendsetter, dear old Dad, seems as if all of his business associates quote-unquote divorced their spouses, too. One minute they're rosé all day-ing on a cruise and the next they return possessed by homicidal demons."

"A perfect murder when there's still a body walking around. I wonder how many more people in Naples, outside your father's social group, are possessed by blood-thirsty wanderers."

"No se."

"As it is, this tentacle is kinda flimsy evidence-wise, and it wouldn't exactly bolster up our case against your dad in a court of law. Or we could be completely off the mark, and it is just an alien sea creature. We need more proof, like actual proof."

"Bell, we're beyond the judicial system. You want proof? It and my mom could be beyond that chaosgate. C'mon." Ambling that way, knight-errant Sir Kimball brandished his mighty silver-dipped stake, ready to rescue his queen Bunny.

Before questing onward, before chaosnauting through the portal, Pepper snatched a chair and propped it between door and jamb. As one of Sir Kimball's retinue, Pepper's duty was to protect The Precious at all costs. That, and being locked out of their only known way out, wasn't exactly wise.

Alas, an invisible force propelled the chair to the other side of the room right as the door snapped shut.

A dank cellar, cloaked in shadows, resided at Point B. Water splashed in the distance, but nothing more. And as for the smell, well, that reeked of hot garbage and bleach. Sticking to the shadows, they tiptoed about and scaled the walls.

Light splashed from around a corner, and Pepper stole a peek. The gruesome spectacle caused her breath to hitch. If only Kimball had heeded her warning to not look, his face wouldn't've blanched with terror.

Sprawled about the wet cement was a soaked-to-the-bone teen girl, her eyes lifeless and frozen. A hose lay nearby, errant drops of water trickling out. Bits of flesh and hair tangled in a drain's metal crossings. Pepper's eyes trawled from the corpse to an active chaosgate affixed to the wall directly behind the dead girl, its destination unknown.

Kimball broke Pepper's concentration and then, with a quivering finger, pointed to a free-standing trough sink in the far-flung corner of the cellar. A barrel-chested man scrubbed his gore-stained hands, globs of blood trickling down the sink's lip and pooling on the cement.

Departing ASAP! would be the wisest course of action. But not before Pepper retrieved a backpack slumped against the wall, most likely belonging to the girl. Deftly, Pepper crouched and reached for the straps. Just one more stretch.

Right as Pepper's fingers grasped the fabric, the killer shut off the water, then walked their way. Sir Kimball laid down his mighty sword, left the refuge of the shadows, and bolted towards the way they came, a cowardly act that gave them away.

At that precise moment, the man sprouted fangs and levitated. Then tore through the air like a speeding bullet. Kimball didn't have a chance. With one hand cinched around Kimball's throat in a vise-grip, the killer lifted Kimball's body in the air as if he weighed next to nothing. In broken English, he demanded to know who Kimball was, who sent him.

Kimball choked out "Shelly Garcia" right as the stake slipped out of Kimball's grasp and clanged to the floor. Which didn't exactly build trust between the two.

Still cloaked in the shadows, Pepper whipped out the blowpipe, wrapped her lips around it, and huffed and puffed. At least one poisoned dart landed on the vampire, his jugular, to be exact. Poison darts didn't do a damn thing to vampires, duly noted!

The bloodsucker whipped his head around, then spotted Pepper. In a dialect most likely Russian, he either cursed her, laid out his plans for her demise, or all of the above.

With a flick of the wrist, he summoned the blowpipe to come into his possession. It slipped out of Pepper's grasp like a Water Wiggler and soared to its new owner. Fright rooted Pepper to the spot; she couldn't tear her eyes away from the death-dealing weapon now in the hands of her enemy.

What about not *venturing outside your home after dark, didn't you understand?* the voice chided as he took complete control of Pepper, forcing her to run toward the vampire.

The tower-tall Russian thundered towards Pepper, his lips wrapped around the blowpipe.

A game of deadly chicken was not what Pepper had in mind. Though, try as she might, she couldn't stop her forward momentum. Right before she smacked into the vamp, and moments before a poisoned dart landed on its intended target, Pepper crashed to the floor, the dart soaring over her head. The built-up momentum aided her in slipping along the wet cement as if on a macabre slip-and-slide. The ride ended right at the stake's location. In no time flat, she wielded the vamp-destroyer and prepared for battle.

However, the vamp outmanned her with his strength. In a snap, the Russian had Pepper in a chokehold, the pressure mounting, airflow constricting.

Sir Kimball didn't do a damn thing. Didn't move a muscle. Only cowered in a corner, rocking back and forth, like the paper tiger he truly was.

Pepper thrashed. Kicked. Arms pinwheeling in an attempt to gain purchase. Pinpricks of stars fluttered at the edge of her vision and were scudding ever closer over her entire line of sight.

Reaching backward, Pepper barely grabbed hold of his neck with one hand, his head with the other, then channeled every ounce of strength she had and pinched. A guttural growl escaped from her mouth as she continued applying pressure. The martial arts move worked like a dream; the chokehold loosened, and she slipped out of his grasp.

When the Russian's arm thrust Pepper's way, she snatched it and yanked him into her. The vamp's back to Pepper, she jabbed the back of his legs near the knees with her sandaled feet, knocking the bloodsucker to the ground.

She jumped atop him and sat astride, thighs squeezing and pinning him to the ground, her forearm pressing on his neck. For a brief moment, she glimpsed an animated tattoo on his neck—fire spurted from the mouth of a black and ancient dragon, and the flames took on the form of a firebird.

Alert once more, Pepper grabbed his meaty head and pounded it into the flooring. Once he was distracted enough, his brain addled, Pepper extracted the stake.

Now thrust it with all your might into his heart. One shot is all you've got. The paladin's words dripped with urgency. *Do it NOW!*

Pepper stabbed the vampire in the chest in one fell swoop, burrowing the silver stake deeper and deeper until it hit gold—the cement flooring. The vamp's eyes popped wide open in stunned disbelief as he clung to the death-dealing weapon, struggling with all his might to extract it. And he had a lot of might.

The Russian's veins ran black with poison. His eyes bulging, ready to pop from their sockets.

You must decapitate him.

And how do you propose I do that? With a paring knife? And why aren't you possessing me and doing it yourself?

You need to learn.

No time!

Pepper, spattered in blood, slipped into the dead girl's back-pack, retrieved her blowpipe, and paused before the chaosgate. With a sidelong glance, she coldly asked Kimball, "You coming?" It would be an exercise in futility to unscrew the disgust from her face.

Through whimpers, Kimball breathed, "Your calmness, it's disconcerting."

Pepper disregarded his remark. Mostly because she didn't want to admit that Kimball's observation was dead-on. Still, she helped a corner-bound Kimball to his feet before questing onward.

CHAPTER 13

When Time is freed, it liberates not the mind but caged anxieties. And when left alone with Free Time, lurking worries step out of the shadows and demand to be heard. As for Pepper, after countless weeks passed by, and she was no closer to discovering the truth about her past, the demands were deafening.

Helpless and hands bound were foreign concepts to Pepper, but that was exactly how she felt after the vampire attack.

Ever the coward, Kimball had bailed around o'dark-thirty shortly thereafter, leaving Pepper to fend for herself should a vampire hunt her down. Or Sawyer, for that matter. If Pepper even attempted to venture out past sunset to hunt for vampires or to go to the grocery store, chances were she'd meet the same fate as the murdered Initiate, Valerie. Valerie, that was the dead girl's name. At least according to the stitching on the inside of her back-pack. But an Initiate she most certainly was, according to the bloodied Karma Academy missive, tucked into a zippered compartment.

To make matters a heck of a lot worse, Pepper couldn't do a damn thing about defending herself from the danger lurking outdoors, at least not in her magicless state. And she couldn't in good conscience further anger the paladin and place herself and him in unnecessary danger. Those near-death encounters—two in the same day—still haunted Pepper, left her feeling uneasy.

So, she hunkered down in her house, became a veritable shut-in, and quickly convinced herself that Jhi would return with good news in tow. Had no choice, really, but to adopt that belief. More-over, they had brokered a deal, vowed to help each other, so all she had to do was bide her time until then. Stay indoors and under the radar, and all would be well.

Week one exile, after the vampire attack: drowning in Free Time, a graduation hangover seized Pepper something fierce. Not even a month ago, Pepper had spent sleepless nights toiling away for umpteen tests, poring over godawfully tedious textbooks and notes, all that in preparation for Graduation Day—the first day of the rest of your life; a day that arrived and disappeared at whip-like speed.

Still reeling, the graduate then had to contend with a "what-now?" vibe thrumming bone-deep, along with heaping doses of fear. Freedom and adult decision-making at such a young age were downright terrifying, and being told to choose a forever career even more so. Overwhelmed, Pepper succumbed to a crying jag and drowned her face and snot-choked nose in an ocean of pillows.

She tragically missed the crutch of mandatory education, a schedule to adhere to, even a routine, but mostly her dad and his loving arms. To her credit, the ugly cry lasted for about fifteen minutes, and she dried her eyes, then called her pops. Misty-eyed, Pepper stifled her tears and relished in hearing his voice, hated having to lie to him, but oh well.

Week two exile spotlighted the blithering mess that Pepper'd morphed into. Thoughts of Jhi and his protracted absence and theories as to why ran on an eternal loop through her mind, driving her mad to boot. Perhaps soul-brokers didn't have cell phones, or they couldn't communicate inter-dimensionally.

Or perhaps Jhi was in danger and needed to hide out until the coast was clear, and calling Pepper would put her in unnecessary peril. Then a heavy-hearted Pepper realized how ridiculous she sounded.

Bottom line, if Jhi wanted to talk to her, he'd finagle a way. Abashedly, the Jhi-crushing quantum-leaped to obsessive levels. A pox on you, Free Time!

Exile, week three: nary a word from Jhi or Kimball. And Pepper was still a basket case. Irrationally, Pepper cursed Karma for somehow thwarting her efforts to attend the goddess' eponymous Academy, thereby flushing Pepper's destiny down the toilet!

And screw you, Jhi! Not just a soul broker, he trafficked in lies on the side. He got the intel he needed from Pepper, then bolted. How very demonlike of him.

Hermit Pepper got reacquainted with another old habit—emotion-eating sessions six ways from Sunday, her stomach a bottomless pit. A throwback from her days in middle school. Pepper whipped up mainly carb-laden Eye-talian (as her pops pronounced it) delicacies, the Food Network Channel her sole form of companionship.

There was some good news to be had. Pepper self-diagnosed her Jhi-obsessing as a chronic affliction—a one-sided crush. Bright side, Pepper had plenty of practice on how to get over said affliction—Time, and she had nothing but time to do just that.

Exile, week four: sweat-coated, Pepper awoke from a reoccurring nightmare—trailing after a shadowy Jhi, vampires hot on her heels—and proclaimed, "No more!" She'd wasted enough time on waiting around for a boy to reach out and call her. A boy whose heart belonged to the elusive JD. A boy who had clearly gamed her.

The hell she'd let more precious time slip through her fingers. So, Pepper untied the proverbial binds that were cinched around her hands, removed the blindfold, and made amends with Free Time. It was safe to say that Pepper Li Bell got back her groove and finally took destiny by its horns.

Not wanting to be dependent on the paladin, and until she reunited with her magic, Pepper decided it was best to seek out other means of defense.

It was amazing what one can find in the shadowy corners of the Interweb, bitcoins the currency. If in the market for vampire-slaying accoutrements, then one needn't look further than the Starless Souk, a black market rife with supernatural goodies.

One seller, in particular, M, hailing from Morgansk, apparently located near Russia, perked up and offered to share her (or his) erudite knowledge in the art of vampire slaying, especially after hearing from Pepper how Naples, Florida was ostensibly blighted by a vamp infestation. By the time the duo concluded their emailing back and forth, Pepper purchased a cadre of armaments and anxiously awaited their arrival.

Exile-no-more, today was turning out to be a red-letter day! The graduation hangover subsided. Thanks to her moonlighting as Alonzo Steele, she had a forever career in mind—joining the sisterhood of assassins overseen by Karma and whatever work that entailed—so having a direction to move in was comforting. All in all, things weren't *that* life-ending as once thought.

Pepper's crush fever broke, and she was on the mend. Sadly, she had no other choice but to amicably call it quits with Jhi (which is easy to do when engaged in a one-sided relationship, but still). And thinking about Jhi produced neither a heart spasm nor a swarm of butterflies, and her blood failed to boil. A red-letter day, indeed!

The doorbell sounded, and Pepper walked briskly to the front door. When she looked through the peephole, an "ugh" escaped from her throat. If not for the obnoxious ringing of the doorbell every two seconds, Pepper would not have opened the door.

"Here, this was resting on your doorstep." As Kimball, glassy-eyed, let himself into Pepper's dwelling, he proffered a box with no return address or recipient name, just a leather-thick postage stamp depicting the wind in the shape of a disembodied hand. "Whoa, Bell, looking ... Well, you've seen better days."

Pot meet kettle. One whiff and Pepper nearly choked from the miasma of alcohol and marijuana-laced fumes blanketing Kimball.

"What do you want, Kimball?"

"Give me a minute, would ya?" Kimball plopped down on the couch, extracted a flask, and swilled its mood-enhancing ambrosia. "Anything fun?" He glanced at the box Pepper greedily ripped into.

The supplies she had ordered from the seller M on the Starless Souk had arrived. Nestled inside were silver-dipped stakes and blades, garrotes, and sunbursters, along with laconic how-to instructions: *Aim for the heart, then decapitate. Pull grenade pin and throw. Good luck, M.*

The vampire-annihilators were no sooner tucked away into their new home, Pepper's go-bag. Should she encounter a vampire, she'd be armed and ready. A victim no more.

"No bag? Wait. Are you back living at your house?" For weeks on end, Kimball had been couch-surfing, according to chatter on Naples Teen Scene.

"Sure am." He collapsed on the couch and ran this fingers through his curly golden locks. "Daddy-O laid down an edict. Said if I ever wanted to see my mother again, I was to return home. Pretty much confirming he's involved in my mom's disappearance. Furthermore, Shelly said he'd sic the Hounds of Hell on me, whatever those are, if I didn't abide by his demands, if I didn't attend some upcoming gala, but more on that later."

The pleasure Pepper derived from Kimball's summoning back home somewhat lessened the anger she harbored against him for not living up to his end of the bargain—serving as eyes and ears on the ground.

"You are aware that Shelly's using your mother as leverage for whatever sick and twisted game he's mired within. As if you didn't know she was, in fact, dead." Twisting that knife into Kimball felt oh so good.

Shock seized Kimball for a spell. "But she's not—Don't say

that! He hid her soul somewhere in the house. I just know it. And I certainly can't quest for it unless there."

He drained the dregs of his flask before fishing out a curious-looking envelope from his jeans pocket.

"Back to the matter at hand. The why I'm here, gracing you with my manliness. And you're welcome for that. While I was motoring around town, this invitation addressed to me materialized on my car's seat by way of sorcery. Milady," he bowed, twirling his hand in a flourish, "I would be ever so grateful if you'd agree to be my distinguished guest. So, what say you?" he asked without preamble, to which Pepper emphatically replied with a hard NO. "Wise decision on your part. As I stated earlier, this is an invitation to the aforementioned gala. The one where my attendance is mandatory."

Pepper tried to pluck the elegant envelope from Kimball's grasp. "Ah-ah, not so fast. Before you open that. Besides moi, the who's who of Naples have been cordially invited as well. Which would explain why you haven't received an invitation."

Pepper rolled her eyes in response before exploring every inch of the velvety crimson and ebony envelope, which, interestingly enough, didn't contain a return or recipient address, just the calligraphed name Sheldon Kimball Garcia II.

"The time has come for the unveiling. *Dun-dun-dun!*" Kimball slurred.

A foreboding air wafted about right as Pepper lifted the fold of the fuzzy envelope and extracted the ornate request for attendance. Written in calligraphy, the words, dripping in scarlet, had to be charmed, their message included, for Pepper felt a tug like a magnetic pull daring her not to show up to the gala. In fact, she could barely hear the taunting whisperings: "You know you want to go. Everyone who's anyone will be there."

"Ha, you heard it, too, didn't you?"

Pepper was too taken aback to respond.

"At first, I thought I was still tripping, but now I know I didn't imagine it." He then whispered the taunt verbatim.

Pepper read the invite aloud: "Greetings and salutations, Mr. Sheldon Kimball Garcia the second and plus-one: Come one, come all to a masquerade ball, where evil's forbidden to pass through the walls. Should you opt to stay home, you'll surely take fright, once the sun paves the way for the moonless night. At the stroke of midnight on All Hallows' Eve, the streets'll be teeming with demonic thieves. They'll seek out their prey one by one, and not a soul can stop them, only the sun. So come one, come all to the masquerade ball, where evil's forbidden to pass through the walls ..."

Date: October 30th

Time: 9:01 P.M.

Place: Port Royal

1881 Jolly Roger Court

Reminder: A mask is a must for the black-tie affair. No excuses, for you've had plenty of time to prepare. We have it on good authority that you're just dying for a good time, so no RSVP is necessary. Trust us, it'll be a night you won't soon forget!

Port Royal, a sprawling community hugged by the beach and bay and dotted with palatial estates, seamlessly bled into Aqualane Shores, where Pepper and Kimball called home. Evil had set up shop in her neck of the woods all right. But, begged the question, just what did *It* have in store for Neapolitans?

"Didn't that murderous carney Miles mention getting some practice in imbibing stolen magic from slain mages before All Hallows' Eve?"

"Yep. Whatever's planned for that gala, it doesn't bode well for guests, the plus-ones, me, that's for damn sure. So, Kimby came through with quite the clue and another lead. Am I right?" He nudged Pepper on the arm with his own. "Now be a dear and tell me when the man of mystery himself is scheduled to arrive, so I can be the bearer of glad tidings. Prove my worth."

"Who?" She affected a cool-as-a-cucumber attitude.

"She says 'who.'" He clucked his tongue. "Jhi requested that I meet him at your house today. I assumed you received the same ensorcelled missive. Why else would I be here?"

Pepper's heart didn't bounce about like a drunken fool upon hearing Jhi's name, proof positive that she was handling the breakup with Jhi like a champ.

A knocking sound emanated in the distance. Kimball averted his eyes to a painting that shimmied against the wall. "Speak of the devil!"

Jhi sauntered out of the chaosgate. He ended at Pepper's side, brushing his shoulder against hers by way of greeting, then said, "I tracked down the fixer who stole your magic. We must leave for Hell tonight!"

CHAPTER 14

The words "come again," and "where the hell have you been, besides Hell," were locked and loaded, ready to fire off Pepper's tongue, but Jhi drew first. "Reconning took me longer than expected. Sorry about that. Then I had business to attend to …"

"I'd say. You've been gone for *weeks*," Kimball said, unfazed.

Jhi had the chutzpah to smirk. "I probably should have mentioned that time doesn't run at the same speed in other dimensions as on Earth. Same goes for certain territories of Hell. Business elsewhere required my immediate attention, and I didn't think about the time difference. Sorry. If it's any consolation, on my end, I haven't been gone all that long. And I chaosnauted here as soon as I could."

So Jhi hadn't gotten the intel he needed from Pepper and bolted? Their verbal bargain was still active? Desperate to unscrew the look of embarrassment from her face, Pepper plucked Kimball's flask from his grasp and swilled a few fingers' worth.

Jhi focused his attention on the grandfather clock. "Looks like we've got some time to kill until H-hour. Till we journey to Hell."

"Here, bona fides for inter-dimensional travel." Jhi handed

over a forged visa with Pepper's mug plastered front and center. The pic must've been covertly snapped sometime after they'd first made each other's acquaintance. Boy, was it ever unflattering, bad lighting, her bangs a righteous mess. Hell, it gave her DL photo a run for its money, and that's saying something.

"Marie Smith is my name? This seriously necessary?" Pepper asked.

"Listen, your life is in danger, so I need you to be incognito. As for the visa. No passport, no entrance. We, too, have borders and rules and more rules and ridiculous bureaucratic regulations. Who do you think your bloated government learned the ropes from? Speaking of ropes, I'm showing them to you, soul-broker recruit. The reason for visiting Hell. Once there, follow my lead, and all should be well." Pepper hung on to the *should* as if she were a hanging chad.

Pepper perused the visa, which slightly resembled a passport; stamps from—other dimensions?—marred a handful of pages. Not that she could comprehend the dialects.

"Pandæmonia's rife with ever-eyes and ears, watching all and sundry, so keep your hoodie up and wear the ID on your person at all times." Jhi proffered said hoodie to Pepper, which amounted to a creepy cowl stitched to a sooty black robe lined in crimson.

After divesting himself of the life-size tool of many deadly weapons strapped to his back, he folded himself on the couch. His beanie was the next item to be removed, and his fingers wasted no time in taming his tousled chestnut-auburn locks.

Jhi went over the bare-bones of what he'd garnered on his end: the good, the bad, and the ugly. After scouring the Records Section of the Department of Soul Brokering, Jhi couldn't find any evidence of Sheldon Kimball Garcia I entering into a soul contract. Ditto for Miles Leagan and Jeremiah Olsen.

"The fact I found nothing smacks of a conspiracy—all the more reason for us to get a move-on. Now for the good news. Tracked down our fixer friend to his last known whereabouts.

Name's Bhi'gow. He's also the proprietor of Skulduggerer's Lair, an enchantment shop and museum of sorts in Pandæmonia proper. I figure we'll pay this Lair a visit, which is where Bhi'gow was last seen, and see if your presence triggers anything." Jhi's piercing eyes and raised brows hinted he had discovered more than he let on.

Kimball excused himself from the reunion and headed toward Pepper's bathroom.

The moment Kimball closed the bathroom door, Jhi whispered, "I thought we had an agreement?" A note of annoyance coated his tone.

"What are you implying, Jhi?" Pepper matched his tone. She, too, thought they had an agreement. He could have called, at least once, and checked in. Was that too much to ask?

"Anything you'd like to share, anything at all you forgot to mention about that mysterious robot voice that wasn't a voice?"

Kimball returned, interrupting Pepper and Jhi's heated chat, and plopped back down on the sofa. "Whatcha guys talking about?"

Pepper ignored Kimball and brought Jhi up to speed on the alpha to the omega, since his protracted absence, save for her mood swings. "So, as you can see, it's all interconnected, that's for damn sure. Kimball's father. How wanderers have possessed the spouses of Shelly's business associates like Bunny. Sawyer. The curious firebird that ensorcelled a way-sign from out of thin air. The masquerade ball invite and vampire that nearly killed us."

"My question is why not just kill your husband or wife instead of siccing a wanderer on them and having to deal with the hassle of keeping the demon on a tight leash," Jhi added, his tone matter-of-fact.

Pepper and Kimball were noticeably taken aback by Jhi's blasé attitude when it came to homicide.

"Speaking of murder. Bell, ever figure out who the dead girl was?" Kimball asked. "Any identifiers in her backpack?"

"No," Pepper lied.

"Probably was a mage, like the girls my father killed." Kimball shifted his weight from off the couch. "I can't unsee my father killing that lavender-haired girl." Kimball rubbed his eyes with the palms of his hands. "Her face is plastered all over the news. Same with the other girl. Their mothers are on TV begging people who have any information to come forward. And it's not like I can call the Sheriff's hotline to submit an anonymous tip."

"You think they uncovered a local mage's guild and ID'd their members?" Pepper asked, sickened by the prospect.

"Not sure. Last I heard, there were six girls and a guy reported missing. The number is climbing by the day. And those are the ones we know about. At least two of the missing girls on the news were mages. And all the missing persons ran in the same circle. The other day, I overheard Miles mentioning to my dad how they recruited someone to help track down mages in hiding. Ven-ad't-say." He slurred the word. "Roughly translated to the Hunter. That's what they called him. God, is that ever creepy. Well, I better get back before Daddy Dearest notices my absence. He's been watching me like a hawk."

"Yes, Kimby, you do that." Pepper directed her attention to Jhi. "Our fellow soldier here deserted us while you were reconning. He only just returned to his pre-agreed assignment."

Kimball then addressed Jhi's reproachful look as to why Kimball had left the den of iniquity in the first place. "I needed me time. So fret not. Your mole is back and has burrowed deep inside Evil's lair, aka mi casa. Maybe when you return from frolicking about Hell, I'll have advantageous news to report. If I'm not dead." With that, Kimball bid adieu and shuffled home.

Once the front door closed, Pepper jumped right in and said, "About the voice ..."

At the same time, Jhi blurted, "You lied about the girl?"

"Yes, and I'll explain why. But you first. C'mon, don't leave me hanging in suspense!"

Jhi squeaked out a smirk. "According to my contact, Bhi'gow is the only fixer with a capuchin partner in crime. Capuchin. Ring any bells?" Jhi noted Pepper's eyes floating down to the sprinkle of freckles on her wrist. "Yep, explains why the branding is in the shape of a monkey. Now, as for the animation, he's not just any capuchin. He's a ruachti." Sounded like rue-AK-ti, the "r" rolled.

Jhi described ruachtis as descendants of an ancient line of warriors, all animals, or hybrids thereof, who were charged with protecting deities. Because of their storied acts of valor, they achieved demigod status.

"To this day, the magic ruachtis wield is formidable, as are their combat skills. Where is all this leading? This ruachti is none other than your mysterious voice. And that's not a branding on your wrist as once thought. There was no need for the fixer to brand you. Not when the ruachti has burrowed inside you. But you already knew this, didn't you? Pertinent details you neglected to share. His name is Loki, if you're curious."

"Honest to God, Jhi, I couldn't tell you about him, er Loki, even if I had wanted to. He wouldn't let me. Tied up my tongue, in fact, the few times I tried to come clean."

Jhi's shoulders dropped, and his eyes softened. "Fine. I'll drop it. But moving forward, full disclosure."

Pepper nodded her head in agreement.

"What still doesn't make sense is why the ruachti had to burrow inside you, an extra layer of protection, if you will, not counting whatever the fixer was tasked with doing. Pepper"—his face grew serious—"this ruachti burrowing inside you, it's extreme and, quite frankly, unheard of. And if you are indeed under a cloaking spell, like I believe you are, it isn't permanent. Otherwise, you wouldn't be cohabiting with a ruachti. The fact remains that it's been biding its time, waiting for a showdown. But for how long? And a showdown with what? Whatever is after you, present tense intended, it must be big and nasty."

Slack-jawed, Pepper did everything she could not to raid the pantry. *Whatever is after you must be big and nasty*, kept running on a loop in her mind.

"Here's the interesting part. The duo of Bhi'gow and Loki fell off the face of Hell around twelve years ago. Haven't been heard from since. Yet all that time, it was business as usual regarding Bhi'gow's enchantment shop."

"That's odd. When would I have developed magical abilities?"

"Adolescence. Hormones are a catalyst to a human's unCloaking or coming into their powers. But not at five years old, I can tell you that much."

Lost in thought, Pepper nibbled on the skin surrounding her fingernail. At the earliest, she would have been twelve when she summoned the demonic duo. Kimball had morphed from bestie to enemy then, so that explained his cluelessness regarding her powers. But what tragedy befell her, forcing her to enter into a devil's bargain?

"Apart from the hell that was middle school, I lived a charmed life with my pops. Or is that belief manufactured?" She blurted out, panic taking over. "Are any memories real?" Larry was her everything. Love like that couldn't be made up.

Jhi latched his sea-glass eyes on Pepper. "How long have you had those freckles on your wrist?"

For some reason, that question chilled Pepper to the bone. "Since I can remember."

That wasn't the response Jhi was expecting, as evidenced by a slight tilt to his head. "Or that's what you've been made to believe. It's entirely possible that your life now is a fabrication, memories altered. But it ill behooves you to entertain the what-ifs. Not when we're hours away from finding answers. Here's the plan. Once we step inside the enchantment shop, Loki'll pick up Bhi'gow's scent and take control of your motor skills. Then he'll lead us directly to Bhi'gow. After all, the only one who can exorcise this hitchhiking ruachti from your body is his fixer companion. Until then, you'll have Loki to fight against whatever danger is coming."

Pepper could feel Loki stir whenever Bhi'gow's name was mentioned, her wrist prickling, a painful sensation akin to when she and her pops got matching tattoos on her sixteenth birthday. If she wasn't mistaken, Loki wanted to return to Hell. Pepper tapped her wrist and conveyed mentally, *Soon you'll reunite with your fixer and I with my magic.*

"Now, onto the bloodsucker and the dead girl."

"Her name was Valerie, and she wasn't just a mage, but an Initiate, like me. But what I can't figure out is how the vampire even knows about the existence of Initiates, let alone where to find one? Not even the Karma Academy invite was addressed to me. Our identities are supposedly cloaked in secrecy. Or they were." Talk about a terrifying thought. "Valerie had the Karma Academy missive in her backpack. It looked identical to the one I received, complete with the how and when to chaosnaut to the Academy."

"Which means she had one day to chaosnaut there—the day of her death, correct?"

"Yep. Begs the question: did the vampire snatch Valerie before or after arriving? If after, that lends itself to a disturbing possibility that Karma Academy could very well be under siege or close to being. Either way, Sawyer van Arsdale has been outed as a traitor to our kind. How else would vampires know about Karma Academy and Agents? What if Valerie wasn't a one-off? Who's to say we're not all in danger of being assassinated? Is our magic the reason?"

Jhi imperceptibly tapped his index finger on the tip of his thumb. "Assuming Hounds have murdered more girls. Technically, we know of only one. And Sawyer tried to kill you for loose-end purposes. She has no idea you're an Initiate."

"And it's vital to keep *that* under wraps."

Jhi nodded in agreement, then said, "Now, as for vampires, barring the supernatural speed and hyper-strength, they aren't blessed with magical powers. Still, the vampire killing the Initiate wasn't just for her magic alone, not when Earth is teeming with mages. And in my experience, vampires are too unruly and impetuous, which means they're not calling the shots. No, guaranteed, their boss is Sawyer's boss."

"That means Sawyer is definitely connected to Valerie's murder."

"Agreed. But I can't see a correlation between Agents of Karma and Initiates, your next-door neighbors, vampires that can now do the impossible, that is, absorb magic and cast spells, and All Hallows' Eve. What do they all have in common?"

Pepper was in her element, puzzling out mysteries. "Fair question. Here's another. Wouldn't Karma know that Agent Sawyer's gone rogue? Or that an Initiate was murdered on her way to the Academy? I mean, she *is* a goddess."

"For all we know, the goddess could be just a figurehead as far as the Academy is concerned."

"But don't you find it odd that I, a magicless amnesiac, as you've basically implied, received an invite to attend the Academy? All hell's breaking loose, and it's business as usual?"

"Now that you mention it, yes, that is odd. The invite said, and I quote, 'we've been observing you for some time now.' If that was true, then these observers would've known you were not a mage and had no means to chaosnaut to the Academy." Jhi, too, enjoyed a good brain teaser, judging from his rapid-fire responses. "Just speculation, but it's almost as if someone sent you that invite as a Mayday call."

"Maybe you're onto something. With Sawyer in the mix, Agents of Karma's cover will be blown to smithereens, if it hasn't already. Same for Initiates. Then it's open season on Agents, the vampires, the hunters. Then again, if not for the ruachti, I'd be dead."

"Nobody but you, me, the ruachti, and whoever sent that invite, if it wasn't Karma herself, was aware that you're an Initiate. You have the advantage. And as for Agents of Karma, they're highly trained assassins, and in the least, they have sorcery on their side. You don't. Which is why it's more imperative than ever we find that fixer. As it stands, only Bhi'gow knows who you really are and what danger you were running from."

The sun began its nightly descent, casting an amber glow about the living room.

"Might wanna get some sleep before we chaosnaut to Hell. Something tells me we won't get the chance once there." Jhi's suggestion had an ominous ring.

CHAPTER 15

Pepper's goal of catnapping before Hell-venturing had been dashed, anxiety to blame. So what better way to work off some steam than baking and noshing?

Buttery light limned the laminated counter, along with a rolling pin drenched in flour, errant chocolate chips that escaped death by melting, bits of chopped walnuts scattered about. A kitchen sink full of bowls glared back at Pepper. As for cleaning, that wasn't on the agenda.

Soon Pepper had another mouth to feed. "Smells delicious." An aroma of freshly baked cookies greeted Jhi. He brushed a finger along Pepper's cheekbone. Noticing her obvious freezing in response to his touch, Jhi added, "Just removed stray flour that took a liking to you is all. Can't say I blame it." Was Jhi flirting?

Damn that Jhi and his chiseled arresting features, perennial stubble intact. The way in which his tongue sultrily moved over his plump lips, as if moisturizing them, preparing for a kiss, or cookie-devouring, the latter being the case. And those eyes, dear God, those piercing eyes that reflected every shade found in the deep sea. When Jhi engaged in conversation, those piercers anchored onto you and refused to unmoor.

Pepper gave in to lustful musings, imagining tracing her

fingertips along his bushy eyebrows; were they as silky as they appeared, or more coarse? One way to find out. And while her hungry fingers were in the general vicinity, they might as well gently sweep to the side of the wild forelock that graced his prominent forehead.

Oh, how Pepper longed to run her fingers through his wavy chestnut locks, that frankly she preferred liberated more than corralled in a ponytail. Tonight, auburn threads, usually buried beneath the chestnut, glistened in the warm glow of the kitchen.

His understated choice of wardrobe received Pepper's seal of approval: jeans and a T-shirt. Yet Pepper couldn't help but wonder what his tattoos looked like without clothes impeding her ogling. Because she could have sworn she spied a scaly tail coiling around his forearm over a month ago, but it seemed to have since retreated.

To top it off, Jhi's mixed messages weren't helping matters. Nor did she appreciate her emotions being toyed with. A relationship firmly stuck in the realm of flirting, with no hope of ever evolving into that which your heart so desperately desired because one party had otherwise promised themselves to another, fueled a slow burn that, if persistently fanned over time, would rage on unabated until you were a pile of cinders; while the other party was left unscathed. So Pepper asked herself yet again, *What game was Jhi playing?*

Before the words traveled out of her mouth, they got tangled up with roiling frustration, and she lightly barked, "I take it you didn't find your girlfriend!" The oven timer dinged. She removed the gooey cookies, then gruffly set the baking sheet on the counter.

Poor refrigerator doors. They received the brunt of her mounting frustration as she swung them open. Scouring the shelves for milk, she whined, "Only two percent? Ugh!" A tinge of annoyance contaminated her tone, and try as she might, she couldn't purify her thoughts, her words; the only course of action was to marshal them to avoid sticking her foot in her mouth.

Balancing glasses of milk and a plate of cookies, Pepper clunked them down on the dining room table, bits of liquid splashing over the rims. This boy set her aflame in more ways than one. Admittedly, Pepper cursed herself for permitting Jhi to drive her crazy. A pox on him! And his girlfriend!

A few sighs and emotion-eating later, Pepper entertained heaps of guilt. Jhi's girlfriend was missing for God's sake and could very well be kidnapped or worse, and here Pepper wished he'd make a move on her.

"I'm sorry if that sounded harsh. It's just that I'm scared." She half-lied. "Hell's usually a place you do everything in your power to avoid."

"If you're picturing gurgling pits of lava-laden hellfire, the deafening screams of the soul-selling damned, that's Gehenna, or more specifically, a territory in Gehenna that is home to Oblivion's Fortress and the Pits of Tartarus."

Jhi described the Fortress as the main prison and the Pits as a separate entity on an island surrounded by lava; jailed in actual pits were humans who had committed untold acts of savagery while on Earth and elsewhere.

"Hell's a dimension, just like Earth. And Gehenna is merely one small section. But unlike Earth, time there moves at a different pace, more like a crawl. Worry not. We will not be going anywhere near there."

That explanation did nothing to chase away the worry. If anything, Pepper felt more terrified and took out her stress on the plate of cookies, shoving nearly a whole one in her mouth. After swallowing, she hesitantly asked, "So, the damned burn in Oblivion's Fortress or the Pits, like, forever-forever?"

"Let's get something straight. Burning in Hell for all eternity, or however you have heard it described on Earth, is more figurative than literal. Depending on the evil deeds the damned committed Earthside, their mandatory sentence in Oblivion's Fortress or the Pits could be anything from a decade, a century, to consecutive life sentences. And the daily torture meted out could consist of burning, sure, but there are so many other creative ways to maim."

Another cookie flew into Pepper's mouth as worry was quickly morphing to fear.

"For the damned, their souls are eternally bound in Hell. Yes, that part is true. But the Fortress is a prison, and just like a prison, you serve the required sentence and then you are released … er, transferred elsewhere. Now, back to your question. No, there is no forever-forever burning in Oblivion's Fortress. Then again, I'm sure those who have been incarcerated in the Pits for centuries would disagree with me." Jhi finished his glass of milk and wiped his mouth with his forearm.

In response to Pepper's question regarding what those people did back on Earth to have received such horrific sentences in the Pits that spanned centuries, Jhi said, "The atrocities they committed would make Lucifer blush. After all, they are truly ruthless, deranged, and evil."

Curiosity getting the best of her, Pepper asked, while wiping away chocolate crumbs from her lips, "If these humans have committed such barbaric atrocities, then why wouldn't Lucifer put them on his payroll as opposed to locking them up?"

"Because eons ago, Heaven and Hell halted the warring, forged a rapprochement, and entered into a covenant with The Man Upstairs. Demons agreed to accept the damned with open arms, while Heaven takes the righteous."

Jhi then mentioned that the damned are essential to daily life in Hell, their magic chief among them, and how souls of the damned made up a large percentage of electrical and mechanical power, along with serving as a form of currency.

Jhi used a mage as an example. "Before they've served their sentence in Oblivion's Fortress, the damned's magical powers are transferred into magic gems. Gems are a form of currency and the most coveted."

Jhi plucked one such gem out of his pocket. It resembled a

vintage collectible cat's eye marble; only this one had indigo vapor pinging about its circular walls.

"Even though demons are naturally gifted with magical abilities, only government officials, i.e., those working for the Ministry of Mischief and Mayhem, are authorized to use their Devil-given powers, while all others are forbidden. This is why magic gems are a black-market darling and heavily sought after in Hell, along with other magically enhanced objects. Because casting magic is banned in Hell, we have no choice but to rely heavily on enchanted objects, and gems are the batteries."

Jhi placed a marble in Pepper's hand. "Aside from powering objects, gems are veritable magic boosters that enable demons to tap into our manacled magic and cast spells. Can you feel anything at all from the gem?"

Heart revving, blood surging, Pepper nodded and explained how she felt a power, a tug of energy, like a vibrational match to her being.

"That's a good sign. Still, law enforcers monitor the use of magic in Hell, so once we retrieve your stolen magic, use these gems sparingly to not draw attention to yourself. Or you will have mala'khas to contend with."

Jhi further shed light on the grim fate of the damned sentenced to eternal punishment in Hell. Once the damned endured torturing for however long in Oblivion's Fortress, their handed-down sentence completed, mala'khas turned them over to the Department of Soul Sundering and Assignments. Taking into account the crimes the damned committed against humanity, parole officers then determined where they were to be transported next and in what capacity.

Some souls were sundered from the bodies of the damned, and their bits and pieces shoved into soul shards, thereby entering into monetary circulation. Others were severed, and their body parts grace the walls of Pandæmonia businesses and private homes like trophies—Talking Heads, the locals called them.

Many unlucky damned were used as sacrifices at the various

shrines sprinkled about. While some were used as carrion for gargoyles—the law enforcers in Hell, patrolling the skies, watching all and sundry. Some were even considered a delicacy and sold in butcher shops.

Boiled down, the fate of the damned all hinged on the evil deeds committed during their time on Earth, the amount of innocent blood shed by their hands, et cetera, et cetera.

Jhi noted Pepper's terror-stricken eyes and gaping jaw. "Okay, so we punish those from Earth? Someone has to do it. Demons are perfect for the job because they have a stronger conviction for torturing and maiming. Bottom line, we have a helluva lot more fun in my dimension. Just you wait and see."

With each passing minute, the dread inside Pepper at the thought of journeying to Hell in a few hours mushroomed. She needed to switch topics before fear got to her, and she called the whole thing off.

"So, tell me about this JD? If I'm going to be helping you find her, it would be nice to know something about her. Like, how did you guys meet?"

One side of Jhi's mouth tugged upward into a half-smile. "Through work. She's a fellow soul broker. What to say about JD ...? Well, she's intoxicating. You can't help but gravitate to her and want to be in her orbit to soak up her rays of warmth and charm. It doesn't hurt that she's unassuming and physically striking. But at her core, she's sweet and"—his eyes narrowed, and a sly smile ghosted over his lips—"intuitive, whip-smart, and resilient."

Pepper instantly regretted asking about the seemingly perfect JD and had to blink slowly to calm her throbbing heart and to chase away any telltales of jealousy that might have appeared on her face.

"I take it you didn't drum up a lead on her whereabouts while you were away, or you would've said by now?"

"You are correct. And the longer she's missing, the colder the trail becomes."

"What's your theory as to what's happening next door with the Garcias?" Pepper nibbled on a cookie, the chocolate melting in her mouth.

"Definitely something to do with soul contracts. Only whoever drew them up didn't put them through the appropriate channels. See, my dominus, Mephistopheles, First Underlord of Hell and Deputy Director of the Department of Soul Brokering, oversees every contract."

According to Jhi, soul contracts adhered to a chain of custody that began and ended with Mephistopheles, from the time a soul contract left the Department to its execution and filing in Records. And every contract contained Mephistopheles' official seal. That way, Jhi's dominus had omnipotent knowledge of who was rendering up their souls, the when, the where, et cetera.

"So if Kimball's father sold his soul, which I'm certain he did, then there would be a record on file, along with the identity of the soul broker, only there wasn't. I don't want to involve Mephistopheles just yet. Not until I've culled more proof."

"Let me get this straight. JD, a fellow soul broker, has up and disappeared. Along with this mysterious soul broker, who has dealings with Kimball's dad and has taken a fancy to sunshiny Naples and its denizens. So much so that said broker has successfully peddled his wares around my turf, yet all proof of signed soul contracts was scrubbed from the Ministry of Mischief and Mayhem Records Department. And your adopted theory is that JD somehow stumbled across the conspiracy involving unsanctioned soul contracts, probably began sniffing around, and was caught by the perps?"

If she's not *the* corrupt soul broker in question. Yes, Pepper immediately jumped to that conclusion but sagaciously chose not to voice it.

Too busy masticating, Jhi nodded his head in response.

"You never explained what led you to follow Sawyer to Naples in the first place? Or her connection to JD's disappearance."

Jhi swallowed slowly before replying. "Sawyer was one of the last people to see JD alive."

Turned out, Jhi had shown up early for a dinner date with JD at a bar on the outskirts of Pandæmonia. There, he spotted JD and Sawyer arguing behind the establishment and described their encounter as contentious. He mentioned his surprise at seeing them together; he had no clue they even knew each other. In fact, their acquaintance struck him as odd. When JD tried to grab Sawyer's hand, Sawyer pushed her away. Then JD fled. Sawyer, too, right after JD.

"I immediately tried to get in touch with JD, but she must have disconnected all communication devices. So, when I eventually tracked Sawyer down a few days later, she was in Naples, engaged in a bloody battle with you in the marina. And the rest is history."

"Hm. Arguing to me indicates a history, like the girls had dealings together in the past. And it's not like we can interview Sawyer, so we're SOL on that lead."

Jhi agreed with Pepper's sentiments.

"Alright. Sawyer, Kimball's dad, and now someone close to you are all enmeshed in this conspiracy. So, where do I fit into the equation once I get my magic back?" How could Pepper possibly aid Jhi in tracking down JD?

"To be determined. Something tells me, though, that once we get to Hell, and we find this fixer, that status will change."

"Jhi, we'll find JD. I promise." For the record, Pepper identified herself as a masochist. And after that verbalizing, Pepper's emotions needed feeding, so she devoured another cookie, as did Jhi.

"Pepper, you're one hell of a baker. I mean, these cookies are—"

"Orgasmic, right?" Secret ingredient—Pepper's tears.

"They're good, but not *that* good."

Right as Pepper noted the glint of mischievousness in his eyes, heat mounted in her cheeks. Nervous, she changed the subject. "I find it odd that nobody's broke inside my house to kill me. It's been quiet since the marina and vampire attack. Not that I'm complaining."

"They might have tried but couldn't infiltrate the defensive wards surrounding your home." Jhi noted a look of confusion painted on Pepper's face. "I drew sigils on your exterior walls before leaving. Nobody but you or I or Kimball could enter through a chaosgate inside."

"Jhi, always assume that I'm not a mind reader. If only you woulda mentioned that you drew wards around my home. Males, I tell ya. My dad's the same way."

"Females, I tell ya." Jhi met Pepper's gaze, then raised her a cheeky grin. "Speaking of your dad, is he in a safe place?"

"Yes," she responded curtly. The subject of her dad was off limits. In Pepper's mind, the less someone knew about him, the better. "And your parents, they call Pandæmonia home?" she asked via deflection.

Sadness ghosted over his features. "No. They're dead." Before Pepper could apologize, he pivoted the subject lightning-quick back to Pepper. "I like how close you are to your dad though, it's sweet. You both must keep in constant contact?"

"Often enough. I kinda feel like shit having to lie to him, though. Should the worst-case scenario happen—" She stopped herself from saying more, as that would bring up the taboo subject that was her dad.

If Pepper were to meet her demise, her dad wouldn't know the truth of what really happened. Protecting him was paramount, so she'd continue to keep him in the dark and, most importantly, his whereabouts a secret from prying eyes and ears. Not even Bunny Garcia knew where Larry had ventured off to, just that he had left Naples. Still, Jhi's insistence about learning things about her dad made Pepper feel uneasy, a feeling that betrayed her otherwise cool demeanor.

"You needn't worry." Jhi cupped his warm hands around Pepper's, and it was a good thing she was sitting because her legs felt like jelly. "I pledge to you, Pepper Li Bell, an oath of protection. I will serve as your stalwart defender and will continue to do anything and everything in my power to keep you out of harm's way. My word is my honor, and I'm bound by the laws of Hell to uphold my sworn oath to you, so help me, Lucifer. Do you accept my order of protection?"

"Yes." A smile traveled from ear to ear, prompting Pepper to ignore the uncomfortable throbbing in her wrist and nervously drain the contents of her glass. Absolute trust set up shop within Pepper when it came to Jhi, the last of her defenses crumbling.

"I guess now is a good enough time as any." Jhi depressed a button on the lower end of the hilt of his jack-of-all-weapons and out popped a mechanical spider. Roughly the size of a dime, the enchanted object that resembled an arachnid scampered on his calloused palm. "Our dialect in Hell is as ancient as it is impossible to learn. But this Lingua Franca will bind to your thalamus and enable you to not only comprehend Laramaic, but speak it fluently."

Pepper golf-clapped. "Well played, Jhi. Springing this on me so late in the game."

Like receiving an inoculation, just bearing the suspense of the parasite setting up shop within Pepper's innards was torturous. Not one for dawdling—the automaton spider leaped onto Pepper's arm, scuttled like the blazes up her limb, then burrowed within her ear. Eventually, the arachnid discovered the perfect place to lie down its roots and get busy translating.

Jhi flicked his eyes to the clock. "T-minus ten minutes till Hell-venturing." He held out his glass. "Before we make final preparations. A toast for good fortune. As we say back home, 'May Seren protect you, Mala'dayyas accept you, Mischief find you, Mala'khas look past you, Demons respect you, and Pandæmonia welcome you.' Cheers." With that, they clinked their glasses together, then drank, their eyes all the while locked on each other's.

"Uh, what's a mala'kha? You mentioned it earlier. And should

I be concerned?" Pepper wasn't sure she wanted the answer. "And mala'dayyas, for that matter?"

"The former is more sinister than your human mind can possibly conceive. Their demonic forms are terrifying and grotesque to the human eye. They are Hell's assassins, the soul-reapers who drag the damned to Hell, the wardens in Oblivion's Fortress. Inflicting misery and eternal torment is an aphrodisiac. Now, the mala'dayya are a whole different breed of demons. They are the princes of Hell, archdemons, fallen angels cast out of Heaven alongside Lucifer, the King of Hell. And all serve in prominent positions within Lucifer's ranks. Technically Mephy is one, but he isn't like the rest." Jhi's voice softened a tad whenever he spoke of his dominus.

Pepper gulped in concert with the grandfather clock croaking out the chimes of doom, signaling that showtime was nigh. According to Jhi, when chaosnauting to Hell, lowlies should do so at 3:00 A.M., when the veil separating dimensions was at its thinnest.

Pepper shimmied into the gifted hoodie. All that was missing was a basket to take to Grandma's, as in the hoodie somewhat resembled a Hellified Little Red Riding Hood cloak. Happily, her messenger bag, crammed with vampire-destroyers, wasn't at all burdensome or blatantly obvious, more like blended in with the cloak. One final cursory search of her go-bag remained.

Once satisfied that all travel essentials were present for the umpteenth time, to wit water, snacks (a hangry Pepper wasn't pretty), forged ID, Pepper recounted the gifted Pandæmonian currency before tightening the strings of the velvet money pouch, sundry magic gems clinking within, then slipped it in her jeans pocket.

Scant minutes ago, Jhi shot off an aside before busying himself with final Hell-voyaging preparations: "Make sure to have your bona fides in easy reach and magic gems at the ready for bribes and shakedowns of Hell's enforcers or others should the need arise." Then he followed up with a jumbled mumbling, something that sounded an awful lot like "or for ransom if dealing with a kidnapping." That chilled Pepper's already iced-over blood.

Before exiting her bedroom, Pepper had a moment of dizzying clarity. In a few moments, she'd be journeying to Hell. Hell, the very place populated by demons, where the Devil reigns. Her heart thumping uncontrollably, skin coated in a sheen of sweat, Pepper nearly succumbed to fear and calling off the entire operation.

What if she was making a huge mistake by leaving? Then again, homicidal vampires and an Agent of Karma could be moments from hunting her down. Decision made. Bedroom lights extinguished, loins nice and girded, the time had come to make haste into the bowels of the living room.

"The dimensional border between Hell and Earth is made up of chaotic dark matter and, as such, it's unstable and always moving," Jhi explained. "Beings cannot survive that crossing over unless they're already dead, their souls untethered. Forget the chaosgates you've experienced. Forget the chaosway tunnels." Jhi had put the finishing trimmings on a proper gateway to Hell, which resembled a two-dimensional drawing of a door without a knob. Only the gateway remained inert. Perhaps the way-sign bearing the inscription: *Lasciate ogni speranza, voi ch'entrate.* (Abandon all hope, ye who enter.) had yet to be rendered. A chill slithered up her spine at the mere thought.

"The only way for the living to reach Hell is by way of rukba —an inter-dimensional transporter. And the vessel must be summoned."

As Jhi chanted, a discordant sound resembling one of Larry's vinyls playing backwards, arcane symbols winged off his tongue; the moment they commingled with the balmy air, they materialized and marched in single file to their new home—the chaosgate frame—then lit up like a blazing inferno.

Before Pepper was none the wiser, Jhi sliced her forearm with a dagger. "What the …?"

"You must make an offering to pass through the gate. Just follow my lead."

The moment Pepper's bloodied arm was flush with the door-frame, what felt like tens of suction cups latched onto her flesh. But that wasn't the most uncomfortable part. Following suit were incorporeal sandpapery tongues and tiny teeth that licked and bit and gulped. Pepper felt woozy.

A vast network of arteries materialized on the chaosgate frame, all surging with her life force, with Jhi's. Blood dripped down and up like rainwater on glass, painting in every nook and cranny of the rendered chaosgate.

For a beat, the erstwhile beige wall flickered in and out of sight as the elevator doors struggled to come into view. In short order, the doors parted open like curtains, and a plate-glass window glided down, akin to those found in banks, recessed cash tray, voice portal, and all.

A wizened old man, north of ninety, played the role of Hell Inter-Dimensional Protection Agent-cum-rukba operator. Perched on a stool, he looked rather dapper, what with the Scottish pocket cap riding atop a cloud of hoary hair. Matching puffs of hair colonized his chin, eyebrows, and ears. Skin and bones aptly described his body from head to toe.

"Shlamlak. Dakhee toon?" his gravelly voice asked in Laramaic through phlegmy coughs. Luckily, the glass partition doubled as a spit-catcher.

"At dakhee vit," Jhi responded.

"Sheol B'arQoa mah'kom nomine?" The language itself sounded churlish, fearsome, and beyond ancient, or perhaps the elevator operator's tone could be attributed more to his demeanor. He very well could have been at the tail-end of a rather lengthy double-shift.

Jhi responded. Only Pepper couldn't understand a lick of what he said. Unfortunately, the Lingua-Franca parasite hadn't gotten into the groove just yet, as in it wasn't automatically translating Laramaic into English.

The rukba operator made a curt demand, as evidenced by the inflection of his tone. Jhi slipped his passport through the cash tray, and Pepper did the same.

The demon slipped a monocle over a rheumy eye. "State your reasons for visiting Pandæmonia."

Jhi explained it was a business-only trip for the two of them.

Once the operator was satisfied that their mugs matched their bona fides, he granted them passage and triggered the teller window to glide upward.

At the precise moment Pepper and Jhi were safe and snug inside the suffocating space, the rukba doors snapped shut, a sobering reminder that there was no way out.

Mantled in rich cherry wood, a guard rail journeyed along the three walls of their Hellride. Bubbly muzak served as disquieting ambiance. New-car smell with notes of hickory wood wafted about. Or perhaps the smoky scent was attributed to the pipe the operator held in his veiny hands, spindly fingers busy tamping down tobacco within the bowl before lighting.

Imitating Jhi once again, Pepper grabbed hold of one of the *oh-shit!* straps dotting the perimeter of the cable car, then hoped against hope she remained one of the living. That death wasn't a prerequisite for entering the not-so-pearly gates—an addendum that perhaps escaped Jhi's memory, like the time-lag in Hell.

Not a beat later, the darkly intro to *Danse Macabre* filled the airwaves. The discordant melody resonated in concert with the liftman, who mimed the sliding of a bow along the strings of an imaginary violin. The Devil's Chord could very well have supplied the power to the elevator because off they went helter-skelter.

As if a giant's hand picked up the cable car, then tossed it like a frisbee, so too did they spin and twirl in a counterclockwise motion like a demonic Tilt-A-Whirl. Pepper's insides were agitated and were ready to pop, like the shaking of a bottle of bubbly before uncorking. Then utter stillness reigned.

The door dinged open. "Welcome to Hell." Only it was voiced

in Laramaic and sounded incredibly ominous. Merely a prelude to what resided beyond.

And judging from the brief glimpse Pepper snatched, she entertained the idea of turning tail. An idea her gut wholly concurred with.

CHAPTER 16

The rukba's doors glided shut and then poofed out of existence, leaving them stranded in No Man's Land.

The thrill ride to Hell had disgorged the duo at an open-air terminal without a ceiling. Where the rukba once stood, now a solid, obsidian-and-jade marbled wall long enough to house fifteen rukbas stared back at Pepper; the flooring seamlessly blended in with the wall. Save for a few braziers with bright blazing hellfire dotted about, this terminal was bereft of beings, directionals, anything really.

That was a lie. There was one directional, a gleaming jade-and-obsidian marbled pathway, bracketed by an endless valley of rust-colored soil. The path offered no other recourse but to follow its sinuous curves—curves that abruptly ended on a riverbank up yonder. So follow it they did, one foot in front of the other.

Jhi threw his arm out, halting Pepper's forward momentum moments before wayward balls of hellfire flames tumbled across their paths like deathly tumbleweeds; the heat they emitted was palpable. That near miss caused Pepper to become nimble-minded and ever aware of the environs at all times.

The word "B'a'i'Ra'Hccendo" soared out of Jhi's mouth in all its gutturalness. Loosely translated into English via Lingua France to that of firebushes, their leaves licked by dancing flames swathed the crimson-soiled terrain and would intermittently spit out the incendiary tumbleweeds.

Not even the balls of inferno themselves would dare engage in a tryst with the milky-white papery plants that resembled scrub bushes, in height only; so sharp their fronds, one touch would slice skin down to the basal layer. Undoubtedly, the scar would serve as an indelible warning to never, ever, molest a *Papyrus mactabilis* again.

"Tell me again why the rukba couldn't've just dropped us off at Skulduggerer's Lair?" Pepper whispered, the creepy environment to blame for her hushed tone.

"Being a demon has its privileges. And seeing as how you're not one and have never technically traveled to Hell before, even though your bona fides say otherwise, I had the rukba operator drop us off where he does all first-time visitors. The fringes of Pandæmonia." Jhi adopted a strictly business tone. "There's a method to my madness."

First-time visitors were forbidden to enter through Hell anywhere but the chaosport the duo had been dropped at, and the reason was simple. Traveling across the River Acheron was essential because it recorded a being's essence into Hell's visitor registry system. The recording also allowed the visitor to chaosnaut in the future to other chaosports throughout Hell's vast dimension.

"Once we cross over the river, it will have recorded your soul as belonging to that of your assumed name. Just as no two fingerprints are alike, the same can be said for souls. And as far as Hell is concerned, your soul belongs to Marie Smith."

"You're pretty impressed with yourself, aren't ya?"

Jhi's lopsided grin by way of response caused butterflies to stir in Pepper's belly.

"Jhi, you're one-hundred percent positive my assumed name won't raise any red flags? Like, the River won't realize my assumed name and real name don't match up."

"Ninety-nine point nine percent certain."

Pepper stopped walking, the point-one percent rooting her in place.

When Pepper innocently asked what would happen if they tried to chaosnaut elsewhere without crossing the River, Jhi stated that her body would explode.

To calm her frayed nerves, he placed a comforting hand on her shoulder. "Listen, there's no record of a Pepper Li Bell in Hell. Your name isn't on any registry as far as the Ministry is concerned. Believe me, I searched. The River doesn't even know your real name or have a record of it on file to compare to the assumed one. But if it didn't work, for whatever reason, we'd know from the swarm of mala'khas waiting for us on the other side."

Jhi's matter-of-fact response robbed Pepper of a reply, and she nearly vomited on the spot. His assuring her that all would be well didn't assuage her fears. Not in the slightest.

Noticing her apprehension of walking toward the River, he grabbed her hand and pulled her onward.

To make matters worse, a vibe of unease, edged with panic, coated the air molecules in Hell, evocative of the times during Pepper's youth when she'd rotate the crank on a Jack-in-the-box, discordant barrel organ music lilting. She knew the demonic clown would pop out, yet the anticipation mounted within, nonetheless, and when the clown would rear its twisted head, she'd lurch and scream all the same.

What wasn't helping with the off-the-charts creep factor was the tomb-like silence permeating about, save for the duo's shoes slapping the volcanic-glassed pathway, which, Pepper was convinced, only alerted the lying-in-wait beasties of their presence.

Pepper's nearly frost-bitten hands (by a Floridian's standards) sought refuge in her cloak's pockets before cinching the thick cloak ever tighter. The biting chill's jagged teeth must have gashed the atmosphere before moving on to gnaw at Pepper's cheeks because the sky appeared to have sustained mortal injuries, its ichor bleeding outward, canopying the dimension in a blanket of myriad shades of fierce reds and blazing oranges.

The bluest of blue sun, threaded with orangey-yellow arteries, throbbed like a heart. The subtle *thump-thump-thump*-ing pumped swollen clouds, resembling blood vessels, into gear, casting them horizontally across the heavens. As they scudded past, they appeared as tubelike fingers, angrily clawing the sky, digging and gouging into the already festering wounds. If this was Hell's daytime, Pepper wondered what nighttime had to offer.

The path ended at the black-as-pitch choppy waters of the River Acheron. Scrunching her eyes, Pepper couldn't even discern the shoreline on the other side. Unfortunately, not a single vessel was docked at the end of the deserted pier, and the one and only cab parked nearby certainly wouldn't do the trick, so how they were going to ferry across and reach Pandæmonia proper had yet to be determined.

"Here"—Jhi shoved a wad of Pandæmonia currency into her sweaty palm—"tender these flesh notes to the cab driver."

A tad smaller than dollar bills, flesh notes were fashioned from the flayed dermis of the damned and threaded with varying denominations; some "fleshies" contained a network of veins, others a patch of curly hair, a few wrinkly sunspots and liver spots here and there, but all were oily and porous. And gross. Tactility speaking, the flesh notes felt like tuba noodles, only a touch firmer.

Charon's Cabs was rendered along the chassis of the convertible, a jalopy reminiscent of her dad's old station wagon. Only this jalopy was headed for the junkyard.

Behind the wheel that resembled an airplane yoke slept a … well, a proper demon. Too bad a chauffeur's cap occluded his face. The sound of the waves crashing on the shore twenty-odd feet away must have lulled him to sleep. That, and sheer boredom.

Jhi cleared his throat, which woke the cabbie up from a deep slumber.

"Good afternoon." Like a parody of evil, Demon Earp's voice was high-pitched and not at all frightening, so Pepper's shoulders slackened a tad. As he exited the vehicle, he asked, "Where can I take you fine folk?" His breath stank like that of brimstone-laced cigarettes.

The driver was precisely how Pepper pictured your garden-variety demon—skin the hue of utter darkness, a visage born from nightmares, teeth like railroad spikes, blood-ringed eyes and lips. Horns that spiraled outward with endpoints that yearned to gut a human. But not the ensemble. Channeling an Old West gunslinger, pistols dangled from his belt, a sated bandolier rested on his barreled chest.

After a harmless go-round of haggling over the ridiculously inflated fare into Pandæmonia proper, Jhi and the driver reached an agreement, and Pepper forked over the price-gouging fee.

Hands the size of hams patted the chassis, which prompted the backseat door of the convertible four-seater to click open. "Hop on in. Name's Spade."

Jhi and Pepper's bums slid along backseats that were uphol-stered in human skin, hair, and all. Demons prided themselves on recycling efforts; *can't let the damned go to waste,* was their motto.

With a torque of a key, the ignition fired, and up they rose, hovering about scant feet or so above the jade-and-obsidian marbled roadway. Pepper could have sworn she heard muffled screams from inside the vehicle but remained mum. Gale force winds buffeted the cab as it veered onto the pier and continued navigating further and further. Black murky water crashed against the tall piles, crawling upward with every hit, wooden planks moaning.

No, no, no, the car wasn't seriously going to … Oh, God! Pepper dug her fingers into the seats, grabbing on for dear life as the Charon soared over the lip of the pier, then down, down, down it fell—were they going to be submerged?—until the cab halted, barely hovering over the surface, sooty water spraying on Pepper's face. Spade hit the gas and thundered forward and, soon, nothing but wide open waters surrounded them.

"Looks like we've got ourselves some company." The headlights cast a haunting green glow over the inky river of glass and moved about like searchlights, seeking out the sea creatures lurking beneath. A wormlike leviathan slithered just beneath the surface, keeping pace with the Charon.

Pepper held on for dear life, her eyes riveted on anything but the leviathan.

Unruffled, Jhi's head canted slightly as he relished the chilly air nipping away at his cheeks. "Home sweet home." The brimstone and briny air coaxed his lips into a half-smile.

"Land ahoy!" Spade proclaimed.

Though nightfall stirred, in the far, far distance, Pepper eyed towering obsidian skyscrapers with spires like that of black daggers that pierced the bleeding sky, stabbing away.

Spade navigated the Charon onto terra firma and breathed a sigh of relief. "Oh, merciful Seren. We made it in one piece."

Pepper couldn't agree more. Still, she wasn't off the hook just yet. Her eyes raked over the shore and craggy cliffs, on the lookout for mala'khas lying in wait. When Jhi gave the nod indicating they were in the clear, she dropped her shoulders and sank back into the bucket seat.

"So, what brings you all to Pandæmonia? Business or pleasure?" Spade asked.

In the throes of childlike wonder and too awestruck at the hauntingly sinister beauty of the terrain, Pepper struggled to form a semblance of thought, let alone respond. Truth be told, Pepper couldn't reply as her mouth was otherwise occupied breaking down the handful of mini peanut butter crackers she had shoved into her mouth, frayed nerves to blame, so the carrying on of small talk fell on Jhi's able-bodied shoulders. "A little of both."

Mimicking a skiff, the taxi skimmed over the glassy roadway, now spangled with spidery veins of quicksilver. Jhi, a closet mechanic, ventured to respond to Pepper's innocent inquiry of what powered soulcars if not gasoline. The fuel was comprised of souls fresh from serving time in Tartarus.

When the engine was ignited, so too was the hellfire within. Catalyzed by the fiery inferno, the combustible souls bounded every whichaway throughout the chassis, fought to escape, howled to be rescued, all the while whirling and whirling like an F5 tornado. Like chaotic atoms, their disorder is what enabled cars to soar. Sometime during Jhi's dissertation of Hell mechanics, Pepper zoned out.

The River Acheron was but a speck in the background the further inland the car juked. Eventually, the craggy mountains gave way to red sand dunes. At first blush, a graveyard of triangular mausoleums, reaching heights of fifteen-odd feet, was sprinkled about the crimson soil, sand eddying about their peaks. But in actuality, the mausoleums were the apexes of pyramids, containing solely a doorway aboveground. Most of the private residences found in Hell were subterranean.

In the field up ahead, a being clawed along the ground, its sallow body mangled as if it had been deboned. It picked up its pace once its beady eyes latched onto fresh meat—Pepper.

Closer and closer, it crabbed, one arm in front of the other, swimming on the ground, moving faster and faster, keeping pace with the cab. Until a gargoyle whooshed down like a dragon and plucked the damned—perhaps an escapee from the Pits of Tartarus—from the gleaming roadway and knifed its claws into a protruding rib.

A zephyr of wind created from the flapping of the gargoyle's wings blew back a strand of Pepper's locks; it had ventured *that close* to the convertible soulcar.

Gargoyles were the watchers of Hell. And if not a gargoyle, then the damned would've been devoured by a hellfowl, what with the damned serving as their carrion, Jhi had whispered. Should the damned perish, not a problem, because, in short order, they'd regenerate, doomed to live a life of misery and everlasting torture.

At long last, the taxi floated within the innards of Pandæmonia proper, joining the already soulcar-choked roadway. Scads of gleaming obsidian skyscrapers loomed high above, their towering forms glassed within the same marbled sidewalks. The hopping metropolis bustled with oddities, demons, and other beasties milling hither and yon.

Lampposts graced every corner, orange-red hellfire roaring within. Rush-hour traffic navigated along with the current, as in the road mimicked a river. But it was only a trick of the eye, an eerie effect caused by the undulating flames cast by the lampposts and myriad braziers.

Half-beasts and bent-bodied wendigos prowled down the gleaming avenue, bypassing store after not-so-quaint shop and within pouncing distance from Pepper. Then there were unidentifiable beings cloaked from head to toe, the midnight-hued fabric of their robes trawling along the sidewalk. Vintage strollers rolled of their own accord, with multiple snakelike limbs peeking out of the seat.

Spade, noticing in the rearview mirror Pepper's frightened expression when she spotted a terrifying creature, said, "Try not to pay any attention to ghouls, or you'll have a dickens of a time getting rid of them. Pests, the lot of them." Easier said than done.

The ghouls' grotesque features, curtained by straggly, oily hair, flickered in and out of sight like static. They seemed to jump through time when they'd come back into view, which was prime for pouncing before their prey was any the wiser.

One such ghoul caught Pepper in its sights. It disappeared and then reappeared right by her door. Its oily hair brushed against her skin, its talon-like hands reaching through the lowered window for her.

Before a yelp escaped from Pepper's mouth, Spade shouted, "Get out of here!" Spade swerved the taxi to another lane, and

Pepper's door swung open, which knocked the ghoul off the car, then slammed shut just as quickly.

Establishments appeared to be in various stages of melting, facades warped and crooked. Side streets and alleys were bent and zigzagged and led to warrens, aka places Pepper wouldn't be caught dead within.

The Yarn Harvester bookstore grew upward; actual floors were stitching together before Pepper's bulging eyes. For the Love of Cerberus offered the latest accessories for the beloved hydra-headed hellhound. Succubi's Secret—lingerie, heady perfumes, and otherwise sold within. Enchanted window decorations graced each and every establishment; truly, they were eye candy for the demented.

Take Succubi's Secret, for instance. Vignettes played on a loop, showcasing ensorcelled succubi mannequins demonstrating the merchandise, spotlighting humans in the midst of being ensnared, bewitched, falling prey to the eponymous antiheroes. The further inside the metropolis they ventured, the creepier the sightseeing.

In the city's center was a roundabout, with a macabre fountain in the middle, ultraviolet-blue hellfire flames pirouetting atop the bloodied water's surface. (An aside, the roundabout was invented in Hell.) Straight, left or right, whichever direction the denizens chose, they'd eventually wind up in one of Hell's many Suburgatories: Oblivion's Bluff, Vale of Naraka, the Fields of Lament, and more.

On cue, tens of hundreds of hands-free umbrellas snapped open. Replacing handles, disembodied hands latched onto shoulders or arms. Begged the question, what was the flash mob a prelude to?

Spade flicked a switch and closed the cab's retractable roof in preparation. Jhi, picking up on Pepper's curiousness, discreetly pointed upward.

Wow, was Night ever the grandstander, pulling out all the stops to eclipse Daylight. A legion of darkness converged from all corners of the heavens as it commenced its doctoring to cauterize the festering wounds inflicted during daylight hours. Like a spilled inkwell, blackness slinked inward, blotting out all colors. The cerulean sun was now ringed by a pool of ink.

Unsatisfied, Night applied more pressure, its fingers squeezing the sun, which had no choice but to acquiesce and cave in on itself, bending to Night's will. The sun mimicked an hourglass before it exploded. *Pop! Pop! Pop!* The sound of bubble wrap being strangled filled the airwaves, merely a prelude to kaleidoscopic stars jutting from the heaven's belly. Then pinkish-silver rain-drops sifted down.

Hellfire-laden lamps kicked the blazing inferno up a notch as if being doused with vats of kerosene and drenched the cityscape in an orangey-crimson glow.

The taxi stopped abruptly. "This is as far as I can go. Rush hour's a bitch. Lair's a few blocks up."

While ambling down the street, Pepper's attention riveted on a faceless, featureless man who bypassed her. Donning a suit and bowler hat, his swinging briefcase was in lockstep with the tick-tocking of his stride. His shadow was not in lockstep; it was strolling about freely.

Another faceless man walked in the opposite direction. When their paths crossed, their respective shadows stopped for a chat. At first, appearing as long silhouettes on the blackened sidewalk, limned by the orangey hellfire, their ambulant forms slithered up the wall of The Torture Chamber; their shadows reflected on the glass of the furniture store chatted away, face to face. To make matters even creepier, sadistic contraptions beyond the paned glass window were visible and stole Pepper's attention: a hang-man's noose, an iron maiden, and a dangling coffin torture device.

Pepper, mentally reminding herself to not gawk, met Jhi's stride a few blocks later. They halted before Skulduggerer's Lair.

"Something's off." Jhi surveyed the area.

Pepper tuned out the din of grumbling horns and the general hustle and bustle of the city and raked her eyes over a vendor, a random taxi driver, then landed on the bay window of The Skinstress directly across the avenue. The window dressing showcased mannequins adorned with couture fashion weaved from human dermis.

Then she caught a movement, a reflection in the window of a handful of wanderers hovering idle, their forms crooked, features warped, no lips, just box-cutter sharp teeth, watching with their silver orbs and waiting. Pray tell, for what? A disquieting shiver snaked up Pepper's spine.

A discordant childlike humming stole Pepper's attention. A girl—thirteenish—skipped down the sidewalk, her head a tad engorged and disproportionate to her petite frame. Her lime-green and yellow flowery dress sashayed with each bounce, the crinoline underneath peeking out with each bop. Thick bangs and pigtailed locks, mirroring the hue of Pepper's silky black, tumbled down the girl's wall-flat chest, then went airborne with each gleeful leap. Completing her oh-so-sunny ensemble, white bobby socks crowned with lacy frill graced her alabaster limbs.

Arguably creepy, undeniably whimsical, this girl radiated an ethereal vibe, her facial features perfectly symmetrical. Hell, the tweenlet even carried a teensy patent leather purse that perfectly matched the Mary Janes on her feet.

"Oh, shit! A Lolly'ka. Get inside, quick!" Jhi gruffly ushered Pepper through the front door of Skulduggerer's Lair, then barricaded his body in front of the only visible point of ingress.

Resplendent in a crimson cape and satiny top hat, the shopkeeper, in the midst of dusting display cases, remained still but not his head. That swiveled ninety degrees. He bade the newly arrived a "Goooood eve-ah-ning," his tone grim and ghoulish.

All legs and no torso, the thin demon's appendages mimicked that of a daddy-longlegs. As for his features, those were cadaverous. Unhurriedly, the shopkeeper's spidery-thin lips bowed in a sneer, further accentuating his harshly pointed chin.

"Cadabra's the name, magic's the game. Speak up should you need assistance or have questions that are dyyyy-ing to be addressed." He returned to dusting.

"The hell is going on?" Pepper squeaked out, barely above a whisper, as she lowered the hood of her cloak. Getting into a melee in, well, Hell wasn't exactly auspicious for their survival. "For a hot second there, I wanted to have pretend tea-time with the cutesy doll child."

Jhi wouldn't peel his eyes away from the street to address Pepper. "Yeah, she's about as sweet and innocent as Jack the Ripper. Listen, Lolly'ka's are cold-blooded mobsters that run Pandæmonia like a shadow government. Shaking down businesses for payment, their protection in return. They kill for sport. Need I go on?" Jhi wasn't a fan.

"You're telling me that little girl is a Mafioso?" Pepper laughed.

"Chuckle away, Pepper. That little girl is about as old as Lilith. Y'know, the erstwhile queen of Hell, before Lucifer ousted her from her throne. Some even believe the Lolly'ka's to be Lilith's direct descendants. Point being, they're not to be trifled with. And I'd advise anyone to tread lightly should you cross their path. Seren willing, the Lolly'ka skips right on by."

What at first began as a prickling in Pepper's wrist soon morphed into a legion of rubber bands snapping away at her skin, pulling the hairs out of their roots. A beat later, Pepper's wrist mimicked a divining rod, Loki the controller. The capuchin began scouring the entire square footage of Skulduggerer's Lair for his partner, Bhi'gow. Her skin squirmed, giving the impression that hundreds of worms were embedded within the epidermis itself. Make no bones about it. Loki wanted to escape from his prison cell, and he was bound and determined to do just that.

Loki propelled Pepper around Skulduggerer's Lair, an establishment that was light-years from a fly-by-night operation; scads of Pandæmonians' Choice Awards graced the walls.

The Bellowers, Pandæmonia's premier news source, vaunted the Lair as the best in the biz for bespoke possessions; from the mundane to the grand, you name it, the Lair would possess it. The store's most buzzed-about achievements were on display, like a creeptastic museum of sorts. All one need do is peruse the bevy of captions for a pithy history of the haunted whatnots. Each item could be recreated on request.

Awards weren't the only things gracing the walls. Decapitated human heads were scattered about. Pepper couldn't escape the notice of one such head, a man, in the prime of his life when he kicked the bucket. His eyes followed her, watching her every move.

Soon Pepper was immersed in a Petri dish of enchanted and erstwhile possessed artifacts: accoutrements for the budding magician, maniacally giggling clowns, dolls, typewriters, mirrors, mummies, TV's, wedding dresses, paintings, and so on, even a vintage horse-drawn funeral coach that occupied the far-flung corner of the gargantuan emporium.

Not to mention the macabre tableaux vivants that punctuated the lair; a veritable graveyard of "living pictures" if you will, what with the taxidermal bodies of historic mages—or in Earthly parlance, illusionists—evil mages, and serial killers alike populating the staged scenes.

What the …? Ew! Interesting were a few of the more colorful musings occupying Pepper's mind as she became absorbed in the stuffed remains and their grotesque reenactments.

It appeared as if Loki had picked up a stronger scent. Pepper's body gravitated towards a disappearing box, about six feet high; nearly there and inches away from the box, a lifelike doll impeded Pepper's forward momentum.

The Lolly'ka from before, the very Mafioso Jhi had warned Pepper about, capered round Pepper, singsonging adagio, "'A *ring, a ring o'roses, a pocket full o' pepper, atishoo atishoo, we all fall down.'*"

Abruptly, the skipping ceased, and the Lolly'ka stood stock-still, engorged head canted, while her wrist flicked a yo-yo up and down, its movements hypnotic. "Wanna play a game?" she asked Pepper daintily, her tone found in the higher treble clef region. Blunted bangs barely graced the tip of her ebony, arching eyebrows. Her anime eyes emoted impish intentions as they fluttered open and closed ever so innocently, while her rose-bud lips bowed into a pout.

Pepper replied, "Oh no, but thank you."

Wrong answer. The Lolly'ka's eyes snapped to full alertness, her upturned nose bunching together, lips pursed.

Monkey on a mission, Loki flung Pepper inside the magician's box. Unfortunately, the zipping-closed door drowned out Jhi's scream of "NO!"

Pepper pleaded with Loki to stop, even dug her nails into the box's velvety walls, rending the fabric, but the monkey wouldn't listen.

Of its own volition, Pepper's hand unlatched the hidden door, and her feet barreled over the threshold and into a secreted room, awash with a fiery glow. Tall shadows cast from hellfire-lit braziers danced a macabre number about the gleaming obsidian-and-jade walls.

"You shouldn't've come." It was any wonder the below-basso voice didn't cause the room to quake, but Pepper sure did from the ominous tone alone.Once Pepper's eyes adjusted to the dim light, she set her sights on the stranger.

In a far corner, a gnarled beast rested his head on his knees, his flaccid arms wrapped around the tufts of his tawny-furred legs, matted and stained with blood. Distorted horns jutted out from the demon's forehead, horns coated in liquid blackness. The tongues of ultraviolet-hued fire licking the tips of the demon's horns weren't so much a blazing inferno but dying embers, sputtering to be fed tinder. Like that of steel blades, the pronounced facial bones threatened to slice through his charred-gray flesh at any moment; the same was true for all the cartilage.

Even if this demon posed a viable threat, which he most certainly did, he couldn't harm Pepper because his fetlocks were shackled to the wall, his flesh pierced through and through. However, the same couldn't be said for his black-as-pitch eyes—pools of fathomless nothingness locked onto Pepper, threatening to pull her into oblivion, cursing her to eternal damnation once there. Other than those frightening features, this demon was severely emaciated and badly beaten, a constellation of old and fresh wounds marring his charred leathery skin.

Within an arm's reach of the demon was an amorphous dipping pool. Sulfuric spring water flowed freely from a water-spout fashioned from the mouth of a damned, its decapitated head affixed to the wall, its eye sockets sewn shut. "Lethe water. Too much'll," the demon paused as if exhausted from speaking, from moving his black-lipped mouth, "divorce the imbiber from reality … and trap them in a world of their own design. Too little'll render you immobile, and muscles will atrophy. Like mine. So I'd stay away from it if I were you."

Barring a tone that wavered between thunderous and affable, his seven-foot-something form—cloven hooves and backward knees and all—if not a tad shopworn, struck fear in Pepper's heart.

A riot of tally marks marred the variegated walls, all overlapping, crisscrossing, scratched out, and what appeared as blood oozed from within. A soiled rib and femur, humanlike, the marrow long sucked dry, rested nearby.

Pepper lurched, not so much from the demon but from the walls. Were they sentient? If not, then why were they concave for a beat, then convex, and so on? Like an inhale, then an exhale?

Before Pepper could utter a remark, a burning sensation lanced through her being, then mushroomed into searing pain. She grabbed her wrist, biting back screams. For a beat, her dermis rippled before the capuchin leaped out.

At first, looking like a cartoon, the second the furball met the air, his body transmogrified into a living, breathing primate. A primate that soared into the demon's arms, his long prehensile tail coiling around the demon's hands.

"Loki?" the demon's voice trembled, and eyes glinted with a hint of recognition.

To finally see Loki, Pepper's paladin, in the flesh … was

surreal. A cap of brownish-gray fur and even darker sideburns hugged his tiny grayish-white face with a splash of vanilla along his neck, and fur the hue of burnt brown covered his tail. Though he couldn't have weighed more than eight pounds and reached the height of a six-month-old baby, this capuchin possessed an air of gravitas and came off as formidable.

Through and through, Loki radiated regality. The only feature that separated him from a common capuchin was his horns; they were small but deadly, just like Loki.

When Loki's bulging orange eyes glinting with ancient wisdom met Pepper's, he smiled, his needle-like teeth on display, then nodded his head once in what Pepper read as a gesture of "hello."

Pepper replied in kind.

Loki then returned his attention to his partner-in-crime and plucked half-spectacles from the floor with one lens fractured and perched them on the demon's strangely sculpted nose.

"Blessed Seren! Loki, it is you!" Tears trickled down the demon's pointy cheeks and tumbled onto the matted fur of his long-lost friend.

So this was Bhi'gow. The infamous magic-pilferer had turned into a blubbering mess. Tears flowed unabated as he cradled Loki. Responding in kind, the capuchin hugged and nuzzled his bygone friend.

Pepper wished the lovefest would conclude, for there were more pressing matters to attend to, like, *ahem!*, where's her sorcery?

Overcome with anger, she leveled a revolver on the demon. "You stole my magic, fixer, and I'm here to take it back!"

"Go ahead and shoot me. I'm already dead. As you will be soon."

CHAPTER 17

Jhi thundered over the threshold of the disappearing box and smacked right into Pepper's back, which knocked her off balance and caused her gun to slip through her fingers and skitter across the marble flooring until the dipping pool swallowed it whole.

Falling towards the obsidian marble, Pepper was a hairsbreadth away from smashing into the unforgiving floor when she felt her shirt collar digging into her throat, her body airborne for a heartbeat and corkscrewing around till she was face-to-face with Jhi.

In the span of seconds, his movements on fast-forward, Jhi had thwarted Pepper from kissing the marble, and before she landed on her feet, he had unsheathed, then brandished two scimitars. His legs assuming a ready-for-battle stance, Jhi cocked an eyebrow at Pepper as if saying, *Why are you standing there, weaponless?* As if she wasn't already noticeably discomfited from her blunder.

"There's no leaving. We're trapped, so it's best to save your energy for what's coming down the pike." Bhi'gow was resigned. "And I'm afraid this is one battle Loki isn't prepared for. He's weak. His muscles have atrophied from dormancy, much like mine. Time is what my friend needs to replenish his energy reserves."

Loki wasn't exactly spry at the moment, his movements arthritic, so Bhi'gow appeared to be speaking the truth. Pepper had just barely survived a brush with a rogue Agent of Karma and a bloodthirsty vampire only because of Loki. How could she possibly survive without his magic? Without his supernatural everything else?

Jhi loomed over Bhi'gow, inspecting the demon, figuring out if he should release him from his chains or challenge him to a duel. Meanwhile, Loki stood in between, chittering angrily. The ruachti's message was received loud and clear: *You touch Bhi'gow, you die.*

"I'm neither your enemy nor whom you should be concerned about." Bhi'gow addressed Jhi. "The Hounds of Hell are on their way to collect their ensnared prey—the girl."

With that revelation, Jhi betrayed every emotion possible in all manner of "oh shit!" He aggressively attempted to journey back to the shop proper. He sliced his palm and, with his blood, traced what looked like runes, or maybe they were sigils, or a combination thereof. Either way, they appeared ancient, arcane even. He drew a chaosgate in the center of the sigils, but it wouldn't activate. Then he chanted an incantation, but nothing transpired. Not one to quit, Jhi kicked the barrier, but it was still impenetrable. Like a caged lion, he paced, his head darting high and low.

"Jhi, who're the Hounds of Hell?" Pepper's voice was tinged with panic. "Kimby mentioned them in passing right before you showed up at my house."

"A sadistic and violent vampiric criminal organization—Dammit!" Jhi huffed, running his fingers through his hair. "Would have been great if Kimball mentioned them to *me* in passing," he snarked.

After taking a few calming breaths, he said over his shoulder, "The vampire you ran into"—Jhi continued inspecting the premises, not making eye contact with Pepper—"the one juiced up on magic who nearly killed you and would have if not for Loki, guaranteed he was a Hound." Jhi pivoted on his heel, his attention riveted on Pepper. "Listen, we're gonna be in for quite a battle. As in kill or be killed." Jhi made no qualms about being brutally honest. "But we can get through this. Only if we watch each other's backs."

He extracted an orb from his mobile armory, like one of those stress-relieving balls that humans savagely molest; the ones that don't curb stress whatsoever. "You behind this?" Jhi snapped at Bhi'gow as he tore the malleable glob into several pieces, then hurled the bits. Soon the room fell prey to a creepy-crawly infestation; the globs scampered everywhere, like cockroaches.

"No. Just bait. It's the girl the Hounds want. And the girl they'll get."

Though it appeared as if Bhi'gow had made peace with death long, long ago, Pepper hoped Loki would chitter some sense into him. Besides, the fixer was no use to her dead.

Once invisible to the naked eye but now fiercely glowing by dint of the globs, a scattershot of spheres filled with runes and sigils stained the floors and walls, greasy and undulating in appearance, like heat rising off pavement. Some symbols radiated, like if you touched them, they'd melt the skin right off your bones; and appeared to be dynamic, insofar as they switched, changed patterns.

As Jhi inspected the magical curiosities, flickering firelight reflecting on piercing orbs, he was silent for a beat before explaining his findings. "From the bits I can translate, a mage has thwarted all magic casting, and their blood bound the spell. Activated it. Magic in motion. This is good. I can't cast magic, but neither can they. So hand-to-hand combat it is." A slow smile spread across his lips.

But not Pepper's. "And the parts you can't translate?" Pepper dreaded the response.

"They could literally spell out our death for all I know."

Can-can't you break whatever the spell is?" Pepper's voice

broke. "And what about that glob thingy? That's magic in motion."

"Not without the mage's blood, I can't. But even that isn't a guarantee. The elements are at the mage's mercy, have bent to his will. We're sealed inside this chamber with no chance of escape. Not unless the mage breaks the seal. And as for the rune-revealer, it's classified as an enchanted object with a sole purpose, a far cry from magic casting."

"Yeah, okay, but you obviously understand the language written, so write us out of this deathtrap."

"Easier said than done. I can find a crack in their security system and break the spell for the parts written in Laramaic, but the same can't be said for this other strange language interspersed —" He was referring to the dynamic script that seemed to take on a life all its own.

"Tun-fendin'ga, the tongue of the mystical Ancient Ones. The darkest of dark sorcery. *That* is what's trapped us here, and *that* is why we'll all be slaughtered shortly," Bhi'gow said, and left it at that.

Loki squawked, his ears perked up, his attention focused on the barrier.

"Get out a sunburster, now!" Jhi commanded.

From that moment on, all events were a blur. One moment Pepper had somehow extricated a sun grenade, the next four Hounds of Hell with their animated firebird-dragon tattoos on full display stormed into the room, outnumbering the trio, Bhi'gow excluded.

Pepper yelled, "Get down!" before pulling the plug on the grenade, then ducked and averted her eyes away from the blindingly bright explosion.

One surprised vampire took the brunt of the blast, fire devouring his blackened skin, his body licked in flames. Jhi's aviators shaded his eyes from the simulated Florida sunshine and permitted him to move about the blinding blaze unfettered, like the converse of night-vision goggles. He donkey-kicked the suffering vamp to the ground and burrowed a silver stake right into his cold, cold heart. One down, three to go.

Like a heat-seeking missile, one Hound singled out Jhi. Before Jhi could defend himself, the Hound uncorked a bottle, then tossed the corrosive liquid at Jhi's face. The enemies had done their homework, pre-calculated who the major threat would be, and acted accordingly. The goal to blind Jhi and therefore destroy the strongest link first had been foiled thanks to Jhi's sunglasses, but his skin suffered the consequences, welts formed and bubbled, his skin sizzled. Agony seized Jhi long enough for the bloodsucker to kick away Jhi's scimitars, leaving him weaponless.

After spiraling through the air, Loki suctioned onto the face of the attacker heading straight for Pepper. However, Loki's intentions of gouging out the bloodsucker's eyes were for naught because the vampire tossed the flying capuchin into the wall as if he weighed next to nothing. After crashing to the floor, Loki remained motionless.

Pepper screamed, eyes misting with tears. Then a blast of heat ignited within Pepper, and she wanted for nothing but to destroy these Hounds of Hell, snap them in half, vengeance her fuel.

Body revolting from abject pain notwithstanding, Jhi went to intercept the vamp dead set on harming Pepper. He shoved the acid-flinger bloodsucker out of his way as if he were an inconsequential afterthought, but another Hound lassoed Teflon-thick cable ties around Jhi's hands. With that, Jhi's efforts to aid Pepper in battle had been temporarily waylaid.

Sandwiched in by two vamps and hands bound, Jhi struggled with every ounce of strength he had left, but the enemies had gained the upper hand. In their respective hands, they brandished dual-bladed knives, ready for gutting, and they got to work in haste. They slashed and sliced the air, Jhi narrowly avoiding the razor-sharp blades.

Confident Jhi would be the victor, Pepper focused on not dying herself, because frankly, that wouldn't help anyone. Besides, the hell she'd give the Hounds the satisfaction.

A barrel-chested, bloated-necked, roided-out bloodsucker took advantage of Jhi's apprehension and decided to make Pepper his plaything. Nostrils flaring, the bloodsucker stampeded her way like a bull in a ring, long determined strides eating the distance between them in no time flat.

Hoping her muscles would recall every move learned from her brief stint kickboxing during DVD workouts, Pepper braced herself for a battle royal and assumed the fighting stance, stake at the ready. Even so, her adopted steely posturing belied the terror gripping her, along with a heart that wouldn't stop banging against her rib cage.

Pepper lunged forward at just the right amount of distance between them and attempted to drive the stake right through his heart. The vamp swatted the stake from her grasp, exerting little to no energy.

She connected her fists to the bloodsucker's stomach. Jab, jab, jab. Though her fists smarted something fierce as if she were pounding a brick wall, she continued jabbing, one arm extended outward, elbow straight as a board, then the other arm as she scrambled backward.

But her actions had zero effect on the vampire, which tickled him silly. A quitter she most certainly was not. She rained down more of those boxing moves, one after the other, regardless of encroaching exhaustion, regardless that her knuckles were raw and bloodied. Still, she couldn't steal a moment to extract another weapon, and she was tiring fast.

Extracting the last trick up her sleeve, she bunched her fingers together and glided them directly into his larynx to cobra strike him, but he thwarted her advances.

Attempting to dodge his advances, Pepper jumped, bending one leg, while the other thrust outward, but the vamp caught her foot midair in a viselike grip, nearly snapping her foot in two.

Pepper yelped out in pain as he whirled her onto his shoulders in a fireman's carry. So powerful his grip, no amount of squirming or biting on Pepper's part would extract her from prisoner mode.

The vampire bit into his finger, and blood gushed, which served as a medium for his rune-drawing. He was writing a way out, breaking the spell. Then what would become of Pepper?

Pepper squirmed and struggled and kicked and fought to escape, but that only incited the Hound to hold her tighter. Loki's stirring gifted her with the second wind she so desperately needed. But Pepper's fugitive relief came and went as she focused her attention back on Jhi. Jhi had dodged, dipped, dived, and ducked every death-dealing blow by the vamps, accomplished fighters in their own right, and delivered a few blows himself, all the while keeping them more than occupied and away from Pepper, but was bloodied and carved, nonetheless.

All that changed the moment Jhi hazarded a glance at Pepper, who was moments away from being taken to who knew where. Injuries and pain all but forgotten, Jhi jumped in the air, grabbed each of the bloated Hounds' heads, then let out a guttural grunt as he smashed them together. The impact nearly killed them both. While Jhi finished one off, beheading the sucker with his own weapon in one fluid motion, blood dripping from the blades and cascading down Jhi's arms, the still-standing vampire grabbed Jhi from behind and began slashing his neck, an eye for an eye in action.

A helpless Pepper screamed for Loki to do something.

Jhi banged his head into the vampire's Cro-Magnon brow, a maneuver that ended up saving Jhi's hide.

A sword whipped through the air and landed in Jhi's bound hands. He nodded thanks to Loki. Then he spun back around. Fighting with his hands zip-tied, Jhi proved that his skills as a swordsman were unparalleled. All Pepper could do was hope and pray that that Goddess Seren demons invoked would shower them with good luck because the barrier leading out was breaking.

Clashing and banging, swords pummeling swords, Jhi was engaged in a battle to the death with a bloodsucker, who was bent on demolishing Jhi and downright incandescent that Jhi had stymied the Hounds' ambush. Jhi and his blade went to town. His body moved as if floating on air as he spun the weapon, slicing vampire skin with every graceful whirling motion.

It truly was a breathtaking sight watching Jhi attempt to destroy the night-walker while his hands were bound. The curve of the sword, dipped in silver, gleamed as it disarmed the vampire, wresting away his dual-bladed weapon.

Not a problem, because the vampire produced a Glock.

As the bullet whipped around the space, Jhi jumped on the man, and they spun around, engaged in a deadly waltz, each vying for the lead, each vying for control of the gun. The deathly spectating ended for Pepper because the vampire began to break the barrier. As the vamp neutralized the runelike sigils with his blood, a doorway struggled to materialize, here one second, gone the next. As if a strobe light were on, Pepper snatched glimpses, more like flashes, of the Lolly'ka behind the door, kicking and pounding the barrier.

When the doorway flickered back into existence, a battle cry proceeded the Lolly'ka as she soared through, holding tight to one end of a hangman's noose. Was *she* Boss Lady? That thought sent a wave of defeat crashing through Pepper. But then reality twisted and turned, and when finished spinning, the unfathomable unfurled before Pepper. The Lolly'ka tackled the vampire like a defensive back and sent him reeling, and Pepper crashed to the floor.

Not about to give him a second chance, Pepper crabbed backward and as far away from her captor as possible.

The pint-size bandit wrapped her stockinged legs around the Hound's chest and squeezed and squeezed like a boa constrictor. Surely his soul would be emitted out of every available orifice from the sheer pressure the Lolly'ka exerted, her face rivaling that of a sunburned British tourist in Florida. Lightning fast, she doubly wrapped her yo-yo around the vampire's bloated neck. Grunts escaped her rose-bud lips as she pulled as tight as could be, leaning backwards, yanking and squashing until the vampire's head popped right off his square shoulders.

The Lolly'ka punted his decapitated head away from his body as if it were a football. Blood spattered her otherwise peaches-and-cream complexion.

Aware he was outnumbered, that his comrades were dead, the last vamp standing tried to turn tail. But Jhi gutted him and burned the body with nothing but what appeared to be a lighter. Then took out plenteous aggression on the dried husk of a blood-sucker. A nimbus of the vampire ashes swirled around Jhi's head, and at that moment, he resembled a dark angel.

The Lolly'ka hurled a switchblade Jhi's way. He snatched it midair, then liberated his hands of the Teflon-strong cable ties.

After pocketing her newly returned switchblade, the inter-loper-cum-rescuer yanked the chains from the wall, liberating Bhi'gow. Then she stated in a huff, "Quick! Follow me! We don't have much time!"

CHAPTER 18

The Lolly'ka was oblivious to the coterie of transfixed eyes glaring her way. Instead, she bent down to grab hold of the noose while simultaneously grousing about the state of her soiled, dainty dress. "Fuh'karity fuh'karing fuh'kar!" A stream of even more vulgar profanity sallied forth. "This was my favorite dress, too, those bloodsucking douchelords. See what they did to my eye? Socked me and knocked me out for a spell and kept me from saving your asses sooner! I swear to Lilith, next one I see, I'm gonna tear apart, slowly."

They all clung to the hangman's noose that also served as a grappling rope, an anchor to Skulduggerer's Lair that would allow passage back and forth through the spaces. The only instruction was to not let go, not to remove contact with the rope while crossing the heavily fortified barrier, lest they be blown to smithereens. Naturally, the Lolly'ka delivered the foreboding warning while tittering.

A gargoyle stood sentry at the front door of Skulduggerer's Lair. Pepper lurched backward and smacked into the once-possessed piano, her bum pressing down on the untuned keys.

"Calm down, sweetling." There were notes of superiority in

the Lolly'ka voice. "Trixie's with me." Trixie joined her pint-sized boss, who clocked in around five-foot-three.

Tucked behind the gargoyle's back were bat wings of gunmetal and inky-black—a hue that seamlessly matched the variegated marble texturing the being's leathery skin. Standing nearly eight feet tall, the demon loomed sinisterly over everyone, Bhi'gow included. Vested in an armor breast-plate, she was all lean, corded muscle, not an ounce of flabby fat could be found save for her chest, and even that wasn't so much flabby but pronounced; if anything, the hilly orbs revealed the gargoyle's gender.

Pepper finally found someone whose chest was a smaller cup size than hers. So, what if it was a gargoyle? She'd take it.

Although Trixie's features were about as demoniacal as one could imagine, forked tail and tongue, fangs for teeth, to say nothing of her terrifying presence, yet her eyes leveled the ratio of evil to virtuous, smoothed out the tangled feelings of fright and fear. Eyes never lie, a maxim of Pepper's, a belief that rang true and hadn't let her down yet. And this gargoyle hadn't proved Pepper wrong. Her slit eyes of mercury with flecks of green shimmered with honor, with loyalty. Still, the gargoyle would rip Pepper to ribbons on Perrin's command.

"Store's surrounded." Trixie's sonorous tenor possessed the ability to chill human blood.

Two more gargoyles joined Trixie. One of them, who went by the name Minx, growled, "Two wanderers dead ahead, two more at three o'clock. They brought along ghouls for backup."

The third gargoyle, Gamble, added, "Counted about eight or ten Hounds around the corner, idling in the shadows."

"We're outflanked and outnumbered." Perrin snuck a peek out the window before returning to the center of the Lair. "There's no way we can take them on. The best bet is to distract them and slip away undetected."

While stealing a glance out the window, Jhi said to the Lolly'ka from over his shoulder, "Very convenient that you're here. *And* had a way out of that prison, smattered with copious amounts of runes." Jhi's voiced suspicions were met with a hyper-dramatic eye roll. "Moreover, am I supposed to believe that a Lolly'ka all of a sudden not only hatched a soul, but has good intentions and wants to help others? What, did you actually pay heed to the proselytizing Born-Again Demons, denounce Lilith and join the ranks of the Almighty?"

The Lolly'ka remained poised. "First of all, the name's Perrin, so use it. Secondly, regarding the noose, this isn't my first rodeo, dickwad!"

Seriously bizarre, the watching of a tweenager not only fend off vampires but spew such vitriol in a voice coated in pixie sticks and pink lemonade while simultaneously batting her baby blues. Her mouth was worse than Pepper's, worse than a drunken sailor's even.

"It's only a matter of time until those fuh'karing"—a fusillade of expletives followed—"craplords outside realize their comrades-in-arms aren't returning and charge into the Lair. What're you gonna do then? Sweetling here is about as useless as the damned praying for absolution. And the even is too much to can't with this limp-as-a-noodle demon and his sidekick gimpy monkey. Then there's you. A fuh'karing mess. You're bleeding out like a sacrifice to Seren." Drops of Jhi's blood marred the flooring. "So, by my calculations, I'm your only hope of staying alive. Just consider me your vessel to safety," Perrin proudly proclaimed.

Jhi remained mulish, despite grimacing from his festering wounds. "When you crossed the barrier," Jhi said to Pepper, "you must have set off an alarm, alerting the Hounds to our presence." He switched his attention to Perrin. "Now, why are you here if not working for them? If not their backup? After all, the Lolly'kas, *your* mob, are allied with the Hounds of Hell."

"Hold up! You have no idea why you were ambushed, do you?" A wicked grin slowly formed on Perrin's spackled bubblegum-pink lips. She seemed to derive pleasure from having the upper hand.

"And you do?" Jhi growled.

"Eeny, meeny, miny, moe," singsonging, Perrin waggled her finger to and fro, "catch a human by the toe, if it hollers devour it whole, eeny, meeny, miny, MOE!" Her finger landed on Pepper. "Sweetling, you're a wanted girl. Wanted fully alive, that point's stressed. Helluva price on your head, too."

Jhi stood in front of Pepper, as did Loki, who pulled his lips back in a snarl for extra effect.

"Hey, hey, I didn't say *I* put the bounty on her head."

In two strides, Jhi devoured the distance between him and Perrin.

Perrin held her hands up in defense. "Hey now, lover boy, if I wanted sweetling, I wouldn't be standing here playing games with the likes of you. Instead, you'd all be dead, save for sweetling." Though haughty, that admittance must have had a harmonic ring to it, because Jhi backed off.

Recalling Jhi's warning about what to do in a bind, Pepper whipped out her forged ID and stated her assumed name, occupation and purpose for visiting Hell. She dipped her other hand into her go-bag and extracted magic gems of various colors, some green, others red, yellow, blue, indigo, violet, and orange. In hindsight, she probably should have asked what the colors represented.

With her palm facing upward and full of magic gems, Pepper said, "These in exchange for your silence."

"Oh, sweetling," Perrin said, her tone condescending, "that's so adorable. But it would take a helluva lot more than magic gems to buy my silence, Marie Smith. Or perhaps I should call you by your real name. Pepper."

Pepper did not expect that response and tried her damnedest to tamp down a reaction. As it was, her nails begged to be chewed. "You must be mistaken—"

"If not gems, then name your price? We'll offer more than the bounty," Jhi prodded.

Perrin sighed histrionically while ironing out the wrinkles on her summertime dress and adjusting the unruly crinoline beneath. "Tempting, but no. And it's not like a magic gem or fleshie amount is being offered for Pepper's abduction. No, I'm here because the enemy of my enemy is my, well, not friend but associate. So, let's go, associates."

Jhi remained skeptical, so Perrin revealed more of what had sent her into a fit of pique. Pandæmonia was Lolly'ka turf, and Perrin didn't take kindly to the Hounds storming in and running their shadowy operation like a bunch of discourteous ruffians sans asking permission from the Lolly'ka's.

"Y'know, the lack of respect and being kept in the dark is appalling. I can't even." She placed her dainty little hand out and huffed, then deeply inhaled a centering breath. "Something's going down, something big and I have a right to know what that is, dammit! Moreover, the damned're restless. Now, as for the why exactly, I'm not sure yet, but sweetling here's the linchpin."

"From my vast experience, the Lolly'ka's are accomplished liars." Jhi's spoke in a monotone, just stating facts. There had to be unresolved history between Jhi and the Lolly'ka's that would explain his mistrust.

"Get all your info from Wicked-pedia, did you?"

Jhi opened his mouth.

"Rhetorical question. You should know then that I'm not a bounty hunter, dimensions from it. Besides, I have bigger beasties to fry than hunting down the likes of Pepper."

"If not in collusion with the enemies, then how did you know to come to Skulduggerer's Lair at precisely the time of our arrival?"

"It's a good thing I showed up when I did, or the lot of you'd be dead." Jhi wasn't amused. "Dear Lilith, are you ever xykree-headed. Okay, fine! Earlier, at the Tenth Circle, while kicking back and nursing a Cocytus-cold ale after a long day of queenpinning, I overheard the Talking Heads mantled about the Tavern mention something about their freedom; now what would give those good-for-nothing damned the idea that they're gonna be liberated soon? What is this, the Harrowing of Hell part *deux*? Unfortunately, one of the Heads caught me eavesdropping, and the rest clamped their jaws shut." Perrin noted Jhi's ears perking up. "Ooh, I've got your full attention now."

The damned, or their decapitated heads to be exact, apparently populating this Tenth Circle watering hole like macabre artwork, were apprised of not only Pepper but her goings-on since landing in Hell, her final destination a constant on their flapping lips.

"If Pepper did, in fact, seek out Skulduggerer's Lair, then that right there proved she was *'the girl.'*" Perrin air-quoted. "Well, at least according to the damneds' argle-bargling. And I must say, sweetling, they described you to the letter—hair, eyes and all. So, if they know what you look like, then chances are the mala'khas do as well."

Loki jumped on Pepper's shoulders, then squeezed them. She touched him back, acknowledging his concern that she, too, shared.

"Xykree got your tongues?" Nobody answered. "Oh, my fuh'karing—Hey, your funerals, but I'm not gonna die. So who's coming with? Because we have a few minutes at the most till the Hounds, ghouls, and wanderers bust through the windows and door!" Perrin rubbed her tiny hands together, suggesting she was done with the matter, her ruby red nails as sharp as tacks.

Pepper grabbed Jhi and pulled him away so they could chat in private. "I'm freakin' out, Jhi! Whoever is after me knows my real name. Does this have anything to do with the River and soul registering?"

Jhi swore up and down it didn't. They wouldn't have made it to shore if that had happened. She'd be a corpse right about now or in the Pits if so. That this was something else entirely, something far more worrisome.

Pepper rejoined Perrin and the others, Jhi on her heels. "I don't care if Perrin eats hearts for snacks, shops at the Skinstress across the street, whatever, she saved me, so in my book, she's an ally!

Now can we please leave, like now!" Before she went catatonic from fright!

If only Pepper could draw her way out of this nightmare by rendering a chaosgate. Alas, the forbidden fruit that was chaosnauting inter- and intra-dimensionally, sketching her way outta Hell or the Lair, was expressly forbidden and not possible under Lucifer's forever reign.

"The Hounds are advancing." Jhi quickly retreated from the window and stood beside Pepper. "What's the plan then, Perrin?"

"The Lolly'ka's have ways ye not know of, but will after today." With pride coating her voice, she elaborated. "The Lolly'kas have made certain that every Pandæmonia establishment has access to the warrens—"

"All the better for shakedowns," Jhi added.

Perrin ignored his snide comment. "And it just so happens that the one inside Skulduggerer's Lair resides underneath the funeral coach."

"The River Styx is underneath us." Jhi was beyond incredulous. "Negative. Not happening!"

"I know the warren of tunnels like the back of my hand, 'kay? I'll get us to safety in one piece. Hopefully. Points for at least trying? Yes, no?" Perrin's incessant giggles didn't have company. "You guys are so serious."

Tens of Hounds charged the Lair. "Go! I'll fend them off." Trixie thundered to the front door, silver blades a-swingin'.

Perrin popped open the elongated back of the hearse, then hoisted up the carpeted bottom. Underneath was a stairless hole that led to that which couldn't be discerned because of the crushing blackness. With the flick of a switch, gears grumbled, and a staircase grew, step by metaled step. Another flick of a button and the stairs crumbled, folding downward to make a slide.

Wanting to be as far away from the vamps as possible, Pepper jumped first and slid her way to oblivion. The slide was shellacked, and the fall at the craggy bottom was rather painful.

It would have been lovely and most appreciative if Perrin had warned them that the agitated water of the River Styx was inches from the slide's end. Not that anyone could see the river wall or the water, not as long as the warren was black as pitch. The swirling and crashing of the river through the tunnel was booming, a torrent of spray lashing at their arms.

Perrin lit a lucifer by rubbing the match on the stone flooring, sulfur wafting about, then flicked the burning stick into the air. The match kissed a wick in a lantern feet away and dressed it with its warmth, then hovered to the next lantern and the next, continuing down the tunnels like a ghostly lamplighter.

Seeing as how magic was forbidden for civilians, Perrin must have magic gems, Pepper deduced. That, or the match was an enchanted object.

The warren aglow in cobalt hellfire, Pepper eyed shadows of demonic-looking creatures undulating on the moldy walls, but no bodies were to be found. Perrin maneuvered to a central control panel hidden within the rocky walls. After entering a code, the stairs whipped up, annihilating the slide, then folded upward like a yo-yo.

A flat-bottom boat crashed against the urchin-crusted river wall. Jhi unmoored the skiff while Perrin grasped hold of a ferryman pole, then pushed the skiff away from the dock. And off they sailed.

Pepper had been whitewater rafting before with her pops in Colorado, but that exhilarating yet terrifying experience was nothing compared to the River Styx; in fact, it was akin to sitting in an inflatable tube in a kiddie pool.

The labyrinthine tunnels that they whirled down were too narrow for the great breadth of the River Styx and, as such, caused much turbulence. Waves crawled up the curved walls. Water splashed into the skiff, drenching its passengers. Before the gang even began their perilous journey, they were soaked.

The skiff spun like a whirligig; round and round they went. If your hands weren't grasping on for dear life, then you were a goner.

Perrin was laser-focused, robotic were her movements as they changed course left and right and straight. Every moment was precious and couldn't be spared for contemplation.

After some time, Perrin sat down on a bench like a flight attendant preparing for a crash landing, and calmly stated, "Hang on! This part's the roughest."

The rapids tossed them forward and forward as if a swell belonged to the hand of Poseidon, and the god, deeply angered, hurled them away from his dominion. So great the forward thrust, Pepper could've sworn they were airborne for a beat.

All eyes riveted on a stony gaping maw that was dead ahead. Seaweed stuck in its jagged stone teeth. "Is that a waterfall?" Pepper stuttered.

Perrin giggled, which was more than disconcerting. The River Styx and the skiff were vomited out of the mouth of the warrens. The prow dipped, then took a nosedive, dragging its passengers down and down. Tens of hundreds of feet separated them from the bottom—the bottom where the water crashed and churned.

Pepper's screams rent the air as she held on to the bench, plummeting to her death.

CHAPTER 19

Without warning, the skiff righted, morphing into a flying palanquin of sorts; gargoyles Minx and Gamble were the bearers.

After squaring her shoulders, Pepper hazarded a glance over the lip of the vessel, her fingers death-gripping its rim. Below was the confluence of all five Rivers of Hell. In every direction, the tempestuous waters smacked into one another and tempered, forming Lucifer's Bog, a belching swamp thinly veiled by gaseous mist and alight with bioluminescence.

Fret not intrepid adventurers, directional signs were abound hither, thither, and yonder, some even marked with: BEWARE! *Lucifer's Bog is cursed with spontaneous vortices.* And as for the gnarled-limbed woodlands girding the swampland, adventurers should be on the lookout for creatures most foul, lurking in the shadows, waiting for their dinner to breeze by.

In response to Perrin's asking, "Where to?" Bhi'gow offered his dwelling as a hideout shelter.

"That's the last place we should be heading. Meaning the Hounds're expecting us to do just that, and we'd be falling into a trap, yet again." More than a hint of anger coated Jhi's words.

To be fair, all and sundry were thriving on roiling adrenaline from the earlier battle, so tempers were flaring.

A gargoyle groused, said the winging around aimlessly needed to cease lest they be spotted, so someone better bark out a direction, or they'd take matters into their own wings, whatever that meant.

"Well, if it's any consolation, I don't recall my address, so consider it a safe house." Bhi'gow readjusted his position and winced, his wounds getting the better of him. His charred hide had been worn down to the bone on his wrists and ankles, where the shackles had called home for years. "That salient knowledge, among other things, rests with Loki and Loki only. See, at the conclusion of every fixing job, I always empty my memory bank of all intel, a standard industry practice, I assure you. And I must have done just that before I was apprehended, for, during the years of torture, I told the Hounds nothing because I knew nothing."

Jhi mulled that discovery over for a beat before he felt assured and nodded.

Loki's teensy hands got busy navigating the flying skiff to the destination, and the gargoyles slightly changed course. Pepper stole a final glance back and eyed a scrim of fog veiling Pandæmonia's imposing skyline that grew smaller and smaller the further away they journeyed. Until it morphed into that of an indelible memory.

The flapping of the gargoyles' wings, as they picked up the pace, incited zephyrs of icy wind to nip Pepper's cheeks. While tucking her freezing hands inside the insulated sleeves of her robe and tightening the hoodie, she caught Jhi stealing glimpses.

Jhi crossed over a bench to sit beside her. "How you holding up?"

"Not sure just yet. Everything happened so fast," Pepper lied. Actually, her emotions were a cauldron of untold fear and shock, and more shock, and a dash of anger. The adrenaline from the battle only compounded the already caustic mixture, threatening to boil over at any moment.

"You did good back there, at the Lair. That sun grenade, nice touch," Jhi said as his arm brushed against hers. "Fighting side-by-side for our lives is just about as intimate as two people can get." Matter of fact morphed into flirting.

Twitterpated, Pepper felt a blush creep along her cheeks and elsewhere. That futile bliss was quickly dispelled when Pepper reminded herself that Jhi is scouring dimensions for his missing ladylove, and once they reunite, then buh-bye Pepper. Dammit! Not again. Pepper meets boy. They flirt. She crushes hard. Only to find out too late that his heart belonged to another.

The word "no" was not in Pepper's vocabulary. And when she wanted something and could not have it, the want turned to need. Unfortunately, that spelled trouble when the something was a some*one*. If anything, history should have taught her by now to get off the emotional roller coaster—passenger of one—before it crashed and burned.

Angrier at herself more than anything, she darted her eyes and attention elsewhere, seeking out a distraction to stave off screaming bloody murder or connecting her fist to something, to someone.

"Fixer, how long exactly did the Hounds hold you prisoner?" Pepper's question took on an undeniably hostile edge. She traveled to Hell for this moment, and she wasn't about to let more time pass before she got answers.

"Twelve long years."

They fell off the face of Hell around twelve years ago, Pepper recalled Jhi saying about Loki and Bhi'gow.

"Is that how long you've been holed up inside Pepper?" Jhi asked Loki, disbelief wrapped around every word.

Loki chittered and nodded his head.

"For *twelve years*, the Hounds kept you prisoner?" Jhi, like Pepper, was stitching the pieces together.

"Yes. It was an ambush from the start. And we escaped, just barely."

The Hounds had been one step ahead of Pepper this whole time. They anticipated her traveling to Hell. Begged the question: What other deathtraps did they have in the works?

"Bhi'gow's the only insurance the Hounds have against losing track of me, so does everybody here seriously believe that they're gonna let him escape? Just like that?" Pepper shook her head. "No way. They're after me, Perrin said so herself."

"For fuh'karing sake. Is everyone here brain dead?" Perrin huffed.

Pepper's jaw opened, a retort locked and loaded.

"Rhetorical question. The Talking Heads? Remember them? They're under the assumption that they got a ticket outta Hell. Sorry to burst your 'it's all about me' bubble, sweetling, but whatever's in the works is epic. We're talking about an operation of tragic magnitude that far surpasses little old you. Sure, you're an integral part of the operation—"

"I think you're right." Not that that admittance by Pepper blunted her fear any. Or at all.

"The Hounds never let their intentions slip, nor any viable intel"—Jhi pinned Bhi'gow with a sharp look—"*not once* during your time in captivity?"

Before the fixer could say "no," Pepper added, "Does All Hallows' Eve ring a bell? Because whatever's in the works culminates on that day."

"Yes, it sounds familiar. I caught wind of the Hounds mentioning that particular day, but thought nothing of it or that it correlated with my abduction. Now, I can't tell you what's going to happen then, but whatever it is has attracted players from Hell and Earth alike, all having equal stakes in the spoils, that much I ascertained."

If Pepper's blood hadn't already been chilled from the Arctic temperatures, that ominous delivery did the trick.

The stars impaling the heavens were ever so close, so much so that if Pepper extended her hand outward, the kaleidoscope of glistening daggers would surely slice and dice her skin. If only that were so. If only she could feel some pain, save for numbness.

Bhi'gow added, "Of note, whoever's in charge wants Pepper alive. And that matter is nonnegotiable."

"Ooh, I wonder if it's sacrificial in nature, like a demonic resurrection on All Hallows' Eve, why the Hounds want sweetling. Like the blood needs to be pure. You a virgin?" Perrin might as well have said, "pass the potatoes."

As for replying, Pepper's narrowing eyes took the reins.

"Rest assured, after my goyles are done *chatting* with a few Talking Heads back at the Tenth Circle Tavern, we'll see what they had to say under duress, like who's calling the shots," Perrin said while flicking open a compact, then powdering her button nose.

"Perrin, why are you here, helping us?" Jhi's eyes narrowed with suspicion.

"I made myself perfectly clear why back at the Lair."

"Yes, Pandæmonia's your turf and the Hounds of Hell usurped your position of power and insulted your faction in the process, and you're gonna get even, but—"

"This isn't merely about bloodsuckers treading on my toes. Eons ago, a line was drawn in the sand, a mutual understanding forged between our factions. How I see it, the Hounds of Hell crossed said line and woefully broke ancient rules, albeit unwritten. Now the truce our factions once had has been rendered obsolete, and there is no going back. Heed my warning. I sense a war is brewing, and it's gonna be messy. So, you're either with the Lollyka's or against us. And those who choose the latter … Well, they'll have far more than a curse from Goddess Shi'rue to contend with. Now, I know where the Hounds of Hell stand." Perrin locked her orbs on Pepper and Jhi. "What say you, sweetling, Jhi?" Perrin reproached Pepper with mistrust aplenty.

Stalling for time, Pepper offered, "Tell you what. I'll share what I know. But only if Bhi'gow and Loki do the same first, starting with when and why they stole my magic and memories.

That is the key to understanding why a homicidal vampiric cartel is after me. It has to be. I mean, what could a five-year-old possibly have done to land on their radar?"

"Sweetling, it's not just the Hounds of Hell that are after you. One thing you should know about the Hounds is that they are militaristic in their organization. This means they have a leader, someone who gives the Hounds their marching orders. Another thing to know is that while they're formidable opponents, they can be bested with magic."

"Not anymore," Jhi amended. "The Hounds can now cast magic like proper demons. What was once unheard of is now common practice on Earth and in Hell. And unlike the rest of us in Hell, they can cast spells without the need of gems. Yet, their magic isn't drawing the attention of mala'khas. Why is that?"

"That's a big fuh'karing problem." Perrin exchanged looks of concern with her goyles. "Well, I'd worry about the whys later and focus on how to stay alive. As it is, you probably have, what, days at the most until you're spotted, until the Hounds hunt you down." Perrin's wide eyes pinned Pepper in place as she glided a lip-gloss wand over her smackers. "Of course, I could offer you protection in exchange for information. Starting with who you are and why you're so fuh'karing important."

Pepper added a valuable tidbit to the conversation herself. "Well, we already know who's calling the shots. That would be a female. Goes by the name Boss Lady. She's who the Hounds most likely report to." She instantly regretted sharing, and not because Jhi lobbed icy daggers her way.

Perrin perked up, her large eyes narrowing. "Ooh, really? What else do you know, sweetling?"

Pepper shivered and cinched her robe ever tighter; the frigid temperature wasn't to blame.

Perrin slipped her compact back into her purse and extracted a new object—the yo-yo-slash-garrote. While playing with the death-bringer, she tossed it dangerously close to Pepper's neck before snapping it back. Rinse and repeat. Unless Pepper willingly spilled her guts, she feared Perrin would do the same to her. Literally.

The anxiety too much to bear, Pepper's heart rolled in her chest, feelings of lightheadedness resulting. Before getting down to the nitty-gritty, she needed to simmer down her thoughts into some semblance of order. So, what better way to do just that than distracting herself by focusing on the terrain below—terrain that grew exponentially forbidding.

The skiff glided over rocky canyons and craggy cliffs—Pepper could've sworn she spied a cave or two—over deserts with rolling dunes, nary a pyramid to be had, to fields of hovering bioluminescent flora and fauna. Within all the environs, Hell-creatures with bat wings and odd-numbered limbs scampered about, some mid-devouring their hunted prey, some mid-stalking; either way, it was a bloodbath below. And just like the prey below, Pepper, too, was being hunted from every direction, or so it seemed. She desperately needed allies.

As it was, Pepper shakily walked along a threadbare tightrope that threatened to snap at any moment; if she fell, did she trust these strangers to catch her? Or would they let her free-fall to her death? And who's to say they weren't working for the enemy? So what was Pepper to do? To tell or not to tell the truth?

Honestly, she wanted for nothing but to curl up into her pop's arms and have a long-overdue crying jag. But she couldn't. And she most certainly wouldn't put Larry in danger. Instead, she opted to have what Perrin just quaffed—Grissel's ale. Flask now in hand, Pepper sipped the contents, an internal thermostat warming, edge-blunting, sweet-and-briny concoction, with hints of pomegranate.

"*Ahem*, Pepper," Bhi'gow started. "Bound by the rules of Hell, Loki is unable to share with me the events of when and why you entered into an unholy bargain, your magic and memories the price, allegedly—"

"While Loki might be contractually forbidden to share with you the events that transpired after meeting with Pepper, that's not the case for Pepper, now is it, Bhi'gow?" Jhi donned his soul broker hat. "Always read the fine print. The laws of Hell permit fixers to divulge the inner workings of an operation that pertain to the signee, should the signee inquire. Pepper has, and now you are legally obligated to answer her query."

"While that may be true, need I remind you that I erased my memory bank of our encounter? And Loki doesn't speak, so I'm afraid that knowledge stays buried with him." Bhi'gow might have been tortured senseless for years on end, his body a battleground of evidence thereof, his muscles atrophied, but that wasn't the case for his mind. Memories or no, it was as sharp as a devil's pitchfork. And that tongue of his, slicked with silver.

"Not necessarily." Perrin jumped into the conversation. "I have a way to extract Loki's memories. But I'll hold off on the how until sweetling spills."

Bottoms up! Pepper gulped back more of the sweet and briny ale for much-needed liquid courage, then dramatically wiped her mouth with her forearm before beginning with the epic yarn spinning. "It all started when I received a call from my next-door neighbor, Kimball …"

From a wanderer possessing Bunny Garcia and many others to her encounter with Sawyer, meeting Jhi, the mysterious All Hallows' Eve ball invite—Pepper vouchsafed all the events that led her to Hell, save for Karma and her agents. Because Pepper wasn't sold on Perrin's loyalty or the gargoyle's, the same goes for Bhi'gow; any scene involving the goddess, the Academy, and Agents of Karma wound up on the cutting room floor. Keeping the edited-out clips company were all mentionings of Jhi's girlfriend, JD. While Pepper trilled like a canary, Jhi's glares spoke volumes: JD was off limits.

Perrin slightly nodded, a gesture that stated, "you've chosen wisely," and pocketed her yo-yo.

"Your turn, Perrin." Pepper couldn't wait a moment longer for life-saving answers.

"Unless you're a fur'moria"—a memory thief—"there's no

way to steal Loki's memories without killing him. And you'd have to go through me first," Bhi'gow growled.

Loki whipped out a quarterstaff and held it out defensively.

"Now, now. There will be no killing." Perrin unfastened her patent leather purse, and out popped a … "Sprites are curious little devils." Size-wise, the creature resembled a starved sparrow. "And harder to find than a chaste soul in an archdemon." She slipped on a ring with a chain attached to the collar coiled around the sprite's neck.

It was hard to tell where the sprite's tail began and ended or if the sprite even had a torso. But the noodle-like hands and arms attached to something. As for its teeny face, no bigger than a fingerprint, that was humanoid, right down to its lips, aquiline nose, and arched brows. But not the jet-black horns that stabbed upward or its charcoal-colored form. Though it had no legs, it curved its tail into a U-shape and then rested atop Perrin's shoulder on its tail's arch.

"You ventured into the caves of Gehenna and not only lived but bagged a sprite. Nice." Jhi gave credit where credit was due. "Still, sprites aren't fur'morias, what with their diet consisting of brains. Not to mention how they torture and KILL THEIR PREY!"

"Torturing is fun. Up to a point." Perrin cast her eyes elsewhere as if she were wistfully lost in days of yore, days spent torturing and dismembering. "But when you're not getting results, it becomes a real drag. Until I found Tavi. Now, when boredom strikes, I unleash him."

"From your purse," Pepper pointed out.

Responding to Pepper's judgmental looks, Perrin replied, "What? It reminds him of home. It's cavelike. Or dark. Whatever!" She slackened the tension on Tavi's leash. "Can everyone shut the fuh'kar up and let me explain my plan?" After a sigh, she continued. "Something to do with their organic makeup, a survival instinct of sorts. It allows sprites to hunt their preferred prey with remarkable accuracy. They do make for the best trackers. So, I had a theory and needed a sprite to test it out."

Jhi tossed his hands up in a "that's what I basically said" gesture, his nose bunched up with annoyance.

"Yes, Jhi, their diet consists of brains. But it's what happens after ingestion. A chemical breakdown occurs, which results in a reaction much like with LSD. And the hallucinations experienced by sprites thereafter aren't hallucinations but memories belonging to their last prey. Now here's the trippy part, when my hypothesis was proven correct. I, too, can experience those foreign memories myself, as if I was the prey, the events happening live and in living color. All senses felt."

When Perrin scooted on a bench to get closer to Loki, the capuchin went on the defensive, his quarterstaff at the ready.

"Loki, I'm gonna need you to concentrate on the fixing job in question, to the moment when it all began. Tavi will sense the electrical impulses crackling inside your hippocampus. He'll then chew—or nibble a hole in that area of your head and suck out the activated memory. It shouldn't—it won't hurt. At all. His saliva will salve the gushing wound. So, no worries, you won't bleed out. It's instinctual, the saliva, the better to keep prey alive for snack time—"

Loki angrily chittered and nodded assent.

After Perrin loosened the leash, Tavi zipped to Loki and began nibbling on his head, to which Loki clenched his fists and winced from what was most likely untold pain.

Perrin yanked on Tavi's chain, forcing the sprite to zip back to his master, blood coating his razor-sharp teeth and chin. Holding a vial in one hand, with a finger on her other hand, she poked the sprite's doughy belly, and he vomited a bloodied green concoction into the vial.

Perrin handed the puke to Pepper. "Cheers! And enjoy the trip!"

Pepper cringed as she drank the chunky, bloodied vomit, its consistency much like spoiled milk. Feeling woozy, drunk, endorphins surging, though she remained in one spot, she felt as if she were on a roller coaster going zero to ninety in two seconds flat.

Then everything stilled. And another type of thrill replaced the high.

Pepper's mind was transported to another time, another place.

She was inside Loki.

She had become Loki.

CHAPTER 20

In an alley, a gaggle of kids ushered in the Lunar New Year by waving sparklers and igniting whizzing ground spinners. Loki scampered past them, sight unseen, as he surveilled the seemingly abandoned warehouse for points of infiltration.

Sigils smothered the exterior walls, prohibiting chaosnauting inside or out. No less than two lowlies, armed with Uzis, were positioned 24/7 outside the only entrance—a steel door. That left one option, and even that was dicey. As for the hostiles within, they weren't going anywhere until sunset. So Loki had no choice but to strike in the dead of day to rescue his client held captive inside.

Boom! Boom! Boom! Fireworks exploded in the Manila sky, drowning out the beating drums in the distance as Loki jumped up the wall and navigated along the corrugated roof of the warehouse, bypassing window after window, their panes stained black, questing for the one riddled with bullet holes. The one that would—hopefully—allow him to steal inside undetected.

At the infiltration point, he gingerly removed the fractured bits of glass, creating a wide-enough space for his tiny body to squeeze through.

After diving inside the dimly lit warehouse, he landed on a

rafter and was immediately assailed by the ubiquitous stench of decay and butchery, of urine and feces and the juices corpses released after death. The stifling humidity only intensified the stomach-roiling stench.

Thank Seren, the defense wards did not detect his presence. And neither would his client, seven-year-old Kassendra Li, for Loki was cloaked in shadows.

Loki's client sat twenty-odd feet below him, manacled inside a very large birdcage that hovered midair by way of sorcery. And below Kassendra, shadowy tendrils, appearing like a sea of serpents, slithered about the floor and walls, devouring all illumination on their quest to dominate every inch of the sprawling space but for the suspended birdcage. That jaundiced light was spared, always, to keep an eye on the youngling within.

Kassendra lifted her weary head from her knobby knees right as a door at the farthest reaches of the desolate warehouse groaned open. As the door promptly slammed shut, terrified whimpers and beseechings from beyond the sole point of escape were silenced.

Loki winced and cursed Goddess Seren, as he had arrived too late.

The Hound of Hell, unrelenting in his quest for vital information at his overlord's behest, gruffly shoved the newest slave forward, all the while holding a serrated knife to her throat. Her flats, unable to gain purchase, slid on the slick cement floor, the chains secured around her hands and feet clanking with each step. And like Kassendra, this girl was a mage, her magic choked.

In broken English, the slave girl regurgitated the memorized script, like all the others before her, demanding Kassendra spill where she'd hidden her baby sister, and then the Hounds would release them both.

But when Kassendra remained mum, the girl, panic-stricken, unrelentingly begged in her native dialect and screamed fiercely at Kassendra, her pupils bleeding out like droplets of oil. So strong the slave's will, Loki could feel the ghost of her spindly fingers strangling Kassendra's already battered and burned arms, violently shaking her to trill, to say something, anything, that would stay the girl's inevitable slaying.

"Forgive me," Kassendra responded stoically in her native tongue. "It'll all be over soon. Just picture a happy place." If that was even possible for the slave girl.

Unfortunately, the slave didn't understand Kassendra's words because she didn't speak a lick of Tagalog or English, nor did Kassendra speak Munhwaŏ.

Loki could sense Kassendra's frustration, her wrathful thoughts—she would have done everything in her power to rescue this girl, and all the others before her, and the others to come.

If only her hands weren't bound.

If only her magic wasn't lost.

If only Kassendra hadn't made a deal with the devil, her magic the ultimate price.

The Hound wrenched the slave girl's head back. Seized by terror, rivulets of tears gathered on her chin.

Seconds before the Hound delivered the coup de grâce, Kassendra mouthed silently to the slave girl, "You're not alone."

The Hound of Hell applied more pressure to the girl's skin with the gleaming blade as it slid across her neck, nearly decapitating the girl in one fell swoop. Arterial spray soaked her camisole and soaked the monster's hands. He slurped the viscous matter off his stubby fingers and the serrated edge of the knife, but that wasn't enough to sate his thirst.

Murder reflecting in his ebony eyes, he tossed the girl to the side before lunging Kassendra's way, his fangs hungering for her life force, for her magic. Which meant the monster was nearly out of juice and needed to replenish his supply.

A tremor of fright coursed visibly through Kassendra, rattling the chains clenched around her limbs.

Growling, the Hound prattled off threats impregnated with

vivid descriptions of what he planned on doing to Kassendra before his master returned.

Loki needed to drain the vampire of all magic before he harmed the ruachti's client. Thinking fast, Loki tossed a throwing knife at the rectangular row of glass panes behind him. Jagged ebony fragments rained down.

Vagrant shafts of sunlight lanced through the newly made openings, then refracted off the myriad shards of glass before assailing the Hound, flash-pointing his flesh. Boom-boom-boom, arms and face and legs caught fire. Skin ablaze, he lobbed expletives as his meaty limbs bounded into the shadows. The hands of gloom swathed the savage man and salved his smoldering body. Skin reweaving over bone, his flesh was made whole again. But not his magic, as the healing drained that.

The Hound turned on his heel and disappeared behind the point of egress, returning to his crew held up within. Loki heard their drunken laughter and ribald comments for a split second before they were snuffed out by the closing door.

A whimper escaped and hitchhiked on the fetid air—a whimper belonging to yet another slave. And within the hour, he'd be dead and his magic drained.

Loki had one shot at rescuing Kassendra, so he waited for a beat to ensure the coast remained clear before commencing the rescue operation, his eyes anchoring on the youngling.

Kassendra gingerly plucked away stray locks of her tangled raven hair that were glued to second-degree burns that charred her sunken cheek and hooked them behind her ear. A river of sweat poured down her dirt-coated arms and pooled in the myriad blistering burns and slashes, turning a muddied pinkish-brown.

Sunbeams surged through the shattered window, illuminating the once darkened space surrounding Kassendra's cage. The shadowy tendrils on the concrete below aggressively swam towards the light to snuff it out, their swirling motions mimicking a feeding frenzy of piranha.

Cocooned in haunting silence, save for a *drip-drip-drip* sound, Kassendra's terrified eyes trawled along the newly illuminated cement ground. Rills of viscous matter spilled down a centrally located drain, smack dab under the floating cage.

Body after lifeless body was scattered about. Their throats slashed. Each of them so, so young, no older than sixteen. Thirteen? Ten? But one commonality forever bound these individuals: they were all mages.

Fragments of the dearly departeds' pleas still lingered, clawing away at Kassendra. A sea of terrified wide-open orbs drowning in their own blood all locked on her, causing the youngling to bury her head in her knees.

Though Kassendra was merely a child through and through, Loki reckoned she had been around for much longer than seven years, if not centuries. How else could this youngling have been skilled beyond her years in the mystical dark arts? Aware of worlds far removed from her own? Of otherworldly beings? Of fixers and ruachtis?

Or how Kassendra had astral projected to Witherwhere, her baby sister, Pepper, firmly by her side. Or how the eldest Li sister had known the invocation to contact Bhi'gow and Loki therein?

At first blush, Loki liked Kassendra, respected her even. This youngling might have been sweet like pixie pie, but make no bones about it. She beguiled those pixies with her charm, then butchered them and served the minced pixies up with a smile. Loki sensed that same edge of darkness in Pepper, too. Then again, a few telltales led Loki to believe another had instructed Kassendra. And that same being had lent Kassendra a portion of their magic—the ancient bits—and guided Kassendra every step of the way.

Like when Bhi'gow, in Witherwhere, had singsonged to the Li sisters, "I can fix your perilous plight, for a price, as nothing in life is ever truly free," then produced a furled contract, Kassendra didn't bat an eyelash.

Or when Kassendra had replied, as if by rote, "*He*"—venom

coated that word—"and his Hounds won't stop until me and my sister are dead. This is the *only* way to stop him. At least for now."

Not even a wince escaped when Bhi'gow had sliced Kassendra's palm (the same couldn't be said of Pepper), then dipped a talon-like pen in the reservoir of her blood. Boldly, she'd signed her signature on the dotted line—a reaction Loki had never experienced in his few centuries-long career of fixing. Then again, their innocence would shine through at times, reminding Loki they were just a four- and seven-year-old child, respectively.

With the ever-binding contract activated, Kassendra and Pepper had forever signed away their magic, their only line of defense. Even then, the youngling hadn't shed a tear.

"Escaping the Hounds of Hell and their vengeful overlord is worth the price," Kassendra had stated as if by memory, her tone resolute. When it was said and done, she had whimpered, "I want the bad man to go away." Her diction had turned more childlike as she veered away from the rehearsed script. "I want it to be over. I don't want to run anymore."

Until the time of rescue, Bhi'gow had instructed Kassendra to carry on with the ruse that she was still a mage and to deliver stern warnings to her captors that she'd obliterate the Hounds if any harm befell her. They knew all too well her warning wasn't a bluff because they'd witnessed her power first hand, her soul-devouring fury, hence the manacles and the suspended cage.

It was go-time!

Loki's tail coiled around the metal rafter, and he propelled his body forward and backward, building momentum before he swung to another beam. Then another. Until he dropped to the final destination—the cage.

After uncloaking himself from the shadows, Loki chittered, "Hello."

Misty-eyed, Kassendra sopped up an errant tear with her knee, a smile spreading on her lips.

He climbed down and moored his tail to the oxidized bars.

While hanging upside down, his fingers fished through a miniature satchel festooned around his teeny waist. Now upright once again, he placed his finger on his lips, silencing his client's apprehension, then flashed a radiant key.

The key's teeth slipped inside the cage's padlock. One torque later, and the locking mechanism melted, and the magical wards disintegrated right along with it. With that, the cage door squeaked open. After another twist of the smoldering key, the manacles bounding Kassendra were no more.

Once liberated, Kassendra rubbed her abraded and bloodied wrists and ankles, shaking back sensation, all the while intently watching her rescuer for salient instructions.

Loki pantomimed the master escape route and plan, then liberated a fighting quarterstaff that had been slung across his back, tailor-made for the vertically challenged capuchin. He sliced the gleaming quicksilver weapon through the fetid air. Glowing sigils materialized along the shaft as the creature traced a figure-eight pattern, his movements nimble, fluid, the thrum and pulsation emanating from the staff nearly imperceptible.

In response to the summoning, scattershot shadows from all corners of the dank space aggregated, then crawled along the cement, over corpses, and veiled over the monkey, cloaking him and Kassendra from sight. The youngling already knew the drill: as long as their hands stayed linked, the invisibility spell would remain intact.

Kassendra counted to three, and they sprung out of the cage and landed on the concrete.

On the way to the solo exit, not sliding on the viscous matter mantling the ground proved challenging as they weaved around the bodies and jumped over stray slithering sentinels that crossed their paths.

They halted at the door. On Loki's command, it whispered open, just a trace. He tugged Kassendra's hand, but she wouldn't budge. Her rational mind, most likely, was hard-pressed to believe the men, the soulless Hounds of Hell, couldn't see her, couldn't discern her whereabouts.

Grazing his finger along her cheek, Loki mopped up a trickle of fear-imbued tears, then squeezed her hand as a reminder that he was there, protecting her, and they were still invisible. Kassendra nodded, and they stole inside the room.

The Hounds of Hell gathered around a table in the nexus of the cramped space. They'd already divested themselves of their sidearms and knives and placed them next to nearly drained bottles of vodka on a lazy Susan.

All muscles and bravado and serrated fangs were on display as they placed wagers in a game of Russian Roulette. A handful of young mages were chained to the wall behind them, some already dead, gulches of blood marring their necks and wrists.

The animated fire-breathing dragons inked on the necks of the Hounds seemed to serve as sentries, on the lookout for things not of this world, for things unseen. The dragons patrolled the circumference of necks and shoulders and arms and faces, stopping for a beat and smelling the air before marching on.

Laughter boomed out as the loser of the Hounds' sick and twisted game loaded his revolver with a single silver bullet, flicked the cylinder round and round, then closed it. The vampire handed one of the captive mages, a young boy, the gun, then wrenched the barrel, along with the boy's quivering hand that gripped it, against his temple. Should the mage think himself clever and brave and kill a vamp instead, the Hounds trained their weapons on him.

A Hound growled, demanding that the mage pull the trigger. He squeezed his eyes shut and acquiesced. The gun clicked. Sorrow reflected in the mage's green eyes and downturned mouth.

Loki pointed to the escape route—a sizable dry sink directly underneath a stained-black window. A Hound opened the sink's cabinet and produced a bottle of liquor, leaving the door ajar.

On her knees, Kassendra crawled within the bowels of the cabinet that provided just enough room for her and the simian.

Before proceeding onward, Loki quietly secured the cabinet door behind them, the monsters disappearing from view. Behind a tarp that mantled the cement wall was a hole. After squeezing through the hole, Kassendra's feet touched down on the pavement.

With barely enough room to maneuver, because a Dumpster concealed the aperture, they shuffled sideways in the narrowed space. Loki noted a smile emerging on the youngling's lips, her hopelessness waning. Still, her heartbeat raged on, her palm as sweaty as ever.

As they ran down an alleyway, the Dumpster a speck in the distance, Loki hazarded glances over his shoulder, looking for day-dwelling eyes and ears, for the team of snitches the Hounds had on their payroll. But no one suspicious caught his eye.

After a quick sprint, the alley's mouth regurgitated them into a market in Binondo proper—Manila's Chinatown.

A fusillade of firecrackers whistled and exploded, sparks raining down, merely a prelude to the fearsome blood-red dragon that winged across Kassendra's path, momentarily halting their great escape. Its motions fluid and nimble, it soared on the balmy air, sidewinding and undulating. Underneath the dragon, puppeteers glissaded along the street as hundreds of locals and tourists alike cheered them on.

In the sweltering heat, Loki and Kassendra threaded their way through a pedestrian-filled central walkway, past a galaxy of lean-tos and storefronts and traders hawking their wares.

Loki pointed to the blue-tiled archway standing regally in the distance, a beacon of hope, of safety and freedom. Just one more block to go. Kassendra's breath hitched, her eyes swimming with tears, as she was so close to reuniting with her baby sister.

Loki narrowly avoided a moaning motorcycle and jumped onto the hood of a jeepney to avoid being crushed.

Kassendra's foot fell into a gaping hole. Her sweaty palm

slipped out of Loki's grip, severing the shadow-cloaked spell, casting the shadows back whence they came.

As misfortune would have it, the jeepney driver recognized Kassendra's materializing form. He slammed on the brakes, leaped out of the vehicle, and grabbed her arm. Kassendra squiggled free and rocketed across the street, in the opposite direction from the snitch and Loki.

Signaling to other Hound associates nearby, the ratty driver whistled loudly with his fingers.

Loki screeched for Kassendra to stop, but she couldn't hear him over the din. Running and running, she crashed into a man. Cars squealed and fishtailed to a stop around them, just barely avoiding a pile-up.

A hooded motorcyclist threaded through the traffic. With one hand steering, he tossed Chinese stars with the other—Kassendra's back was their programmed trajectory.

Spotting the death-dealing weapon, Loki soared off the hood of another car. Airborne, his body corkscrewed as it fought to catch up to the Chinese star, spinning Kassendra's way. He snatched the star right before it struck Kassendra.

Unfortunately, Loki failed to see the second man and the hurtling star he tossed that successfully made its mark on Kassendra's neck.

The impact catapulted Kassendra into the stranger's arms. Loki tried to hoist her up to usher her away, believing there was still hope, but her legs gave out. The sunburnt stranger stopped the little girl from crumpling to the asphalt.

Kassendra, in the throes of death, fixated on the stranger's belt buckle—a bull that glinted in the sun and reflected in her caramel-hued orbs. "Golden Bull." Kassendra's eyes, shimmering with intimate knowledge, journeyed upward to meet the stranger's. Her mouth formed an "O," and a wan smile touched her lips. With her last breath, she whimpered, "It's … you." Then the spark in her eyes was all but snuffed out.

Loki bowed his head, paying his final respects to brave

Kassendra. Then he sized the stranger up for a beat, reading his energy to determine if he was friend or foe. He had tucked a wrinkled map in his shirt pocket, so he was most likely a tourist. Cradling Kassendra, the man refused to leave her side and screamed out for help in English, a southern twang coating his pleas, shock etched into his features. So friend he was.

The ghost of the recently slain slave girl blinked into existence next to Kassendra. She raised her arm and pointed behind Loki.

The capuchin whipped his head around. A handful of the Hounds' daytime snitches, armed to the teeth, were barreling down the road, their weapons trained on Loki and the American.

Loki quickly cloaked himself in shadows once more, right as the American began sputtering nonsense—something about a magical monkey—to a concerned crowd that fenced them in. Locals frantically called for help and tried to help Kassendra any way they could.

Loki removed a pinch of fluster dust from his satchel, then blew the blue particles right into the American's face. After a few chokes, the American stopped talking and donned a goofy look, his eyes unfocused, his body swaying.

The ghost nodded her head, communicating to Loki that she would take care of Kassendra from here on out.

Loki nodded assent. Capitalizing on the fracas, Loki dug his claws into the dazed American, and they slipped away unnoticed. The capuchin took a hard right into a pharmacy and waited until the American crossed the threshold before bolting the front door shut and flicking the sign to CLOSED.

Passels of herbs that smelled like hot garbage were suspended from the ceiling and tangled with the American's head as he drunkenly ventured into the inner sanctum of the pharmacy. Sizable apothecary drawers mantled the walls.

Loki materialized into view before a wooden counter smothered with scales, herbs, oddities, and hellish curiosities galore.

"WHERE'S KASSI?" Bhi'gow growled as he exited a back room. He then directed his wrath at the American. "AND

WHO'RE YOU?" The suspended herbs quivered, and apothecary drawers shook as the sizable Bhi'gow stomped towards the human.

Hands up, Loki jumped in the middle of the two and wildly chittered to Bhi'gow the entirety of the operation in a language that only the demon and ruachti understood.

Nodding his head in understanding, Bhi'gow somewhat relaxed, the ultraviolet flames licking the tips of his horns changing from raging inferno to smoldering.

Bhi'gow's pitch-black eyes locked onto the American, who was crouched in a corner, trembling. "We don't have time for dramatics, Mister ...?"

"Bell. Larry. Larry Bell," he sputtered.

"Okay, Mr. Bell. Scoop your jaw up from off the floor and tell me why you're in Manila and how you know Kassi Li." His booming voice put the fear of death into the disheveled and addlepated American. It was impossible for the forty-something man's pupils to grow any larger.

"How I wound up in Chinatown is beyond me, and my jeepney driver actually"—he paused, his sun-beaten brow puckering with confusion—"especially when the driver was headed to the Coconut Palace, the first stop on my spur-of-the-moment day trip, which is nowhere near here. Now I'm lost, and my cruise ship is leaving port—"

"Mr. Bell, how is it that Kassi recognized you, a lost tourist, as you allege?"

"Who's Kassi?" From a simple energy reading, Larry was telling the truth. That much Loki ascertained. "I was trying to hail a taxi, and that's when this child slammed into me."

"Well, Kassi certainly knew you, Mr. Bell. And my partner seems to think you're telling the truth." The flames on his horns swirled and sputtered, a sign that Bhi'gow was deep in thought. "I didn't have a Plan B." He clasped his hands behind his back and paced, talking to himself, his hooves scraping against the floor. "I'm bound by the caveat Kassendra included in the contract: Everyone is to be treated as an enemy unless Kassendra says otherwise. Most curious how she recognized Larry—"

The demon's tongue switched to Laramaic as he went over the newly hatched Plan B with Loki. After pivoting his body ninety degrees, Bhi'gow said, "Pepper, you can come out now."

A little girl toddled out from behind a silk screen. Unlike her big sister, Pepper's brown skin was buffed and unblemished. Pigtailed, her sable locks appeared to have been ironed straight, and a few errant strands escaped from their binds and framed her oval face.

Upon seeing Larry, tears of fright threatened to spill forth from her whiskey-hued eyes. She extended her arm and curled her index finger repeatedly, beckoning something to come hither. Her shopworn teddy bear glided through the air and landed in the child's arms—arms that no sooner strangled the poor stuffed animal. When the little one smiled at her teddy, a lone dimple popped into existence on her right cheek.

Unlike Kassendra, Pepper struggled with being rendered magicless, acted as if all limbs had been amputated. Loki had predicted that eventually Pepper's doe eyes and all-around preciousness would beguile Bhi'gow into giving her a fix— borrowed magics. Oh, how right Loki was.

Bhi'gow scooped Pepper up. "Remember what I told you? About being brave?" Pepper kindly placed her dainty fingers on Bhi'gow's charred-gray face, as though in benediction. A smile sprung on her lips, and the fixer's, too. "Pepper, this is your tatay."

When Bhi'gow placed the youngling in the arms of a very slack-jawed Larry, the American's body shot to ramrod straightness. But the moment Pepper put a tender hand on Larry's jowls, a smile tugged at the corners of his mouth, the wrinkles around his eyes crinkling—an auspicious sign as far as Loki was concerned.

The initial stages of the plan were working out like a charm until Larry must have mentally translated tatay from Tagalog to

English—Dad. "Um, no. NO! I'm a bachelor, a wanderluster, not dad material. Listen, I live on a cruise ship—"

Time being of the essence, Loki tossed a heaping amount of fluster dust into Larry's face, then wiped away the remnants from his hands. When Larry's prattling ceased, Loki's lips curled back in a grin of satisfaction, his yellowed needle-like teeth on full display.

"No, you listen to me, Mr. Bell." Bhi'gow's tone went beyond stern. "Enemies are on their way to kill Pepper, and now you. I entered into a covenant with Kassi and Pepper. As such, I am bound by the rules of Hell to protect this child from the forces of darkness. And protect her, I will. End of discussion."

Larry stood stock still, his mouth catching flies.

"The child's name is Pepper Li," Bhi'gow said. "She's four going on five and an orphan. You're all she has left in the world. And for reasons that are beyond our understanding, Kassi placed her trust in you. Now, whether or not I agree, I must obey her wishes." Bhi'gow then focused his attention on the capuchin. "Loki, come, come."

The monkey scampered the demon's way. Perched on the counter, Loki listened intently to his friend. "You know the drill, friend. I'll be in touch soon. In the meanwhile, protect Pepper from mortal danger."

Loki nodded assent and then leaped into the air. He could feel his body shrink as he soared to Pepper. Then, arms outstretched, fingers steepled, he dove into Pepper's wrist and plumbed the depths of her dermis, burrowing deeper and deeper, getting situated.

Concentrating, Loki tuned in to Bhi'gow's closing remarks, the sounds distant and echoey as if in the bowels of a cavern.

"In the interest of full disclosure, Mr. Bell, soon, while you and your daughter are fast asleep, you will be visited by a fur'moria. As an independent contractor that I oft do business with, this memory thief prefers to remain anonymous. So, in the future, should you ever demand that I return that which was taken from you, I know nothing. With that said, before the fur'moria can do his job, he must receive your express permission."

Silence pervaded.

"Need I remind you, Mr. Bell, that either you say yes or you die?"

Larry sputtered, "yes." As the word marched off his lips, it took form and winged onto a contract that Bhi'gow held and then soaked into the vellum.

Bhi'gow furled the contract and secured it with twine. "Wonderful. Now, the fur'moria will erase this encounter, along with you making the acquaintance of one Kassendra Li, from your memory bank and filling in the missing pieces with manufactured ones, e.g., how you became a father, which for you, Mr. Bell, amounts to an hour of your life stolen."

"But what about Pepper?" Larry choked out.

"All memories of meeting me and Loki will be extracted from her mind, but nothing else, for she's still young and will succumb to childhood amnesia."

"Wha-what about the men ... the ones who killed her sister?" Loki could barely hear Bhi'gow over Larry's pounding heart. "I—I need to sit down." When Larry's legs gave out and he nearly crashed to his bum, Bhi'gow magicked Larry back on his feet and held his swaying body in place.

"For protection, I will weave a spell over Pepper, cloaking her from those that wish her harm; it's in the contract and what my client, Kassi, desired for her baby sister, should the worst-case scenario happen."

"For how long?"

"In the event of my untimely death or worse"—Bhi'gow adopted a strictly business tone—"and my whereabouts are unknown, the cloaking spell will be severed on Pepper's seventeenth birthday. I'm afraid that's all the time I'm allotted. It's the least I could do for a client dying on my watch. Now, Mr. Bell, from here on out, Pepper'll be under your purview. You'll believe her to be your own flesh and blood, and she'll believe the same of you. May Goddess Seren's blessing shine upon you both."

The front door buckled as men smashed their bodies against it. Boarded windows rattled in their frames.

"We've got company!" Bhi'gow growled. "Name of the cruise ship and cabin number? NOW, LARRY!"

Preparing for battle, Loki took control of Pepper's being.

With his needle-sharp nails, Bhi'gow sliced his palm and, with the reservoir of blood, drew the shape of a door on the mildewy wall and transcribed Larry's sputtered reply above the doorway. With that, the bloodied barrier ignited and the wall within dissipated, making room for a chaosgate.

The front windows shattered, and men tumbled through. Their death-dealing weapons at the ready. Bhi'gow willed all furniture, items, or otherwise to levitate. Then, with a thrust of his hands, he crashed them into the interlopers.

Creating a barrier between Pepper-slash-Loki and Larry, Bhi'gow barked, "Run! Now!"

Under compulsion, Pepper grabbed Larry and then jumped through the chaosgate.

Free-falling, down and down, Pepper plunged. All around her, nebulous vignettes of memories not-her-own whooshed by. Then stillness.

Woozy, she nearly tipped over on the bench she sat upon, burped, and then vomited into a vial Perrin held out, a rancid aftertaste leftover. Pepper slowly pivoted her head to the left, then to the right, recalling where she was, *when* she was.

High in the sky, the skiff continued careening through Hell's nightscape, its passengers staring fixedly at Pepper: Jhi, Perrin, Loki, Bhi'*gow.*

Like a feral being, Pepper jumped off the bench and dove towards the fixer. "Kassi trusted you! And now she's dead!" All memories experienced were front and center.

"Who's Kassi?" Jhi asked as he darted between Pepper and Bhi'gow.

"My *sister!*"

"That must have been one helluva trip," Perrin tittered.

Pepper shoved Jhi out of the way. "This fixer"—she angrily pointed her finger at Bhi'gow—"wittingly took a four- and seven-year-old's magic in exchange for protection! And my sister still died! If she had her magic, that wouldn't've happened! So, you owe me answers, fixer! Who is *he, the bad man* who ordered my sister's death? This overlord who's still after me? *He's* who's calling the shots! Not Boss Lady!"

"Pepper!" Pepper could feel Jhi's fingers digging into her arms, tugging her backward, but she refused to budge.

"It's okay, Jhi. Let her go," Bhi'gow said calmly.

"My sister bargained away our magic to save us from him. Yet she died in vain, her sacrifices for naught, because of me. Because, like an idiot, I walked right into this overlord's trap. And now he and his Hounds have me in their crosshairs. They won't stop hunting me until I'm dead." Pepper needed some outlet to let off steam, more Grissel's ale, something, because she was a second away from losing her ever living mind, from crying, tearing out her hair, screaming.

"Can't say I've ever been afraid of a four-year-old mage or a lowlie, nor have I been pathetic enough to sic an army on one," Perrin chimed in.

Pepper switched her attention to Jhi. "Wait! Didn't you say that young mages come into their powers around puberty?"

"Yes. Why?" Jhi asked.

"Well then, how do you explain a four-year-old mage?"

Jhi tapped his index finger along his thumb and slowly blinked his eyes before responding, reactions Pepper attributed to emotion controlling. "I can't. Other than saying it's unheard of, for humans at least. Getting back to this overlord." Jhi's interest was piqued. "You must have something he wants or desperately needs, some vital knowledge, and just don't remember." He focused his attention on Bhi'gow. "You stole her memories, demon. Where did you put them?"

"Childhood amnesia is the memory thief, not Bhi'gow," Pepper said, deflated. "He only removed the memories of my encounter with him and Loki."

Pepper felt bound and gagged and defeated; the only means of escape were the answers her sister took to her grave. Still, if Pepper learned anything from her time exacting vengeance for her clients, it was that when stuck solutions would eventually present themselves; she just had to take a step back and see the big picture, ask the right questions, dig in the right spot, and no matter what, never submit to defeat.

"It's worth mentioning that my sister never once mentioned Boss Lady, just this overlord and how he wanted the Li sisters dead. He and his Hounds were hunting us down, had been for some time, from the sounds of it. I can't shake the feeling that my sister knew him, this *bad man*, as she called him, like they had a past. Ditto for my pops—" Pepper's hand shot to her mouth, covering it. Her eyes widened, her heart tightened, and she could only take in shallow breaths.

Larry—he wasn't her biological father. Pepper's vision blurred.

"If he's not my dad, then how did Kassi know him? Because she did! She recognized him! *Trusted* him even—" This overwhelming feeling of protecting Larry at all costs enveloped her. "Changes nothing!" Pepper snapped, her tone gritty. "Larry is and will forever be my everything, birth father or not. He raised me as his own. And I can't imagine a life where he's not in it. Wouldn't want to live that life! Larry is my father. End of discussion!"

Jaw clenched, hands as well, but Pepper's eyes either didn't get the orders for toughness or broke rank. A few tears slipped out, but she swatted those traitors away. "My eyes are sweaty, is all. It happens," Pepper lied.

Nobody seemed to care; they all wore disinterested expressions.

"So, twelve years ago, some overlord was hellbent on making

you worm food, and, what, he just stopped? Took a breather?" Perrin asked while filing her nails to a fine point. "And in his absence, this Boss Lady assumed leadership?"

"Hm. Sawyer answers directly to Boss Lady," Jhi stated. "And the Hounds never once mentioned an overlord to Bhi'gow. Same goes for Kimball's father, so chances are all parties mentioned aren't in direct contact with this overlord—"

"But the Hounds *were* twelve years ago," Pepper added. "And as far as Sawyer—wrong place, wrong time. She tried to kill me only because I was a witness to her crime. A loose end. That much had been made clear tonight. Otherwise, she and her army would have come after me, on Boss Lady's orders, which is what you originally thought would happen, Jhi. And the cloaking spell hiding me from this overlord was broken on my seventeenth birthday. Yet nobody knocked down my door—"

"Because they figured a cloaking spell hid your whereabouts," Jhi added, "but didn't know when the spell would expire. Plus, you didn't even know who you were, so they couldn't track you by your essence or triangulate your location. Your thoughts, memories, and energy were of someone entirely different and foreign to them."

"So, the Hounds played the long game by setting up a trap, Bhi'gow the bait, and bided their time, wagering that one day I'd hunt down the fixer who had my magic. Only then would they be able to find me." Hope waned with each throb of Pepper's head. "They were right. The only thing that will truly protect me is my magic. And it's forever gone. As is my sister. Leads too, because those have dried up."

"Not necessarily. Like I said earlier, my goyles will get the Talking Heads at the Tenth Circle Tavern to provide us with a lead if they want to keep those flapping lips of theirs." The idea of torture tickled Perrin to death.

Some hope in Pepper remained. "Tavi can eat the memories of the Talking Heads—"

"Sorry, sweetling. Sprites don't eat the dead, so the damned are off limits."

Loki scampered to Pepper and placed his hand over hers.

Bhi'gow spoke for his partner. "Loki wants you to know that your sister fiercely loved you. Because Kassi died on our watch, Loki and I have agreed to return your birthright, along with your sister's. Thank Seren, I never got the chance to render the magics into currency, so they're yours for the taking."

Choked up and vision doubling then tripling, Pepper could only nod a "thank you."

"A kidnapped fixer, a wanted Pepper, an All Hallows' Eve ball, and an MIA overlord. Except for the Hounds of Hell, how do these mysteries connect?" Perrin asked. "Tick-tock, says the clock. All Hallows' Eve is fast approaching. Doesn't give us much time."

"We're all exhausted, so I suggest we try to relax and clear our heads. We'll regroup once we settle at Bhi'gow's." Jhi focused his attention on Pepper. "In the meantime, why don't you fill us in on what happened twelve years ago?"

After composing herself, Pepper did just that.

CHAPTER 21

The skiff began its descent as they entered the outskirts of Bhi'gow's hamlet—the Isles of Obolus, where the climes plumbed the depths of frigidness, plumes of Pepper's breath visible. The River Cocytus surrounded the lush Isles, along with aqua-hued glaciers floating about in gunmetal gray water.

Loki chittered and jabbed his furry finger at the last pyramid located at the dead end of Elysium Lane. Bhi'gow had the isle all to his lonesome. The next property, "his neighbor," could be found on an island miles and miles away.

As the skiff cozied up to a skiff-less dock, the gang disembarked, and Pepper hared it to terra firma, only to halt at a thicket of sod. The gargoyles refused to touch ground and hovered above, their flapping wings drumming up gale-force winds.

The sprawling grass was terribly deceiving insofar as the blades of grass channeled the literal sense of the word "blades." Though dwarfed, the stalks bit and lashed and wanted for nothing but to slice through dermis. "Feed us your blood!" they surely demanded. They even tormented the address plaque 664 ELYSIUM LANE as it creaked back and forth on its rusted chains.

Jhi produced his jack-of-many-weapons, the scythe to be exact, and whacked a trail for venturers, leading directly to the front door of the pyramid, then he wheeled around and headed for the riverbank, landing at the firebushes; the lot of them colonized the bank and were stuck in their own circle of Hell; water not-iced over would ebb and flow onto the dry land. Valiantly defending its territory, the firebushes would blast a fusillade of flames at the encroaching enemy, only to sizzle as the water outgunned the milky-white flora every time—a forever war raging on.

After uprooting a few firebushes, Jhi gingerly held the rhizome, a plexus of sooty spidery roots, and the only part of the plant that wasn't licked in flames. Jhi pithily explained how the plant was medicinal, styptic in nature, and would cauterize his impressive collection of festering wounds. From there, he'd concoct a paste from the unused parts and should be doctored up in no time flat.

The limestone pyramid resembled those dwellings Pepper had glimpsed on her journey into Pandæmonia proper. Judging by the eight-foot-tall gargoyles who stood sentry before the sole entrance, the pyramid's apex towered roughly twelve feet. Still, the mind was hard-pressed to believe that a residence resided underground. That this wasn't a pyramidal mausoleum, but a subterranean dwelling.

A fiery keyhole on the massive stone door like that found on a chaosgate barred entrance. An impatient Perrin grabbed Bhi'-gow's leathery palm and dragged her absurdly sharp nail down its length. When enough blood had been drawn, she fed the lock its owner's blood. Once sated, a click sounded.

Jhi pushed the door inward, and the stone entrance dragged along the silty ground. A zephyr of dank air howled past as if warning newcomers to *Beware! Enter at your own risk!*

The sound of mechanical whirring and churning, albeit faint, and muffled howling, mimicking that of a gust of wind, could be heard. But the utter darkness beyond made it impossible for Pepper to discern where the sounds originated from. Though they were close.

As Pepper crossed the threshold, her shoulder brushed against an object affixed to the limestone wall. A burst of hellfire sizzled along the wick contained inside a sconce—the object in question—illuminating just enough space to reveal a vast staircase that descended into the bowels of oblivion.

Inside the sconce's bulbous base, souls acting like chaotic gaseous molecules swirled viciously, howling to the newly arrived for rescue. Bouncing and slamming against their glassy prison, their speed mushroomed. Though their efforts of howling for help were futile, the built-up pressure inside the base had intensified just enough to have pushed an alloy-coated lever against a whirring steel wheel. Born from the sparks, hellfire sizzled along a wick, burning ever bright, and the captured souls quieted, their howls extinguished. Sconce after soul-powered sconce flared fiery heat right as Pepper passed them by.

The last step disgorged visitors into the main chamber of the pyramid. Various other chambers were sprinkled about here and there and connected via tapering corridors.

Bobbing gently in the air like helium balloons were swarms of souls of the damned. Auras of buttery light emanating from their centers chased away the shadows crowding in corners. Each soul was tethered to a ceramic pot. Inside the pots were bouquets of yellow magic gems pulsing with energy. A lum'bhra—what passed for a lamp in Hell—reminded Pepper of jellyfish that frequently washed up on Naples beaches.

At first blush, 664 Elysium Lane appeared not to be abandoned as once thought but well-taken care of. Not even a speck of dust latticed the corners. The demons thought nothing of it, so Pepper adopted their blithe attitude; perhaps they knew something she didn't.

Barring a subterranean pyramid mantled in floor to ceiling stone, the home echoed that of, well, maybe not an American home, per se, or even an Earthly one at that; actually, the dwelling smeared with macabre furnishings was otherworldly in nature.

Yet despite all that, it felt cozy, what with Bhi'gow's fondness for grandpa gliders (a fondness shared by Pepper's dad); ditto for the patchwork rugs and antimacassars that were draped over the shopworn furniture, both weaved from the skin of the damned. Runners accented the great room, carpeted the corridor ahead, the bedrooms beyond that, and Hallelujah! There was a bathroom. Pepper rock, paper, scissored Jhi for first dibs, Pepper the victor.

Now, as for the otherworldly parts that Pepper couldn't stop ogling and shaking off the Willies—a coat rack and *the* Talking Heads that Perrin had cavalierly mentioned back at the Lair, which were nothing more than the dismembered heads of the damned.

Beginning with the coat rack, in place of pegs were disembodied human hands, their fingers flexing and un-flexing, as they reached out and accepted Pepper's cloak that she had no other choice but to shimmy out of to avoid getting hoisted and hung on a rung herself.

Dotting the walls were the Talking Heads of actual Homo sapiens, jaw-jawing away with each other. Human heads and dismembered appendages, not stuffed, graced the walls and floor. Legs in various staged poses, some daintily crossed as if sitting upright, and hands clasped as if an invisible head rested upon them, all served as shelves.

Arms drowning in jewels, fingers drenched in diamonds served as … Pepper's mind drew a blank—perhaps an artsy jewelry stand? As for the chairs, sofas, and coffee tables sprinkled about the great room, their legs took on the literal sense of the word, and the bottoms were actual feet of the damned, some hairy, some not. Torsos served as seats, human dermis as the fabric.

As for the Talking Heads, some had their lips sewn shut like the one Pepper had briefly noticed in the great chamber, some with lips and tongues missing. The eyes on a few had been plucked out, some stitched shut to match their lips, ears missing altogether—gave a whole new meaning to see no evil, speak no evil, hear no evil.

A shopworn Bhi'gow opted to catch some Zs and tasked Loki

with navigating Pepper and Jhi to Pepper's magical powers.

"I didn't want to say anything on the skiff," Pepper whispered as she and Jhi traversed an anorexic corridor, "but I find it wholly disconcerting that the Talking Heads at this Tenth Circle Tavern knew me by name. Unless Perrin lied, but I don't think so. How could the Hounds of Hell possibly have caught wind that we'd chaosnauted to Pandæmonia?"

Speaking of Talking Heads, scads of them lined the walls, and those with eyes followed the interlopers' every movement.

"Yeah, I picked up on that." Jhi raked his fingers through his unkempt mane, then suffocated his cinnamon locks with his beanie. "I need to go visit this hopping tavern. Listen, no matter what, don't let your guard down with Perrin, or anyone else. No one is to be trusted."

Pepper nodded in agreement. "At least Perrin detests the Hounds just as much as we do, so we have that in our corner. The enemy of our enemy—"

"Hey, wait up!" Perrin gamboled their way. And, with that, discreet speak concluded.

Eventually, the corridor ended at a crocodile crafted of stone. Its grotesque and demonic likeness eclipsed the swollen rays of sun haloing its neck, as in there was nothing sunshiny about the demonic creature. Nor the snaggle-toothed snout jutting out from the wall; that feature didn't precisely temper the forbidding vibe.

The interlopers' presence set off a daisy chain of mockery; the Talking Heads dotting the corridor couldn't stop their silver tongues from flapping.

"Bet they don't know the magic word," one damned jeered.

"Oh, goodie, we haven't seen a death in for-ever!" The Greek chorus was a twitter with anticipation.

"How could they possibly know the code? They're intruders. Still, this should be fun," another chided.

"Won't be intruders for long. Mistress is on her way. Nanny, nanny, boo-boo!"

"Bite your tongue! Why'd you have to go and tell them and

ruin all the fun?" It was hard to discern which head spoke. "Can't wait for that. Whatcha gonna do then, thieves?"

Loki glanced at the Talking Heads; his eyes narrowed with suspicion.

Pepper would have given more thought to Loki's reaction if not for the heart-pounding anticipation of reuniting with her magic.

A beat later, Loki lavished his attention on the doorway and chittered, which amounted to pronounced inflections, guttural growls, and a whole lot of spittle. In response, the maw unhinged and gaped wide open. Voila! The crocodile had permitted them passage into the laboratory, much to the dismay of the damned. Pepper thundered down the steep staircase. As she passed by soul-powered sconces, they woke up and blazed fiercely.

The laboratory served as a mecca for the budding alchemist. There was no rhyme or reason to the placement of the floor-to-ceiling bookcases. If anything, they turned what could have been an organized space into a chaotic mess, creating a maze of sorts. Ever-burning candles, their tapers bearded with wax, illuminated every oddity and curiosity housed within the lab, some even resting on bookshelves, the books themselves, and steps of rolling ladders. Herbs hung from the low ceiling and exploded from out of the drawers of apothecary cabinets. Cupboard after overstuffed cupboard colonized the walls. On display were reliquaries containing elixirs that bubbled, churned, swished, dematerialized only to rematerialize. Bolts of lightning flashed in a few of the reliquaries like a strobe light. Sunlight blazed in others.

A workshop perfect for experimenting appropriated the far-flung corner, aft to a bank of locked cages; inside the prisoners were none other than manacled damned, their bodies intact, for all intents and purposes. To put it mildly, if given the option of being a Talking Head or one of these lab rats, Pepper would choose the former hands down. Pepper paid the damned no mind and continued bobbing along, exploring in the forefront of her mind. If Pepper were stolen magic, where would she be?

Loki served as their docent in the alchemist museum of sorts and pointed to a curio cabinet housing Bunsen burners, beakers, hellfire lamps, unidentified minerals, siphon bottles, and baskets of magic gems, all blanched of color, the cat's eye designs, double helixes, and so on, bone white.

"Bhi'gow's a drainer." Perrin sidled up next to Pepper. "Good to know! They're as rare as fur'morias. The Lolly'kas just lost ours. Took a tumble down the stairs, broke his neck." Perrin clucked her tongue and rolled her eyes. "Now we have a surplus of mages, not enough jail cells to hold them, and no one to siphon their magic, let alone transfer the unstable substances into fulgurite gems. It's a real bummer. Y'know, the creating and selling of magic gems is an enormous source of our income."

Noting Pepper's confused look, Jhi added, "Ever wake up feeling tired? Fatigued, even after a long sleep? You've been drained. Even lowlies have sparks of magic. A sixth sense, I believe you call it."

Terraced reliquaries of different shapes and sizes towered to lofty heights, some labeled, most not, but only one or two contained swirling vaporous magics that strained against their glassed cells; the rest were drained.

Pepper's eyes were agog, for she'd found what she had been seeking. "The reliquaries, they're cataloged by year, then by the given name of the seller." The *want* jumped to *need* when it came to finding her magic.

As Pepper traced her finger along the Ps, she felt like a Jack-in-the-box, one more crank, and she'd pop off the tightly wound coil. Wait, something was wrong. There wasn't a Pepper to be found. Or a Kassendra. "No! NO, that can't be!" Her eyes flittered back and forth from Olek to Peta, willing "Pepper" to appear.

The lab rats broke out in gales of mirthful glee. Pepper whipped around, fists clenched to her sides. Seeing red, she was overcome with a foreign sensation to make the damned pay for their actions, ready to silence them once and for all; the wrathful fury brewing inside her was at the helm.

"Fight! Fight! Fight!" Perrin sure hankered for blood spillage.

Jhi grasped her arms, his lips moving, but Pepper looked right past him, couldn't hear him, her eyes myopically focused on the pallid, boney beings fettered in their cages, beings that she was going to torture unmercifully.

" … note left …" The words "note left" obliterated the red occluding Pepper's vision and snapped her back to reality. Jhi repeated, "Someone left behind a note where your magic would've been."

With shaky hands, she held a piece of dermis like that of a flesh note. The blood-red writing was hurried and spidery: *Meet me at hearth and home. Come alone!*

Behind them, what sounded like a rifle had been cocked.

"Hands where I can see them. And no funny business, or I'll shoot." The voice was reminiscent of a vinyl record being played backwards, its gender unarguably female. To further emphasize the female's "I mean business" stance, she hurled a ring of fire that pinned them in, its fiery border menacingly eating the space between the trio and the blaze. A blast of heat stung Pepper's skin.

A feral, vicious snarl sounded when Jhi went for his weapon. "Hands up, boy, or I'll immolate you lickety-split, then I'll let my hungry xykree, Balakai, finish you off. I'm talking to you, too, Perrin. Now, turn around slowly and don't try any funny business."

Choices abound; where to look first? The rattle-sabering xykree would suffice. The furless, flesh-toned chimera set Pepper's teeth on edge. Balakai's silicone-hued oily hair swept back and forth along the floor, keeping in rhythm with its twitching tail. Crimson-rimmed oval eyes narrowed at its prey; one false move, they warned, and the xykree wouldn't hesitate to rip the intruders limb from limb.

Two small slits for a nose bunched together as if memorizing their scent, all the better for hunting them down should they escape. A lipless jack-o'-lantern mouth curled back in a sneer, exposing teeth like needles, ready to shred them to ribbons. The humanoid part of the xykree was reflected on its front paws or, more specifically, its hands—as in splayed fingers and fingernails as sharp as tacks. Pronounced ribs jutted out from its torso, but the human similarities ended there. Its hind legs were all feline.

As for threat number two, the one holding the locked and loaded bazooka that rested on her slight shoulders. The demon's hair was a skein of polyester, like the packaged decorative cobwebs sold during Halloween season. And judging by the way the puff of snowy locks had been unceremoniously piled atop her crown, how they tangled with rose-like thorns protruding from corkscrewing horns, how they'd ensnared bits of twigs that stuck out willy-nilly, it was as if an unskilled decorator had been at the helm, hadn't quite perfected the art of cobwebbing.

About five-foot tall, bark-like striations made up her ashen arms and legs, along with legions of watchful eyes impressed on the skin, her elbows and knees gnarled. Though a homespun, dung-hued shift hid the woman's trunk, it, too, most likely possessed features found on a birch tree. As for her face, that was glasslike and angular, that exuded a malefic beauty, along with curious eyelashes, if that's what they could be called, fashioned from clumps of snow or branches of teensy snowflakes jutting out from the lashes themselves. Brows mirrored the lashes as far as the snowy element was concerned. Evolving pupils and scudding sclera, misshapen teeth and elven-like ears—yes, she was a demon through and through.

But there was one feature that stood above the rest, one feature that quelled Pepper's restless heart and convinced her erect arm hair to stand down—starkly contrasting her ashen skin and translucent visage were ram-like horns that appeared to have been recently dipped in oil, black violet spitting flames licking the tips; perhaps a Bhi'gow family trait, the flames?

"Thought I recognized those goyles keeping watch outside. Can't leave well enough alone, can you, Perrin? Give the Lolly'kas an olive branch, and they decide to rob your place in exchange."

Branch-like fingers hovered over the trigger of the bazooka. Homicidal rage reflected in the now flickering ultraviolet orbs of the ageless creature. This demon meant business and would think nothing of blowing them to smithereens.

"Zho'zho, it's not what it looks like, honest to Seren." Perrin kept her hands up. "Everyone, meet the owner of my favorite tavern, the Tenth Circle."

Loki, upon hearing the name, peeked out from behind Pepper. The instant the bazooka-wielder set her sights on the ruachti, milky tears, thick like molasses, ran in rivulets down the demon's cheeks. With that, she lowered the bazooka and extinguished the ring of fire before careening the capuchin's way. Meeting in the middle, the dearly departed friends fiercely hugged one another.

"You haven't changed a bit in the eons since I last saw you. I thought you were dead, like my brother. May Seren bless his soul," said Zho'zho.

Loki pointed to Pepper and the others, then crossed his heart. Fingers crossed that sign language in Hell mirrored that of Earth.

"Loki seems to be under the impression that you're not foes, but friends," Zho'zho said. "Heed my warning: if it turns out that you tricked Loki, you'll be dead with the snap of my fingers. I've fortified my home with A-one defensive measures, from incendiary wards to bloodthirsty bogeys to Talking Heads. If I receive one inkling that you're lying, consider yourself gifted with a one-way ticket to the Pits." After delivering the warning, she divested herself of wrath and shimmied into hospitality, which fit her well.

The minute Perrin divulged Bhi'gow was alive, the demon spun on her heel and ran like the blazes, her xykree and Loki following suit. Perrin declared she was bored and skipped off, leaving Pepper and Jhi.

Pepper surmised that no doubt their burgling had been reported to the mistress of the manor by a Talking Head, but how?

"Interchangeable body parts, that's how." Jhi further explained that while one Talking Head's eyes and lips are in the pyramid, its ears could easily be found on another Talking Head at Zho'zho's tavern. So, in essence, one being, though its body parts had been sundered, could have eyes and ears on all comings and goings.

Pepper wasn't following, so Jhi boiled it down. "In other words, Zho'zho's enchanted the Talking Heads to be CCTVs."

"Oh, like a Mr. Potato Head." Jhi didn't get Pepper's reference. Didn't this boy play with toys as a child? And then Pepper had an epiphany. "Wait, then that means that some of the Talking Heads, personified CCTVs, could be eyewitnesses to whoever stole my magic, the Li sisters' magic. To who left the note behind!" Pepper felt giddy with hope.

"Yes, but Pepper, take a step back for a second. Doesn't something feel off? Out of all the taverns in Pandæmonia, and there are many, us demons take bacchanalia seriously. It's like a dimensional pastime. Bhi'gow's kin's tavern is where the Hounds decide to do business? Coincidences are things of fiction. What if Zho'zho is Boss Lady? If you recall, Bhi'gow said that nobody knew where he lived save for Loki. Bhi'gow never once mentioned a sister. I could be wrong, but we should keep a close eye on her all the same."

"True, but the note-leaver sure knew who Bhi'gow was, what he did for a living. Where he lived. Hello! And they knew about me!" Pepper nibbled her thumbnail. "We need to see if these Talking Heads can provide detailed accounts of the thievery and the thief in question ASA—"

A deafening explosion aboveground interrupted their terrifying musings. As a swarm of cavalry stormed down the main staircase, silt sifted down from the laboratory's ceiling.

The Hounds of Hell had smoked them out and obstructed the sole point of escape.

Jhi charged up the stairs, his weapons brandished before him, and disappeared from sight.

As for Pepper, fear was front and center, but she palmed the last sunburster, then barreled in the commotion's direction before second thoughts reared their ugly heads.

CHAPTER 22

F alse alarm. Gargoyles had caused the commotion, three of them to be exact, Minx, Gamble, and their captain, Trixie.

Without missing a beat, the hostess with the mostess, Zho'zho, welcomed the newly arrived and served noshes and libations for all: salted pixie wings, damned jerky, Bonnacon ribs and blood sauce for dipping, ale-battered feet of the damned, sugary pixie pie, pomegranate wine, and the like.

Pepper lost her appetite … for food, not libations—first time for everything. Who was Pepper kidding! Her food strike lasted all of ten minutes before hunger struck. In no time flat, Pepper went to town on the noshes and nibbles, devouring everything in sight but remnants of the damned, raw, boiled, fried, cured, or otherwise.

Before the intel debriefing commenced, Jhi placed his finger over his lips, silencing further chatter, and darted his eyes from Talking Head to Talking Head smattered about the great chamber. In response, the decapitated damned averted their orbs elsewhere, some even feigning sleep, while others remained mum.

His movements nimble, Jhi removed a few magic gems of varying hues from his pouch, then sliced his finger with a dagger. His blood the medium, he traced arcane sigils in the air. The gems were blanched of their vibrancy as molecules bent to Jhi's will and vaporous aetheric threads of air weaved on an invisible loom, piece by gaseous piece, until the latticework dome of silence cocooned all concerned parties. "We have rats in our midst, but more on that later."

The rippling, energetic charge of the translucent barrier *zinged* Pepper when she touched it.

Blood stained the gargoyle captain's leathery skin. "Tell me the enemies look far worse?" Perrin asked Trixie, her tone deadpan.

Once Trixie knocked down a few mugs of warm blood-infused ale and shoved sustenance down her gullet, the gargoyle brought everyone up to speed on what she'd garnered since the gang had escaped Skulduggerer's Lair.

"Aye, mistress, the enemies're dead. Well, save for one," Trixie savagely growled, a measured tone for her ilk. "That spindle-shanked bottom-feeder, Cadabra, pulled a disappearing act on me back at the Lair."

Cadabra, a sleeper agent for the Hounds of Hell, played the role of a shopkeeper at Skulduggerer's Lair. His mission was to be on the lookout for anyone searching for Bhi'gow.

"Before that insolent fuh'kar Cadabra skipped out on our *little chat,* he warned that it's too late. The operation's already in motion and can't be stopped. Come All Hallows' Eve, his over-lord'll be resurrected from Hell, and demons, mages, and lowlies alike will rue not joining the Firebird's ranks."

"Well, looks like my goyle solved the mystery of the disap-pearing overlord. He's a fuh'karing damned whose brain is clearly scrambled from torture. Resurrecting from Hell," Perrin laughed, her goyles too, "what fuh'karing nonsense."

"Wha—what makes you think this overlord and my overlord are one and the same?" Shock was making it difficult for Pepper to register the gravity of the reveal. "And is resurrecting from Hell even possible?"

Jhi responded to the latter with a hard "No."

Nobody chimed in regarding Pepper's overlord question, which, frankly, equal parts pissed her off and chilled her blood.

Fragmented mental notes began to stitch together into a cohesive whole. "The tattoos," Pepper blurted out. Then she brought all up to speed on how the Hounds of Hell were branded with a dragon and Firebird. Strangely, nobody seemed to care about that either. Pepper then harkened back to what had resulted after Kimball set flame to the business card, sharing every detail. "The Firebird. Could it have been a calling card—Boss Lady and Firebird? What if they're one and the same?" Pepper finally garnered everyone's attention, except for Perrin's.

"You know who'll rue the day? This Firebitch who's infiltrated my turf. Just wait till I unmask her." Perrin was impressively reserved in the face of disaster. Daresay she was in her element. Dipping her hand in a snack bowl, she stuffed crunchy pixie wings into her mouth. Perhaps a kindred emotional eater like Pepper?

Trixie verbally rebuked herself for not picking up on the hints that Cadabra was a necromancer; otherwise, she would've anticipated his gimmick ahead of time and acted accordingly. The shopkeeper reanimated a bevy of corpses populating the tableaux vivants dotted about the Lair and sicced them on the gargoyle. While she fought them off, Cadabra vanished in a poof of smoke.

"Team, any word yet from Vixen regarding the loose-lipped Talking Heads at the Tenth Circle?" The very Talking Heads Perrin had overheard argle-bargling regarding Pepper since she chaosnauted to Pandæmonia.

Gamble cleared her throat, which nearly rocked the foundation. "Aye, mistress. Vixen's been surveilling the Tenth Circle, but said it's too dicey to steal inside and interrogate the Talking Heads. The Tavern is swarming with Hounds. Vixen counted at least ten vamps lurking outdoors in the shadows, and who knows how many are planted inside? It's almost as if they're expecting Pepper to show up." Her slit pupils locked on Pepper for a beat.

"Zho'zho, is it common knowledge that Bhi'gow's your brother?" Jhi asked offhandedly, which was pure fishing on his part. He didn't appear to trust Zho'zho whatsoever.

"My life ain't anybody's damn business," she replied coyly, sitting next to Bhi'gow on a loveseat covered with a riot of leathery, hairy pillows.

Bhi'gow answered the same question. "What my sister meant was that no, our kinship isn't common knowledge. Besides, it wouldn't've mattered much if the Firebird's minions paid Zho'zho a visit. It's been many lifetimes since I last laid eyes on my sister, let alone spoken to her and vice versa."

Time and estrangement make strange bedfellows. Time might heal wounds, but not the phantom twitches that linger on indefinitely. And the longer loved ones engaged in bitter conflicts spend apart, the more missed epochs pile up, the harder it is to forgive and let live, for the fortified resentment is unable to be exorcised, and the awkwardness felt becomes unbearable. But a funny thing happens when tragedy strikes. Those life-changing events have an uncanny way of reuniting the estranged, of soothing resentments and unease, time be damned.

Looking at Zho'zho and Bhi'gow with their arms wrapped around each other, Pepper would never have guessed that it had been centuries since they'd last spoken.

Jhi's patience was threadbare. "Zho'zho, out of all the taverns in all of Hell, don't you find it awfully coincidental that the Hounds of Hell picked *your tavern* to conduct their business? That they're swarming the place *right now* as we speak? Or that someone stole *only* Pepper and her sister's magic from Bhi'gow's cache?"

Pepper took that as an in to enlighten all regarding her missing magic and the mysterious note left in its place.

"*Who else* had access to this pyramid besides you, Zho'zho? Access to the *heavily warded laboratory*? *Who else* knew about Bhi'gow's profession, where he stored the reliquaries of procured magic?" Jhi pressed, his tone intimating that Zho'zho was complicit in the unfolding conspiracy.

Zho'zho empurpled, her vexation palpable. "Every week, year after year, I made sacrificial offerings to Seren, bled and gutted the damned after damned, to safely bring home my brother. And in all that time, I never once gave up hope that Bhi'gow was alive and would one day return home to me. So, I don't take kindly to anyone insinuating that I'd ever harm a horn on Bhi'gow's head." Zho'zho's words were so biting that Pepper could almost feel a whip crack against her skin. Furious, Zho'zho marched toward Jhi, her fists clenched.

"Hey now, no need for bloodshed." Jhi raised his hands. "All I'm trying to do is unravel this maddening mystery. As it is, Bhi'gow doesn't have much time left. Should the enemies find him, they'll kill him on the spot with extreme prejudice. Now, Zho'zho, you're connected somehow to the conspiracy. We just have to puzzle out the how. And doing just that could very well be your brother's one and only lifeline."

Zho'zho went from enraged to calm in a snap. "How can I help?"

Jhi continued. "Did anyone else know about the network of enchanted Talking Heads linking the pyramid to the Tavern? Or that you used them as camouflaged CCTVs? Think, Zho'zho, anyone at all?"

"Not that I'm aware of ... Well, perhaps that's not entirely true. A former barkeep of mine was rather ingenious and daresay crafty when it came to transforming the ordinary into extraordinary. It was she who enchanted me with the idea to upcycle Talking Heads from that of bargain-basement ornamentation to CCTVs."

"And did this barkeep know about your brother's disappearance?"

"Oh, dear. I don't recall. Isn't that strange?" She scratched her head.

Jhi sighed. "Let me guess, it was this barkeep's idea for you to install Talking Heads in Bhi'gow's home *and* at the Tavern. That way, you'd be apprised instantly should your missing brother return home. She probably even helped you install them, only you don't recall."

"Rings true, but why *can't* I recall?"

"Probably because she's a fur'moria, or she hired a thief to steal your memories. Just a guess. It's my belief that this barkeep needed a way to break into the pyramid, and what better way than having security cameras and recorded footage she could tap into at will, study the pyramid's schematics, get the lay of the land, and did just that by toying with your sympathies."

"That's how she knew the password to the laboratory and where to find Bhi'gow's cache of rendered-up magic," Pepper offered.

Jhi nodded and said, "Not only that, but this barkeep could very well be watching us right now. So, we need to have a little chat with her mole. Just point us in the direction of the Talking Head that notified you earlier the pyramid had been breached?" Jhi broke the Dome of Silence spell.

Zho'zho chimed in. "To be fair, my brother already had a few ornamental Talking Heads sprinkled about, but she convinced me to add a few more in what I now see as strategic places. She removed an eye here, an ear there, placed them on Talking Heads at the Tenth Circle, then enchanted those sundered body parts to record all goings-on and mentally save the footage, both at the Tavern and home. 'For my protection,' she said. With Bhi'gow missing and me being a single female living in the middle of nowhere, her concerns seemed valid." Zho'zho hit her horn in exasperation.

"Very manipulative," Perrin said. "I kinda like this barkeep. Unless she's the Firebitch."

Talking Head Nancy, the mole, was mantled in the great room, with a bird's-eye view of the entrance and corridors that branched out in myriad directions from the great chamber. Zho'zho enchanted Nancy's orbs to serve as CCTVs; one rheumy eye was situated in the pyramid, while the other was at the Tavern plugging the eye socket of another Talking Head. Cursed with a fivehead and jiggling jowls, the older woman was quite the eyesore. Not even her dangling mother-of-pearl necklace helped matters in the way of aesthetics. Bless her heart, as Larry was wont to say.

The moment everyone descended upon her, Nancy saw the writing on the wall and feigned innocence. Said she was downright dyspeptic at the libelous claims of spying hurled at her. "Well, I have never been talked to so rudely. Uncouth rubes, the lot of you. Like I said, I know not what you speak of."

Pepper expressed that interrogating Nancy was an exercise in futility. Not only was she d-e-a-d, but a decapitated head at that, so what incentive did she have to come clean?

"Sweetling, we'll get the truth out of her yet. Regardless of decapitation, dismemberment, whether the damned are steed for human-drawn carriages, fully fleshed ever-regenerating sustenance for us demons who fancy human offal"—simultaneously Perrin and Zho'zho licked their chops at the mere thought—"or sacrificial offerings, you name it, the damned are cognizant and wholly conscious of where they are and what they are, the pain felt at all times, and their status will forever and ever be that of thralls, Amen," Perrin said impassively.

Which prompted Jhi to further school Pepper in eternal damnation 101: Soul Continuity. The soul's presence is what enabled emotions to be felt, body or no. So, whether the soul occupying a human vessel was at full capacity or five percent, the amount mattered not, for a soul is a soul, regardless. It was imperative that the damned continue to feel inflicted pain and untold misery throughout the course of their eternal damnation. Otherwise, Hell would be a delightful experience. Thus, the delineation between Hell and Heaven would be blurred. Now, where was the fun in that?

At Perrin's command, Trixie began "little chat" time with the haughty Talking Head and "accidentally" choked Nancy with the strand of pearls twined around her engorged neck. Darling Nancy trilled like a canary through fits of choking. "There's no handler, I swear! I communicated with no one!"

"I don't believe you!" Trixie "accidentally" ripped out Nancy's earring, lacerating her earlobe.

In between screams of pain, Nancy explained why she could not hear the goings-on at the Tavern, let alone speak, what with her ear-and-lipless status. But what her eye had perceived was more than sufficient for the culling of answers. A while ago, the Hounds of Hell began loitering around the Tenth Circle. From what Nancy had garnered, they were not so much up to no good, but meeting an associate on the sly.

"Who's the associate?" Trixie yanked on the dangling earring of Nancy's other ear.

"I don't know!" Nancy sputtered through whimpers. "Only have my vision to rely on, remember?" Trixie applied more pressure. "Ow, stop that, you heathen! Okay, fine! Hounds' contact was a female! Looked human. Then again, she could've been one of the elven folk. Darkish hair. Young and cute in that annoying rah-rah sort of way. But that disarming smile of hers, now that was blindingly bright, and no charm could replicate that. Pre-damned, I would've hired her on the spot as my spin doctor."

"This girl, was she a barkeep at the Tavern? What business did she have with the Hounds?" Jhi inquired.

"Don't know and doesn't matter now, because the girl disappeared soon after, as did the Hounds, come to think of it. The vamps only recently resurfaced because of this Pepper. See, one of the Talking Heads at the Tavern also has an eye on things at Skulduggerer's Lair."

Nancy, the crackerjack lip reader, stated that at the Tavern, the Hounds offered a quid pro quo; the Hounds would liberate the damned in exchange for the Talking Heads serving as eyes and ears on the ground and relaying what they'd gathered.

"Soon, the vamps said. They have a way to free us. All we had to do was report to the Hounds immediately if us heads heard anything suspicious or anything about *the girl*. The damned, we're all desperate to get outta Hell, and we'll do anything to be freed from our eternal damnation. And before you ask, I don't know why they picked the Tenth Circle. The other Talking Heads are unaware that Zho'zho's related to Bhi'gow. And it's not like I can communicate that salient point to them, even if I wanted to."

"That explains why the Tavern is surrounded by the Hounds. It's a contingency plan in the event Pepper evaded capture," Perrin said.

"Why would they assume Pepper would flee there?" Jhi was utterly flummoxed but more visibly angered that he didn't have all the answers.

"That makes no sense. They're acting as if I've been to Hell before." Pepper could feel a migraine brewing. "What about the other Heads here in the pyramid? Anyone else have contact with the outside? Anyone else we can have a quote-unquote little chat with?"

Trixie swiped a dagger along Nancy's cheeks—more of a threat than anything. "NO! Just me!" Satisfied, the gargoyle halted the torture.

"Nancy, would you recognize this girl, the Hounds' associate, if you saw her again?" Teary-eyed, Nancy emphatically replied to Zho'zho with a "yes."

Zho'zho retrieved a Limnocular; the memory visualizer resembled an antiquated projector cast in bronze. Must've been one of those enchanted whatnots, like the rune-revealers that Jhi mentioned were sold on the black market, along with magic gems. The center of the peculiar device housed a lens that jutted outward like a spyglass. The machine was dressed in pistons and tubes that ran hither and thither, along with knobs and doohickeys aplenty, including a coin mechanism like that found on a gumball machine.

Once Zho'zho fed the projector the activating ingredients, a stream of red, orange, and yellow magic gems, and cranked the bronze mechanism clockwise, the machine belched steam and groused as the pistons worked out their kinks and various aches. On an attached touchscreen monitor, Zho'zho typed in commands for the enchanted Talking Heads to rake through their memories, homing in on the day that Bhi'gow's house had been burgled, using keywords such as "thief, breaking and entering, laboratory," then hit enter.

Images and words visibly flickered on the pupils of a handful of Talking Heads from the great chamber on. Once the Heads executed the operation, pools of illumination flooded out of their orbs like high-powered beams, some refracting off walls, bouncing here and there. All sources of light, containing the culled data, fused together into a collective whole, then surged into the Limnocular's receiver, nearly knocking it off its pedestal.

The footage was then spat back out through the spyglass lens and projected into the center of the room. Though the recorded footage contained various perspectives spliced together, it remained seamless.

In 3D Technicolor, what was clearly a female, donning a hoodie, pussyfooted into the great chamber. Her face remained obscured from view, most likely done by design. Locks of her caramel-shaded hair, the ends appearing as if they had been dipped in gold, peeked out from her hoodie and tumbled down her chest.

As she ventured down the scores of chambers, she avoided making eye contact with the Talking Heads that recorded her every movement. The cat burglar ignored the spewed gibes of the Greek chorus as she beelined to the laboratory. Nor did she falter at the crocodile divinity; instead, she held a device that played a digital recording of what sounded like Zho'zho reciting the password in flawless Laramaic and another indiscernible language.

Inside the laboratory, her greedy fingers plucked two reliquaries from the bunch and slipped them into a satchel before leaving behind a note. An adept cat burglar, she remained incognito the whole time.

A ferociously hissing Balakai, blocking the only exit, caught the girl red-handed while she snuck inside the great chamber. A blustery mewling howl blew back the thief's hoodie, exposing a singular beauty who wasn't that much older than Pepper.

"That's the girl from the Tenth Circle!" Nancy was now conditioned to squeal, torture no longer necessary. "The associate of the Hounds of Hell! Not a coincidence that the bloodsuckers only started appearing when *she* was around."

Zho'zho paused the footage on the 3D image of the thief and walked around the girl, inspecting. Pepper couldn't tear her eyes away, and every part of her being felt clammy, sick and twisted byproducts of when you stumble upon a cold hard truth.

"Bhi'gow, do you know this girl?" Jhi's finger tattooed the tip of his thumb.

"I have never met this girl before, and the same goes for Loki. I'd surely remember those emerald eyes." The dusting of shimmer shadow on the girl's monolids made the emerald hue of her eyes pop.

"Well, I certainly know her. That's the aforementioned barkeep, Jaylyn." Zho'zho didn't hide her anger over being swindled. "She kept mostly to herself. Rented a room upstairs in the Tavern and would retire there nightly after work until the day she disappeared a few weeks ago. That was the last time I saw that manipulative, lying bitch. Pray tell, why else would she want Pepper's magic if not for being in collusion with the Firebird? Or *the* Firebird?" The inferno licking Zho'zho's horns blazed angrily.

"If Jaylyn colluded with the Hounds, she wouldn't've left a note behind, so that dispels that ridiculous theory." Jhi reproached Zho'zho, and his beetled brow looming over narrowed eyes served as a warning that he'd do the same to anyone who conflated her with the Hounds. Again.

There was no mistaking that patent longing stare of Jhi's—JD, the object of his affection, otherwise known as Jaylyn. Pepper's traitorous heart plumbed new depths of dejection, regardless of uncertain death looming over her. If only she could flip a switch whereby her heart would morph to stone. If only.

Still, the cold, hard truth remained: nobody could ever come between a boy who had fallen head-over-heels for a Sunday kinda girl. The girl who moved past the scheduled Saturday night dinner date and seamlessly glided into the next day. Easily, she could kick back and hang with her guy for an all-dayer, be blanketed in companionable silence, get lost in football, happily chow down on carbs, knock back drinks, exchange ribald-laced jokes. From one stolen glance at the Sunday goddess cursing at a fumble on TV, as she whipped up her no-frills hair into a messy bun, the interested guy's heart revved, making him forget all about the football game.

Smitten, forevermore, his thoughts would be pinned on all manner of the girl, and no other female could ever compare. He gladly spend all his free time with her. Should she ever be in danger, he'd kill for her. Lost? He'd scour the face of Hell and Earth to find her. The hell he'd ever let a girl like that get away.

"I know Jaylyn or JD. That's the name she went by. So, trust me when I say she's a sweet girl and not in cahoots with the Hounds." Jhi left it at that.

Pepper tried with all her might to remain stony and to not only weigh each word before voicing but enunciate them with as little emotion as possible. "Okay, so why did *she* steal *my* magic, then, if she's all sugar and spice and everything nice?" Pepper failed epically in that endeavor, her trembling voice betraying her so.

"*You* don't know *JD*, sweetling?" The sadistic Perrin uptalked, feigning shock.

"Yeah, Perrin. We go way back! No, of course I don't know this chick!"

An indestructible flint glistened in Perrin's wide eyes as she fished through her purse, an action that was met by a collective hush. And when she hooked a tube of lip gloss instead of the head-eliminating yo-yo, a collective sigh resulted. With an audible plop, she uncorked the bottle, then spackled her lips. "I like this salty side of yours, sweetling. A lot. No, I simply asked if you knew Jaylyn because one, you haven't stopped glaring at her. Two, Jhi knows her, and I just figured you did, too. And three, why else would she pinch your magic?"

"Maybe, possibly, gee, I don't know, because she's a THIEF! And also because—"

"Don't say it, Pepper!" More than a hint of fury gleamed in Jhi's eyes.

Button pushed. Pepper didn't take kindly to being told what to do. "Don't say what? That JD is clearly the Firebird? I'm just voicing what everyone else is thinking."

"Speak for yourself, sweetling."

"I pride myself on being an excellent judge of character, and to date, I have yet to be proven wrong." Jhi's words were like finely honed scalpels, cutting Pepper's heart into itty-bitty pieces.

"There's a first time for everything." The millisecond Pepper uttered that rejoinder to Jhi, she regretted it, but did a bang-up job concealing her shame.

Jhi lobbed a look of reproach Pepper's way, and it crushed her, so she holstered her tongue for the time being—an arduous task in itself. Perhaps in time, Jhi'd reach the same conclusions as the others had about the Firebird's identity, that his precious JD was corrupt; Pepper just hoped that by then she hadn't irrevocably destroyed their friendship.

"I think we can all agree that JD, Jaylyn, is a pro when it comes to enchanting the damned. We've seen her masterly skills first-hand." Pepper darted a glance at Jhi, hoping the compliments she lavished on his thieving girlfriend would temper his ire. But when he shimmied back into his mask of impassivity, it was anyone's guess as to what he was feeling. "What if there are legions of other Nancys scattered about? Which means that even if we tried to escape from the bowels of Hell, we'd have to contend with an endless sea of eyes and ears scourin' the environs twenty-four-seven for Peppersightings. Not to be confused with the legions of gargoyles already observing Hell's denizens. And I need more ale!"

"Thank Seren, sweetling, that mala'khas aren't after you, 'cause then you'd be fuh'kared."

Pepper nearly soiled her undies, picturing Hell's assassins out for her blood.

"Even if you did leave Hell, where would you go? Without being armed with knowledge or magic, you're like one of the damned," a gargoyle posited soberingly.

"Trixie's right. We need to stop speculating on whether or not JD, Jaylyn, or whatever the fuh'kar her name is has been drafted by the Hounds and pivot back to the Tenth Circle." Perrin was in her element. "Zho'zho, is there something else that you found odd about the goings-on at your tavern? Need I remind you, your brother's life is on the line."

Zho'zho went all squirrelly, and the flames coating her horns were close to extinguishing. "If word gets out that I ratted, I'm afraid that I'll be killed, or worse. This demon is well-connected."

Everyone present swore to Seren that mum was the word.

Zho'zho took a measured breath before proceeding. "First Underlord Mephistopheles, he began slipping me pouches of Vs and Indys when he'd pay his tab. Money was tight, what with paying nearly half my income in taxes, and I couldn't possibly turn down the highest denominations of magic gems, not when selling magic that formidable would keep me afloat for a long while."

"Okay, so Mephistopheles ponied up hush money. Was he by chance a tavern regular?" Jhi asked.

"As regular as the chimes on the temples of Seren."

"So, he established a pattern." Jhi remained the picture of calm under the circumstances.

"I'd say. Been a patron for centuries. But some time ago, he started paying me to keep quiet and carry on as if nothing had happened. As if he hadn't slipped into the back storeroom of the Tavern and vanished without a trace."

"Vanished? For how long?"

"Ten minutes max. Then he'd return and pick back up, reading the Bellowers' paper and sipping his ale."

"Sounds like he was being shadowed and had to shake off

whoever it was." Jhi's mind was racing. "Notice any Hounds? Any strange beings milling about? Anyone who caught Mephistopheles' eye?"

"No. The less I knew, the better. My patron saint is Seren, not Shi'rue."

"Did Jaylyn ever have any contact with Mephistopheles while barkeeping? Or perhaps lurk around during the times the First Underlord had vanished?" Pepper pressed.

"Yes, to both. But it's not what you're thinking. You see, most demons don't know who Mephistopheles is. Let's just say he does a good job of blending in with the locals. But I had a sneaking suspicion Jaylyn knew all along. She'd have his ale poured before he even waltzed through the door and then delivered it to him right as he sat down at his favorite spot in the back of the Tavern. I knew that special attention she lavished upon him was an excuse to chat, but she was a good employee, did a good job attending to all the patrons, so I didn't mind."

And neither did Mephistopheles. According to Zho'zho, the archdemon had taken a liking to Jaylyn fairly quickly, and wanted to engage in conversation with her, even made it a priority. But when Jaylyn just up and disappeared not too long ago, with no warning, and Mephistopheles didn't ask where his favorite barkeep was, Zho'zho figured he pulled some strings and got her a job.

What, was this Jaylyn the hot TAMALE in Hell? Did anyone *not* take a shining to her, well, save for Pepper?

"Looks like we got ourselves a new lead." Jhi sported a wicked grin. "And as soon as possible, we'll be paying the First Under-lord a visit."

Perrin spittaked Grissel's ale all over her dress. "You'll never be able to steal inside the Ministry of Mischief and Mayhem. It's been tried time and time again. Instant death for those caught trying."

"We'll see about that." Mischief glinted in Jhi's sea-glass eyes.

CHAPTER 23

"Wait! I think I spotted it. Nine o'clock. And Jhi, step on it before that slippery shit outwits us, again!" Myopically focused on the task at hand, the hell Pepper was going to fail at her *one job* of spying with her little eye the shimmering ball-shaped orb that maddeningly blinked in and out of existence on the sandy, desert terrain.

After losing sight of the bouncing orb going on five times now, Pepper eventually deciphered that it hopscotched about in a pattern like that of a pentagram, so all they had to do was outsmart it. But their luck was about to run dry like the Crooked Dunes they were adventuring within, so the pressure was on. No more screw-ups allowed.

"Hold on tight!" Jhi floored the soul-powered convertible and veered sharply to the left, the exhaust pipe belching puffs of fire and brimstone, the howls of the souls within reaching a fever pitch.

Pepper's ebony hair haloed her pinched face as she gripped the passenger side of the vehicle. The wind generated from the lightning-fast velocity sent the sand cresting the dunes into eddying frenzies, exhuming gobs of tens of hundreds of thousands of sundry coins times infinity that winked in the afternoon scorching sunlight.

Scant time ago, Pepper and Jhi had journeyed to the land of Miserer's Hollow, home to the Crooked Dunes and Dreaded Gulch, *and* the Lu'kowsa, a fearsome breed of dragon that roamed the skies of the Hollow, fiercely defending its cache of ill-gotten gains. So far, Goddess Seren had kept Jhi and Pepper off the Lu'kowsa's radar, but her Grace would only last for so long.

While Jhi kept a weather eye on the bloodred skies and artfully navigated the soulcar through an anorexic gorge, one false move and the soulcar would crash into the craggy walls, Pepper quested for the shimmering orb, prepared to assume the role of dragon-slayer should the apex predator spot them.

"Remind me again, Jhi, that there's no other way to steal inside the Ministry of Mischief and Mayhem."

The municipal building was where all governmental officials presided, even the reigning King of Darkness, Lucifer, himself, which explained why there were scads of impenetrable security barricades and pitfalls throughout the Ministry and why Jhi and Pepper were forced to seek an alternate route inside, discretion the name of the game.

Once they reached the predicted spot on the crown of a sand dune, Jhi quickly programmed the soulcar to return to Bhi'gow's pyramid. Watching the matte-black auto rocket over the dune crests and then disappear from sight kicked Pepper's anxiety into overdrive.

Keyed up, Pepper couldn't talk, couldn't do anything save peer at what currently amounted to heaps of sand scant feet away from her and Jhi. She prayed to God, Seren, whoever would listen really, for the glimmering ball to appear. That she hadn't made a grave misstep in her calculations. Because then what?

Earlier, when Pepper'd plied Jhi with pertinent questions on their way to Miserer's Hollow, like what the plan of action was, Jhi'd responded in hypotheticals. Though intra-chaosnauting in Hell was forbidden for demons, that wasn't the case for upper echelon Ministry officials, *allegedly*. Hidden chaosgates leading directly inside the bowels of the Ministry of Mischief and Mayhem were sprinkled hither and thither about the ever-sprawling Hell Dimension, *allegedly*, the bouncing orbs serving as cairns. When caught, an orb, or shard of pure, unstable chaos, much like a lodestone, would transport the victor to its vibrational match—a hidden chaosgate.

If you managed to hunt an orb down, which was tricky in and of itself, what with having to remain stealthy to not advertise your presence to ice-breathing dragons patrolling the not-so-friendly skies, all the while flying around in a soulcar like an idiot chasing after the glimmering orb, you still had to contend with the unseen Sentries, whatever that entailed.

To not appear hostile to the Sentries, Jhi clicked a switch on his enchanted jack-of-many-weapons, currently a quarterstaff, and it collapsed like a folding ruler. Deftly, he slipped it inside his back-pack, then said, "On my mark." He cupped Pepper's hand in his. "Get ready, set."

The key to grabbing hold of a hopscotching orb was to "simply" jump onto the iridescent-flecked mirage, so when it demate-rialized, it would take them right along with it.

"Go!"

Right as the orb materialized, the duo soared onto the surface and was immediately catapulted to wherever, then all movement halted, save for Pepper's stomach, which was still back at Point A.

Though their precise location was unknown, they were still in the Hollow, for whatever that was worth, inside a darkened underwater cave with one visible point of egress carpeted in bones and skulls. The hidden chaosgate, flanked by hellfire braziers, was now visible and located on the only other dry land in sight—only a jump away. But the duo couldn't move from the craggy rock island they stood upon, a rock barely big enough for two, muddy water, no more than a handspan away, splashing the edge.

Pepper might have feared slipping on the slime-coated rock

and falling into the water if not for the invisible force pinning them in place. If not for the booming roar of a Lu'kowsa emanating from the only way out.

"Remind me again that this is the only way to Mephistopheles?" Wrought with fear-laced anticipation, Pepper was about to lose her ever-living mind, wondering *where* the unseen Sentries were, what they were, what they'd do to her. Let alone the dragon nearby, its roar getting closer by the second.

Meeting with Mephistopheles, *the* preeminent soul buyer, and collector, who just so happened to be Jhi's mentor-slash-dominus —that latter intel Jhi only shared with Pepper—was the sole reason they'd risked life and limb to breach the Lu'kowsa's realm.

"There's no other way inside the Ministry that would ensure we stayed under the radar," Jhi replied.

Wind, or what sounded like it, susurrated, the water rippling all around the tiny island, waking up what looked like a predator from underneath the surface, its jagged fin meeting the air.

"Don't move a muscle. The Sentries have arrived," Jhi warned Pepper.

A greasy barrier materialized and then spit out two amorphous Sentries that went to town sniffing the interlopers. Before Pepper could inquire about what was happening, one of the gossamer blobs rudely shoved itself right into her body via a nostril. Not exactly pleasant, the sensation; it was as if she'd swallowed icicles that began stabbing away at her innards. Breath stilted, eyes burned, from inside her body, legions of pinpricks were knifing her arms and legs and chest and neck and throat—

Pepper stifled a scream as she regurgitated the amorphous being from her mouth and nose.

"Let's go," Jhi said, "before they change their minds!" They leaped to the shoreline and then barreled into the chaosgate. Before Pepper could count to three, a supernatural force yanked her through another archway.

"We're inside the Ministry." Jhi retrieved his jack-of-many-weapons from his backpack.

"Inside" was a ghostly-lit chamber, nondescript and compact, with no visible way out.

"What exactly happened back there?" Pepper's hands were trembling, her voice reedy.

"Soul verification. Your mind was free from plots and schemes to usurp the King of Darkness, his comrades-in-arms included."

"I'm afraid to ask what the Sentries would've done to me if I hadn't passed soul verification?"

Jhi ran his finger across his throat before clicking a switch on his quarterstaff and out popped a gun, which he slipped into the waistband of his jeans. As for the quarterstaff itself, he strapped that to his back.

"Seren willing, we get in and out unnoticed. If by any chance we're approached by a mala'kha, remember your cover—your name is Marie Smith, you're a soul-broker recruit, I'm showing you the ropes, and immediately hand the mala'kha your bona fides. No matter what, act normal. Leave the rest up to me. Ready?"

"Uh-huh," Pepper lied.

CHAPTER 24

Following Jhi's lead, Pepper glided along the volcanic-glass flooring and ended at a wall that pivoted ninety degrees, revealing a staircase. Actually, not a staircase, but a spiral escalator tucked within a pocket-sized space.

The escalator corkscrewed around a transparent newel, more like an engorged tube in appearance, like those found in aquariums that traveled endlessly upward. Water surged through the newel, carrying writhing bodies of the damned that wailed for help, their mouths curled back in rictuses of torment, their hands clawing and pounding the glass as they choked on water. Pepper watched in horror as they drowned, only to be regenerated moments later, their agonizing deaths playing on an eternal loop.

"Here, hold on to me," Jhi said unfazed, offering his hand. "There aren't any rails, and the conveyor moves fairly quickly."

She laced her fingers through his, hoping he wouldn't feel her pounding heart.

"Not for nothing, but don't you find it odd that Mephistopheles was incommunicado for days on end, then out of the blue, returns your calls?" Pepper dealt with the bad feeling by munching on barely there fingernails.

"Yes. So, don't feel slighted when I suggest he and I have a chat alone first."

Climbing and climbing, Pepper lost count of how many times they'd revolved. Strangely though, no other floors of the municipal building were proffered for visitors to get off at. At least not from what Pepper could tell. The motion halted right as the wall pivoted ninety degrees. The escalator riders were disgorged on a vaulted-ceiling floor allegedly reserved for the First Underlord of Hell, Mephistopheles.

The duo glissaded down the smokey veneered river-of-glass that provided an A1 view of the damned in extremis. Their staccato rappings on the glass floor for rescue from their watery prison, along with their muted caterwauling, were in perfect rhythm with the click-clacking of Pepper and Jhi's heels; the sounds generated were much like that of a macabre concert. The lobby-cum-hallway, save for the interesting choice of floorscape, was mantled in reflective obsidian and crimson, with spindly branches of quicksilver threaded about.

At the end of the vast hallway sat Mephistopheles' assistant, Sala'dee, as per the nameplate, comfortably resting behind a wavy half-wall, her back ramrod straight. Two grainy, walnut-shaded horns were mostly curtained by her bobbed green hair, shot through with black. Her youthful, sylphlike face, covered in beetle-black skin, was all sharp angles, as if razor blades had been implanted just beneath the surface of her cheekbones, brow, and jawline. Wow, talk about devilishly mesmerizing, her appearance. And the etherealness she radiated, so much so it quantum-leaped to off-the-charts status.

Through smacks of gum and filing her horns, she advised, "His Liege, First Underlord to Lucifer, Mr. Mephistopheles, will be with you shortly. Please have a seat." The demon was a parody of wickedness, for when she spoke, her voice sounded like daintily knelling wind chimes. Her slender fingers double-clicked her ear, and then she moved her lips as if speaking, but no sound came out. "He's ready for you." Sala'dee's smile was scorchingly bright, but Pepper noted a hint of disingenuousness buried beneath. An observation that chilled her.

As Jhi disappeared within the bowels of Mephistopheles' office, Pepper readjusted her weight on the velvety sofa that was far from cushiony and commenced the waiting game. Nary a glossy for perusing about, her sole accompaniment was the lilting soporific muzak in all its instrumental creepiness.

While Pepper surveilled the premises—having an escape route mapped out was a must—a muffled sound stole on the air, emanating somewhere in the vicinity of Sala'dee. Pepper tuned her ears to the disembodied beckoning and was no sooner interrupted by a wilting damned who tried to hail her attention, pounding on the glass underfoot. "Go away, creeper!" Pepper snapped right as the water current carried the damned away.

She turned her attention back to the disembodied voice calling her name, her eyes scanning every nook and cranny of the hallway. But it disappeared. Not only that, but Pepper could not discern an exit anywhere, so that was *fan*tastic and not at all alarming. What *was* undeniably alarming were the holes Sala'dee bore into Pepper's being, a consequence of the assistant's vetting Pepper's every feature, every movement. Yet Pepper continued on with her oblivious posturing, that she didn't detect the assistant spying her whatsoever. Talk about challenging.

Save for the assistant's desk, the only doors dotting the hallway were those leading into the First Underlord's office, which resided directly before Pepper. Eventually, Pepper's roving eyes had no choice but to meet Mephistopheles' ogling assistant straight-on, and Sala'dee darted her silvery orbs, with scarlet flecks that pirouetted about like prima ballerinas, to that of her desk.

"You've reached the office of His Liege, First Underlord Mr. Mephistopheles, Sala'dee speaking. How may I be of assistance?" Her response to the caller from that point on was suppressed, yet her lips flapped zippily, like one of those wind-up, chattering, red-lipped mouths.

Pepper continued sleuthing for a way off this floor—where did Sala'dee go when she clocked out for the day?—and, more saliently, for the haunting voice that summoned Pepper something fierce, like a magnetic pull.

Sala'dee's office occupied the end of the lobby. And on one side of her desk was a refreshment area and on the other was something that currently was out of view, perhaps a hallway containing a point of egress. Only one way to find out. Pepper moseyed in that direction.

Not a hallway, unfortunately, but a recessed wall like that of a turret, and housed within was a stone effigy of Mephistopheles, as per the wall plaque. The statue depicted a slick-suited business-man, his stare pensive; he proffered a scrolled contract in one hand and held a quill in the other. Archdemon or human? Pepper couldn't tell, as there were no horns to be had, nor tail, just a handsome man with a prominent goatee and eyes that glinted with mischief. Then again, Perrin, a demon through and through, was hornless.

Before Pepper spun on her heel, the softest of whispers, reminiscent of the voice beckoning her to open the Karma Academy invite, instructed her to not leave, not yet. Pepper's eyes scrubbed the area around the effigy and landed on a curious round button sitting all by its lonesome on the wall to the left. Oh, how it begged to be pressed. Acquiescing to the inanimate object, Pepper introduced it to the face of her sweaty palm.

A silvery female voice diffused about the recessed area. "After the dawning of civilization, God and the impartial Universe Elect selected a handful of gods and goddesses to oversee certain aspects of life throughout the cosmos. They picked the unassail-able Goddess Karma to assume the weighty responsibility of preserving cosmic law and order upon Earth and ever balancing the Scales of Justice. After Karma accepted the onerous position of judge, jury, and executioner, she solemnly vowed to reward the righteous, defend the oppressed, and persecute the unjust. Chari-table acts would yield blessings while unsavory deeds inflicted upon innocents would come back to the perpetrators, in their current life or future one, however Karma saw fit.

"'And the consequences will be unfavorable,' a sworn oath Karma recited at the time of her induction. Should the Scales of Justice that she vigilantly watched over unbalance in the slightest, Karma would swiftly and blindly right the Scales with nary a second thought or question the reasons why. With that, Earth ticked on like a dream. For a time.

"Not long after our wickedly wondrous and most gracious King of Darkness, Lucifer, conquered Hell, ousting the erstwhile Queen of Hell, Lilith, from her throne, Lucifer's most valued soldier and fellow mala'dayya, Mephistopheles, convinced his commander-in-chief that Earth held boundless opportunity for all demons. One word: souls; moreover, what they could do with them. The notion of reaping piqued King Lucifer's curiosity. So, he sanctioned the enterprising Mephistopheles to abandon his Hellside post and join the flocks on Earth. His mission was to return to Hell with scores of collected souls.

"Mephistopheles' scheme of soul-brokering, in exchange for coveted unimaginables and inconceivables, would systematically and fundamentally change Earth and Hell alike. In the meantime, unruly demons scorched the Earth, mischief and mayhem blazing in their wakes. Demons whispered sweet-nothings in the ears of the corruptible and schooled nascent dictators in the art of oppressing the masses and other fiendish whatnots. They riled the plebeians and lathered them into fits of abject misery and fatalism. Elicited barbaric crusade after bloodied crusade. 'Kill all infidels for your god,' the demons whispered. 'Bloodshed is what he wants.' Then gleefully watched from the sidelines as humans torn one another limb from limb.

"'Overwhelmed from the spate of injustices and people beseeching my name from every corner of the globe, my plate wasn't just full but broken,' in Goddess Karma's own words. Yet that didn't stop resolute Karma; she fathomed out ways to carry on with her solemn vow. Practices that, to date, are considered proprietary and top-secret classified. 'Did she multiply herself?' Demons have posited. Though we'll never know how Karma answers all the cries for help and stays sane.

"Only one time in recorded history has Karma's 'proprietary methods' not proved victorious. One time where the Scales of Justice faltered and found themselves askew. The culprit was Mephistopheles when he irrevocably bent cosmic law and order with the signing of the very first absolute, magically binding, soul-selling contract. Take a gander for yourself."

By way of demonstration, a papyrus contract materialized and hovered in midair. Only a tiny section of the scroll was exposed, as the rest was hidden within engorged rolls at the top and bottom. The magnified fine print read: PURSUANT TO THE SOUL-BROKERING ACT OF 2 ANNO DAEMONUM DOMINI (A.D.D.), P.C. § 666(f)(6), POSTERIOR TO THE BLOOD-SIGNING OF THE MAGICALLY, EVER-BINDING CONTRACT, THE SELLER WILL CONTINUE TO DRAW BOUNTIFUL BREATH FOR THE REMAINDER OF THEIR TIME LEFT ON EARTH. AS SUCH, UNDER NO CIRCUMSTANCES SHALL THE SELLER BE HARMED IN ANY WAY, SHAPE, OR FORM; NOT EVEN A STRAND OF HAIR ON THEIR HEAD SHALL BE TOUCHED. THIS CONTRACT IS ENFORCEABLE IN EVERY PERCEIVABLE DIMENSION. VIOLATION OF THIS ORDER WILL SUBJECT THE OPPRESSOR TO SEVERE PUNISHMENT AND/OR DEATH, OR HOWEVER THE SOUL BROKER DEEMS MOST JUDICIOUS.

"Needless to say, Karma and Mephistopheles entered into a bloody battle of words that spanned eons. Skipping over the unpleasantries, lest painful unproductive memories resurface, Karma and Mephistopheles eventually called a truce. And the truce between Hell and Earth couldn't have come at a better time for Underlord Chaos, a former disciple of Lilith's, who switched sides when the odds waned in his Queen's favor.

"On the outs, Chaos was attempting to carve out a place in King Lucifer's ranks. To curry favor with King Lucifer's regime and to sweeten the pot with Karma, the underlord proffered the use of chaosgates for Earth-dwelling humans. It remains a horn-scratcher for young demons to think that for eons before Under-lord Chaos granted us the use of his portals, forged from his powers, inter-dimensional travel was arduous and dicey at best.

"Our silver-tongued Mephistopheles sold Chaos' offering to Karma as a goodwill gesture, swore that chaosnauting would undoubtedly broker peace between the species. 'Picture it, Karma, you, human mages, and demons alike, all prospering and mingling and making merry.'

"Karma upped the ante and said she'd only accept the deal if one: intra-dimensional chaosgates were added for Earth, a way for mages to move about the earthly dimension freely and easily. Two: rukbas were to be made available to Earth-dwellers so they could freely travel to and from Hell and other dimensions for business or pleasure and vice versa for demons. And three: unruly demons were to be subjected to the rules of law while on Earth.

"'A goddess after my own heart,' Mephistopheles said. With that, they reached an amicable agreement, shook hands, and drew up a peace treaty. First order of business—demons wreaking havoc on God's Green Earth. Pursuant to the Ministry of Mischief and Mayhem, Department of Possessions and Hauntings: said possessions and hauntings are solely permissible if a human has verbally and-or mentally invited, invoked, conjured, spirit-boarded or the like, the demon in question to their person and-or dwelling.

"Furthermore, said demon is therefore sanctioned to possess and-or haunt the body and-or dwelling in question until they, themselves, decide to vacate and-or move on to greener pastures. So monumental was that decree, it permanently corralled and tamed the unruly demons and bestowed upon them a sense of purpose.

"And last, but certainly not least. Karma agreed to turn the other cheek for any human who has entered into an eternally binding contract with a soul-broker for the agreed-upon ninety-nine years, and as such, said human will remain untouched by Karma or anyone under the goddess' purview for said amount of years, regardless of any misdeeds and unlawful behavior or the severity thereof.

"When the ninety-ninth year arrives, and not a millisecond later, a mala'kha will hunt down the soul-selling human and drag the entirety of him, or her, to the Pits of Tartarus, a prison within a prison ringed by lakes of fire, where only the vilest of soul-sellers are imprisoned. Henceforth, the human, body and soul, is the rightful property of Karma for exactly ninety-nine years, in accordance with the Luciferian calendar.

"Every horrific act meted out by the damned, during their time on Earth, will be repaid in kind by Karma and her unique brand of retribution, usually in the form of abject torture, but not always. Vengeance is very subjective. Once Karma's time draws to a close, the human is then turned over to the Department of Soul Sundering and Assignments.

"To this very day, Mephistopheles and Goddess Karma have remained staunch allies and friends alike. We sincerely hope you've enjoyed this presentation brought to you by Demons For a Better Tomorrow, and do have a pleasant day." The voice dissipated.

Addlepated, Pepper stood rooted to the spot, mouth agape.

"Would you like a beverage?" Pepper barely overheard Sala'dee mutter while on a call but opted not to make eye contact, should the demon think she was eavesdropping. "Yoo-hoo! Er, human?"

Pepper twirled on her heel. "Oh, sorry, didn't know you were talking to me."

Sala'dee showed off her pearly whites—so blindingly bright and perfect, an audible ping was all that was missing. "Some sparkling plasma?"

"Only if it's infused with pomegranate." Pepper joshed in the name of fitting in.

In a snap, Sala'dee switched gears, her mask of congeniality all but wiped away by graveness. "A wicked storm's brewing outside, and clouds are rolling in. I'd say there's a good chance for torrential blood showers." Sala'dee studied Pepper for a beat, her head cocked as if waiting for Pepper to respond.

Pepper patted her messenger bag. "It's a good thing then that I carry an umbrella with me at all times." Summer weather in Naples being mercurial and all. Still, that dialogue exchange was odd. "Say, Mr. Mephistopheles must be one hell of an archdemon for Karma to call him a friend," Pepper said, fishing.

For a beat, Sala'dee's limesicle-hued brows knitted, then ironed out just as quickly. "Oh, yes. Thick as thieves. You've reached the office of His Liege, First Underlord Mephistopheles, Sala'dee speaking. How may I be of assistance? ... Certainly. I'll be there in two shakes of a damned's leg." A section of the wall behind her pivoted open, and she, along with her poofed-out skirt that looked like a Judy Jetson collection from summers past, disappeared within the dimly lit hallway beyond.

A beat later, the hidden door rotated back to its rightful position, but not before a zephyr escaped. Not a wink later, a piece of parchment fluttered off Sala'dee's desk.

Pepper harmlessly nosed around the desk a bit before plucking the parchment from its final resting place. She gasped, and her hands trembled as she stared at a wanted poster from the Department of Inter-Dimensional Security and Intelligence. An exact rendering of Pepper's visage glared back. Not to be excluded, Perrin's mug was included on the wanted poster. But not Jhi's.

Along with mugshots and physical descriptors was: *Mala'khas working in conjunction with DISI are asking for assistance in locating lowlie Pepper Li and Lolly'ka Perrin. They are suspected to be members of an inter-dimensional terrorist organization.* ARMED AND EXTREMELY DANGEROUS. DO NOT APPROACH IF SPOTTED. IMMEDIATELY NOTIFY AUTHORITIES. HANDSOME REWARD FOR ANY INFORMATION ON THEIR WHERE-ABOUTS. WANTED ALIVE.

Was this why Sala'dee had been staring at Pepper earlier? Was she comparing the rendering of Pepper to the wanted poster? What if Sala'dee had notified the authorities? What if they were on their way to Pepper at this very moment?

Oh, shit! Running on pure adrenaline, Pepper barreled through Mephistopheles' office doors.

CHAPTER 25

Regally perched on a glassy throne behind an executive desk, Mephistopheles didn't seem at all perturbed when Pepper plowed into his office, nearly tripping over her feet.

In fact, the Prince of Hell, who predated the dawn of civilization, appeared delighted, an impish grin spreading on his thin lips. His arched brows bespoke a permanent expression of naughtiness; that same attribute was reflected in his intense violet eyes. Hornless, tailless—at least from Pepper's angle—nary a glaringly obvious demonic aspect could be found on his person. And she would know, for she gave Mephistopheles a thorough inspection.

Rooted in place, her heart fluttering, happily sighing and smiling, Pepper took comfort in the fact that she'd do anything for the First Underlord of Hell.

At the edge of her mind, Pepper heard Mephistopheles ask, *Would you brush my lush, darkened, wavy hair?*

Yes, please, she mentally responded.

Trim my dark, wiry goatee that perfectly compliments my rugged square jaw?

It would be an honor.

Kill for me?

Absolutely, master.

"Ahem." A hand cinched around Pepper's arm and then forced her down into a chair. Pepper snapped to full alertness and jerked her head to the left. Jhi's eyes spoke volumes. To Pepper, they communicated something like this: "Stay focused."

She mouthed back, "Sorry!"

Mortified, Pepper tried to avert her lascivious eyes elsewhere, away from sex in a silken pinstripe suit, with a tie dangling care-free, all the while trying to recall exactly why she had barged into the office like a damned out of Hell.

Barring the smattering of Talking Heads mantled to the walls, all sneering, their eyes locked on the newly arrived, Mephistopheles' office possessed the usual trimmings of any high-powered Deputy Director's: wood floors and walls, a desk and bar, well-fed bookcases.

Behind the desk and beyond the French doors unfurled a terrace with a picturesque view of Pandæmonia's haunting skyline. And judging from how close the studded night sky appeared, Pepper figured they were pretty damn high up in the Ministry of Mischief and Mayhem complex, if not on the pent-house floor.

"Funny you should be joining us, Pepper. Jhi was just about to retrieve you." The First Underlord's voice was deep and smooth like molasses. Each word was given special attention, sensually massaged, treated as if it was the most important word spoken—

A gust of icy wind blew open the French doors and, with its teeth, bit Pepper's cheeks and hands. She bristled and cinched her cloak tighter.

Mephistopheles rose from his glass throne that was clouded and … swimming with souls, almost like one gigantic soul shard (a form of Pandæmonia currency that reminded Pepper of micro-scope slides, the souls the specimens). Vapor formed into melted faces and then howled from inside the throne as they, the souls, desperately attempted to pound their way out; Pepper wondered why she hadn't noticed that avant-garde design element from the get-go. In fact, she was having a thorny time staying focused.

Her eyes riveted to Mephistopheles as his long limbs sauntered to the wet bar. Oozing oodles of testosterone, he had to be about six foot who-cares-just-drape-your-body-over-mine-sexy, all corded muscle and not an ounce of fat. And his shoulders—

Jhi pinched Pepper's arm and attempted to communicate something.

Mephistopheles interrupted Jhi's concerted efforts of silent communication and offered his guests a drink, to which they kindly passed, then decanted what smelled like single malt Scotch (her pop's favorite stress-reliever) into a rock glass. After plopping three ice cubes within, he took a sip, the ice gently clinging against the glass. His back to Jhi and Pepper, Mephistopheles could still view his company through the wet bar's mirror.

Jhi's index finger tapped the tip of his thumb, a sign that he was on high alert. But why?

The moment Pepper caught Mephistopheles' reflection in the mirror, specifically his violet eyes, Jhi clasped Pepper's hand in his and squeezed. Their color shifted, albeit briefly; in fact, if she blinked, she would've missed the silvery blob, like that of a worm, sliver over his pupils.

This wasn't Mephistopheles but a wanderer that had possessed the First Underlord's body.

The realization that the wanderer had overpowered a high-ranking officer in the King of Darkness' army, a mala'dayya that fell from Heaven alongside Lucifer, sobered Pepper right up. She squared her shoulders and gripped Jhi's hand ever tighter, lacing her fingers through his. An action that let him know she was lucid and spellbound no longer.

Mephistopheles noted Pepper's raised hackles and produced a sidearm, then trained it on Pepper and Jhi. "What gave me away?"

In a measured tone, Jhi responded. "Mephy doesn't take his Scotch on the rocks, for one."

"Tis a pity. Well, I had you there for a while. You can at least give me props for that. Now hand over the girl, and I'll let you walk out those doors alive. If not, and you try to kill me, I'll destroy this meat sack that I'm wearing before you pull the trigger. Then you'll never be able to see your precious Dominus again. Tsk-tsk, such a shame should that happen, really, because this is a fine specimen of a demon. Wow!" He let out a breath in a low whistle. "That spellbinding ability—didn't think I'd master the art of it so quickly. Probably'll get me a whole lotta tail when I venture to Earth shortly, if Pepper's reaction is any indication."

Jhi whipped his head to Pepper's and mouthed, "When I say 'go.'"

"Go!" Jhi jumped up, and his chair soared backward, crashing into the door.

Still holding on to Pepper's hand, Jhi brandished a semi-automatic with his other. In one fell swoop, he shot the pistol right out of faux-Mephistopheles' hand. Then, with the gun's grip, butted the parasitic wanderer right between the eyes before raining down crippling blows. Once disarmed, the wanderer wasn't exactly adroit with hand-to-hand combat, an observation Pepper mentally filed away.

"You're in way over your heads." While struggling to lever himself to his feet, faux-Mephistopheles fired off a fusillade of more warnings. "The penultimate stage in our operation has been activated. And now we wait for All Hallows' Eve, the day we declare victory before the war *officially* begins on Earth."

Pepper and Jhi stopped dead in their tracks.

"For over a decade, we've been engaged in a silent campaign, ever so slowly tipping the Scales of Justice in our favor. But then that meddling archdemon put his nose where it didn't belong and tried to stop our operation—stop *us.*"

Jhi spun on his heel, his eyes set in an expression of murder.

"Mephistopheles failed. So what makes you both, a low-ranking soul broker and a magicless human"—arrogance and disgust tangled with his words—"think you can do what Mephistopheles couldn't? The Syndicate has infiltrated society on Earth and recruited lowlies to join our cause. Now our numbers are legion. We are your neighbors, your coworkers, your friendly delivery man. But in a few days, we'll be your enemy."

Jhi lunged at faux-Mephistopheles and then wrapped his hands around his throat and began squeezing.

Faux-Mephistopheles choked out, "Remember. You kill me, you kill Mephistopheles."

Jhi retreated. "Where does Pepper fit in? Why is *she* so important?"

Pepper panicked and wondered why Jhi was courting danger. Faux-Mephistopheles was obviously stalling, waiting for backup to arrive.

Rubbing his throat and gasping for breath, faux-Mephistopheles responded, "Don't know; don't care. If it were up to me, I'd turn the lowlie inside out and feast on her entrails. But it's not."

The floor quaked. Reinforcements were on their way. "Jhi, we have to go! Now!" Pepper tugged Jhi's arm.

But Jhi wouldn't budge, not until this trip yielded beneficial intel, that much Pepper was certain. "Pepper a sacrifice needed to resurrect your overlord? Once your overlord resurrects, will he be launching this war?"

Faux-Mephistopheles remained silent, a reaction Pepper noted, especially the part where he didn't dispute the resurrection.

With his gun trained on faux-Mephistopheles, Jhi called his bluff and inched backward toward the French doors, pretending to escape.

"No. But the girl's important, *very* important, from the little I gathered. Not to be harmed in any way, shape, or form. No, that act is reserved for the overlord—"

"All I need to do is get word to the mala'khas in the Pits and they'll put your overlord under extra lock and key."

Faux-Mephistopheles laughed. "Go ahead and try—"

The doors from the hallway blasted open, torn right off their hinges. Mala'khas, wretched-looking beasties with bloodred eyes, giant-tall and sumo-big, terrifying sooty wings aching to be extended, their limbs gnarled, stomped inside the room, all armed to the teeth.

Jhi and Pepper bolted to the terrace.

Emboldened, faux-Mephistopheles continued taunting. "You can run, but you can't hide. You're stuck in Hell. It's only a matter of time until we find you."

Palming magic gems, green and blue matter swirling within, Jhi whispered an incantation, the winds drowning out the words.

"We're monitoring chaosgates and all rukbas. The comings and goings of all are being recorded. We have eyes and ears everywhere—"

The French doors disappeared, a solid wall taking their place. "We have a few minutes before they shatter the spell," Jhi warned.

The heavy, frigid winds buffeted Pepper's body, the tempest nearly pushing her and Jhi over the edge of the terrace. Hair whipping about her face, every inhale burned her throat. That, and she could hear her heart frantically beating in her ears.

Inching forward like a glowworm, Pepper's furnace-hot palms death-gripped the frozen balustrade, ice dripping and puddling by her quivering feet. Queasy, she forced her eyes to begin their journey down, down, down to—up this high, terra firma wasn't even visible. The Ministry of Mischief and Mayhem dwarfed the Burj Khalifa, made a mockery of it even.

The sobering truth whipped Pepper backward. They were trapped in a veritable fortress at the apex of the Ministry of Mischief and Mayhem. Death by jumping, or death by mala'kha?

"We have to jump." Jhi wore an impassive expression.

"Come again?" Pepper gulped down frigid air, her lungs paying the price.

"Once we're airborne—"

"Ha, ha. Funny. You said 'airborne.'"

"Yes. So, when we're *airborne*, don't let go of me." Jhi grabbed her hand. "We're gonna do a running start, 'kay?"

He wasn't joking. And no, it was *so* not okay.

Noting Pepper's flirtation with an epic freakout, Jhi asked point-blank, "You trust me?"

Time of the essence and all that jazz, Pepper replied, "Implicit-ly," and meant it.

With matching strides, Jhi and Pepper thundered towards the railing, then sprinted over. Free-falling down and down, Jhi fought the Herculean winds and wrangled Pepper into his chest. On his orders, she wrapped her legs around his stomach and her arms around his neck and held on for dear life.

Jhi yanked on a cord. Then with an audible whoosh, a para-chute burst open, wrenching the duo upward, straight into the star-studded heavens.

While soaring, Jhi held tightly to the steering lines and banked right toward Pandæmonia proper that could barely be seen in the distance. Pepper hazarded a glance back at the Ministry of Mischief and Mayhem. A massive and fearsome fortress that towered to epic heights, the Ministry resembled a deconstructed Rubik's Cube. Obsidian squares precariously dangled atop squares, some sections rotating, others not. Spires jutted out from the fortress' crown and jabbed the night sky, gargoyles perched at the top.

Pepper didn't have time to ponder what it felt like to be wrapped in Jhi's warm embrace, his stubble tickling her cheek, nor could she get lost in his scent, hints of cinnamon and sandal-wood, what, with Pandæmonia's skyline, at first a suggestion, becoming more and more focused, as was the road below. "Holy shit!"

Following Jhi's terse instructions, Pepper plucked gems from his jeans pocket and nearly dropped his switchblade, but caught it in the nick of time, as she picked out violet and blue gems.

Jhi gruffly corrected her, reminding her they were moments from death. And that she had less than ten seconds to distinguish between violet and indigo before their guts were splattered on the volcanic glass ground.

The ground was rushing towards them. Ten, nine, eight …

Hands a quivering mess, Pepper prevailed and palmed the two magic gems of the required hues—she hoped.

"Now cut me! And draw enough blood to make it count for the offering." Noting Pepper's panicked expression, Jhi barked, "DO IT!"

Pepper flipped open the switchblade and sliced Jhi's forearm. Blood gushed down his arm.

Jhi hastily fired off an incantation, which drained all magic from the gems, the multicolored vapor commingling with his sacrificial blood. Frankly, Pepper was too freaked out to pay that close attention to his words, what with a painful death at hand.

A scream lodged in Pepper's throat as her foot scraped the ground. And then the road—they were moving away from it. Soaring higher. If Pepper wasn't mistaken, the *wind* had scooped them up.

Their speed mushrooming, the wind rocketed the duo into the city center of Pandæmonia. Then into Pandæmonia's version of a parking garage. A hulking structure that had sheer drops on every floor. The summoned wind unceremoniously dropped them near the top, and they rolled to a stop.

Wordless and darting glances over their shoulders, they bypassed an unmanned security booth, then continued skulking on squishy flooring, making their way to what Pepper deduced was a contingency reserve, a getaway car. The garage resembled a honeycomb; little caves cocooned slumbering soulcars. Jhi unlocked one such soulcar, its windows heavily tinted, and told Pepper to jump in.

After firing up the ignition, they were off. The road ahead ended abruptly, and the soulcar motored right off the side of the building. Once the two-seater met nothing but air, Jhi goosed the engine, and the vehicle drifted downward like a shorn feather from a mala'dayya's wing.

Near enough to the ground, Jhi continued to navigate through the backstreets until they reached the roundabout in the city center and touched down on the road that would deliver them to the Isles of Obolus, according to the road sign.

Chalk it up to nerves or the uncomfortable silence, Pepper blurted out A to the Z, the wanted poster, how a bounty'd been put on her head and Perrin's. But not Jhi's. "Don't you find it odd that DIDI didn't list you as an aider and abetter?"

"Not at all. It's merely a ploy to cause dissension." Jhi's demeanor was icier than the temperature outside.

His arm grazed Pepper's knees as he reached inside the glove compartment and extracted a slice of dermis, or rather a stamp fashioned from skin, along with a fountain pen.

He asked her to transcribe. "Weather's dicey, rain with a chance of hail imminent. Best to stay indoors until the forecaster predicts blue skies once again." He told her he was finished with the dictating, then continued on. "Seal the message in the envelope, then address the letter to Tranquility Avenue, apartment number seven-two-five Necropolis."

Jhi sliced his finger and dropped dollops of his life force on the flap of the envelope as if it were a wax seal, then recited an incantation. "Aeolus, Keeper of the Winds, behold the letter." In response to Pepper asking who he had warned, Jhi said, "My partner."

Zephyrs of howling wind buffeted the soulcar back and forth, and it nearly skidded off the volcanic glass road until Jhi got a firm handle on the yoke. A whorling black hole blinked into existence and kept pace with the speeding vehicle, its aperture bleeding open wider and wider, revealing absolute nothingness beyond. Until an enormous hand made of air punched out of the black hole. Its wispy fingers plucked the correspondence right from Pepper's grasp before an inhalation vacuumed the mystical hand and letter back into the gaping maw. The hole sealed shut. Then stillness.

Jhi curtly explained that the blood was an offering to Aeolus— the demonic Keeper of the Winds.

Keeper and apparent postmaster, Pepper thought.

As the environs morphed from pyramid-choked suburgatory into desolate craggy mountain terrain to icicle-coated bent-treed forests, Jhi's silence and his apparent refusal to discuss what the hell had happened back at the Ministry or why he never once mentioned having a partner other than Jaylyn only mushroomed and smothered the airwaves. A cauldron of fear—was a war on Earth with a demonic regime imminent?—adrenaline, confusion, exhaustion threatened to combust within Pepper, and she unholstered her tongue, ready to lash it at Jhi.

But his tongue-slinging skills trumped that of Pepper's, and he fired first, "Who the hell are the Li sisters?" He pivoted his head to look at Pepper head-on. "Better yet, who the hell are *you*?" Eerie calmness dripped from his tone. "You must've done something pretty awful to—"

Burning with rage, Pepper interrupted. "Great question, but alas, I'm unable to come up with an answer. I'd ask my sister, but gosh darn it"—she theatrically snapped her fingers —"she's dead. Perhaps we should ask your *girlfriend*. Jaylyn seems to know an awful lot about the Li sisters."

"Yes, let's do. Oh wait, shoot"—he aped Pepper and snapped his fingers—"JD's otherwise preoccupied at the moment. Her schedule's most likely jam-packed with torture. An unforeseen byproduct of crossing paths with the Hounds of Hell."

Pepper bristled from the coldness he exuded. "Chances are that Jaylyn most likely escaped and is in hiding. She left that note for Bhi'gow not too long ago." It took everything in Pepper not to refer to Jaylyn as the Firebird. Though that conversation was drawing nigh.

Jhi took a measured breath and nodded in agreement. "What I meant to say before you interrupted me is that whatever you or your sister, Kassendra, had done, or possessed at one time, or knowledge you discovered, it's big enough to have attracted the likes of Lucifer's regime."

"If not Lucifer himself." Pepper's stomach revolted from the mere uttering.

"No way the King of Darkness is involved in the conspiracy. His megalomania ensures that there's only one sun in his orbit. Besides, Lucifer holds all the power as King of Hell and has a mutually beneficial relationship with Earth. There's no advantage to him declaring war on Earth, or he would have done it eons ago. Moreover, he wouldn't need to engage in subterfuge. He'd just prohibit the resurrection of this overlord and call it a day."

"Yeah. Now that I think about it, a king would never allow another to declare war on his turf. Well, if not Lucifer, faux-Mephistopheles received help from someone high ranking. How else could he have possessed your dominus? I mean, Mephistopheles is a prince of Hell, for God's sake. Is there even a rank higher than a prince besides a king?"

"Mephy's a prince of Hell in name only. He never assumed the mantle of responsibility that goes along with that title. He always felt more comfortable in his role as archdemon, a rank lower than a prince, less pomp and circumstance, more anonymity. Still, over-powering Mephy is damn near impossible unless a close confidant betrayed him."

Close confidant like Jaylyn, Pepper thought.

"Mephy could be the first or one of many archdemons to be possessed. In the least, the Department of Soul Brokering has been infiltrated. Just have no way to prove it. The Firebird's syndicate is conducting one helluva pinpoint operation, Pepper, you being the target. The Ministry is monitoring all chaosgates and rukba travel, for Seren's sake! That responsibility falls under the purview of the Department of Inter-Dimensional Security and Intelligence. So, have they been infiltrated, too? After what happened today, I'm led to believe yes. High-ranking Ministry officials have colluded with the Firebird. But how many and how far up the chain of command that goes—there's just no telling."

"Pretty high up, seeing as how the DISI put out a BOLO for Perrin and me. Well, I guess now we know the mystery of how the soul contracts bearing Kimball's father's name and his murderous cohorts weren't put through the appropriate channels in the Department of Soul Brokering. The unnamed soul broker, the mole, is faux-Mephistopheles."

"Negative. The mole isn't a wanderer. This mysterious individual is highly intelligent, calculating, patient, trusted."

Trusted like Jaylyn? Pepper nearly blurted that out. "You said that your dominus possesses esoteric knowledge of who's rendering up their souls. Do you think Mephistopheles is still alive?"

"Yes. The question is, for how much longer?" Jhi chuckled weakly. "That sly devil left a trace of his essence behind for me to find. Think of it as a breadcrumb. Only I was too distracted to pick up on the clue. Thankfully, you cued me in when you fell into a lusty trance." In response to Pepper's knitted brows, Jhi added, "Lowlies are more susceptible to spellbinding. Of note, that ability is fixed to Mephy's soul, not his 'meat sack' as the wanderer called it."

"Is' lusty trance' the technical term, Jhi?" Pepper joshed.

In response, Jhi couldn't stop his lips from curling into a lopsided grin.

Holy moly! If a mere whiff of the archdemon spellbound Pepper, what would happen should she be in actual-Mephistopheles' presence? Blushing a beet red, she shuddered at the thought, as did her nether regions.

"No, Mephy's more valuable alive than dead, so I reckon he's being tortured yet unbowed all the same. Seren willing, faux-Mephy makes another blunder, and someone else notices in the interim."

Pepper asked Jhi to elaborate further.

"Mephy detests Scotch. He's more of an ale kinda archdemon. I knew something was off from the beginning. Let's just say faux-Mephy is unskilled in the art of delay tactics. So, I hatched an escape plan, but then the plan went flaccid when you thundered into the office."

"Well, Sala'dee had to've noticed something was awry, yet didn't warn us, so—"

"On the contrary. The wanted poster conveniently left on Sala'dee's desk? That was a heads-up for you. She's playing dumb, which is why she's still alive."

"Jhi, what're we gonna do?"

When Jhi shrugged his shoulders, then chased that response with a heavy sigh, Pepper refused to entertain the hopelessness knocking at her door. But given the gravity of the situation, she couldn't see a way out of this nightmare. They had hoped that visiting the First Underlord would have produced a viable lead, but that hope remained unfulfilled. The note left by Jaylyn remained the last clue they had collected, and unless and until they decrypted the coded message, they were stuck in Hell. Still, she donned her karma-for-hire hat and racked her brain for solutions.

"I take it this overlord's incarcerated in the Pits? Faux-Mephistopheles didn't exactly dispute what you had said. Aren't only the vilest of soul sellers held there?" When Jhi nodded his head twice, she swallowed a lump of fright before continuing. "So, we know we're most likely dealing with an entity that should never be allowed to tread on earthly soil again. What if we killed him or took his soul before he could resurrect and nip this whole thing in the bud? We are in the same dimension as him. Being a soul broker, you must have connections with Fortress wardens. What if you pulled a few strings?"

"I thought of that, and even if I had connections inside the Fortress, I don't in the Pits. Besides, both prisons are heavily fortified and magically warded, the Pits even more so. That heist would require hardcore planning and time, which we don't have. Even so, we can't rob the overlord's soul because it already belongs to another. You can't steal Lucifer's souls. Period."

"What do you mean, we don't have time? Wait, what is the date today?" One day bled into the next, and it wasn't long until Pepper lost track of time.

"We have until tomorrow to stop the war—"

"TOMORROW?" Pepper's heart dropped.

"Yes. The All Hallows' Eve ball is tomorrow night. I, too, lost track of time until today. Bhi'gow's island runs on different time than Pandæmonia or Earth, slower, like the glaciers all around us. A few days here is the equivalent to a few weeks on Earth." Jhi placed a hand on Pepper's knee. "Pepper, if we're unsuccessful in stopping this overlord's resurrection, he won't stop hunting you—"

"Am I missing something? You all said it was impossible for the damned to resurrect from Hell, and I believed you, but now you're acting like it's a done deal unless we stop it." Panic coated her vocal cords. "You figured something out, haven't you?"

He nodded solemnly and removed his hand from her knee. "When I said it was impossible for the damned to resurrect from Hell, I lied. But in my defense, loopholes *are* considered rumors, hellfire tales spread by the damned. During daily torment and merciless torture, the damned cling to the hope that a way to be exonerated from their sentence of eternal damnation exists. What fools! Then again, I know mala'dayya, and they derive pleasure from watching the damned lose faith. So, I wouldn't put it past them to sneak in damn-near-impossible-to-achieve loopholes, to be executed in an impossible amount of time, only to watch the damned jump through hoops and eventually lose. Yet the Firebird and her minions are awfully confident that their overlord's success is a foregone conclusion."

"And let me guess. Loophole exploitation involves soul contracts? That's why we can't steal his soul and why it belongs to Lucifer."

"Yes. There are two stipulations involved for anyone even thinking about escaping Hell. One, the damned in question must have signed a soul contract. And two, discovering what the loophole is and exploiting it, which the Syndicate already figured out. I'd bet all my magic gems that this overlord was taken to Hell exactly twelve years ago, according to the Gregorian calendar. It would explain his disappearance all this time. And all that time, the Firebird, his right hand, has been figuring out a way to exploit a contractual impossible-to-achieve loophole at her master's behest, seeing as how he's been otherwise indisposed."

"And you think that's what Jaylyn uncovered before she went missing?"

"Yes, and Mephy." Jhi downshifted right before the road abruptly ended. They zoomed feet above arctic waters and floating icebergs housing beasties with blood-soaked muzzles, the air rife with the pungent smell of death and decay. If there was another road for them to follow, the blanket of icy fog veiled it from sight.

Some aspects of the story revolving around Jaylyn just didn't hold water, and Pepper couldn't be convinced otherwise that Jaylyn and the Firebird were not one and the same. Now all that remained was for her to persuade Jhi.

"Why did Jaylyn, a soul broker who just uncovered a conspiracy that involves soul contracts and demons declaring war on Earth, decide to take a job as a barkeep at Zho'zho's tavern? And don't tell me for extra money."

A smirk ghosted over Jhi's lips. "I thought that was obvious. JD was following a viable lead."

The thrumming of the soulcar's engine awoke a hell-bear resting on a nearby iceberg, and the ferocious beast leaped into the air to take down the vehicle and its passengers—food for later. Jhi swerved just in time, narrowly avoiding a run-in with the beast's massive claws.

Though rattled, Pepper carried on. "Yes, I get Jaylyn was following a lead, but we only knew about the Tavern through Bhi'gow. So, how could Jaylyn possibly have known about Bhi'-gow's connection to this conspiracy, let alone that he had a sister and that she owned the Tenth Circle?"

"You're actually wrong. We didn't find out about the Tavern through Bhi'gow."

The curtain of fog lifted and revealed another island a klick away. Jhi stepped on the gas pedal when another hell-bear came into view.

"You're right." Pepper deflated, her *gotcha* moment fizzling out. "Perrin's who first mentioned the Tavern."

"But I don't think Bhi'gow is who JD was initially after. I think it was Mephy. I have a question for you? Let's say JD is the Firebird, because that's clearly what you're getting at. Why not surround Bhi'gow's pyramid with Hounds like she did the Lair, waiting for you to show up? Taking it a step further, while keeping in mind that Bhi'gow hasn't spilled any valuable intel despite years in captivity, explain to me what would have brought the Firebird to the Tenth Circle in the first place. What purpose would the Tavern have served? And why would the Hounds even think you would go to the Tavern? You, a lowlie, who has never stepped foot in Hell before."

Dammit, Jhi, and your logical explanations. "Not sure yet about the pyramid. That is a tad odd. And I agree with you that Mephistopheles is at the center of this. But why meet up with him at the Tavern?"

"JD needed to fill Mephy in on what she had discovered, a conspiracy that seems to have originated within his department, while also ensuring he wasn't involved. She needed to protect herself first and foremost. I'm guessing she tailed Mephy to determine where he regularly visits. And the Tenth Circle was a safe enough place to initiate contact. What better way to blend in with the clientele and not draw attention to yourself or your mark than working as a barkeep? Remember, Zho'zho said JD only worked there for a brief spell. Now, I've answered your questions, but you have yet to explain why the Hounds would be waiting for you at the Tavern?"

"I don't think they were waiting for me to show up. That was Perrin's theory, and actually, I think one of her goyles had mentioned it first."

Jhi seemed just as relieved as Pepper when they reached another island. "Finally, something we can both agree on."

Jhi landed the soulcar on the narrow volcanic road that ran parallel to the murky water.

"Faux-Mephy said the Syndicate has eyes and ears everywhere," Jhi said. "And the Tenth Circle is one of many establishments where the Talking Heads are part of that surveillance system. For all we know, the Hounds could be surrounding the Tenth Circle because of Mephy. Maybe he somehow found another body to inhabit and escaped capture. The Hounds realized, just as Jaylyn had, that Mephy frequents the Tenth Circle, so the vamps have the place surrounded in the event he shows up. It's all conjecture at this point. Are you even going to try to convince me that JD is the Firebird, or have you realized the error of your ways and given up?"

Pepper's competitive spirit came out to play. She'd stump Jhi yet. "Why did Zho'zho say Mephistopheles had taken a liking to Jaylyn, as if he didn't know who she was? Wouldn't he have recognized one of his own employees?"

"Pepper, does the CEO of a conglomerate know all of his underlings? Of course not. JD was fairly new to the trade, and considered rank and file at that. So, it's entirely possible that Mephy did not know who she was. But you also have to understand that that was Zho'zho's recollection of events, which doesn't make it a reality. Now, whether or not JD and Mephy knew each other or even shared gathered intel with one another is a moot point, as they're both missing. But thanks to Seren, we're still in the game, and we must stay focused if we have any hope of surviving. What we shouldn't be doing"—he peeled his eyes away from the volcanic roadway to look Pepper dead in the eyes —"is wasting time on your irrational distrust of JD. So, can we move on from this line of questioning?"

No can do, Jhi. Pepper then fired off another question. "You have presented a compelling argument; I'll give you that. But you still haven't explained why Jaylyn needed to break into Bhi'gow's laboratory if she's not, in fact, the Firebird."

"As we know, the timeline of events is sketchy. But what we have ascertained so far is that Jaylyn went missing shortly after stealing your magic and before we chaosnauted to Hell. Also, you don't convince an untold amount of Talking Heads overnight to serve as snitches in exchange for freedom. Regardless, that endeavor of setting up eyes and ears all over Hell must have taken six months in the least. During her time at the Tavern, I'm guessing Jaylyn overheard the Talking Heads mention the Lair and eventually figured out Bhi'gow was the owner. Only problem, the trail of clues ran dry."

"Why would Bhi'gow's name ring a bell if she's not the Firebird?"

"Enter Zho'zho, the happy accident, otherwise known as the Grace of Seren. Sometimes you're meant to run into certain people." Jhi tossed Pepper a flirtatious wink. "Zho'zho intimated that she and Jaylyn became fast friends. In the least, she liked Jaylyn. Allowed her to rent a room at her tavern, so trust was established between the two. I can see them tossing back a few Grissel's ales after the last of the customers have gone home, and in a tipsy state, defenses lowered, Zho'zho mentions her brother, Bhi'gow, who's been missing for twelve years. That might have been before or after Jaylyn overheard the Talking Heads. The order matters not. Once JD heard Bhi'gow's name, the trail of clues picked back up, and she needed to break into his pyramid to look around for information."

"But why the laboratory?"

"As you and I realized, during our stay at Bhi'gow's pyramid, only one room is locked. If you were looking for information, would you not target that room?"

"Of course I would." Pepper was bound and determined to throw him for a loop. "Okay, going along with your theory, then why take magic belonging to my sister and me, then leave a ransom note for Bhi'gow when she knew the fixer had been missing for years? What was her rationale for that? Kinda pointless, if you ask me."

"Pepper, that's what we're trying to find out. We are exactly where JD was in the investigation at one point, only she moved forward while we've stalled. And I'm betting she garnered intelligence from Zho'zho and then ensured nobody else would learn that knowledge when she stole Zho'zho's damn memories."

Pepper couldn't argue with that fact. Zho'zho's memory had been wiped clean, so there had to be a good enough reason for the memory stealing.

"And before you delve into the minutiae and ask why *your* magic when there were others available. According to Bhi'gow's filing system, yours was the most recent, and he hadn't gotten around to draining it. There were only a few other jars with bits of magic inside, but not like yours."

"The amount of money Bhi'gow would have made from our magic alone is a shit-ton, from my paltry understanding." Once she got a head nod from Jhi, she carried on. "So, you think she was holding magic for ransom, and it was purely a coincidence, even though you don't believe in coincidences, that it happened to be mine?"

"You're right. I don't believe in coincidences. There's something else to the ransom note."

The fact that Jhi wouldn't even entertain the possibility that Jaylyn was the Firebird sent Pepper into a fit of pique. "But why not tell you what's going on? You could have helped Jaylyn. You're searching Hell and Earth for her, for God's sake!"

"She didn't want to put me in unnecessary danger, probably, at least until she had gathered more intel. This conspiracy involves powerful players who wouldn't think twice about killing someone who could sabotage their plans. They murdered your sister and kidnapped Bhi'gow. JD and Mephy have gone missing after following the same trail as us. We just narrowly evaded capture ourselves. So, the fewer people who know, the better. Any more questions?" He didn't really mean the latter; annoyance peeked through his otherwise unflappable demeanor, his hands strangling the car's yoke.

"Why don't you want the others to know you're a soul broker and that Jaylyn was, too? What's the big secret?" Pepper needed to voice all her concerns. This could be the last time they'd be alone for a long while.

"Why don't you want them to know you're an Agent of Karma?"

Touché, Jhi. Always play your cards close to the chest.

Jhi had valid answers for every question Pepper lobbed his way, which was nothing short of infuriating. But she still wasn't wholly convinced that Jaylyn was on the up and up. Unfortunately, all she had to go on was her gut, so she had no choice but to table her suspicions for the time being.

"So, what I was about to mention before we went off track with your JD suspicions—"

"Oh yeah, the loophole."

"Yeah, that little thing. So as I was saying: A prize awaits those who manage to exploit a soul-contract loophole. As in invincibility."

"And by its very definition means unstoppable." Dread enveloped Pepper. She foraged through her go-bag for food, but all that remained was a stray salted pixie wing and a lone chocolate raisin—not nearly enough to feed the mounting stress and worry! Still, she inhaled them both and chewed slowly.

"True, but I firmly believe that every being, gods and goddesses included, has an Achilles heel, invincibility notwithstanding; the tricky part is uncovering what that is. To defeat an enemy, you must know him better than he knows himself. What makes him tick. His habits. Preferences in lovers and the like. Unfortunately, gathering that kind of intel requires patience and time. One of which we don't have much of."

Hands tied and her back to the wall, defeatism was chipping away at Pepper's resolve, and she averted her attention to the environs, the better for stifling tears of frustration.

Jhi cupped his hand over hers and gave her a gentle squeeze. "I've been in my fair share of situations that spelled certain death, where I was surrounded by hostiles, and I couldn't see a way out, yet I never once gave up the hope that Seren would come through. There's a reason she's the patron saint of thieves and assassins."

"Well, you're alive, so clearly luck is perennially on your side. Or you're just a modest badass. Or both."

"Can't argue with the truth." He half-smiled. "You know perfectly well what I'm trying to say."

"Yes. While I appreciate your pep talk, you have magic on your side, and I don't," Pepper barked.

"We have a lead on your magic, so I wouldn't give up on that so quickly."

"I wouldn't call an encrypted ransom note a lead. Even if we could decode the message, we're trapped in Hell. Let's face it, I'm a dead girl walking." Pepper wanted her dad more than ever. And food, lots of carb-ridden food.

"You burning what little time we have for a pity party no less is fruitless. I need your head in the game, Pepper. And that demand is not up for debate. You have two choices: to live or die. By choosing the former, you think of nothing but survival and how to achieve it. If the latter, then tell me now, and we'll call it a day." Ruthless, that's how Jhi came across.

"We. Are. Trapped!" Pepper reiterated. "Unless faux-Mephistopheles is a lying liar, and the Syndicate isn't monitoring rukbas. I mean, is that even possible to accomplish?"

"Hell is the epitome of a surveillance state. Freedom is an illusion. Eons ago, the King of Darkness mandated that all ever-active inter-dimensional rukbas—think of them like regular doors in your home, as in they don't require summoning, and are permanent—were to be destroyed. Now, they're operated by civil servants assigned to the Inter-Dimensional Protection Agency. And all inter-dimensional chaosnauters are delivered to various chaosports throughout Hell. That way, his draconian regime could monitor all comings and goings. Don't get me wrong, unauthorized rukbas exist. But between paid snitches and a harsh sentence in the labor camps at Oblivion's Fortress for law-breakers, even if you ferreted out one, chances of not getting caught are slim at best. But that's what I excel in—not getting caught!"

Pepper stewed in terrifying silence as they soared back to de facto mission control.

Whether it was the silence; Jhi's sobering pep talk; Pepper's will to survive; not disappointing her father; wanting her magic, dammit!; Jhi swearing up and down that his precious JD was innocent, the hazy mystery began to sharpen. Jhi might have had his theories about his girlfriend, but Pepper had her own.

The Hounds of Hell started sniffing around the Tavern not long after Jaylyn took the position of barkeep, then disappeared around the same time as Jaylyn. Jaylyn only worked at the Tavern for a few months, tops, long enough to get what she needed to break into Bhi'gow's laboratory—the goal all along. Once the Syndicate put their surveillance system into place, perhaps a daisy chain of Talking Heads on the Firebird's payroll alerted Jaylyn to the connection between Zho'zho and Bhi'gow.

While working undercover, maybe Jaylyn gave the Hounds a heads-up when she first spotted the First Underlord. So were the vamps stalking the Tavern because of Mephistopheles, or were they hired muscle for Jaylyn? Talking Head Nancy asserted the Hounds were meeting up with Jaylyn at the Tavern. But was Nancy even a reliable witness?

Jaylyn disappeared shortly after stealing the Li sisters' magic, which was around the same time as her fight with Sawyer, so had she stolen the magic before or after meeting up with the rogue Agent of Karma? Is that why the girls were rendezvousing, to discuss the stolen magic? If so, the girls were in cahoots. Perhaps they had a falling out, and Sawyer offed Jaylyn. Even so, both events took place a short time ago, right around Pepper's seventeenth birthday.

What made little sense was the encoded ransom note. Zho'zho had taken a liking to Jaylyn and probably divulged some closely guarded secrets; Pepper agreed with Jhi on that front. Unfortunately, Pepper couldn't prove this, as a fur'moria had most likely scrubbed Zho'zho's memory clean of all conversations between the two.

Still, why would Jaylyn, the Firebird, leave a ransom note for the very demon she was holding prisoner? Not even Jhi had a good explanation for that.

A frisson of fear shot through Pepper. The note wasn't meant for Bhi'gow. The magic might have been precious to the fixer, but it was even more precious to its rightful owner—Pepper!

Then there was the missing First Underlord. Mephistopheles' patronage of the watering hole had continued until recently, up until his disappearance. All that time, the First Underlord was aware he was being watched by the Hounds, even gave Zho'zho hush money, and had to resort to subterfuge. But who was he meeting in secret? Someone who was in danger? Someone the Hounds were after? Someone important enough to the First Underlord that he would endanger his life for them?

As she began piecing the puzzle together, her mind was inundated with images and remembrances. Miles Leagan on the news saying Karma is dead. The world in a crime-ridden state. People committing crimes with impunity. Injustices not righted. Pepper receiving the Karma Academy invite in the mail. Sawyer, an Agent of Karma, gone rogue. The slaying of an Initiate who had allegedly attempted to chaosnaut to the Academy. Karma Academy's supposed infiltration. Jaylyn, the Firebird, taking the magic belonging to an Agent of Karma Initiate and leaving behind a ransom note. The disembodied voice guiding Pepper to Mephistopheles' effigy. The history between Karma and Mephistopheles. The peace treaty between Hell and Earth. Mephistopheles' disappearance. What did they all have in common?

"Goddess Karma!" Pepper squirmed in the bucket seat, adrenalized as all get out. "That's who Mephistopheles was meeting! 'Thick as thieves,' those were Sala'dee's words regarding Karma and Mephistopheles. Jhi, what if that's who the Firebird is after?

What if they want to kill Karma, and to do so, they have to first get rid of her Agents?"

Jhi's eyes were fever-bright. "Pepper, you might be on to something. What if Agents of Karma are the goddess' Achilles Heel, and that's why their very existence is cloaked in secrecy? Or *was* cloaked and would explain why the Syndicate needed to recruit Sawyer? Which means right now, if your theory is correct, Karma could be severely weakened."

"Oh God, that would explain why justice isn't being served on Earth. Why good people are being punished while the wicked are rewarded."

Jhi's face screwed up with concern. "And if Karma is no longer presiding over Earth, then this overlord, after his resurrection on All Hallows' Eve—tomorrow!—will take over Karma's reins. Making war on Earth a foregone conclusion."

"*They've* had the upper hand for over a decade, essentially engaged in psychological warfare, convincing lowlies to join their cause. Bunny was just one of many victims. Once the war officiates, nothing will change." Pepper's blood chilled. "At least not for lowlies who are oblivious to the existence of magic and other dimensions, of demons champing at the bit to inhabit their bodies. It'll be business as usual. The wolves are wearing sheep's clothing."

"No, the wolves are the sheep. Lowlies agreed to sell their souls. Agreed to turn on their neighbors. The ability to wield magic was the sweetener, a sample of what's to come."

"We need to contact Karma, summon her! There has to be a way!"

"You don't summon gods. They come to you. Mephy obviously had a direct link of contact with the goddess, but by kidnapping him, the Firebird's syndicate cutoff Karma's support system and all lines of communication."

"If I had my magic, I bet I could initiate contact with her. Don't ask me how I know that. It's just a gut feeling. But seeing as someone stole my magic ...!" At the brink of frustration, tears stung Pepper's eyes. She couldn't warn her sisters-in-arms, who were in imminent danger, nor could she help Goddess Karma. For as long as she was magicless and trapped in Hell, powerless Pepper would remain.

Then the hitch in her throat stilled, and it was almost as if she could hear her father, as if Larry were sitting beside her, whispering a message he'd drilled into Pepper time and time again: *If you ever find yourself lost and are stumbling around a dark path, there's always a way out. Remember, Pepper, I'm always with you, heart and soul, so use that certainty as a beacon to banish the darkness and find your way back to me. We are each other's light.*

A *beacon* ... or signal fire. The business card at Walt's marina. Kimball setting it aflame, revealing a way-sign, the Firebird's MO, if you will. All the remembrances flitted in her mind's eye. *Meet me at hearth and home.* Jaylyn and the Firebird used the same MO, the same calling card. Could that be the smoking gun, proving that the Firebird and Jaylyn are actually the same? Jaylyn didn't uncover the conspiracy; she had been spearheading it the whole time.

"Hearth and home is another word for fire." She swallowed lumps of hysteria that threatened to surge. The trail of clues hadn't run cold, but was a blazing inferno. "Jhi, we have a destination! Now, all we need is one of those ever-active rukbas. Here's hoping Seren can spare us some more of her Grace."

CHAPTER 26

After Pepper and Jhi divulged the whole schmear of their time spent gallivanting—Perrin's choice of words—around Hell, Perrin said in a huff, "Nothing more than a sidekick to a lowlie, that's what the DISI painted me out to be! What the fuh'kar? Consider my reputation sullied!"

A furious red blotted out Perrin's peaches-and-cream complexion. Her wrist flicked up and down as her death-dealing yo-yo ate the string, then vomited it back out, the second verse the same as the first.

Noting that Pepper and everyone else not-Perrin wore looks of concern, she spat, "WHAT? Yo-yoing calms me, so it's either this or heads will be rollin'." She sighed. "Please tell me it was at least a flattering mugshot?"

"Perrin, your support and concern for my well-being truly warms the cockles of my heart." To match her sarcastic tone, Pepper affected being choked up by pursing her lips, placing her hand over her heart, and nodding in solidarity before getting back on track. "So, as you can see," Pepper said, wrapping up her appeal to the room full of allies, "we have to figure out a way to reach Karma because her life's in jeopardy. Now, I think I scored us a ticket outta Dodge with that note Jaylyn left behind. Slight hiccup though, it's null and void without an active rukba. No pressure, but we have until tomorrow to stop the resurrection. To stop the looming war. To stop my inevitable death! So, if anyone knows of one such gate, *please* speak up now."

Bhi'gow and Loki exchanged knowing glances before communicating covertly.

"Scuttlebutt has it that Karma is not to be trifled with. Tread lightly, they say, with that goddess," Zho'zho simply stated. "Now, Pepper, I'm not at all contesting the veracity of your claims, but do you and Jhi firmly believe that Karma is truly in danger?"

They nodded assent.

"Karma's the enforcer on Earth. She keeps humans and demons in check, no? So, if she were to disappear, then ..." Perrin proffered that what-if in hopes it would incubate.

"Then that would mean that an evil unlike anything the Earth has ever known will be unleashed, and Karma'll be powerless to stop it." Bhi'gow said, after wrapping up his tête-à-tête with Loki.

"Then, once Karma's out of the picture, the Firebird's syndicate would rule the Earth like warlords, committing sundry execrable act after another with impunity, and the free world we know would cease to exist. But that scenario blighted Earth eons ago, which was the reason behind the forging of the peace treaty, the very one enacted by Karma and Mephistopheles," Jhi stated.

"Let's say I happen to know where one could find an active rukba." Bhi'gow adjusted his wiry spectacles. "But I'm going to need some reassurances before I spill. Should you be walking into a trap set by the Firebird, have any of you conjured up a plan of action?" The hellfire devouring Bhi'gow horns gleamed with concern, which mirrored his expression. "Loki and I are in agreement that there's an air of deception around Jaylyn. And the Firebird's identity remains a mystery. Who's to say she isn't this Jaylyn or wearing her face as a disguise?"

Ah-ha! Bhi'gow and Loki were on the same page as Pepper. This couldn't have been more perfect. Bhi'gow just gave Pepper the ammo she needed for a full-blown assault against Jaylyn. Trafficking in duplicity, Jaylyn had clearly been living a double life that didn't include Jhi. Hell, he didn't even know her real name until recently. But that painful truth had yet to put a kink in the man of mystery's unflappable demeanor, which burned Pepper up something fierce.

"Excellent points, Bhi'gow," Pepper said. "No, we haven't whipped up a plan. And we won't until we're all in agreement that Jaylyn choosing to sling drinks and tend to rowdy tipplers at the Tenth Circle was a calculated maneuver on her part so that she could steal my magic—"

Jhi cut Pepper off. "I thought we went over this already." His eyes bore into her. "If JD's the Firebird, then what was her motive in stealing your magic and leaving a note behind for the very fixer she's holding prisoner? What if JD was bewitched? A few short hours ago, you would've done anything for a certain archdemon who shall remain nameless."

Pepper's nostrils flared, her mouth bowed in a wry grin. The hell she'd lose this verbal sparring match, stiff competition notwithstanding. "What's her *motive*? Uh, catching me at all costs. A Plan B, if you will, should we foil her dastardly Plan A. It's not like Bhi'gow was making like a canary. Why else would the Hounds of Hell, who work under the Firebird's purview, have picked the Tenth Circle as a prime spot for conducting their nefarious business if not for Jaylyn? Plus, Jaylyn's using my stolen magic as bait, same MO with holding Bhi'gow. Also, she didn't leave that ransom for Bhi'gow by mistake, Jhi. She left it for me! And you know what, her plan's working. I'll do whatever it takes to get my magic back." The more something seemed out of reach, the more Pepper wanted it. Needed it.

While dueling, the tongue-slingers were oblivious to all save for each other. Meanwhile, their captive audience, gargoyles included, watched with rapt attention, their heads pinging back and forth from Jhi to Pepper.

"And, Jhi, seeing how you're afflicted with selective memory, do allow me to remind you of the eyewitness testimony of Talking Head Nancy. She ID'd Jaylyn as the associate slash boss the Hounds of Hell were meeting at the Tenth Circle."

"So said the earless and therefore deaf damned with cataracts, and with those winning credentials, she'd never be allowed to sit on a grand jury. May wonders never cease. C'mon, what else have you got, because, sweetheart, I'm on a roll?"

How Jhi valiantly defended his girlfriend like Sir Galahad, the way in which he'd swing his mighty sword and parry every scurrilous claim aimed at Jaylyn, caused Pepper to swallow back bile. "Well, Jaylyn, in the least, is a common thief! You can't deny that!" Pepper's hands balled into fists.

Beetle-browed, a perfect storm scudded across Jhi's sea-glass eyes for a beat before dissipating just as quickly. Then he was back to the picture of unflappability and countered with, "Those in glass houses shouldn't cast stones. JD might be a thief. I can't contest that, but she's an accomplished one, as in her criminal record is unblemished." Unlike Pepper's is what Jhi didn't say. How did he know about Pepper's arrests? "For the last time. JD. Is not. The Firebird!"

Feeling clammy, her heart twisting in her chest, Pepper was finally struck with the realization that Jhi would never valiantly defend her like he did Jaylyn, his girlfriend. Sure, he cared about Pepper, fought alongside her, was loyal, but that's how friends act. Just friends. That's what Jhi and Pepper were to one another.

Perrin noticed Pepper's abnormal silence and proffered Pepper her flask.

"One tenet of enemy-slaying is to destroy them from within." Bhi'gow intervened, his speech directed toward Pepper and Jhi. "All one needs to do is plant the seeds of discourse within a faction and walk away. And I must say, the fighting between you two is not only divisive, but'll ensure the Firebird remains victorious. Now is not the time for disputes."

"Pepper, I'm sorry about what I said earlier—about casting stones. Everyone in this room, we lie, cheat, steal daily. It's in our covenant as demons." Jhi's backpedaling was for naught, as far as Pepper was concerned, so when he tried to meet her gaze, she looked away but grudgingly accepted his apology all the same.

Perrin took the preverbal mic. "Tick-tock, demons … and human. We have a resurrection to stop. Fact, the Firebitch has orchestrated quite the media-savvy smear campaign. Because of her, there's a dimension-wide manhunt for *me*. And the wanted posters with *my* name and face—and Pepper's, too—are making it that much easier for demons to ID me—or us. Hate to admit it, but the Firebitch outflanked us. Pinned us in a corner."

"Which is precisely why we must entertain the possibility that the Firebird's diverting you to a direct route, i.e., the alleged embedded way-sign in the note that was left behind by Jaylyn," Bhi'gow added.

"There were security measures put in place *years* ago at Skul-duggerer's Lair." Jhi's mask of unflappability slipped a tad. "JD only just left this note in recent weeks. Still, wherever that way-sign leads us, there could be another breadcrumb waiting. Another breadcrumb leading us right to JD." Hunger burned in Jhi's eyes, which killed Pepper anew.

"Then, it's settled. Take any magical supplies you deem neces-sary from the laboratory, and once you've armed yourselves to the teeth, we'll rendezvous in the burial chamber. And hopefully, this note will prove fruitful." Bhi'gow rose and excused himself. Loki followed suit.

"Well, I wish you guys well on your journey, and may Seren tag your heels and Shi'rue the enemy's." Perrin began to take her leave into the kitchen chamber, her goyles trailing after her.

"Perrin," Pepper called out, to which the Lolly'ka spun on the heels of her patent-leather Mary Janes. "You can't stay in Pandæ-monia. You're not safe here."

"Oh, sweetling has a soft spot for little ole me." She feigned sincerity well.

Pepper wasn't about to stoop to obsequious levels in the name of convincing the living doll to join their army, but honesty drenched in honey wouldn't do any harm. "I do actually. You're partially the reason why I still have a pulse and why you've earned a few more kill notches on your yo-yo." That statement forced a smile to touch Perrin's pouty lips. "What I'm trying to say is that your prowess for inflicting savagery and your impressive knowledge of battle strategy are vital for our mission."

After much whiny dithering and kicking around limestone silt sprinkled about the floor, Perrin grudgingly agreed to accompany Pepper and Jhi to Earth. "I hate Earth; it's so boring," she said petulantly, more to herself.

"Sweetling, hold up. I'd like a moment, just you and me." Perrin grabbed Pepper's arm and escorted her to a private corner of the great chamber, steps from a crackling fire, and waited for *all* to disperse before speaking, the "all" being Jhi. "We could be chaosnauting into an ambush." Wearing a wise-cracking mask no more, Perrin's grave expression caused Pepper to cringe.

"And …?"

"*And* I'd like to continue being fleshy and living the good life, queenpinning and ruling the warrens of Hell, not become an amorphous ball of ectoplasm, like a common spook. Our team is only as strong as our weakest link. That would be you. So, get your head in the fuh'karing game. Pepper, you won't last a minute when you come face-to-face with the Firebird. Not unless you divorce yourself from your feelings. Feelings get you killed. In the least, they weaken you. Can be exploited. And by looking at your face, I've more than proven my point." Who was this Perrin?

"I—I don't know what you're talking about," Pepper lied.

"No? Well, allow me to enlighten you. Jaylyn might be many things, archbitch to you, master thief to Bhi'gow, *lover* to Jhi." That pellet of truth that Perrin cruelly lobbed felt like a swift kick in the gut. "But the Firebird she isn't, at least I'm not fully sold. Only you can't see that patently obvious truth because jealousy clouds the prism through which you view Jaylyn."

Cheeks ablaze, Pepper cringed with mortification.

Perrin slaked her parched rosebud lips with balm. "I get it. You want what you can't have, and the longer you go without it, the more desirable it becomes until it consumes your every thought. But when balancing on a double-edged knife, eventually, you'll get cut to shreds. Boys like Jhi—they get their rocks off from basking in fawning adoration. Yet *you'll* never get closer than an arm's length to him. No, that spot's reserved for his lover. Still, the moment a boy like that notices you pulling away, he'll step up his flirting, draw you to him once more, till he's got you right where he wants you. And the vicious cycle continues. See, you're hooked, and Jhi's the drug until you kick him cold turkey."

Perrin walked away, but not before she said over her shoulder, "Let Jhi go before you wind up like your sister."

CHAPTER 27

Fluttering heart and creeping blushes, blissful sighs and perennial grins, you're swinging on a star, and the world's your yo-yo when you're in love.

Yes, it was true; romantic love had been dawning within Pepper and was ever rising towards its zenith, coaxed by none other than Jhi's mixed messages. Until Perrin's truth-pellets knocked Pepper off her celestial perch and sent her tumbling down and down. But ecstasy wouldn't be waiting at the bottom to catch her in its arms, not since her romantic stirrings had been downgraded to that of demoralizing puppy love.

For those poor unfortunate souls gripped by that cruel unrequited shade, their falling ended with a crash to the unforgiving earth, all by their lonesome. Nobody ever talked about the brokenhearted or how their fluttering hearts would be replaced by gaping holes that courted the likes of festering misery. As for the creeping blushes, Pepper would keep those on a tight leash. At least, that was the plan.

Honestly, Perrin's words, albeit cruel, scared Pepper. And this wasn't exactly Pepper's first rodeo, her first time grappling with unrequited love, crushing hard on the unavailable. So perhaps it was best to let Jhi go. But not before she said her piece. Then she'd lavish her undivided attention on looming dread and uncertain death that were waiting in ambush.

Go-bag at the ready—her heart not so much—Pepper made her way to the burial chamber reserved for Bhi'gow's ancestors. A chilly zephyr winnowed past her neck by way of greeting. At least, she hoped it was the wind. Plunged in the bleak darkness, Pepper couldn't even see her hands.

Right on her heels was the boy she had to see about. Pepper wasn't sure whether to kiss him or curse him—ah, wasn't unrequited love grand?

As if sensing visitors, hellfire ignited within myriad suspended-and-standing braziers that were scattered about the towering chamber. Barring Pepper's wrath, the air was redolent with an ancientness that predated the dawn of civilization, and ominously lurking in its shadows was the message: *Mind your manners, interlopers, one false step and you're dead.*

Taking that warning to heart, Pepper took catlike steps, but each tiptoe echoed about the dead-quiet chamber, potentially waking up slumbering demons. Her blood chilled from the mere thought. Or perhaps that was attributed to her imminent confrontation with Jhi.

From Pepper's limited perspective, the burial chamber was divided into three sections. Two low-ceilinged wings flanked the towering, cavernous center. And the far walls of the entrance wing resembled cobweb-encrusted honeycombs that cocooned the dearly departed.

Her sneakers scraped along the silty stone earth as they meandered past fresco-like renderings, appearing like wallpaper borders, depicting a bloody crusade that seamlessly hugged the uneven contours of the wall as it curved into the main section of the chamber.

According to Jhi, the sanguinary Battle of Pandæmonia that pitted Queen Lilith against the recently ousted-from-Heaven Lucifer and his fellow mala'dayyas was about as epic as a crusade could get. And judging from the forbidding renderings, Jhi wasn't far off the mark. More like underplayed the holy crusade. Hell's soil was stained eggplant and littered with bludgeoned and impaled corpses of gargoyles, dragons, fork-tailed devils, and mala'kha alike. Decapitated heads were crudely shoved on spikes and sticky gore coated the batons and stained the soil with viscous matter.

Pepper had unknowingly crossed the threshold of the main area. Tearing her eyes away from the violent and beyond savage depictions, she was in awe of the chamber's vastness. The chamber proper was large enough to house a monstrous cruise ship that her dad hosted on. In fact, this chamber dwarfed all the others in the pyramid and made them feel more like cubbyholes in comparison.

At the anterior of the chamber—at the opposite end from where Pepper was stationed—upright sarcophagi held the majority of the walls hostage except for a duet of gilded coffins that rested on a dais, most likely housing the patriarch and matriarch of Bhi'gow's extended family tree if Pepper ventured to guess.

Sprinkled hither and thither—in Pepper's vicinity—were stone benches and altars. Numerous deities' feet were smothered with bearded candles and remains of the damned; yellowy bones and remnants of bloody entrails marred the ground.

Feet away and directly across the entrance wing was another low-ceilinged room. Lines of sundry demons, flawlessly carved into the limestone walls, bracketed the room, the statues brandishing menacing swords. A sea of eyes appeared to follow Pepper's every movement. *Ye intruders, beware!* the sentinels silently warned.

More ghostly zephyrs wafted about the dank chamber. Lashing back at the taunting wind, flames inside braziers sputtered and guttered and cast clawing shadows on the demonic sentries, tricking the eye to make it appear as if the sentries were animated, and that at any moment they would spring out of their stone encasements and lay siege on intruders. A trick of the eye. Yes, that was Pepper's theory, and she was sticking to it.

Pepper hugged her arms around her chest, not so much to ward off the biting chill in the air but the disquieting chill that reverberated up her spine.

After sneaking up on Pepper, Jhi placed his jacket around her, then gently cupped his hands around hers and brought them to his lips, where he blew hot air on her skin.

Her mind was angered at his questionable gesture, but that cursed heart of hers revved, and dammit, was that a blush creeping up her neck? Did he forget about his girlfriend, the putative leader of the Hounds of Hell, or about their quarrel earlier? Pepper wiggled her hands out of Jhi's grasp.

"Sorry about before," Jhi said, his voice echoing about.

"For deriving delicious pleasure in dispelling my theories?" When Jhi nodded assent, Pepper said, "S'kay." Uh, no, it *so* wasn't okay. "Wait. It's not okay." Pepper took a deep breath, hoping to calm her nerves. "I don't appreciate your mixed messages. One second, you're flirting with me. The next, you're sniping at me because I dared to say what everyone's thinking, that Jaylyn could very well be the Firebird."

Jhi's brow and nose crinkled. What about Pepper's statement did Jhi find confusing?

On a roll, Pepper continued. "I'd probably feel the same exact way if it were my boyfriend everyone pointed the finger at, accusing him of committing heinous crimes. It must be soul-crushing to be *betrayed* by the girl you love." She might have spat the word "betrayed," just a tad. "But I'll tell you this much. I wouldn't be holding hands with another boy or leading another boy on! My heart would belong to him and him only, you mixed-signal-giving, two-timing jackhole!" Oh, that felt *awe*-some! Pepper's lips quirked into a grin.

"*Girl I love?* Hold up. So you *are* under the impression that I'm romantically linked to JD?" Incredulousness laced Jhi's tone. "I wasn't sure for a while, but then—" Jhi made no attempts to conceal his mirth nor the barrage of chuckles that vomited out of his mouth.

"Um, gee, I wonder what gave me that impression? Oh, I don't know, perhaps the times you either expressed or confirmed that Jaylyn was your girlfriend. And not once did you ever deny the claim or set the record straight." This boy infuriated Pepper so.

"I refuse to waste precious time and energy correcting people who jump to their own conclusions. They'll do what they want, regardless. Secondly, JD is a girl, and she's my friend who also happens to be in danger. And I'll do whatever it takes to protect my friends. Ever cross your mind to ask me point-blank?"

"In my defense, you care about JD, so I just assumed—"

"What, guys and girls can't be friends?"

"Not when one has feelings for the other." Had Pepper seriously just detonated that truth bomb?

He delicately clutched Pepper's hands in his once again. "I can count on one hand those I would risk life and limb for, and now there's one reserved for you." He sweetly kissed a finger on each of her hands, causing gooseflesh to hatch along her arms.

"A part of me feels like I don't know the real you. That I had you pegged all wrong." Pepper could hear Perrin's warning, appearing more and more like a premonition at the edge of her mind. Was this Jhi's attempt at drawing Pepper back in? Confused, she put some space between them.

"I'm no angel, sweetheart. I lie, cheat, steal, and kill if need be. It's in our DNA as humans, after all." He winked. "I'm perfectly imperfect. An unapologetic, distrusting misanthrope. And that's on a good day. Everything you've seen of me thus far is the real deal. Take me as I am or not at all."

Pepper latched her eyes onto his lips, especially the bottom one, plump and prime for nibbling.

Jhi stepped closer, crushing the space between them. "Should today be my last, and I'm bested by my nemesis Death, I fear that I'll be doomed to spend eternity lamenting for what could have been. For letting a girl like you slip through my fingers." Jhi's mouth hovered tauntingly close to hers, his breath feathering against her flushed skin.

"Anyway. Yeah, so I'm glad we had this talk." Pepper's nerves were awfully chatty.

Jhi's pillowy lips parted ever so slightly. Pepper responded by leaning in with breathless anticipation.

His fingers hooked errant strands of ebony hair behind her ear before they delicately traced the contours of her cheeks, then journeyed lower.

"I, uh, OH—"

Jhi cupped Pepper's slender face in his hands, dipped his head, then silenced her nervous mumblings with his soft lips, lips that tasted like pomegranate-laced nirvana. He didn't need to tug her closer, for she willingly fell into him, snuffing all the space between them.

Her greedy hands traveled the length of his back, up to his shoulders and neck, then to his tousled hair, where she knocked his beanie to the floor so her fingers could happily frolic about.

His tongue parted her mouth and flicked against hers as their kissing intensified. Soft and slow, yet intense all the same.

Jhi's hands adventured down Pepper's back to her bum, squeezed her tush, and pushed her even closer into him. A current of passion carried the young lovebirds away, and they were oblivious to the world around them, lost in each other. Just him and her and no one else.

So, when Jhi halted and stepped back for a breather, a sense of longing struck Pepper down, her lips hungering to be fused to his once again. Eyes fluttering open, she wanted for nothing but Jhi's strong arms to entwine around her waist, for skin to touch skin. To feel his touch.

"I've wanted to kiss you since the moment we first met. There's something about you, Pepper, that drives me crazy."

On her tippy-toes, she responded in the only way she knew how, by delivering to Jhi the Goldilocks of smooches; it wasn't a peck, nor was it a marathon make-out session, but it sure packed a punch as evidenced by his devilish grin and eyes that smoldered with lust. With that, Pepper was victorious in her goal of making Jhi want more.

He pulled back, out of breath, then scratched his head as if he had forgotten his train of thought, to which Pepper silently giggled. After all, she felt the same way, as in her thoughts were myopic and focused on Jhi. And what kind of delicious trouble they could get into.

Jhi extracted an apothecary jar jammed with swirling, multi-hued vapor that *pinged!* off the glass. If Pepper had any hope of surviving, she couldn't exactly venture through the chaosgate to the fearsome unknown sans magic. "Bhi'gow tasked me with doing the honors."

Pepper tried to snag the jar from Jhi's grip.

"Not so fast! Before you imbibe this borrowed magic, let's get some basic sorcery out of the way." Jhi spoke rapid-fire. Magic casting was a two-step process. Thinking about that which you desire, then willing it into existence. "Intention and confidence, a heart-mind coherence, are the foundations for spell casting. Add in gems and blood offerings, and you can summon gods and elemental spirits, et cetera. Listen closely. You must know *exactly* what you want to happen. *You* are in control. Nobody else. Magic isn't lazy. Watch and learn." His eyes looked in a downward direction. "This is what I want to happen."

The zipper on Pepper's jeans navigated downward of their own accord, to which Jhi's eyes smoldered with lust.

"And I channeled the confidence that it is so. Even a kernel of doubt will thwart your attempts. You already know magic exists, so you should exorcise the doubt from your mind."

Jhi pulled Pepper to him, his arms wrapped around her waist, his eyes locked onto hers.

"I should mention that if you didn't want the zipper to lower, it wouldn't have been so easy for me." Jhi smirked and planted his lips on hers once again. He came up for breath, and added, "Try not to overcomplicate spells by overthinking them, like you tend to do about other things best left unsaid." He interrupted his tutelage with kisses on her neck. "Make sense so far?"

"Mm-hmm." Pepper was having a hard time focusing, what with thoughts of her and Jhi getting to know each other more intimately occupying the forefront of her mind.

"Now on to magic gems. The fulgurite gem, the marble that houses the magic, is divinely created. Gems enhance innate magical abilities and help make spells that much more powerful."

Jhi explained how magic gems were only effective for the magically inclined or those who once were and now lived on borrowed magics.

"Reds, oranges, and yellows. Those are fuel for magic, pick-me-ups, should your magic be on the fritz and you're in a bind. Or batteries for enchanted objects. Red being the cheapest and shortest lasting. Magic is like a muscle in the body that, if overworked, needs to be recharged. The greens, blues, indigos, and violets, now *those* are the powerhouses."

Jhi continued to explain how green was connected with matter, so should you wish to change it, that was the gem to use.

"What would blue do?"

"Communication?" How Pepper knew that was anyone's guess, perhaps because of some inherent knowing.

"Well done. And as for your reward …" Jhi's hands ventured into Pepper's jeans, through the open zipper, and over her underwear. "Blue is used in most spells." He kissed her ear. "It's a key ingredient." His tongue tickled her earlobe. "And a conduit. Blue communicates your intentions, magically speaking."

Jhi briefly mentioned how indigo fell in the realm of psychic energy, mind control, protection spells. Pepper was too distracted to ask a follow-up question before he ventured on to violet, the most powerful and sought-after of them all.

"Can mages cast magic without gems?" she asked in between kisses. "Can I? Can you?"

"Mm-hmm," Jhi breathed. "For simple things. Levitate a glass or lower a zipper"—a grin tugged at his lips—"no gems needed.

Big things, like summoning a god, changing matter, defying physics, never. Gems are a must-have for human mages. If not for Lucifer binding our magic, demons and denizens of Hell wouldn't need gems, as demons are directly tied to chaos. And chaos is magic in its rawest form. Mages can innately attune vibrationally to chaos found all around them, in the air you breathe, in nature. And magic-filled gems are the conduit through which mages channel powerful magic, putting them on the same playing field as demons and other beings."

The lesson concluded, and their making out began anew. Hands ventured to new unexplored places, their collective moans of ecstasy the only sound in the burial chamber.

Jhi pushed himself away, trying to catch his breath. "We better stop there before, you know."

Pepper somewhat agreed. They wouldn't be alone for much longer.

"Magic"—he struggled to corral his thoughts—"is … Oh, yes. I nearly forgot." He chuckled, his face flushed. He handed Pepper the jar taken from Bhi'gow's cache of magical powers. "That borrowed magic won't last for long, but in conjunction with your bag of gems and with your recently acquired knowledge, you should be able to protect yourself and not have to rely on others. Got it?"

His instructions were simple in theory, but most likely knotty in practice.

Here goes nothing. Pepper unstoppered the jar and gulped down the paltry contents. The formerly sealed vapor was highly misleading; the smoky mixture tasted more liquidy in nature, like a subzero caffeinated slushy, only without the fruit flavor. It traveled down the esophagus smoothly, then exploded, magic rushing through every vein in her body. Her internal thermostat climbed higher and higher.

Pepper was adrenalized, her body ablaze. In fact, she felt like running a marathon, scaling the walls, parkouring around Pandæmonia proper, making the buildings and roads her bitches, swimming every river in Hell.

Better yet, grabbing Jhi and making haste to a shadowy corner of the burial chamber, then committing acts of yummy foreplay, before ripping off his clothes and—

"Pepper, you okay? Your eyes are kinda bugging out of your head."

"Jhi, I feel—" Her hands trembled as she began pacing.

"Invincible?"

She nodded.

"That reaction should quiet down soon, hopefully."

Stone scraping against stone emanated near the entrance as company pushed the massive doorway open. The gang began trickling in.

An invisible barrier cordoned off the chamber Pepper had yet to explore, the one guarded by a phalanx of demons barring entrance. An offering is required to venture within. Bhi'gow slashed his palms, then placed his bloodied hands on one such guard as though in benediction. Once sated, a rhythmic cadence sounded and echoed about as the demons lowered their swords, one after the other, with mechanical precision. A vibration oscillated and frequency swelled, the bellwether of an enchantment.

The barrier parted like translucent curtains, revealing a chamber, rife with scattershot pillars, that was once cloaked from sight.

While everyone else crossed into the chamber, the lovebirds trailed behind, the overpowering need to be touching one another calling the shots. Fingers entwined. Skin brushing against skin. Short but sensual kisses exchanged discretely behind fat pillars. Pepper and Jhi couldn't get enough of each other. Their fervent mutual desire, the urgent need for privacy, and the inability to be alone drove them crazy.

One last kiss given, then one more, and then another for good luck, Pepper and Jhi reluctantly joined the rest of their party.

Bhi'gow threaded through the cadre of sigil-smothered pillars until they reached the far end of the room. Until they reached an ever-active rukba, arcane sigils thrumming along the curved frame. "Heed my warning: If word gets out about this rukba, the list of suspects will be short. And I won't have second thoughts about killing the rat."

Bhi'gow fed the chaosgate the remainders of his ichor, which triggered a door to snap open with a hydraulic hiss, revealing a stark white space with bench seats running along the walls.

Loki jumped off Bhi'gow's shoulders and stood next to Pepper.

Grinning from ear to ear, Pepper happily shot out her arm. Loki climbed up her appendage, then settled on her shoulders.

"With a heavy heart, I must report that Loki and I sundered our bond." Bhi'gow's eyes swam with sadness. "I wouldn't've agreed had Loki not insisted. He feels he can help you, Pepper, and keep you safe. Can't say I disagree. Though you won't be able to communicate telepathically unless and until you've undergone the Bonding Ritual. Only Loki can conjure *that* spell, and he'll do so at his behest." Bhi'gow devoted his attention to his companion. "Until we meet again, dear friend."

"I'll keep a weather eye on Bhi'gow, nurse him back to full strength, and keep my ears to the ground at the Tenth Circle." Zho'zho sounded like a proper soldier. "May Seren be with you, and Shi'rue overlook you."

Pepper stared at the slice of skin resting on the floor of the rukba at the note Jaylyn, the putative Firebird, had left behind. In her mind, she could see hellfire licking the words "meet me at hearth and home." Pepper felt a thrill snake over her spine; she puzzled out—hopefully—a lifesaving clue, trapped in Hell no longer.

Pepper envisioned precisely what she wanted to happen as she palmed gems of every color, because quite frankly, she recalled very little of Jhi's introduction to magic spiel, then voiced the words "singe JD's note." A flame of fire ignited and ate the words "hearth and home." And really, it wasn't so much hellfire, more of a hellspark, but still.

The note levitated, curled up on itself, then smoldered till it was a heap of ashes. Then the ashes joined forces and ferociously churned into a funnel-like shape. Five distinctive curlicue-ing sigils were spat out of the funnel; the peculiarities glued themselves along the stark white walls and glowed a fiery crimson, then vanished.

Doom befalls those who pluck the Firebird's fiery feather from the scorched earth and set out on a quest to hunt it down. Being right wasn't all it's cracked up to be, and for Pepper, she was downright terrified. Too bad because the hydraulic doors slammed shut, sealing them inside, a sobering reminder that there was no way out!

Why was everything appearing as a blurry streak? Before Pepper's mind could register that oddity, the elevator whipped off, hurling Pepper into the wall.

It was as if the Firebird had sunk her talons into the rukba and carried it and its hapless passengers off to her lair. Round and round the clock, they spun.

Then nothing. All motion halted.

The doors hissed open. Scant feet away was a run-of-the-mill door.

"JD's way-sign is unique to her and her only," Jhi explained. "Think of it like a Universe-issued email address, which means no two are alike. Not only is the way-sign unique, but it's also encrypted, so there will be no replicating it."

"Get ready, team, because once we walk through that door, there's no returning to this rukba." Perrin warned.

Pepper reminded herself that they had exactly one shot at getting this right. One shot to kill the Firebird. One shot at getting their next clue.

"If we're not on Earth, we could be anywhere in the cosmos." Double-fisting, Pepper squeezed the life out of Sawyer's blowpipe in one hand and a silver-dipped dagger in the other.

"That's what's so fun about it." Perrin's exuberance for danger was disturbing. While adjusting her coral headband that inter-dimensional traveling had knocked askew, her breath hitched, and eyes glinted with delight. "I just realized—I can freely cast magic! Without needing gems! Oh, the chaos I'll be creating!"

They established a pecking order for who would enter the Firebird's lair first, from strongest, magically speaking, to greenest: Jhi, tightly gripping a sawed-off shotgun, sated with silver buckshot, and Perrin, death-dealing yo-yo front and center, tousled for first place and ended up deciding to squeeze through the frame side-by-side; a dagger-wielding Loki trailing behind, who truth be told, probably should've been first—he was a divinity after all—then Pepper and that fearsome ability to conjure a hellspark, so that should keep the team alive, at least until the enemies' collective laughter subsided.

Grinning and salivating at the thought of a battle, Perrin simply stated, "Let's go get this Firebitch!"

CHAPTER 28

Not sure what Pepper had expected, but an attic wasn't a possibility, not even a viable contender.

Luckily, impenetrable darkness didn't blanket the attic, not completely, thanks to a scattershot of light lancing through planks of wood nailed over the windows. Spiders, the sole occupants, asserted ownership of all exposed beams and windows, their spinnerets toiling away from dusk to dawn.

Resting aslant, the door, formerly a chaosgate, had been unceremoniously tossed against the wall, doorframe and gargoyle-knocker present. Unable to resist, Pepper depressed the patinated latch and the door creaked open. Moldy wallpaper in various stages of wreck and ruin—an echo of the attic as a whole—greeted Pepper.

Unfurling before Pepper was a graveyard for jettisoned curiosities galore in various stages of disrepair. While joining her troupe, wood-planks griped and groused under her feet, which wasn't exactly helping with stealth mode.

When she toed a tattered baby doll out of her path, and it discordantly cried, everyone cast glares Pepper's way. She mouthed, "Sorry" to the perturbed.

Either that was the wind howling through the teensy rents in the decaying walls that resembled bullet holes, or—Pepper shuddered at the thought of what option number two could be.

Jhi ducked down as he traveled under the slanted walls, his destination the boarded-up dormer windows. Once Jhi freed the circular windows of their oppressors, bountiful sunlight splashed inside, drowning the gloom and doom that had held the attic hostage.

Aft to a cabinet housing the creepiest of porcelain figurines, Perrin stood stock-still and tapped her finger on her berry-stained lips. "Non-tinted windows. A fusty odor sans the delicious miasma of death and decay and abject fear. Ergo, this place is *so* not Hounds-of-Hell-friendly. Ugh, and I'm bored already."

Jhi retrieved a pearlescent glob from his backpack, tore it into bits and pieces, and tossed the scraps to the wood-planked floor. The rune-revealers scampered about, seeking their marks.

Soon, the attic was alight with glowing protective wards, every surface smothered. The arcane ruins forbade unsanctioned chaosnauting inside or out of the premises. No shock there. Not until the globs made contact with sigils written in the tongue of the Ancient Ones.

Pentagrams encased in circles, knots of runes jutting off the curves, each of those containing glyphs that jumped to life, intricate pattern after pattern popping into sight and shifting and changing, as if a ghostly mage were scribbling and erasing and rewriting.

"What's the difference between vocalized spells in conjunction with magic gems and the drawing of symbols in the tongue of Tun-fendin'ga?" Pepper ventured to ask, dreading the response.

"The former's child play while the latter means we're fuh'kared. We're dealing with primeval magic here, magic that comes at a price, more than just taking an innocent's life," Perrin said, her tenor somber. "I might not be versed in Tun-fendin'ga or know the first thing about the dark mystic arts, but I'm smart enough to know not to tangle with one who is."

"We better hope we're on Earth because if not …" Jhi let out his breath in a muffled whistle.

Pepper bristled at the thought and quickly chased away—or at least tried to chase away—her worries with Grissel's ale. Then tendered the flask back to Perrin, who did the same.

"The walls aren't the only thing that's smothered around here," Perrin added. "The air is as well. With spooks."

Far-off murmuring hitchhiked on a phantom zephyr. Though the chitter-chatter was disembodied and incoherent, it was disquieting nonetheless.

An arctic chill slithered over Pepper's cheeks, and white puffs of breath plumed from her mouth. She hugged her arms around her chest. The enemy you couldn't see was far worse to battle. And from the sheer drop in temperature, the unseen enemy was close at hand, like inches away from Pepper.

Pepper joined Jhi at a dormer window that had been relieved of its tyrannical sun-occluders. The roof below sloped dangerously, and its shingles were weather-beaten. But what had seized Jhi's attention was not the cartoonishly steep roofs, nor the absurd amount of chimneys or intricately ornate eaves and gables (and that was just one side of the estate), but what lay beyond.

"Anything look familiar? Anything at all?" Judging from Jhi's tone, he already knew the answer.

The house rested nearby a craggy cliff that loomed over a newspaper-gray ocean. In the distance, waves rolled and crashed ferociously as they crawled their way from horizon to shore, moving in lockstep with the swollen clouds scudding above. The lurking threat began to lay siege to the blazing sun and was moments from declaring victory.

At first, a light drizzle trickled down the windowpane, slightly warping the environs, then morphed into a torrential downpour. Soon, a murky gloom chased away the light outdoors, then stormed through the windowpane and flooded every nook and cranny of the attic.

Parched, unchecked grass mantled the terrain and hugged the

bluff; a klick away, swarms of moss dangled from the gnarled branches of a lonely, towering tree. Wrapped around one of its limbs was the rope of a swing, its tire swaying back and forth as if a ghost child occupied it. Pepper's eyes eventually landed on a pair of tombstones. The dearly departed's final resting spots were feet away from the gargantuan tree trunk and embraced by its canopied leafy branches.

Any minute now and Pepper would have to scoop her jaw from off the floor. "The—the oil painting hanging inside my house. The one painted by my landlord. What the hell?"

Eureka! said Jhi's eyes. The scenery beyond the dappled windowpane was a replica of the artwork painted by artist Wilhelmina Davidson, the current owner of Pepper's home in Naples, Florida.

The canvas Jhi and Pepper referred to—the one gracing the wall in Pepper's living room—depicted a rambling Victorian mansion captured in its heyday. The perspective of the painting would be as if the artist had set up her easel to best capture the lone moss-laden tree, the craggy cliffs suspended over the Pacific, and the manor all in one shot, save for the tombstones; those were recent additions, unfortunately. From Pepper's recollection, there would be a wraparound porch with a swing for two, sprouted turrets aplenty, and a truncated widow's walk.

Pepper and her pops would play a game to pass the time they'd dubbed *Would You Ever and For How Much?* This painting of Willa's, or more specifically the house depicted, would inevitably come up as a scenario every time. *Would you spend one whole night inside the obviously haunted manor alone for $1,000,000?* Pepper unfailingly would answer in the negative. No amount of cash in the world would suffice, yet ironically, here she was, inside the creepy mansion and did so gratis.

The potential for being trapped inside a painting existed, and before she voiced such a spurious claim, Pepper fished out her jilted cell phone (wireless providers weren't exactly Hell-friendly). While

Pepper anxiously waited for the phone to fire up, she prayed they were indeed in the Land of Milk and Honey, the individual liberty-adoring U S of A. Pepper sighed in sublime relief. "Guys, good news. We're definitely not stuck in some painting or in another world. According to the GPS, we're in Carmel-by-the-Sea, California."

At first delayed, a spate of voicemails and text messages blew up her phone, all from Kimball. Her sifting through them was interrupted.

"So, what's the connection between your landlord, Willa, and JD? And are we inside Willa's house, then?" Perrin inquired.

Pepper spewed all the intel that her dad had shared with her. *Money can buy many things, but happiness ain't one of them*, Pops was wont to say. And for Wilhelmina Davidson, that couldn't've rung more true. Before her pops had made Willa's acquaintance, death had ferried Willa's one true love, Willy, to the hereafter. Left with a fortune as vast as her heartache, Willa set out on a world cruise, and that was where she met Larry.

As a host, Larry was paid to entertain the single ladies by mentally flossing their minds with intellectual conversations and, of course, ballroom dancing after they'd devoured their seven-course meals. With a bit of patience and elbow grease, Larry Astaire—his sobriquet in the cruise circuit—not only coaxed Willa's lips to bow into a smile, but she morphed into a veritable Ginger Rogers, something Willa had craved. See, her husband, Willy, had been wheelchair-bound and couldn't waltz with the love of his life.

While Willa and Larry quickstepped to Shanghai, waltzed to the French Riviera, tangoed to the fjords of Norway, a platonic bond was forged. Soon, Willa offered her home in Naples, Florida, to a very homeless Larry with youngling Pepper in tow, with the stipulation that he also serves as a live-in home watch. *Be it ever so humble, there's no place like home*, and for Willa, home was Carmel-by-the-Sea.

"... childless and a widow, Willa lives alone in California.

She's the owner of my home, but in name only. Our rent checks are still cashed every few months. So, that's all I know."

"That so? Here, take a look-see." Jhi proffered his aviator shades to Pepper. After she slipped them on, Jhi stood behind her and took her hand in his, which sent chills to frolic about Pepper's arms, ditto for when he snuck a kiss on her neck, then navigated her fingers to the focus knobs on the shade's rims.

Pepper zoomed in on the two tombstones, then through trembling lips, she read the epitaphs aloud: "Here lies prankster Willy Davidson, a lively chap through and through, he vowed to return to his Willa one day, to dance while sailing the ocean blue." Her eyes journeyed to the second grave. "Here lies Willa Davidson, who bid the final adieu." Pepper gulped back a wad of fright, tightly wrapped in shock. "But weep not for her, for soon she'll return anew."

In utter disbelief, Pepper whispered aloud the year of Willa's passing. Jhi slipped the shades off Pepper's face, then hooked them on the collar of his Henley.

"Willa Davidson. Passed away. Six years ago," Pepper said incredulously. "Then who's been cashing the rent checks? Who's pretending to be her when I call?"

"C'mon, people. Use those pea-sized brains of yours before they atrophy due to lack of exercise, which could be at any moment now. So, here's where I spell out the obvious." Perrin spoke slowly for the thick amongst them. "JD. J for Jaylyn and D for Davidson."

Pepper couldn't join in on the skull session because stunned disbelief had arrested her, manacling her jaw shut. By rote, Perrin shoved the flask into Pepper's sweaty palm. "Maybe you should hold on to it."

"We're burning time. Best to keep moving." Jhi moved toward the stairs.

The attic lorded over a sprawling hallway, dotted by scores of closed doors. The walls revolted and declared war against the hideous rose-patterned paper that most likely colonized their surface well over a century ago, and currently, the walls were winning. They had peeled away vast amounts of the garish enemy. Frankly, the rotted sections of wood beneath that were exposed during the rebellion were more aesthetically pleasing than the former eyesore. As were the smattering of varying-sized portraits and pictures alike that bedecked the walls.

The wind ferried keening sobs and moaning dirges that howled past Pepper, then disappeared around the corner at the far end of the hallway. The lingering sadness was palpable.

"Uh, was that a ghost?" Pepper whispered the last word as if saying it aloud would welcome disaster.

Unfazed, the demons responded with a simple, "Yes."

Distracted, Pepper nearly tripped over a dead mouse, make that three; their putrefying corpses were slumped near the chewed sections of the baseboard. Pepper tore her eyes away from the deathly sight and cozied up next to Jhi, who was keenly observing a ridiculously large portrait.

"Meet the eleven or twelve-year-old version of JD," Jhi stated.

After one stolen gander of said portrait, Pepper immediately uncorked the flask and swilled more mood-blunter. Moments later, eight sundry orbs gawked at the peculiar photo.

At first, the portrait contained only hauntingly beautiful Jaylyn, leaning against the lone tree outdoors, her eyes latched on the tombstones situated off to the side—so she had been orphaned, and at such a young age? Nothing was out of the ordinary, so what had seized Jhi's attention? Pepper inspected further to find out.

Jaylyn's iron-straight ebony locks were perfectly parted down the middle. The white frilly dress she donned poofed out around her calves as if she had been spinning and spinning and the garment had yet to still. Barefoot, she dug her toes deep within the soft loam, so she wasn't exactly prissy by any stretch of the imagination. Though she didn't smile at the camera, the striking girl was due north of sad and squarely on happy; her rich, honeyed eyes reflected as much.

But then, Pepper didn't even know where to begin with the shock that had zapped into her with a vengeance; the ale was seriously slacking in its duties of taking the edge off.

A legion of ghosts materialized around Jaylyn. It was as if the portrait itself was a Halloween lenticular 3D gag, where, depending on the observer's perspective, the benign image morphed into a malevolent depiction. To be fair, the ghosts didn't exactly scream horror, nor did their presence spike terror in the hearts of observers.

In fact, the semi-transparent ghosts were rather jovial, their collective lips pinned back in hearty grins while they undoubtedly proclaimed "cheese" for the camera. And all were resplendent in diversified clothing, most likely denoting the time period in which death had visited them. Sure, the dearly departed made up the sum total of Jaylyn's family, but they deeply adored her.

In all honesty, what had caused Pepper to swill more Hellwater were the individuals bookending Jaylyn—Wilhelmina Davidson and her husband, Willy, standing feet away from their tombstones. Myriad frame photos captured more ghosts. And for years upon years, Pepper had been conversing with one ON THE PHONE! OH MY GOD! A head-exploding revelation right there.

"Look." Jhi pointed upward. "High school graduation class of one-year-ago; that's the JD I know." A festooned banner in the background bolstered Jhi's claim, obliterating any niggling doubts: CONGRATULATIONS JAYLYN. The soul-broker was resplendent in mortarboard and robe, diploma in hand. She stood between her beaming mom and dad—correction, her semi-transparent mom and dad, who could only be described as ghosts.

A furry hand grabbing Pepper's interrupted her stroll down memory lane. Loki guided Pepper to an end table, roughly five doors away, that was under siege by an army of more family portraits, and pointed to one in particular. Willa Davidson, her skin black, her body rotund, was very much alive when this picture was taken; however, Willy, her semi-transparent, lily-white-skinned husband, with a skein of gray hair, was not.

A young girl around the age of seven or eight, her slender legs draped over the kneeling matriarch and patriarch of the rambling Victorian abode, couldn't suppress her grin that traveled from ear to ear as she sat betwixt her parents. Neither could Willa, for her two-hundred-watt smile threatened to blind those in her presence as she wrapped her meaty arms around her little girl in a bear hug.

Ghost Willy echoed the same effervescent euphoria as his wife and daughter. And the cigar parked on his lips, the monocle positioned over his right eye, and jaunty suspenders all lent themselves to the same bubbly vibe.

But it was the girl who stole Pepper's attention. Or more like the scar that marred the right side of the youngling's face, dragging down her eye a tad. From cheek to ear, young Jaylyn's skin had been ravaged by a fiery inferno, from what Pepper surmised, just like she had back then. *Then* being when Pepper had gone back in time and witnessed through Loki's eyes Kassendra's death.

Pepper's heart *thump-thump-thumped* in her ears because she had unintentionally unraveled one mystery but couldn't yet voice the words. Her heart and mind were at odds.

The adjacent wall supported Perrin's weight as she *swipe-swipe-swiped* the point of her switchblade along the tip of her bubble-gum shellacked nails. "To be surrounded by you lot"—Perrin sighed hyper-dramatically—"well, it's not easy, at times exhausting, and it's clearly punishment."

Perrin finished her impromptu manicure and pocketed her switchblade before continuing.

"Being the only human around and an only child to boot, obviously JD was a nascent necromancer, who liberally dosed herself with borrowed magics, hence the raising of the dead and a plethora of playmates to curb the boredom. And I said borrowed magics because she had rendered up hers and Pepper's to Bhi'gow. Look at that. I just solved the mystery of why JD broke into Bhi'gow's home and pinched magic belonging to the Li sisters only. I amaze myself. Everyone, meet the elusive JD slash Jaylyn Davidson slash Kassendra slash Pepper's big sister slash spook girl—boy was that a mouthful."

"For the record, Bhi'gow said my sister died, and Loki was an eyewitness to Kassendra's death, so why would I have ever thought otherwise? Hell, I saw my sister die through Loki's eyes. Even so, in all the other pictures, Jaylyn's scarless."

"Magic. It's a wonderful thing and great for cosmetic enhancements." Jhi's eyes were riveted to the family portraits.

"Say Jhi, did JD ever mention having a sister?" Suspicion laced Perrin's tone. "You two were co-workers, no? And close enough friends for you to be scouring Hell and Earth for her."

"If she had, I would've mentioned it," Jhi responded over his shoulder.

Perrin dropped the subject, along with her keen stare at Jhi.

Pepper, however, couldn't do the same for the subject of the business card left behind by the Firebird and the note written by Jaylyn—both items were enchanted, and when lit on fire, they created secret destinations. Or was that common with mages?

"But then why did JD wait so long to break into Bhi'gow's pyramid? Wouldn't she have taken back her sorcery a helluva lot sooner instead of living off borrowed magic?" Pepper was still having a difficult time processing the news. Until a few minutes ago, Pepper had convinced herself that Jaylyn was the Firebird. What if this was, in fact, a ruse, a mind-screw enchantment of sorts, put in place by the Firebird to toy with Pepper's emotions? And boy, was it working!

"I'd venture to guess that the Davidsons had commissioned a fur'moria to extract memories of a life best forgotten from their adopted daughter's mind," Jhi said. "Who knows? JD could have been gripped by survivor's remorse, believing you were dead, Pepper, or captured by the Hounds of Hell. It's not like Bhi'gow was around to set the record straight. Or Loki. Plus, she bargained away her magic. That's enough to drive a mage into fits of madness."

"That's most likely what happened," Perrin added. "And explains why JD waited so long to take back her magic. Also, there's no way JD would've kept up the charade all those years if she knew who Pepper was, especially receiving care packages from her long-lost kin."

"Technically, the care packages were mailed by my pops, so y'know, it's not like my name was attached," Pepper added from over her shoulder as she padded further down the hallway. "Besides, if Jhi's right about the memory altering, then JD didn't even know she had a sister. Let alone that she was me—Jaylyn's my sister!" Pepper blurted out. "And she's alive!"

Her reaction was absurdly delayed, and she wasn't sure whether to cry or laugh from nervousness, but the sea of sundry orbs staring her way wasn't helping with keeping the salty betrayers at bay. So, in true Pepper fashion, she willed the emotion betrayers to return whence they came. And by will, Grissel's ale was to thank. Chin-chin, *glug-glug*!

Jhi's impatience was visibly fraying and moments away from snapping. "This kicking around of speculation is a colossal waste of time. Scurrilous claims were lobbed at JD, pegging her as the Firebird and Hounds of Hell associate, so we've officially cleared her name. Next on the agenda, locating her ASAP." The hunger in Jhi's eyes was fever-bright. Man-on-a-mission began opening doors to recommence sleuthing.

"What if she's already dead?" Perrin uttered in the background.

Pepper absently meandered away from the mystery-unraveling chitter-chatter and padded down the threadbare runner rug, inspecting a boatload of more photos that memorialized the Davidsons post-death. The Davidson Family sure enjoyed throwing soirées. Hell, this clan would probably throw a Gatsby-esque gala honoring the setting sun.

Yet, in all the photos, one constant remained—Kassendra-slash-Jaylyn's eyes glinting with unadulterated joy. If anything, that observation chased away encroaching melancholy and ushered in solace; as far as Pepper was concerned, Jaylyn deserved nothing but unmitigated joy and much, much more.

She studied Jaylyn for physical similarities. Her sister's skin was a shade lighter than Pepper's, her face round to Pepper's oval. As for her forehead, that was on the small side, unlike Pepper's, which was wide. A dimple graced Pepper's cheek, but the same couldn't be said of Jaylyn's. No, Jaylyn proudly wore her burn scar, almost like an accessory, at least until she reached puberty because that imperfection wasn't present in later photos.

It was hard to tell from photos, but it appeared as if height-wise Pepper clocked in a few inches more than her sister. And a few more pounds as well. Though they shared the same button nose, swan-like necks, and wide-set eyes, their irises twins.

Larry, on more than one occasion, had compared the shade of his daughter's eyes to "the best damn drink he's ever had," a rare 1949 single malt Scotch he had the pleasure of imbibing after returning from active military duty overseas, courtesy of a civilian thanking him for his service. Mirroring the Highland malt, the Li Sisters' eyes were a deep shade of amber with subtle flecks of gold —perhaps a family trait?

A door mere feet away creaked open. Beyond the threshold, the bedroom screamed: *A teenager lives inside me. A teenager who goes by the name of Jaylyn.* Pepper slipped out of her melancholic reverie and crossed over the threshold.

CHAPTER 29

Jaylyn had claimed one of the turrets of the Victorian dwelling and had a bird's-eye view of the lonely, sprawling property, not another residence in sight. Just endless cliffs and nothing but the wide-open ocean beyond.

Inside, a smattering of posters of American boy bands du jour and K-Pop idols alike jockeyed for attention from their positions on the walls. Pepper and her sister *so* did not share the same taste in the male persuasion; Pepper liked them edgier and devil-may-care, not fresh-faced and cloned.

Nor did Pepper share a fondness for neat-freaking like her sister. The bedspread—a riot of happy, happy colors—was ironed to perfection, nary a wrinkle to be found. Frilly accent pillows were perfectly lined up against the headboard. In fact, the bedroom was spotless save for a latticework of dust and could easily serve as a showroom for the latest teen trends in decorating.

The moment the others joined Pepper, the bedroom door slammed shut, locking them inside.

Panicking, Pepper tried to pry the door open. But it wouldn't budge.

A fire blazed in the hearth, angry flames licking the brick and spark screen, the heat intensifying by the second. Whatnots and trinkets shimmied on the fireplace mantel, a prelude to the rolling roar that barreled down the hallway, giving off the impression that a freight train was furiously chugging their way. The very foundation quaked. Windows rattled in their frames.

"We've been warned, so we better make this fast," Jhi said even-keeled.

Perrin stated measuredly that if the spooks wanted them dead, they'd be dead, so the dearly departed were instructing them to ferret out a clue to Jaylyn's disappearance that resided in her room. And should they be unsuccessful, well, Jhi said they'd table that what-if for the time being. Nevertheless, the pressure was on, so they divvied out sections of the bedroom to inspect thoroughly.

Pepper focused on the dual nightstands bookending the bed that served as command central for a cadre of neatly stacked tomes that ran the gamut from the lowlie-approved fantasies with a dash of forbidden romance to how-tos and what-not-to-do-evers! for the budding necromancer.

The haunting lilt of a music box interrupted pepper's frantic perusing. A few of the instruments' teeth were either warped or missing, which caused the melody to distort. In her quest for clues, Perrin had lifted the lid of a jewelry box perched atop a dresser. Inside, the shopworn ballerina drunkenly wobbled on her stage. But that wasn't what stole Pepper's attention. No, it was the cheval mirror next to the dresser and the incoherent whisperings that beckoned Pepper to come hither. Mechanically, Pepper gravitated that way, nearly tripping over wandering rune-revealers

Standing before the mirror, Pepper gazed absently into the glass darkly, beyond her reflection. A feeling of terror and dread enveloped her right as a tugging sensation erupted in her solar plexus. Giving in to the sensation, she leaned forward and—

"Your bangs could use some taming," Perrin said, sidling up next to Pepper in front of the mirror. "But other than that eyesore, you look … Actually, your skin's kinda oily and in dire need of powdering. And is that a pimple?"

"What—Oh, I wasn't checking myself out. I—okay, this is

gonna sound weird, but I swear something inside the mirror was calling to me."

A wayward rune-revealer rolled up the cheval mirror, paused, then rolled back down. Back and forth the glob ventured as if confused.

Perrin squatted down in front of the mirror to further inspect something that had caught her eye. "Looks like blood." Sure enough, a few droplets blended in perfectly with the cherry hardwood flooring.

Intimate knowledge alighted on Perrin's ethereal face. "The Order of Shi'rue, ever hear of it or them?" Perrin asked, to which everyone shook their heads no. "Not surprised. Most haven't. According to legend, the Order trafficked in portents, necromancy, and curses. And they didn't just dabble in the darkest of dark sorcery. They became one with it."

As Pepper backed away slowly from the mirror, Perrin watched her like a xykree.

"Need to transmute lead into gold, hex an enemy, destroy lives, exact vengeance, bring down kingdoms?" Perrin continued. "They were your go-to mages. Supposedly, they derived their godlike magical powers from Shi'rue, worshipped her even. Drank her blood. In fact, legend says they had a direct connection to Shi'rue and other dimensions through mirror magic. So secret was the art form, that only Initiates were taught the ancient magic and runic language used in speculuming."

"And you know this how?" Jhi asked Perrin. Something told Pepper they were one step ahead in the conversation.

"If not for Shi'rue double-crossing Lilith, Lucifer wouldn't be sitting on Lilith's throne right now!" Bitterness coated every word Perrin spoke.

"Wasn't what I asked," Jhi said.

"Let's just say I make it a habit to learn everything I possibly can about my enemies. Satisfied?"

"Someone want to fill me in?" Pepper asked. "Isn't Shi'rue the goddess of misfortune and curses?" When everyone nodded,

Pepper continued. "So, what does she have to do with the mirror or me?"

"Mirror magic and mirror walking," Perrin huffed, "the sailing between speculums—skills only known and practiced by mages in the Order of Shi'rue. Rare skills at that. And by rare, I mean extinct."

Perrin retrieved her switchblade, stabbed her palm, then smacked it on the glass. With the flourish of her hand, she magicked away the bloody palm print.

"Legend says that the Order was wiped out centuries ago." Deftly, and before Pepper could protest, Perrin sliced Pepper's palm and then slapped it against the looking glass. "The how unknown, their knowledge of speculuming dust in the wind. But the legends got it wrong."

Right as Pepper winced from the pain, an intricate knot of glyphs materialized. And just like the tongue of Tun-fendin'ga, they, too, were indecipherable by all present. But not Pepper. "Chaospocket—that's what the enchantment is for. But how do I know that?" A chill slithered up Pepper's spine. The chorus of incoherent voices from inside the mirror that only Pepper could hear reached a fever pitch.

"My explanation of specumuling was idiot-proof, or so I thought. I can't possibly dumb it down anymore," Perrin said deadpan.

Instinctively, Pepper touched the glass again, and it trembled as if some unknown force had rattled it awake from a long slumber. A beat later, the silver-backed mirror swiveled in its frame like a pinwheel, undoubtedly responding to Pepper's chaotic energy, to her tremendous fear of the unknown.

At first, an incoherent whisper, a memory, on the fringe of her mind, its passage into her consciousness forbidden, faintly instructed her to take a measured breath. *She* was in control of the speculum, it said, not the other way around. Pepper did as suggested, and the mirror stopped spinning on its axis and opened like a door.

Darkness pooled from inside the speculum. Tamping down her fear, Pepper pierced the veil of blackened mist with her arm, tingles jabbing at her skin. Blindly, her hand quested about the cramped portal pocket, hitting barriers, until it knocked into one item, box-shaped. Once she extracted it, the mirror snicked shut.

"What?" Pepper asked Perrin, Jhi, and Loki, who all wore looks of shock and awe.

"Pepper, you're a speculumist," Jhi said, alarm coating his tone. "If what Perrin said is true, and the legend is real, you and your sister are affiliated with the Order of Shi'rue in some way, shape, or form. This means you have more than the Firebird, the Syndicate, and whoever they're resurrecting to worry about. If word gets out that the Order hasn't been destroyed, that there are survivors, then magic-wielding soldiers of fortune on the payroll of the richest and most powerful will hunt you down."

Jhi's warning got Pepper's attention alright, but she didn't have the time or the energy to unpack the terrifying realities of what being a speculumist meant or the potential danger it presented. So, she focused on her sister's belongings.

She joggled the standard shipping box and items within rustled. Though the recipient's address had been penned, the individual's name was missing: Peachy-keen Lane, Dillard, GA, 30030. A stamp lorded over its rightful place, its edges jagged, which was to be expected when dealing with necrotic human flesh. The fleshy postage stamp depicted a disembodied mystical hand fashioned from the wind, a hand that belonged to either Aeolus, the Keeper of the Winds, or one of his mail-carrying minions.

"Jaylyn had designs on sending this package right away. She already sealed the postage stamp with her blood, so all that remained was for her to summon the deity by calling out its name —that's it. Yet, she didn't. Which means *something* distracted her." Jhi's face screwed up with fret.

Pepper dumped the box's contents on the bed: a world map, folded umpteen times; an envelope; and a reliquary jar. But not just any old jar. Jarred magic, meet Pepper, your true soulmate. As if sensing its energetic match, its master, the multihued vapor pinged and swirled against the glass in unbridled joy. Unable to resist the urge any longer, Pepper unstoppered the container and greedily gulped down her magic.

Her body was flung off the bed and dragged along the wooden floor until it careened straight into the wall with an audible thump, her head smarting something fierce. Pepper preternaturally skyrocketed to her feet, her skin buzzing and hair electrifying outward as if she'd placed her hands on a Van de Graaff generator—a staple at science museums far and wide. Endorphins within surged like no other. Magic coursed through her veins and symbiotically nested in her cells.

At long last, her sorcery finished unpacking within its forever home. The magic sang in Pepper, in her blood. She felt omnipotent. Magical powers, the wherewithal to create something from nothing, to bend reality to your will, could be a potent cocktail for some if they weren't mindful, a cocktail that could be addictive if over-imbibed, the drunkenness resulting in an insatiable thirst for more and more and more. Oh, the endless possibilities. To form an army of minions to do your bidding.

"Sweetling's got that feral look in her eye."

"I've never felt more alive," Pepper voiced maniacally, her eyes bugging crazily. "Every atom of my being is thrumming, is connected to everything and everyone." She tried to levitate the bed, her finger demanding that it rise—do her bidding now! For a beat, it shimmied, pathetically, before exhausting. "I am un-stoppa—"

Perrin magically hurled one book after the other, Pepper's head the bullseye.

With a casual swipe of her hand, Miss Invincible cast the projectiles into the wall. Until one smacked her squarely in the noggin. "Ouch! What the—" What was left unsaid signaled how fatigued Pepper felt. Drained as if she'd finished an Ironman triathlon in record time.

"Well, that show of marvelous wonder and magic beyond compare snapped you out of your drunken power trip, for the time being," Perrin said while exchanging looks of concern with Jhi and Loki.

Pepper's magical high deflated significantly as her sorcery began to kick back and chillax in its new forever home, or recharge, as was really the case. All thoughts and plots of world-domination seeped away. Well, not quite all.

Jhi unfolded the map and ironed out the kinks. Right off the bat, the bevy of red circles jumped out at the gawkers. Jaylyn had highlighted every major city around the globe, from Los Angeles to Berlin to Cairo to Dubai to Moscow to Mumbai to Tokyo to Beijing to Mexico City to Buenos Aires. According to scribbled notes on the map's margins, an All Hallows' Eve masquerade ball would occur at each location.

And then there was Naples, Florida, a tiny Gulfside fishing village dangling near the end of a peninsula, yet at the epicenter of it all, according to the stars and arrows encircling Naples. Now what exactly the "epicenter of it all" was had yet to be determined.

Pepper ripped open the last remaining item—the envelope. A vial of what looked like blood and an invitation resembling the one Kimball had received a while back slipped out. Elegant in appearance, feathered edges, and calligraphed writing.

"Mmm, a coppery tang." Perrin's tongue flicked hungrily over her glossy lips.

"Invite's written in the recipient's blood," Jhi ventured.

Gracing each side of the request to attend was a trace of a bloodied fingerprint impression, whorling ridges and furrows as clear as day, faint yet clear nonetheless.

Pepper's eyes roved hungrily over the written words: *Greetings and salutations, Mr. Kenneth Bogsworth and plus-one: Come one, come all to a masquerade ball, where evil's forbidden to pass through the walls ...*

Jhi poured a few drops of the curious liquid directly on the bloodied impressions. He instructed all to observe. At that moment of contact, blood to bloodied fingerprint, the words winged off the parchment, and the letters divorced themselves of meaning. Some tumbled down and down off the page, where they exploded into a poof of smoke. At the same time, other letters shimmied and rejiggered, crafting a whole new message altogether, one that was deeply disturbing and entirely sinister.

You sold your soul, Mr. Bogsworth, so you must pay, on this, your final reckoning day. Don't think yourself clever, don't think yourself brave, by trying to hide, or skip town altogether. We'll come for you no matter the weather. If your answer's still no, to Hell you will go. Escorted by demons, you don't want to know. Surprises are many, but choices are few. Just answer the call if, y'know what's good for you. So, come one, come all to the masquerade ball! Trust us, it'll be a night you won't soon forget. You might ask what's needed for the settling of debts: heart's desires on lips and your plus-ones in tow. Once contracts have been signed and wishes bestowed. Just sit back and enjoy the main show.

Reminder: A mask is a must for the black-tie affair. No excuses, for you've had plenty of time to prepare.

Collective jaws were unhinged.

"I take it only those who sold their souls can see past the veneer and glimpse the true message because the letter's written in their blood. So whoever this Mr. Bogsworth is, Jaylyn swiped a sample of his blood and, in doing so, broke the spell," Pepper said.

Jhi raked both hands through his disheveled hair, worry etched on his face.

"'Sit back and enjoy the main show.' For me, the takeaway is that those who sold their souls are safe?" Pepper opined. A chill ricocheted about Pepper's being. "The plus-one's, they're prey for a canned hunt, the Hounds of Hell the hunters. Everything Kimball had said is coming to fruition."

"And it'll be a glorious bloodbath. A smorgasbord of defense-less lowlies, all running around frantic, their screams of terror silenced by the ripping out of their vocal cords, their throats slashed." Perrin could not cork her enthusiasm for mayhem and murder. "I do love a good party!"

Jhi mulled over a thought before giving it a voice. "Judging from the obvious threat, I'm venturing to guess that the individuals haven't sold their souls yet. More like they've committed to a verbal agreement of sorts, a promissory note, if you will. The Firebird needs soul-sellers to be present at the galas, so she gave them a taste of absolute power to get them hooked. Therefore, their attendance must be part and parcel of the loophole exploitation. Otherwise, the resurrection is null and void."

"Shit! There's no telling how many soul-sellers they've wrangled." Fear spiked through Pepper. "Who are we kidding? We can't single-handedly interrupt every ball around the globe. We can't stop the resurrection!" With trembling hands, she picked up the shipping box, then shook it silly, convinced there had to be more items inside.

"There's something far more nefarious afoot than a wholesale soul-selling extravaganza. The only way we'll find out is to attend the ball. We're wasting time! We have to get back to Naples!" Jhi bolted to his feet.

"Hold up!" A rolled-up ziplock baggie fluttered out of the box. Housed inside was a note, along with a wilted flower petal, clearly otherworldly, along with an unassuming piece of paper. Greedily, Pepper unzipped the baggie; immediately, a strikingly familiar fetor assaulted her senses.

When Perrin went to touch the bioluminescent petal, its colors thrumming with life, transmogrifying from glowing indigo to a bleeding puce, Pepper threw the bag. "Don't! That plant's deadly to the touch!" Pepper was met with stink eyes. "You guys don't smell that odor, do you? An orangey java … nestled within a rotten egg?"

The demons couldn't pick up an odor and then stated that they'd neither seen nor heard of such a plant. Pepper then wondered if only Agents of Karma were genetically predisposed to pick up the distinctive scent.

Pepper lavished their attention on the last potential clue—the note. The monogram W & W lorded over the stationary and scrawled below was a note written in haste, blood smears marring a constellation of words. The penmanship wasn't the only thing in dire need of help, so was the writer.

Abort mission stat! Switch to Plan B. Trust no one. DO NOT under any circumstances make contact with Sawyer. She's working for them. DO NOT go to the Tenth Circle as previously discussed. It's no longer safe. The Ven-ad'tsay found me there. I just barely got away from him and ran for my life. But at least I know what he looks like, and he knows I can ID him, so you better believe he wants me dead.

Hounds have infiltrated the Tenth Circle. The blood-suckers didn't see me, thank Seren. The bad news— Mephistopheles is no longer working under the radar. Luckily, I filled the First Underlord in on everything we had discovered on our end, so we can count on him. He's definitely a huge asset to our operation. He'll continue to help the goddess and feed her information while we continue on with our side of the mission. At least that's one concern off our plate.

Unfortunately, the Syndicate must have caught wind that I was alive. Otherwise, they wouldn't have hired that cold-blooded assassin to hunt me down. I don't know how they figured out I had survived that day in Manila. I've been so careful to cover all my tracks. Now our entire mission is in jeopardy because of me. And the Ven-ad'tsay won't stop hunting me, so I can't continue gathering intel. I'm so terrified. I don't know who I can trust. Or where I can run to. I'm seriously freaking out. And I'm not willing to put anyone else's life in danger. So, I have no other choice but to go radio silent, which means you're on your own. I'm so sorry.

Once you've stolen inside the Ministry, immediately navigate to the prearranged meeting spot. There, the contact will recite the code phrase. Your reply of "only if it's infused with pomegranate" will alert them you're the one. Should the contact, at any time, mention inclement weather, they're warning you that it's a trap. Immediately abort Plan B, then return to the rendezvous point and wait for further instructions! Hopefully, it won't come to that.

Anyway, pass along this intel, and then they'll instruct you on the next course of action: The Firebird, along with the help of Vlad and the Hounds, executed the impossible. They figured out a loophole in that man's soul contract and have been working behind the scenes to exploit it. We couldn't identity the loophole. But we have it on good authority that there is a mole inside the Ministry, someone with access to the Pits and the vault of soul contracts within the Department of Soul Brokering. From what Mephistopheles could tell, this mole stole over a million unmarked soul contracts, and we also believe the mole revealed the loophole to the Syndicate. The mole is high-ranking and might not be working alone.

If we don't stop the Syndicate's operation, they will break him out of the Pits on All Hallows' Eve. And when that happens, he'll be invincible. Karma's a dead goddess walking, the Scales of Justice keeping evil on Earth at bay will be destroyed, and the forces of darkness will declare war on Earth. Our contact's mission is to use their resources to figure out the mole's identity and investigate the ins and outs of the loophole. See if there's anything we can do to stop the resurrection before it's too late.

You'll notice that I've included my sister's magic. Thanks to you, our plan worked, and I was able to swipe it from Bhi'gow's cache. As discussed, your mission regarding Pepper is purely reconnaissance. If you find her before I do, do not approach her. Do not give Pepper her magic, regardless of your feelings on the matter. It's just too risky. Unfortunately, I couldn't drum up any information on Pepper's whereabouts or her assumed identity. Bhi'gow must've cast an ironclad cloaking spell, thinking me dead, and erased Pepper's memories. Just a guess at this point.

It's not like I can get answers from Bhi'gow or Loki. Trust me, I tried. I looked everywhere I could think for the duo, even left a note for Bhi'gow, hoping he'd pay me a visit. But he never showed up. Not that I pinned all my hopes on it, but desperate times and all. And I don't want to believe the worst, that that man had Bhi'gow and Loki killed. Unfortunately, that terrifying theory is becoming more and more tangible with each passing day. Which only shows that that man's vendetta against us, especially Pepper, is all-consuming.

I at least have my magic, thank Seren. Right now,

my sister's in grave danger without hers. There was this small part of me that thought what if Pepper got her memories back and, by the grace of Seren, made her way to Hell in search of her magic and stumbled across the note I left behind. Even writing that makes me feel like a complete idiot to have entertained that false hope, to have even thought that was a possibility.

My greatest fear is becoming a reality—that that man will resurrect from Hell and hunt Pepper down, torture her, and then she'll wish she were dead. So, please, please continue doing everything in your power to locate her before he does. Before the Ven-ad'tsay tracks her down. I'll continue on my end as well.

We're Earth's last hope. May Seren be with you, my friend.

Yours in confidence,

JD

PS: I grabbed a sprig of some strange plant from Sawyer. I think she was gonna use it on me. Be careful, though, and try not to touch the plant because disconcerting thoughts and feelings came over me, then lingered for a time before my magic disappeared altogether—all that from just a trace of the oily residue left on my fingers.

The letter and its apocalyptic tone killed Pepper's magical high and sobered her right up.

"Definitely not good news for your sister." Perrin's bluntness felt like a swift kick in Pepper's gut. "Chances are the Ven-ad'tsay found her before she could summon Aeolus and mail the package.

But she might not be dead, though. Not yet. If I were in charge, I'd use Jaylyn as a bargaining chip to smoke out Pepper. Or vice versa."

As for Perrin's brutal honesty, Pepper ignored any possibility that ended with Jaylyn six feet under. "We knew the Firebird and the Hounds were running the show, but who's this Vlad?"

"Dracula, the original fuh'karing vampire. Years ago, he up and vanished from public sight. If one believes the rumor that a rival had vanquished the arrogant, homicidal bloodsucker. But maybe that's what the Syndicate wanted us to believe," Perrin responded, her attention firmly rooted on Jhi. "There isn't much known about Vlad, by design. He's elusive, as the day is long, and filthy rich. Centuries ago, Vlad made his fortune trafficking in illicit you-name-it. It's just so strange that the Hounds allied with Vlad. Unless he killed their leader. And why keep it a secret, from even the Lolly'kas? I don't like this, not one bit."

Made his fortune trafficking … "I wonder if Vlad has anything to do with the plant. I wasn't certain before, so I didn't say anything. But I've seen this plant before." Pepper explained how she had first stumbled across trace evidence of it at Captain Walt's marina. "But it wasn't until I touched it at The Red Snapper …" Pepper described how it made her feel—off, distant, there, but not. "I think this plant is somehow correlated to the demonic possessions back home. But I don't know how or if it goes beyond my neighbor and her social circle."

Perrin's tunnel-vision in all manners of Jhi tuned out Pepper's musings. "Tell me, Jhi. You didn't seem at all shocked to learn about Vlad's involvement, unlike Loki and me." Perrin's eyes narrowed with untold suspicion.

"What do you want me to do, Perrin? Scream and shake in fear?" Jhi contorted his face in annoyance.

"Speaking of fear. Your dear, dear friend, JD, is terrified, doesn't know where to run or hide—and as we all know, fear and feeling trapped are breeding grounds for desperation—but she doesn't reach out to you for help. Why's that?"

"She spelled out the why in the letter. Didn't want to put my life at risk. Look what happened to Mephy. Perhaps we should focus on why JD felt it was risky to reunite Pepper with her own magic, let alone the warning about not approaching her. Just a tad odd, don't you think?" Jhi said coolly.

Perrin's orbs bore into Jhi.

Before Jhi could lob the caustic remark waiting on his tongue, Pepper's phone buzzed angrily from inside her jeans pocket, and she jumped with fright and asked, "What time is it?" Nobody knew.

In light of discovering that Wilhelmina Davidson had died, that Pepper had been conversing with a ghost, learning her sister was alive, along with a bevy of other disturbing finds, Pepper's cell phone and its various practical purposes had escaped her notice, so when she glanced at the reminder screen now filled with missed message after missed message, her heart fell out of rhythm. Frantic, she scoured through the "SOS, 9-1-1, Mayday, expletive-laden" texts all originating from Kimball Garcia—or Blackmailing Bottom-Feeder, which was his new moniker in Pepper's contact folder. He had fired off all texts the day Pepper journeyed to Hell, and they just now appeared. And the last text was a doozy. *You must be dead. Forgive me. did what I had to do.*

Then a few days ago, a distraught Larry had sent a fusillade of texts, demanding to know where Pepper was and why she wasn't answering his calls. Pepper quickly texted back that she was okay, and asked her pops how he was, then panicked when he didn't respond right away. Before leaving for Hell, Pepper'd wisely arranged for pre-written emails and texts to be sent to her dad, but the scheduled programs must have glitched. Thankfully, his cruise wasn't expected to arrive at port until *after* All Hallows' Eve.

"Your dad—he okay?" Jhi asked, concerned.

"Uh, yeah, Pop's fine." Doubt crept into her voice; lest it show on her face, she changed the subject. "All Hallows' Eve, it's in less than six hours."

"Less than that. We're on Pacific time, remember?" Jhi corrected.

Addlebrained, Pepper fired off a text of her own: *WTF?*

Kimball responded immediately: *U not dead?! Can't go home! House surrounded!* Blackmailing Bottom-Feeder then asked Pepper to meet him at a rendezvous point and finished with: *FWIW, I'm sorry.*

Texts weren't exactly conveyers of remorse, so before Pepper lost her ever-living mind, she sagaciously shelved her combustible anger until she heard from the horse's mouth about what exactly had occurred during their lengthy absence.

"Whoever Jaylyn was warning, he, or she, never got the chance to warn Karma. Never received the letter. I mean, we're talking what, a month or two ago, that Jaylyn went missing." Pepper obsessively checked her phone again. Still no response from her father. Lines of worry were etched on Pepper's blooming, fiery red face.

"If a First Underlord had been duped," Perrin said, "Jaylyn's chances of outrunning them are slim to none."

Pepper's phone buzzed, and she immediately lavished her attention on the screen. Relief surged within her, and she choked back tears when she saw the text was from her pops. *I'm fine, Pepper. But you have some explaining to do when I get home. I have to get back to work. See you in a few days. I love you.*

Back in the game, Pepper's magical powers, though recharging, were hungering to be used, hungering to be complicit in acts of Karma-ing.

"I refuse to believe that my sister's dead. Those assholes kept her alive once, in a cage, and it wasn't just to smoke me out, so chances are they'll do the same again. Hey, us Li sisters, we're hot commodities in their eyes, right? Which means she's alive, and I'm gonna find her. And I'll destroy anyone who interferes, or impedes whatsoever, in my bulldozing through every last enemy!" Pepper divorced herself from the bed and stood at attention, as did Loki, firmly planted on her shoulders, ready for action.

"Sweetling, that was beautiful. Now let's go kick this Firebitch's ass and stop war on Earth in the process!"

The bedroom door snicked open. "I believe the ghosts have released us from captivity. See, Jaylyn's family has faith, too. I'll bring her back, alive." Pepper vowed to the empty yet frigid airwaves.

CHAPTER 30

S cant minutes ago, the outline of a door had been magically traced on the inside of a wheelchair accessible bathroom stall moments before a chaosgate popped into existence. Luckily, the loo had been unoccupied; otherwise, that would have been embarrassing.

Three stacked heads and a capuchin on top had cracked open the stall to take a look-see. Once the coast was clear, they shot out of the bathroom and into the bowels of Dillard's department store. But not before Loki insisted with chittering and animated movements that he cloak Perrin and himself in shadows.

When Kimball drunkenly stumbled out of the evening gown section, Pepper immediately plied him with the utmost important of questions. "Did my dad try to get in touch with you?" Her stoic mien belied the terrified little girl within, for when it came to her pops, she was fiercely protective, and that included masking any and all concern. More of a coping mechanism that Pepper had adopted at such a young age. If she didn't draw attention to him, he would be safe and sound.

Pepper noted the bloodshot glassiness of Kimball's eyes as they bore into hers.

"Yeah, actually. I, uh," Kimball sputtered, "intercepted a call from Larry to demonic Bunny. And you're welcome. He said all texts and emails from you had stopped, and he hadn't heard from you in a few days and was equal parts pissed and deeply concerned and *blah blah blah*. So, I told Larry you're fine. Just busy doing nothing at home, not going out with your nonexistent friends, y'know the usual. When he insisted I check on you, I lied and said I did. I just figured he got in touch with you right after we spoke."

"He did," Pepper replied rapid-fire. "But when was this?"

"Sometime yesterday. The connection wasn't the greatest; maybe the satellite phone was to blame."

Pepper discretely pinched her wrist, the discomfort chasing away surging tears of relief. As far as how to keep her pops away from home, she'd figure that out later. One thing at a time. Besides, all that mattered was that he was safe and sound.

"Now, what I *didn't* tell your dad was that the Hounds of Hell have your house surrounded and are waiting in ambush. And, Bell, this crime boss seems to know you. Like you have history with one another. Unfinished business. Just a gut feeling, mind you." He took a hearty pull on his flask. "I'm not referring to the Firebird, by the way. I meant the one they're resurrecting has personal beef with you. Which by the by, that's the whole point of the ball, to resurrect someone."

"This a trap? The Firebird order you to lure us here?" Jhi growled, whipping his head back and forth, inspecting the department store. Nothing but stroller-pushing moms and seniors milled about.

"No, I swear. Hello! Did I not just give you people a tip-off?"

"The resurrection is old news. Do you have any useful info on *who* they're resurrecting?" Jhi betrayed no emotion.

Kimball shook his head. "Though the gala's being thrown in this person's honor, their identity is shrouded in mystery. And nobody, not even the vamps, dares utter this person's name, so methinks that's a direct order, and horrific violence will befall anyone who dare defy said order. I'm telling you right now, come midnight tonight, whatever they're unleashing from its hellish chains and raising from the dead is pure evil." Kimball shook off the willies, then hiccuped.

Myopic, Pepper breathed in rapid staccato, her jaw clenched tight, and could not focus on anything not-Kimball.

She then recalled something he had said in a text: *Forgive me. I did what I had to do.* "What. Did. You. Do. Kimball?" She may have had no other choice but to keep her voice down, but that wasn't the case with her fists. They were fired up and ready to go, begging to connect to Kimball's sun-kissed mug, to yank out locks of his golden curls, perhaps loosen a few of his pearly whites, then rinse and repeat.

Kimball lurched backward and ducked behind a clutch of heavily sequined evening gowns. "Dial down the fury a notch or two, Bell, or you're gonna get us kicked out."

Hindsight being 20/20, perhaps Dillard's wasn't the wisest of venues to hold a covert confab. Granted, the second floor of the anchor department store occupying Coastland Center Mall was usually quiet and sparsely populated at this time of day and, more saliently, out of eyeshot and earshot of acquaintances and demons alike. Yet the stink eyes lobbed at the under-twenties from shoppers weren't at all falling in line with all manner of stealth. In other words, the teenagers gathered in the evening gown section were clearly up to no good.

"Nothing you wouldn't've have done if it came to your dad, and if you say otherwise, you're a liar!" Kimball channeled grit, no doubt a byproduct of feeling safe and secure as he crouched behind the rampart of sequined vestments.

A wildfire blazed through Pepper's being. Of their own accord, Pepper's hands punched through the ramparts and then yanked Kimball out by the upturned collar of his Polo shirt. "Start talking, beta boy."

"*Somebody* needs anger management." He readjusted his molested collar. "Now, if you recall, I warned you, Bell, that Shelly would think it odd if he found out you and I were conniving.

Well, *found out* he most certainly did. The last time you and I spoke, well, shortly after that, Shelly interrogated me. Let's just say that my retort of 'go fuck yourself!' didn't exactly sit well. But when he threatened to kill my mom, for good, I told him everything I knew about you, A to the Z." Kimball displayed not even a trace of penitence. "You know firsthand how sycophantic Shelly can be. How he's a social-climbing opportunist. After relaying the acquired intel culled from yours truly, he ensconced himself good and plenty within the Firebird's ranks. Bell, you pissed off the wrong person."

With that, the remaining holes in the mystery of who apprised the Firebird that Pepper had journeyed to Hell were spackled. "It was you! You're the rat! Do you know the danger you put us in?" The wild pounding of Pepper's heart in her ears drowned out all other sounds. "*We* almost got killed. *Killed*, Kimball, because of *you*." Her voice was strangled, breathing a struggle. "Our blood would have been on your hands! I hope you die in a gutter because that's where rats like you belong." Spittle coated the corners of Pepper's mouth.

"Like I said, if the roles were reversed, you wouldn't've hesitated for a minute to save your father."

"Did Shelly keep his end of the bargain and give you back your mother? Did the wanderer vacate her body?" Pepper asked, her voice shaky, violent thoughts directed toward Kimball occupying her mind.

"Not exactly. The wanderer still possesses her. But her soul is in safekeeping, so says Shelly. Correct me if I'm wrong, Bell, but I thought the plan all along was that you track down my mother's soul and exact revenge on her murderer. Remember? Both of which I handled. No thanks to you. We already knew Walt was on the Firebird's payroll. But he didn't just poison my mom and her friends. The Hounds ran their drug-trafficking operation out of the Red Snapper. They transported the supply through the chaosgates. Captain Walt would then pick up the drug and distribute it accordingly on his boat charters. Walt's gig was to make quote nuisances quote go away for all the soul-sellers in the area; think of it as a perk for those who already agreed to sign devil's contracts. From spouses to anyone viewed as a business threat"—Kimball dragged his finger across his throat—"eliminated via possession. No body, no crime. What I haven't been able to find out is what the drug is exactly. Still, you're oh for two, Bell."

"What exactly did you handle, Kimball? Sounds like your dad is still alive. And we already knew Walt was involved, so nothing new there."

Kimball's utter lack of remorse kicked Pepper over the edge. Surging within her was a ferocious tempest that was fueled by thoughts of maiming, of destruction.

Your wish is my command, Pepper said to her fist. In no time flat, her knuckles walloped Kimball's nose and smarted afterwards. As evidenced by the blood gushing out of Kimball's otherwise perfectly shaped smeller, the strike was a smashing success. She snuck another wallop in for good measure.

"Christ Almighty!" Blood trickled down to Kimball's pink shirt.

The violence caused by her hands, along with the recipient being guilty as charged and thus deserving of retribution, at least in Pepper's mind, left her jonesing, like a meth-addled junkie, to finish the job.

Put him out of his misery, her thoughts cajoled, *do it now!*

She could have easily strangled the life out of Kimball and walked away with nary a regret; that thought alone spiked untold terror through Pepper. Instead, of her own accord, she took a tentative step back, then another.

Jhi stepped up to the plate and served as the goodwill ambassador. "Listen, Kimball, if you want to earn back our trust, I suggest you start plying us with intel." He flipped up his Henley, revealing a Glock, to give Kimball a sneak peek of what he'd be facing should he continue to prevaricate or plead the fifth.

Kimball extracted a handkerchief from his pocket, then shoved it up his nostrils to sop up the blood. Now, when he spoke, his voice was not only slurred but nasally. "Understood, loud and clear. My father's associate-in-crime had a soiree at mi casa, and the guest list extended well beyond the usual suspects. The who's who across the U.S. and well-known tech giants and international robber barons, but I repeat myself, were all in attendance. It morphed into a bacchanalia, which, don't get me wrong, normally I'd be all over that shit, but this was … something else entirely, like *Eyes Wide Shut* creepy. They were all juiced up on magic, demonstrating their newly acquired abilities, forcibly drinking blood from mages, who just so happen to be all the missing persons on the news. Dead bodies dotted the floor." He shook off a case of the creeps.

"I thought lowlies couldn't cast magic"—Pepper focused her attention on Jhi—"not even if it was borrowed." Her heart lurched in her chest at the prospect of sociopaths coming into unlimited magic.

"They can't. It's impossible." Jhi's eyes remained glued to Kimball's.

"I'd say the same thing about someone resurrecting from Hell," Kimball replied. "Y'know, it's smart what they're doing. Giving undecided soul-sellers a sample of magic is a damn good convincer and has them hooked. I saw it happen at the party. And then those soul sellers tell others, and the others tell their friends, and on and on it goes. Word of mouth is the best form of advertising. The Firebird sits back and waits for people to flock to her. And it's not just the Firebird you have to worry about, but some vampire lord and his Hounds of Hell disciples. Oh, my bad, not lord but High King." He affected the words "High King" with an air of snobbery, mockery front and center.

"This High King, he attending the gala tonight? He been holing up at your house?" Urgency bled into Jhi's tone.

"Mind's a little fuzzy, or maybe it's the pain and the fact that my nose won't stop throbbing, so give me a break. Jeez. All I know is that His Royal Highness only just recently rolled into town on his Harley. From the likes of it, he plans on setting up permanent residence in the Glades, naturally with the help of Shelly Garcia, realtor to demons and vampires. An aside, I thought perennial sunlight and subtropical weather were anathema to night-walkers, but apparently, that lore's been debunked. Also, since when can vampires cast magic?"

Jhi took a threatening step in Kimball's direction. "Since never. Where's the King now?"

"Gothic-ifying his fortress in the Everglades? How the hell am I supposed to know? And it's High King, not King, not Lord, and certainly not Dracula or Vlad, as in He Who Impales. Be ever mindful of your words lest you offend the bloodsuckers, the fragile little teacups they are. I know from experience that they don't take kindly to their quote-unquote High King being disparaged by lowering his rank or calling him by his given name. Their feelings get all hurt weally badly. One nearly drained me, but Daddy-O stopped him in the nick of time, only because Shelly didn't want bloodstains on his hundred-thousand-dollar Pashmina-wool—"

"The High King," Jhi snapped, along with his fingers, *"what's his role?"* Another flash of the Glock did the trick.

"The love and concern, it's palpable."

Over the stalling, Jhi tugged Kimball's ear.

"Ow! What is *wrong* with you people? Uh, the High King, he's like the chief in charge of the Hounds of Hell and vampires far and wide. Who knew there's a hierarchy with bloodsuckers?"

Jhi ate the space between him and Kimball.

"Sorry! The High King lent the Hounds out to the Firebird back in the day, an effort at detente, if you will, or maybe the criminal enterprises merged. I don't know. Boiled down, they're all in cahoots. And capital-Evil times evil equals we're FUCKED! Can we pivot back to the topic of vampires and magic? Because I distinctly remember you telling me vampires cannot cast magic. Also, you were misinformed."

Kimball described blood-thirsty Hounds conjuring spells left and right, when not ripping into the jugulars of poor unfortunate souls.

"I. Was not. Misinformed!" Jhi growled.

Then Jhi went over his theory that vampires and the Firebird must have forged a mutually beneficial venture. And how they combined their collective magical powers and preternatural skills to create an unstoppable force needed to raise the damned from the Pits of Hell.

"Just not sure how they pulled off the combining of abilities" —Jhi seemed to talk more to himself—"and I'm sure they'll stop at nothing to keep that knowledge under lock and key. That discovery could be the secret to stopping them ..." his voice trailed off.

Pepper's heart went arrhythmic, breath shallow at that reveal. "Did you uncover anything that could help us infiltrate the ball tonight?"

Kimball's elbow would need oiling soon from its constant bending. Moreover, that flask of his must have been enchanted to hold a never-ending supply of libations.

"Give me credit here, peeps. I'm trying my best to power through the throbbing pain. Okay, listen, people, tonight's merely an appetizer. This whole conspiracy is bigger than we thought. It's gone global. The Syndicate infiltrated society all over the world, and from what I gathered, convinced a legion of people to sell their souls. But that's just the tip of the iceberg. There's something far more nefarious in the works than Team Evil resurrecting their overlord from Hell, and it all revolves around tonight's ball. Which is on the tongues of the Naples elite, so much so it's getting more action than me as of late. The halls of Naples High are abuzz with kids trying to score invites or brainstorm ways of crashing. So, trust me when I say that I worked overtime trying to convince anyone who would listen to not attend. Now, will they end up taking my advice? Very much doubt it."

"Their funeral," Pepper said with about as much compassion as she could possibly muster, which amounted to zilch. Truth be told, the hate Pepper harbored for Kimball colonized every fiber of her being.

"Their funeral, indeed. Revelers have no idea that the good time promised is them and their plus-ones. As in, they're sacrificial offerings, food for vamps."

"I wouldn't be so sure about that, more like vessels for the damned. Speaking of plus-ones. The invite specifically stated to bring one. Non-negotiable. So who's your date?" Pepper grilled Kimball.

"Going stag. Kinda. Last-minute change of plans. I'm actually my father's plus-one." With shaky hands, he gulped more Jack Daniels from his flask.

Pepper couldn't bother to question the last-minute change. She was too busy seething with anger, vividly picturing digging a six-foot grave. Then toeing Kimball's writhing body within and covering his smug mug with dirt.

"Tell me, Kimball, when you weren't ratting me out, did you at all manage to vet the location of the gala?" Panic knifed through Pepper as she stole a glimpse out the doors. Night began weaving its dark veil over the sky, keeping in rhythm with the deafening tick-tock of the doomsday clock.

"I did, from the comfort of my boat. Caterers were buzzing around. Of note, the prep kitchen abuts the bay, so, for the sake of stealth, it's best to arrive by vessel."

Perrin nearly drew blood when she scratched Pepper's arm to steal her attention away from plotting Kimball's death. It probably looked odd to see Pepper crouch down and tune her ear to nothing, and nod her head in understanding.

"Do you really think that they won't have security features set up?" Pepper de-snarkified Perrin's inquiry before relaying it.

"Suffice to say, this is probably one event where party crashers'll be greeted with open arms. As for us, we'll be cloaked in darkness so they won't see us coming." Jhi was pumped.

"So, what's the plan?" Kimball asked, his brows raised. "How're we gonna stop the resurrection?"

The evening gown section serving as de facto command central, the gang hatched a fool-proof mission. They would rendezvous with Kimball at Crayton Cove Marina, then board his speedboat. From there, Captain Pepper would navigate the boat through the Naples Bay and the various canals throughout Port Royal, then moor at a close-enough mansion that's currently on the market. Meanwhile, Kimball would drive to the estate, then march through the front doors of the masquerade ball like a boss.

If unsuccessful in stopping the resurrection, soon Pepper would come face-to-face with the being who had tried to murder not only her sister twelve years ago but Pepper as well.

CHAPTER 31

One needn't venture further than the community of Port Royal—in Pepper's own backyard—to see proof that Naples, Florida, truly was the playground of the filthy rich and not-so-famous, and now add hellspawns to the list. And like any filthy-rich playground, sprawling estates were the jungle gyms.

But the one hosting the All Hallows' Eve ball dwarfed them all; the feudal lands claimed four lots. The multistory Mediterranean residence appeared sentient; it was aglow with hellfire and spewed fog that crawled along the ground, menacing preludes to the mayhem that was about to befall Neapolitans should they dare enter the devil's lair. Which was what Pepper was moments from doing. Luckily for her, she would enter sight unseen.

Earlier on the boat, the quartet decided it was best to split up into duets; Loki picked the teams. Jhi conjured up a signal for an abort mission—four simultaneous slashes scratched on the arm— should the odds not be in their favor. If that should occur, the mission would then become one of intel gathering.

While Pepper moored Kimball's speedboat to the dock a klick away from 1881 Jolly Roger Court, Jhi removed his quarterstaff from its resting place on his back and then traced a figure-eight pattern in the moonlit air, his movements graceful as he summoned shadows to come hither and do his bidding. Pepper caught Loki keenly, yet surreptitiously, observing Jhi's magic casting. Or was it Jhi's weapon that appearance-wise twinned that of Loki's, albeit larger?

Mist-like shadows crawling along the expansive outdoor living area answered Jhi's call and slithered past the guest house and pool to the grass, then over the seawall and onto the dock. At first, pooling around Perrin's Mary Jane's, dark shadows crawled up her knee-high stockings, her waist, over her face, up to the crown of her head, erasing her from sight.

Loki shook off whatever had piqued his curiosity and fed the final throwing star and dagger, their ends dipped in poisonous silver, to his sated bandolier and thigh scabbards. Once he completed stocking his mobile armory, he lavished his attention on Pepper, ensuring she was well-armed: sunburster grenade, silver-tipped knife, blowpipe, and magic gems all hidden on her person.

Quarterstaff in hand, Loki summoned the shadows, a spell divine in nature according to an offhanded comment Perrin had let slip while Pepper motored through the backwaters of Naples Bay.

Though darkness embraced Pepper, she struggled to grasp the concept of being cloaked from sight. Simultaneously, she had to trick her rational mind and deny the reality of her senses; though she tiptoed about and could see all, interact and feel, she was invisible, right? Though wearing Loki like an accessory helped to dial down the level of fear from "Ohmygod, I'm gonna die!" to terrified.

Once the gang reached the stone mansion colonized by creeping vines, they breezed past the pool, cabanas, an outdoor kitchen and landed at a wall of two-story windows facing the bay. There, they initiated the next step of their mission: find Kimball and the Goldilocks of hiding spots therein. Which was an arduous process, seeing as how the mansion was clogged with merrymakers.

Sundry eyes swept over the area beyond the panes. Legions of flames dressing bearded candles and fiery braziers guttered as the silhouettes of masked individuals howled past like dervishes. It wouldn't be an exaggeration to say that all revelers were dressed to kill or dressed to be killed; men were garbed in monkey suits, the women swathed in haute couture ensembles that had to cost a king's ransom. And not one in the bunch dared defy the invite. Though the mandatory masquerade masks ran the gamut from broken porcelain doll to long-nose Venetian, they did share one common feature—all were beyond sinister in appearance.

As if revelers were wickedly stricken with Saint Vitus's Dance, their bodies twisted and strained to the syncopated rhythm of a six-string orchestra and showed no signs of restraint as their heels glissaded about the dance floor.

As for the staged musicians, well, they appeared to be possessed themselves, their eyes devoid of humanity. Sweat sluiced down the violinist's face, his prized instrument tucked under his chin, his body rocking back and forth as if he were a marionette under the mercy of his demonic puppet master. A spotlight originating from nowhere shined on the soloist, then preternaturally zoomed in on the bow he fiercely gripped; it sawed along the strings at lightning speed, which defied all sense of reason. The strings themselves were threadbare and buckled, threatening to snap with one more swipe. The haunting and primal chords crashed at Pepper's feet, amalgamating with the fog, then grabbed ahold, luring her limbs onto the dance floor.

"Found him," Jhi said. "Nine o'clock." Kimball stood next to a towering, potted sea grape tree, its elephantine leaves impregnated with flowers that would swat away any competition in the form of wallflowers. The time was nigh for devil's-lair entering. So, to the kitchen, they went.

Caterers in the midst of a cigarette break whined about this and about that. Pepper couldn't understand a lick of their grousings, because they spoke not in English but Laramaic. It appeared that the lingua franca parasitic translator had huffed its final breath.

To the undiscerning eye, the caterers appeared to be clothed in elaborate Halloween costumes in the vein of kitschy one-size-fits-all packages sold at Celebration Town, guaranteeing that the demons would garner nary a second look from lowlies to blend in. And it was all very meta, demons masquerading as humans costumed as demons. But to Pepper, she knew all too well that their flesh-like masks with gobs of blood trickling down were frighteningly real and, dare say, freshly flayed human skin at that.

Nearly forgetting she was a mage, Pepper plucked out a magic gem from a pouch tied to the belt loop of her jeans, containing bluish vapor. Then, in barely a whisper, she said confidently, "From here on out, I can communicate in and understand Lara-maic." The gems thrummed in her palm, the remaining vapor within no longer vibrant. As the magic settled on her being, her blood sang, her throat tingled, mind buzzed. The sensations were akin to a first kiss, euphoric.

After stealing inside the prep kitchen, not to be mistaken for the primary kitchen that was next on the agenda, Pepper raked her eyes over the general vicinity. Smears of blood marred the tile as if a body had been dragged, the trail ending at a butler's pantry, its door closed.

Whip-fast, Pepper's heart dropped. They had nailed the wanted poster with her mug to the wall adjacent to the pantry, the same poster she had last seen in Hell. Not to be left out, Perrin's was nailed cattywampus next to Pepper's.

Twitchy as all get out and hands a sweaty mess, Pepper chided herself for even entertaining fear. As did Loki, for his talon-like fingernails dug into her shoulders. Message received! Priorities were the name of the game; she had a sister to rescue, a goddess to find, Agents of Karma to warn, intel to garner—oh yeah, and a resurrection to stop.

So, forward and onward, it was. One foot in front of the other. Until she was milliseconds away from running directly into serial killer Miles Leagan. Pepper froze in place. She couldn't breathe lest he somehow hear her.

Frightening to look at, Miles was a vision of pure evil sporting a tuxedo, a horned devil's mask resting atop his shellacked head. He followed the bloodied trail that ended at the butler's pantry and flung open the door. Inside were a dozen males and females, all chained to the pantry wall.

Miles unlocked the manacles of the female closest to him, her face a rictus of hate. "I hope you choke on my blood, you micro-dick shitstain!" she spat, saliva landing on his pockmarked cheek.

While wiping the spit from his face, he barked, "I've had it with that fucking mouth of yours!" He conjured a serrated knife from out of thin air and cut off her tongue. Sliced it right off and laughed as it plopped to the terrazzo floor. He licked her magic-infused blood from off the knife.

The girl's fellow mages whimpered and howled for help.

"Help!" Miles placed his hand over his heart, his facial expression a parody of a damsel in distress. "Somebody help us from the dangerous man!" He derived pleasure out of mocking them. "Nobody is going to help you, you shittards. And if you make one more noise, I'll gut you slowly and play with your innards until you die a slow death, then bring you back to life, and gut you again and again."

With his knife-like fingernail, he sliced the tongueless mage's throat and drank and drank, his imbibing becoming more and more aggressive. Her limp body crashed to the floor, and he kicked her into a far-flung corner as if she were nothing. Using a dishtowel, he wiped his mouth and then tossed it into the sink. He adjusted his tie and lowered his horned mask before returning to the soirée.

The mages were as good as dead, and they knew it. If Pepper helped them, she'd risk exposure. The End. It was Pepper and the gang, or the mages, right now. There was no both in this equation.

Still, what Pepper just bore witness to made her mission that much more realistic, the stakes that much higher, the odds of her surviving the gala—Magic 8-Ball says *Outlook not so good.*

As silent and fluid as could be, they entered the primary kitchen, giving a wide, wide berth to the frenzy of activity that swarmed about a gargantuan island. Hors d'oeuvres and accoutrements for cocktails filled the island's surface.

Betwixt bottles of champagne and condiments were flowering sprigs that reeked of sulfur, but not before notes of orange and java tickled Pepper's nosebuds. Half-butchered, translucent tentacles writhed in agony on the chopping block.

To protect the remaining tentacles within its nucleus from imminent slaughter, the flower's petals, echoing that of Chinese Lantern perennials, clamped shut, its hue fiercely pumping between puce and indigo and quickened, like a frightened heartbeat, as the cleaver hovered over it. The chef swung the cleaver in an arc toward the cowering plant. Its writhing stilled, and its rust-colored essence pooled on the chopping block.

A caterer barked out an order, "Bring me more of the para doxea," which elicited a rapid response. A fellow demon dropped a bundle of the wriggling plants on the prep station.

Pepper recalled Jaylyn's written words of warning: *Try not to touch the plant because disconcerting thoughts and feelings came over me ... before my magic disappeared altogether ... from just a trace of the oily residue left on my fingers.*

A demon, masquerading as a human, hands wisely gloved, added drops of the peculiar plant's blood to a tray of tartlets and a bowl of bubbling champagne punch, then signaled for her associates to deliver the poisoned sustenance and libation to the none-the-wiser humans. "When you're done doing that, take the rest to the mages. Shove it down their throats, if you must. We can't chance their powers returning before the main event."

With that, Pepper discovered the smoking gun—the plant played the devil with one's willpower, lowered defenses, caused obliviousness, giving wanderers an in to possess a body. The plant also stifled a mage's magic, but temporarily, from the sounds of it.

These partygoers did not know the hell that was in store for them tonight.

It was easier in theory than in practice to avoid the frenetic possessed partiers as they showcased their forbidden dance skills; they twirled and dipped, the trains of the elaborate gowns mimicking their owners' movements, swishing and swooshing about, snapping the air like whips.

Once at the sea grape tree, Pepper notified Kimball that the shadow-embraced gang had arrived. From here on out, the plan was to remain anchored to the wall and surveil for any sign of the Firebird, for Hounds of Hell, and this vampire High King.

Hounds of Hell, dressed in tuxes, earpieces visible, dotted the perimeter and flanked all entrances and exits. To the untrained observer, they'd appear like hired security. Some were tasked with handing newly arrived partygoers black velvet gift bags.

Like a choreographed dance, a flash mob even, waiters wearing Victorian garbs and lacy masks, blood-stained tears trickling down their cheeks, gracefully bobbed along the current of wassailers. "Poisoned appetizer or laced libation?" Their movements of dipping along with their trays and narrowly spinning out of the way to avoid run-ins were right on cue and harmonized with the syncopated tempo, the clicking of heels, and the clapping of dancers' hands.

The humans who had wittingly agreed to render up their souls in exchange for boundless who-knows-what—their friends and loved ones be damned!—were easy to spot amongst the clueless flock in attendance. In their collective hands, they clung to the ornate gift bags. Many fostered a shared look of fright and were wrought with anxiety, their bugged-out eyes darting back and forth, as did their feet, which had succumbed to fits of pacing. *Oh God, what have I done? What have I agreed to?* undoubtedly occupied each of their thoughts. Meanwhile, their husbands, their wives, their plus-ones were none the wiser.

Possessed-Bunny Garcia, slinking near Shelly, and Miles Leagan, drunk on magic and acting normal as if he hadn't murdered a mage in cold blood moments before. An animated flame flickered on Miles's neck. As he turned around to grab an appetizer from one of the roaming waiter's trays, his back to Pepper, she could fully see more of the tattoo—a dragon and fire-bird, newly inked from the looks of it.

Shelly scoped out his son, Kimball, then lined him in his crosshairs. Regardless of where Shelly strolled, he ensured his son never, ever left his sight.

A legion of tuxedoed Hounds of Hell exited the kitchen and began making their rounds like sentinels, circulating the venue in toto, sweeping for potential threats, then halted at their respective stations. Arms folded, the bloodsuckers' sooty black eyes made like hawks and scavenged about, sizing up every reveler, or perhaps they were picking out their midnight snacks ahead of time.

A vampire henchman marched Pepper's way and halted ever so close to her she could keenly observe his animated tattoo; the dragon halted its marching on the vamp's neck as its eyes moved left then right, searching for the unseen.

Two henchmen appeared from a closed-off wing of the mansion and flanked an elevator to Pepper's immediate right. The Hound must have received the go-ahead from his visible earpiece, for he nodded in the affirmative, gave a hand signal to his comrades, then pressed the "call" button.

A *ding!* chimed, and the elevator doors fanned open. Three people occupied the lift, two females and a male.

Vlad, the vampire High King, was formally announced. Wearing a tux, he nonchalantly strolled out of the elevator first, his short yet serrated fangs glinting in the hellfire glow. Pepper's attention was drawn to the animated art tattooed on his hands, or more specifically, the swishing tail of a dragon; as for its body, that was inked elsewhere on his person.

His age was north of thirty, but far south of forty. Though average in height, the same couldn't be said about his facial features: sculpted and olive-toned skin; a nasty scar marring his throat; and eyes, cobra-black, that smoldered unimpeded with all manner of desire and bloodlust. Frankly, Pepper wasn't sure what she had expected. Perhaps a mangled, old, death-warmed-over Nosferatu, but certainly not the fine male specimen before her, which made him that much more dangerous, that much more a formidable threat. With one look, he'd seduce you, bed you, before going in for the kill.

Vlad's security detail left their post at the elevator and walked slightly behind the High King as His Highness stalked to his quarry corralled in the great room.

Pepper darted her eyes back to the elevator. Beyond a delicate lace mask, there was no mistaking the icy-blue eyes of the female that had once bore into Pepper's moments before she went in for the kill and nearly succeeded in ending Pepper's life, if not for Loki. Or Jhi. The porcelain British beauty with locks of hair coated in the finest of silver, Sawyer van Arsdale, a rogue Agent of Karma, a sister-in-arms who had been lured to the dark side. While waiting for the rest of her party to exit, Sawyer adjusted the folds of her black dress, a short and flirty affair, more cocktail than black-tie.

They say doom befalls those who pluck the Firebird's fiery feather from the scorched earth and set out on a quest to hunt it down. And hunt down, Pepper most certainly had. Behold the Firebird personified, the third and final person to exit the elevator. Boss Lady would be viewed as pristine, lovely, and regal to everyone not in the know. Not the evil mastermind of a criminal syndicate muscled by bloodthirsty vampires.

Ever so faintly, a note of familiarity regarding the Firebird lurked on the fringes of Pepper's consciousness, just out of reach, followed by an aftertaste of a general malaise that settled around Pepper like a noose. Her heartbeat quickening in response. The feeling was akin to being smacked with déjà vu the moment you crossed paths with a stranger. How could you possibly know this person if you only just met? And it wasn't a pleasant feeling, more like that of unfinished business.

Tendrils of auburn hair threaded with glistening gold splashed down the Firebird's naked back. Her moon-kissed skin was lustrous, pearlescent. And ruby-hued eyes reflected … was it sadness? No, they were hollow, bereft of emotion. For a split second, Pepper pitied her, then snapped out of the spell the Firebird clearly had weaved over the crowd.

The Firebird was resplendent in a bespoke gown mantled in crimson and gold feathers with a train that mimicked the bird of prey's elegant and elongated tail. The arresting ensemble hugged her svelte five-foot-nine frame and gazelle-like legs.

Sparks ignited and burst into flames that licked the bloodred plumage, and hints of twenty-four-carat gold appeared to be melting off and even left behind a trail of glinting gold. And the flames weren't a glamour as Pepper once thought, for they guttered in the wind as the Firebird slinked Sawyer's way, scorching the very ground that she trod upon.

Sheer in the back straight to her bum, or a suggestion thereof, the cinched bustier of the ensemble plunged dangerously low, yet still maintained a sense of mystery. Bee-stung lips that put Perrin's to shame, and a pronounced cupid's bow were a perfect match for the Firebird's heart-shaped face. The mask she wore occluded all identifiable features, most likely by design. But the queenpin was most certainly young—couldn't't've been more than twenty-one.

Once the Firebird assumed her rightful place in the great room, she lobbed a disarming smile to her guests, that was followed by a venomous sting. Then, with a simple wave of her finger, she showboated her sorcery prowess. Fireworks exploded and screamed over the agog crowd. And the pièce de résistance, the booming spectacle aggregated into the letters WELCOME, ONE AND ALL!, then popped into confetti that sifted downward.

Miles Leagan glided over to Vlad to bask in the original vampire's glow. Vlad patted Miles on the back, a gesture that pleased the serial killer.

"Appears as if he's climbing up the ranks," Kimball shared.

A beat later, the High King sidled over to the Firebird's side and whispered into her ear. Not breaking eye contact with her guests, the Firebird responded with a gentle nod of her head, hands clasped behind her back.

According to Pepper's watch, T-minus ten minutes until midnight, until the calendar ushered in All Hallows' Eve.

The resurrection ceremony is well underway; it's actually happening, and our hands are tied; these words played on a loop in Pepper's mind, haunting her. Sizing up her enemy, Pepper felt she could take on the Firebird, a lightweight pugilist vs. a featherweight; hell, a twig outweighed this chick.

Now, as for sorcery, that was another story. But it wasn't just the Firebird she had to defeat. No, Pepper and her army of three would have to battle countless Hounds of Hell, the vampire High King, an Agent of Karma, and demonic kitchen staff—all skilled mages. And in record time, Pepper would be captured and her army summarily executed; in fact, all battle strategies led to that ending. So, the ceremony would go on, and the mission just became one of intelligence gathering.

Perrin and Jhi had reached the same conclusion, for Perrin scratched the previously discussed signal for standing down on Pepper's arm. Defeat made Pepper nauseous.

On Vlad's command, a handful of Plexiglass screens, each approximately sixty-five inches in diameter, materialized and hovered midair. Picture in picture times infinity appeared on the computer interfaces like little boxes, all capturing live footage of gala-goers from all over the globe, awaiting raptly for the grand event.

After nodding her head to Vlad with approval, the Firebird waved her hand in a flourish—palms open, then clenched her hands into fists. A cast spell stole the voices of every person in attendance and around the world, hushing the incessant chatter.

"My sincerest apologies for interrupting the festivities." Depending on the ball's location, the Firebird's words magically translated into that country's native tongue. "My associates will pass out the contracts shortly." Her voice authoritative yet elegant, the Firebird could lull you into a trance and ensnare you in her gossamer web before you even realized what had happened.

Case in point, some people were downright terrified, their hands gripping their throats as they desperately tried to choke out words, pleas for help, eyes bulging, while the majority gazed at the Firebird as if she were their liege, no doubt their blood drowning in para doxea.

The Firebird signaled to a Hound, who then handed a briefcase to Sawyer. Sawyer flicked open the briefcase. Scores of scrolls were housed inside, more than could typically fit, defying the laws of physics if not for magic.

As Sawyer began tendering the soul-selling contracts, pens clipped to each one, it became apparent that she wasn't in charge and wasn't just handing them out willy-nilly. The contracts preternaturally navigated Sawyer to the rightful recipients. The events that transpired in Naples were mirrored at every gala across the globe. How many people did the syndicate convince to sell their souls? A million? Millions?

"Ladies and gentlemen, to fulfill your solemn blood oaths, at the stroke of midnight, you have fifty-nine seconds to sign your given names on the dotted line with the fountain pens provided. We have filled them with your blood, after all, so waste not, want not." That smile of the Firebird's was beyond disarming. "Should any of you renege and try to escape, I have my associates on standby"—the Firebird pointed to the Hounds scattered about, their fangs at the ready—"to aid you in the signing endeavor. Let's not morph what should be a breezy execution into unnecessary bloodshed and carnage."

The Firebird unclenched her fists and hurled the stolen voices into the airwaves. With audible gasps, people coughed and sputtered. Then she magicked flames of fire that blazed into the shape of a tick-tocking clock.

Glassy-eyed revelers clapped like trained seals, as if this was a spectacular show, and joined the Firebird as she began the counting down to midnight along with the magicked clock. "Ten. Nine … Two"—the crowd's excitement reaching a fever pitch— "One. NOW SIGN!"

A handful of cowards who didn't heed the Firebird's warning tried to turn tail but were instead manhandled by the Hounds of Hell. The bloodsuckers gruffly forced their quivering hands to do what they were told. Shed tears mingled with their blood on the contract. Others were patently hubristic and wore a smug smile, like Shelly and Miles, as they proudly scrawled their signatures.

Though the Firebird appeared stately—head up, hands behind her back, one palm resting in the other—Pepper noted the Firebird's bosom rising and falling in a staccato beat, her eyes subtly darting to the elevator every few seconds and then back. And her tight-fitting bustier wasn't to blame.

Once the last letter was inked, the contracts, of their own accord, tightly furled with an audible snap, then whiplashed through the air.

Like a catcher, Sawyer held open the briefcase as the flying contracts smashed into its bowels. One of the madly flying contracts sliced a woman's cheek. When a Hound doctored her bleeding wound with his sandpaper tongue, a tug of war of emotions froze on her face: wariness vs. trust, and the latter proved victorious. Proof positive that whoever had the poisonous para doxea coursing through their veins was dead meat, their body ripe for the taking.

When the last contract soared into Sawyer's glove, the briefcase snapped shut, and crypt-like silence pervaded the room. Those in the know waited with bated breaths, but for whom?

Pepper stifled back coughs caused by … smoke inhalation. Smoke? Her eyes darted to the genesis of the inferno—the elevator scant feet away. A prelude to mayhem, at first smoke bled out of the shaft, followed by a miasma of fire and brimstone. Sentient-like flames clawed open the doors of an elevator. A fiery inferno licking the threshold was no sooner extinguished by the ascending lift. *Ascending?*

But basements were unheard of and close to impossible to have in Southwest Florida, leaving one other option. The resurrection ceremony, the loophole exploitation, had been a smashing success. They had resurrected a being that had once called the Pits of Tartarus home. The very being who wouldn't stop hunting until it captured the last of the Li sisters—Pepper.

For those who tuned in to their sixth senses, they were familiar with the telltales of imminent danger. At first, the feeling was of creeping discomfort, like you'd rather be elsewhere and weren't sure why exactly. But if they failed to heed the warning and leave, the hair-raising sensation morphed into that of a sinking heart and quickened pulse, all smothered in dread. Then it was far too late to run and hide as fast as they could, for doom already tagged their heels. Which was precisely what happened to Pepper.

The moment her eyes hooked on the being, the man, her gut was assailed with a primal familiarity. Something karmic of another life. Could that be? Still, something about him scared her bone-deep. Yet the genesis as to why was shrouded in mystery and locked far, far away, not in the dark recesses of her mind, but in her soul.

CHAPTER 32

Whimpering and panting, the nearly naked man, his pants in tatters, rapidly crawled out of the elevator like one of the damned fleeing his demonic tormentors, his eyes terror-stricken, sweat running in rivulets down his dirt-caked face. Or perhaps his mind hadn't registered that he had resurrected from Hell. That he hadn't executed the impossible, been pardoned from his sentence of eternal damnation, escaped Hell, and lived to tell the tale.

Though he had been the only occupant in the rukba, disembodied whispers, many in number, could be heard before the doors fanned to a close, silencing their incoherent chatter. Phantom hitchhikers? Wanderers? Pepper shuddered at the thought.

Once free of the confines of the elevator and realizing mala'khas weren't at his heels, ever so slowly, he rose to his feet as if being pulled by strings, his spine straightening until he stood erect. He paused, shook out the kinks of his six-foot-something frame, and got a bead on his surroundings, the situation, the slack-jawed audience too afraid to move, to make a peep.

His glacial orbs, the shade of desolate Arctic, froze on the Firebird, and his mouth melted into a smile. It took some Herculean effort on his part to walk in her direction, but he persevered, albeit stiffly, as if he wore chains. He swung one leg outward, then another, his bloodied feet smacking on the echoing expanse of marble.

Bloodied yet unbowed, his body had been beaten unmercifully, flogged, burned, and sliced, as evidenced by the landscape of blistering bubbles and other horrific injuries pockmarking his form. A Grizzly Adams beard colonized a triangular jaw. Buckets' worth of grease dripped out of his stringy hair, his body caked in dirt and filth.

As the man bypassed Pepper, a stench of rot assailed her, terror seizing every fiber of her being. She couldn't possibly dig her back any further into the wall, but that didn't stop her from trying.

The vampire High King was the first to break the ice, interrupting the stranger's forward momentum. "Brother Cazzian," he said in a thick Eastern European accent, "aren't you a sight for sore eyes." Vlad gingerly hugged the battered man, then whispered something in his ear while pointing at the floating monitors, at the ocean of soul-sellers around the globe. News that delighted the stranger, for his eyes crackled with greed, like a soul broker on Capitol Hill.

Not one memory stirred deep within Pepper from the mere mention of the name Cazzian. Perhaps her brain had wilted from the sheer horror of it all.

Cazzian directed his attention to the Firebird. "Ember, it's good to see you. It's been way too long." The Firebird responded with a nod of her head.

On the Firebird's orders, a Hound wrenched two terrorized mages from out of the kitchen. They spent their last seconds putting up a good fight, but they were no match for the Firebird, not without sorcery; they were gnats to her raptor. She sliced the skin on their wrists in one fell swoop and held them in place while Cazzian greedily drained them dry. Their corpses crumpled to the ground, and Cazzian unceremoniously kicked them the side. The waitstaff dragged them away like flotsam.

Cazzian wasn't a vampire, from what Pepper could tell. Pray tell, what was he then? A mage? Magic borrower? Or was the blood of mages merely a pick-me-up?

With an audible sigh of satisfaction, Cazzian juiced up on magic, conjured up a flurry of darkness that churned around him, obscuring him from sight. Pepper's ebony locks billowed back from the spectacle. The massive crystal chandelier quaked, its glass beads clinking.

When the tornadic winds evanesced, a whole new man stood before the room, scrubbed, cleanly shaven, mantled in a tuxedo, the honed planes of his face on full display. Pepper ventured to guess his age to be mid-twenties. He raked his calloused hands through a mop of wavy strawberry blond locks. His brow showed signs of wear and tear, a tad weather-beaten. A suggestion of freckles polka-dotted his fair complexion.

Cazzian received applause and bravos, huzzahs all around. To which he rolled his eyes with disdain.

Like a glitch in the matrix, Cazzian flickered in and out, appearing incorporeal for a millisecond, then solidifying. Loki tapped Pepper's shoulder. He had noticed it, too. As did Ember; a momentary look of panic reflected in the Firebird's eyes before she schooled her features into a stony expression.

Cazzian, the distinguished guest, stood before his rapt audience, and his telegraphic mug appeared on the hovering screens, broadcast for soul-sellers elsewhere. The Firebird stepped to the side to give the guest center stage.

From his pulpit, Cazzian kicked off what Pepper felt would be a rousing soliloquy. "Contrary to popular belief, it's not the Almighty who doles out punishments. No! *He* can't be bothered with such trivial matters and, as such, elected a truly wicked goddess, the Lady of *un*Justice, the consummate *bitch*, Karma, to preside over Earth and Hell as judge, jury, and executioner. *She* picks and chooses who to punish and weighs her options on those cursed, lopsided Scales of Justice, blindfold be damned!"

Pepper could almost feel the acid burning through her skin from the vitriol that he spewed. Whatever had occurred between him and Karma in Hell, he would not soon forget.

"Since my banishment from Earth, twelve years have ticked by. But in the far reaches of Hell, that translates to a century. For nearly one hundred years, I was caged in the Pits of Tartarus and tortured senseless by Karma until I died, only to be regenerated the next day, and the day after that, and on and on, it went. But I took my lumps, knowing full well that *I* had outsmarted the avenging *bitch*. That one day, *I* would serve *Karma* her just deserts. And she'd beg me for mercy, beg me to end her wretched life. When the damned, my Pit mates, beseeched their tormentors, the mala'kha, for mercy, when their plaintive cries and keening wails of abject agony were deafening, I shared with them my game-changing plan and gave them a choice: join me, help me, and I'll liberate your souls."

His basso velvety smooth voice, meant for talk radio, lulled many of the party-goers, the plus-ones, into a trance; blissfully ignorant, their eyes were agog with childlike wonder as if hearing a fireside tale and not the naked truth.

"Soon, my name spread like hellfire, and I became a legend: the man who restored lost hope within the damned, the man who figured out a way to escape Hell. Upon hearing the rumors, the mala'kha roared with laughter and replied with: 'It's easier for a camel to journey through the eye of a needle than for one of the damned to be pardoned from eternal damnation.' Well, I am the camel and have dispelled Hell's proverb. And it wouldn't have been possible without all your support." Though the tenor of his soliloquy was on the side of pleasant, eyes don't lie, and his were crackling with murderous intent. Death was on the agenda for tonight.

"Rest assured, for the faithful amongst you, those disciples who bargained their souls tonight, I will grant you with the ability to slay a mage and drain them of their chaos, their magic-imbued blood, and in turn, you will be able to cast magic freely. The same ability that was once bestowed upon me." Cazzian nodded to Vlad. "An ability that's impossible for non-mages or lowlies, as they call us. Gone are the days of bargaining away your souls. No more soul reapings. Eternal damnation and torture in Hell are a thing of the past. Soon you will be able to manifest your wildest imaginations, do what you want with impunity, and live your lives untouched and forever free from the long arm of the law. Forever free from Karma's wrath. You might not have been born a mage, but after tonight, you will become one all the same."

Pepper was having a thorny time gauging the audience; many were clearly under the influence of the poisonous para doxea, sporting dopey grins and glassy eyes, while others were aware and sweating bullets, regret etched all over their faces. Some wore looks of confusion, refusing to believe in demons and magic and the like. Were they still under the impression that this was an elaborate theatrical production? Because some said as much under their breaths.

Then there were those few salivating and champing at the bit, like Shelly and Miles. To Cazzian's disciples, he wore the mask of The Anointed One, a bringer of hope and change, a wish-fulfiller. Ironically, these disciples were wholly unaware that they were nothing but patsies doing Cazzian's bidding. He cared not for them and certainly didn't care if they lived or died. How could he possibly trust millions of strangers, let alone welcome them into the Syndicate with open arms?

"Before the bestowing of mage-like powers and eternal youth, before I set you free to conquer worlds and live life without consequences, never having to become one of the damned, before you join my campaign to kill Karma, and her few remaining Agents, whereby I assume the bitch's mantle of judge, jury, and executioner, I'll need a show of loyalty. A test, if you will."

Pepper watched in horror as spear-like nails grew on the soul-sellers' fingers, their collective eyes glinting with homicidal intentions.

The Firebird tapped her gold wristwatch, and Cazzian nodded in understanding.

"As per the contracts you signed," Cazzian said, "you have exactly one minute to kill your plus-ones. You'll find weapons in each of your gift bags, or if you brought your own, even better. I can't be bothered with the how. So be creative, and be quick about it. If you attempt to flee, off to the Pits, you go." Cazzian looked in the Firebird's direction. "Ember, would you do the honors?"

Ember half-nodded her head as if bowing, then drew sigils in the air, her blood the medium. Moments later, a countdown clock fashioned from vapor materialized.

Calmly, a soul-selling woman produced a dagger from her clutch. Her plus-one scampered backward, soiling himself from sheer fright, urine soaking his crotch. Like a viper, she lunged and knocked him to the ground, then stabbed him through the heart, repeatedly, his life force spattering her face and ballgown. She stepped gingerly out of the way of his pooling blood to avoid sullying her designer stilettos.

But other soul-sellers weren't so keen about the murdering of their dates. No, they ran every which way.

Through the ruckus, Pepper and the others were able to communicate to each other that it was best to remain in one spot. Which was most wise, for the atmosphere morphed into a churning cauldron of fear and panic and regret that bubbled over with ear-piercing pleas for help.

The Hounds stopped the plus-ones attempting escape and kindly pinned them in place as the soul-sellers murdered them with nary a second thought.

Blood spatter coated the walls, the floor, the drapes, windows. Within no time flat, the great room morphed into a charnel house, a macabre tableau comprised of bodies slumped against furniture, others spread-eagle on the ground, some clinging on for dear life, their eyes fluttering as if calling for HELP! in Morse code.

Blood and carnage took place worldwide; monitors showcased a crush of people stumbling over mutilated bodies as they tried to flee. Their terrified screams pierced the airwaves as they desperately pounded on walls that were once points of entry before being magicked away.

00:00. A collective hush cocooned the environment, courtesy of a spell cast by Ember. Cazzian's eyes ping-ponged from Vlad to Ember and back and forth; a "now what" look cemented on their faces.

Barbed wire chains poofed into existence and ran from inside the closed elevator to Cazzian, piercing the flesh on his feet, torso, hands, and neck.

A newly emboldened Cazzian addressed the soul-selling survivors in the room and around the globe. "Remember, always read the fine print." He finished with a hearty chuckle.

On every screen, chaosgates along the walls blazed into view, their frames licked by hellfire. The same thing happened in Naples. As the chaosgate doors fanned open, towering, bent-bodied beasties with bloodred eyes stomped out of the gates to Hell, their claws wielding enormous scythes.

The mala'kha had arrived to drag their prey to Hell.

These soul-sellers were duped and made the biggest mistake of their lives. Clearly mugged by power-lust, they wittingly entered into an unholy bargain with the devil. And in the span of minutes, they signed their blood on the dotted line of an eternally binding, Hell-forged soul contract, then killed their plus-ones—all part and parcel to the exploiting of a loophole that enabled Cazzian to be pardoned from a devil's contract he had signed however long ago.

Looked like Karma got the last laugh after all.

The mala'kha loomed over the cowering soul-sellers, then abruptly stabbed them in their guts. Serving as a siphon, the scythes sucked souls upon souls from the lowlies' bodies. The souls traveled up and up through the transparent handles and ended in reservoirs attached to each scythe. The mala'kha left fragments of souls intact, the better to feel pain, then maimed and tortured the soul-sellers, giving them a taste of what was to come.

After securing the soul-sellers' necks in barbed wire chains, their flesh pierced through and through, their screams snuffed out by magic, the mala'kha dragged the damned to their new forever home in Hell. In a matter of minutes, nearly every soul-seller worldwide became one of the damned.

Fiery explosions engulfed the galas around the globe, eliminating all evidence of what had transpired at the venues. Out of all the millions of soul-sellers, only a dozen or so in Naples survived the festivities.

As the last lowlie was dragged past Pepper, its flailing hand brushing against her sneaker, as the last chaosgate shut and vanished from sight, the barbed wire chains puncturing Cazzian ejected from his skin. In one fell swoop, they crashed to the floor and slithered on the ground toward the elevator as if mala'khas in the Pits pulled the chain back whence it came.

Ember's shoulders dropped. The corners of Cazzian's lips tugged into a smirk as his flesh became whole. And Vlad heartily clapped and shouted, "Bravo!"

Ding! rang the elevator.

Pepper whipped her head in that direction just as the doors glided open. A crush of nebulous shadows thundered out, their incoherent whisperings reaching a fever pitch.

Over the chaos, Cazzian welcomed the newly arrived. "They're yours for the taking, my friends!" He fanned his arms out, gesturing to the bodies of the plus-ones.

As for his "friends," well, they were his former Pit mates that had joined the man of legend's cause in Tartarus and must have helped him exploit the loophole, from what Pepper surmised. A promise made and kept, the damned were rewarded. They might not have been able to escape Hell with their bodies intact like Cazzian, so new vessels would have to do.

A salvo of undulating forms slinking on the walls, the ceilings, onto the floors, where their crooked silhouettes slithered over the bevy of captured bodies, then into exposed orifices they crawled.

When the chaos died down, Shelly Garcia crawled out from his hiding spot, Miles' plus-one by his side ... well, pieces of his plus-one, and Shelly's—Wait! Shelly's plus-one was Kimball, and they both were alive.

"Pardon the interruption, Mr. Cazzian," Shelly squeaked. His simpering request to approach the makeshift dais that Cazzian, Vlad, and the Firebird—or the trifecta of evil—stood upon was granted. As he shuffled his way there, stepping cautiously over corpses, his eyes darted in Pepper's direction.

Pepper slowly pivoted her head to her left to investigate that which stole Shelly's attention and eyed Kimball, a ball of nerves, fidgety and red-faced.

Ever so slightly, Kimball toed a jettisoned cocktail napkin like a bored kid kicking stones until it was within Pepper's general vicinity. An action that caught the attention of a Hound nearby, who nodded to Vlad.

With a curt nod, Vlad gave an order ... then it was a blur, a phantasmagoria of hellish nightmares made manifest. A visible Perrin stood slack-jawed, shadow-cloaked no more. Pepper searched frantically for Loki, but he had vanished. Jhi, too, was missing.

Pepper didn't dare move, didn't dare utter a word, for fear the shadows that loomed over and around her would scatter like their creator Loki, exposing her to her mortal enemies.

But then ... then Perrin's terrified eyes bore right into Pepper's, her lips mouthing "run" right as a Hound wrenched Perrin to the ground and swift-kicked her in the gut.

Too late. Talon-like nails of a Hound latched around Pepper's wrists. A scream for Loki's help tore from Pepper's throat as an unknown force jerked her through the air. She crashed onto the hard marble, sharp pain lancing through her shins and knees. Though she tried to crab away, the cold muzzle of a gun digging into the back of her cranium thwarted that desire. Her captor forced her back to her knees, the gun pointed at her head cocked. Like a sacrificial offering, a Hound presented Pepper to Cazzian.

Perrin was shoved next to Pepper and forced to her knees. The girls exchanged glances of "What now?" Pepper couldn't reach a sunburster grenade under her jacket. Same for the silver-tipped dagger and Sawyer's blowpipe. Magic gems, on the other hand, she had stored loosely in her pocket. If she could just—

"You make one move, and your friend dies," Vlad warned a wriggling Pepper. She couldn't discern even a shred of humanity in his beetle-black eyes.

Speaking of Sawyer, she snatched her left-behind weapon strapped to Pepper's hip. "I believe this belongs to me."

The moment Cazzian set his sights on Pepper, his face ran the gamut of emotions like flip-book animation, from stunned disbelief to earth-shattering realization to surreality to smug murderous delight. Not wanting to chance the mother lode of prizes escaping, he produced from thin air manacles that clenched around Pepper's wrists and Perrin's, too.

The moment they locked in place, Pepper felt a stinging zap, then another, like static electricity, only more intense. The pain lingered for a few beats before fizzling out, and with it, so too did her sorcery, her last line of defense. That vitality, that thrumming of power, that zest, a sense of purpose, all but disappeared, exhaustion and a general malaise left in its wake.

"Mr. Cazzian, if I could have a moment of your time." Shelly, the toady, attempted to say.

Unable to tear his eyes away from Pepper, Cazzian shot his hand out in a gesture of silence. "Centuries, I've waited for this moment. For centuries the Sisters Li slipped through my fingers like an unfilled dream." His mouth twisted into a grimace, a laugh forthcoming. "Yet here you are."

"She's my neighbor." Shelly inched his way closer. The hell he'd let the opportunity to shine pass him by. "All this time, Pepper's been living next door. How fortuitous."

Cazzian ignored him, though. "My, my Pepper. I believe you

predicted as much, this moment in time. Though probably not you on your knees, bowing before me." That turn of events delighted him so. "How very ... *karmic.*"

Hatred mounting, the bitter taste of anger burned Pepper's throat, and she spewed to the trifecta of evil, "This won't stop me from ripping you all to shreds and bathing in your blood." Where that voice and animus came from was anyone's guess, but it wasn't Pepper speaking. Still, it rang familiar like ... déjà vu.

Cazzian replied, "Funny, your sister said the same thing ... Perfect Kassendra. Always the responsible one. Always stuck cleaning up your messes."

Pepper's heart went berserk like a possessed metronome, and she felt woozy. Jaylyn—had she been captured after all?

Entertaining hopelessness, Pepper looked away and trawled her eyes over the carnage to her reflection in the two-story window. That's when she caught the slightest of movements. In fact, if she had blinked, she would have missed it altogether. A Hound standing under the archway demarcating the entrance to the left wing of the house dropped to the ground in a heap. His body dragged out of sight. But how? Was it Loki? Jhi?

Whip-like, an object sliced silently through the air and found its mark in the neck of a Hound standing sentry by the elevator shaft. The Hound ripped the dagger out of his neck and attempted to shout, but the shout died with him, for the silver had already entered his bloodstream, his words of warning drowning in poison; his plexus as a whole now visible, every blackened vein and artery throbbing and threatening to burst.

But the spectacle was short-lived, for he disappeared from sight before his body could crumble to the ground. Shadow-cloaked, the silent assassin dragged him away. A bloodied trail ended at the wing. But not for long. The silent assassin magically mopped up all the evidence.

Unfortunately, the clang of the bloodied dagger that took the vampire's life hitting the marble floor seized Vlad's attention. He ordered a Hound to inspect the area.

That spectacle was enough to invigorate Pepper. She tried to communicate that all would be well to Perrin by tossing her a half-smile.

Cazzian caught that endearing exchange and examined Pepper like a scientist discovering a new life form. His brows furrowed, eyes narrowed with suspicion. Out of the blue, he barked, "Kill the Lolly'ka!"

The Hound nodded, cocked his gun, and aimed for the kill shot.

"Boss," a voice boomed from the kitchen, "look what I found."

Cazzian waved his hand in the air and gave the Hound holding Perrin captive a stand-down order.

Two Hounds entered the great room, frogmarching their prisoner. Good news: Perrin's life was spared, temporarily. Bad news: the prisoner was Jhi.

CHAPTER 33

Though it appeared as if Jhi had put up a fight, as evidenced by the bloodied lip he sported, the cuts and bruises along his eyes, cheekbones, chin, his collar ripped, his Henley hanging on for dear life.

Briefly, Pepper snatched a glance in the window of a Hound's head, rolling past a potted sea grape tree before vanishing in thin air, his body as well. One by one, Loki—it had to be him—was eliminating threats. Her life and Perrin's, and now Jhi's, rested in the ruachti's hands.

The Hound bypassed Pepper and hurled Jhi at Cazzian's feet. Jhi's back to Pepper, his upper back exposed, she nearly gasped upon seeing his tattoo as a whole. The very tattoo she glimpsed on his forearm when they had first met, or the coiled tail thereof— a fearsome dragon, the very animated dragon inked on every Hound, denoting members of Vlad's criminal syndicate. The winged monster's red eyes glared at Pepper as it spat out fire like a taunt. But the absence of a firebird struck Pepper as odd.

Disconnected, that's how Pepper felt, a tugging sensation mounting, like the greater part of her soul that had vacated her body was trying to yank out the remaining bits so they could be one.

"Fuh'karing backstabbing prick," Perrin said to Jhi under her breath, her face rivaling that of Pepper's pierced heart.

"And this boy's alive, why?" Cazzian, none too pleased, asked the Hounds.

Cazzian canted his head as if he listened to an invisible person whispering in his ear. But the movement was subtle. He executed one tiny nod of understanding and then ordered Jhi to pivot around.

Smirking, Jhi acquiesced and then showed off his tattoo, as per Cazzian's orders. Not once did Jhi make eye contact with Pepper or Perrin.

Cazzian barked to Jhi's captors, "Let him go."

Vlad stepped forward, patted Jhi on the back, and introduced Cazzian to the Ven-ad'tsay, the Hunter, unmatched when it comes to tracking down anyone or anything.

Still wearing that smirk, Jhi sauntered over to Sawyer. And judging from the expression of disgust written all over Blondie's face, she wasn't overjoyed with the recent addition to the Syndicate. But she gave Jhi a curt nod all the same.

Like a fool, Pepper glanced in Jhi's direction, hoping he'd toss her a wink, a half-smile, a sign of some sort that this was all a daring ploy and the only way to guarantee his allies' safety. He made a solemn vow to protect Pepper. He pledged her his loyalty. That no-good, rotten son of a bitch.

And then it happened. Seething hatred usurped shock and rained down its holy terror. "You're a monster!" The object of Pepper's wrath was none other than Cazzian.

"Me? A monster?" A hearty laugh surged from his throat. "That's rich, coming from the likes of *you*."

"Evil like you will eventually get their comeuppance. Karma will see to it! *I'll* see to it!"

"Evil, you say? Well, we certainly have more in common than you thought." He smirked, hidden knowledge etched on his face. "As for Karma, she will do no such thing. She's most likely incapacitated at the moment ..." He probed Pepper again, as if looking for some sign of recognition. "Aren't you ever curious. There are shades of old Pepper but muted. Hmm … perhaps it is you, after all. One way to find out." He squeezed her skull with his hands.

Searing, blinding pain ripped into Pepper's mind. At first, it felt like scalpels cutting her gray matter. She couldn't breathe, couldn't move. Then she was knocked back into the stump-like legs of the Hound, and the pain left, sweat pouring down her brow and cheeks.

"Your memories have been wiped clean." That revelation ticked Cazzian off. "Smart move. Even so, only cowards want to forget and not face their sins. Out of mind, but not the soul, doesn't change who you truly are. You're still the same despicable, sociopathic girl underneath, memories or no … Unless—" His anger escalating, he spun on his heel to face Shelly, then growled, "You brought me a golem and thought I wouldn't notice! Hounds, tie him up!"

Shelly quivered, probably damn near soiled his pants. "Wh-what?" He was handcuffed and held at gunpoint. "That's Pepper Bell, or Pep-Pepper Li, as you call her. I swear."

Cazzian's hands squeezed Pepper's face once again. "Look at me when I talk to you!" He sprayed her face with his spittle. "No recollection of memory in your eyes … You don't recognize me, do you?" His head whipped back to his coterie. "This girl is an imitation, an echo. I met damned with more soul than her. That's why I freed them from Hell."

Vlad intervened. "Brother, she went to Pandæmonia in search of the fixer. No, we vetted this girl, and she's *the* Pepper Li."

"I don't care if you vetted her. She is not the conniving, ruthless mage I once knew her to be." He pinned his focus on Pepper. "I didn't spend centuries hunting down the Sisters Li only for it to end now in a whimper. And I certainly didn't sell my soul only to endure years and years of torment at the hands of that *bitch* Karma; what, so that one day I'd come face to face with this pathetic shell of a once-formidable mage?" Cazzian's face screwed into a grimace of disgust. "Hell, you're not even a worthy adversary. Look at you, cowering, defenseless, a suggestion of sorcery running through your veins. Killing you now would be like slaughtering a baby." Hatred became him, rage bubbling over. "I deserve a proper vengeance." His hands hungered for death, to zap the life of out anyone, anything.

His shoes click-clacked to Perrin. Lips pulled back in a sneer, he gripped her ebony tendrils and wrenched her to her feet. "Your care and concern for this Lolly'ka has brought about her demise. Which will make her death that much more enjoyable."

A *thwomp-thwomp-thwomp* sounded, its origins unknown.

Perrin yelped. Not from the pain, but from being jerked backward by an invisible lasso into nothingness. Ripped locks of her black hair were tangled in Cazzian's fingers. As for the Hound who had held Perrin hostage, he fell forward with a loud thump, poisoned silver daggers jutting from his tuxedoed back.

"A shadow-cloaker." Filled with palpable rage, Cazzian sliced his arm with his needle-like nail, beads of blood welling, and used it as the medium for which he drew sigils in the air that closely resembled Tun-fendin'ga. The script radiated and appeared sentient; the sloping lines, the arbitrary dots, slashes, curves, united and parted, and back and forth, then twisted in on itself before shrinking and expanding and flipping over.

"Hear me, O Shadows. I demand you leave the employ of he who seeks refuge within you. I demand you shroud Pepper, silence her screams, and spirit her away to Witherwhere, to a place therein where only I can find her. Only on my orders will you uncloak her." Cazzian's spoken edict appeared to serve as an activator, for the hovering sigils materialized into view and then pulsated, their velocity increasing by the second until they reached the speed of light and disappeared from sight.

Obedient to their new master Cazzian, shadows swooshed off Loki. Forsaken by the elements, he stood exposed near the kitchen. But Loki cut an impressive form all the same: dagger-wielding, battle-ready, his lip curled back in a hiss, piranha-like teeth on display.

"Retrieve that flea-infested vermin and bring him to me!" Cazzian barked at the Hounds.

Pepper tried to run away, but the shadows found her, gagged her, and coiled tight around her stomach, clenching ever tighter as they dragged her away.

Standing stock-still, Loki's chest, rapidly rising and falling, stilled. His arms, at first pinned to his sides, raised slowly, palms up, as if channeling the manna from a demonic war god, his brown eyes morphed into a shock of milky white.

With a supernatural speed, Loki plucked a tray from a felled demonic server and hurled it toward Pepper. It kissed its target, slicing the head of the Hound holding Pepper captive right off his body, and then continued on its deadly trajectory, beheading the Hound directly behind him.

Not a moment later, Loki magicked every gun to him and fired the weapons until the magazines were emptied. He then hurled every Chinese star and throwing dagger until his bandolier and thigh scabbards were bereft of weaponry. Hound after Hound collapsed to the floor. Sawyer leaped behind a fallen dessert table. Jhi joined her. The Firebird was nowhere to be found. Same for Kimball. Daggers poisoned Vlad, but it wasn't enough to destroy the vampire High King, not by a long shot. Cazzian looked like a pincushion for death-bringing implements. With no effort, he plucked them from his person as if they were thorns.

On Cazzian's command, his will be done, poison-dipped daggers, bullets, and Chinese stars wiggled out of their final resting places, out of the bodies of felled Hounds of Hell, demonic waitstaff, and party-goers, then swiveled in the air until their business ends, dripping in blood, faced Loki.

"Kill him now!" Cazzian ordered his inanimate minions. They tore through the air like a heat-seeking missile to their target.

Loki's movements swift, the air his ground, he torqued his body away from the death-bringers, twisting, somersaulting, corkscrewing, handless cartwheeling. Loki dodged death; the weapons failed at every turn. Until a spray of bullets stopped their forward trajectory and rocketed in the opposite direction, right into Loki's abdomen.

The capuchin halted his forward momentum for a beat, blood coating his furry hands, shock etched on his features. Right before a dagger landed between Loki's eyes, he barreled to the side, then disappeared.

Through the glass's reflection, Pepper spied Loki, mid-glide, whipping out a sun grenade. He pulled the pin, then lobbed the vamp-slayer.

An explosion of once-captured sunlight blasted through the great room like a shock wave, knocking Pepper over. The blinding light chased away the shadows holding her hostage, forcing them to betray their master. Shouts and crashing boomed. Hounds at the point of impact were incinerated on the spot, their ashes eddying about. The body parts of vampires within the radius of the detonation littered the floor.

Lightning fast, Loki's hands scribbled an incantation in the air, rivulets of his blood pooling at his feet. The moment the sigils took form and morphed, then reworked themselves into more complicated patterns and glyphs, streams of symbols, like sentences, sprouting from a single source—Pepper recognized the tongue of Tun-fendin'ga.

As did Cazzian. While cursing and taunting, his rage boiling over, upon noting that Loki was a dangerous adversary who posed a serious threat to his grand plan, Cazzian spotted Pepper at the double entry door and stormed her way. Like parting the Red Sea, he magically cast dead bodies and limbs out of his path. He was out for blood and looked as if he might kill Pepper on the spot.

The dynamic sigils Loki had drawn took flight and zoomed Pepper's way. The sigils knitted together like thread. Over her and around her, they weaved a protective barrier. Loki soared through the air and landed at Pepper's side, beating Cazzian by a millisecond, right as the last thread stitched into place, sealing the dome and Loki and Pepper within it.

Cazzian threw his hand out to stop the barrier from completing, but was too late. Seething, he kicked the jellied dome, pummeled it, tried slicing through it, but it was impenetrable. Cazzian tossed everything he had at it, every ounce of magic, and eventually, the spell Loki had cast weakened. Like a broken polymer chain in stockings, fracture lines spiderwebbed all around the dome.

Knowing the dome was moments from shattering, Loki used his quarterstaff to summon back the shadows, and they responded in kind. Pepper couldn't see Loki, but she felt a furry hand take hers, and with it, the frigid gloom of darkness devoured her once again. They bolted to the kitchen.

In the distance, she heard Cazzian say, "No, let her go. She's no good to me in this condition." Then he appeared to her, in spirit form, and delivered a message, his voice booming as if on surround sound for all to hear. "I have taken what is most precious to you, Pepper. Tit for tat. And if you don't want more blood on your hands, I suggest you find your memories and then" —he screwed his face in abject disgust—"BRING BACK WHAT YOU STOLE FROM ME!"

The all-consuming hatred he felt for Pepper went beyond visceral and took on a life of its own.

In a much calmer tone, yet chilling, all the same, he added, "Maybe then we can end this once and for all. In the meantime, I'll be overseeing your loved one's care, meting out the torturing and resuscitating. What good is a dead body? And no funny business either. Do allow me to jog your nonexistent memory. This is the last life for the Sisters Li. There will be no more running. No more hiding. No more cheating death or Karma rescuing you. You die, Pepper, your soul is mine. Then the real fun begins. Now go and find those memories and what you stole from me. And do so quickly. The clock starts now. I'll be in touch."

CHAPTER 34

Once outside, Loki and a rattled Pepper stopped running when they heard "Psst!" by a pool house feet from their docked boat.

Perrin stepped out of a copse of bushes and yanked on the collar of a hogtied Kimball, the bloodied string of her yo-yo digging into his wrists. "Ball-less wonder here tried to make a run for it and was taken down by a Hound. If it weren't for me and my trusty yo-yo, he would've been worm food."

"Wh-what're you gonna do with him?" Stunned disbelief wrapped around Pepper.

"Interrogate him, for starters. First question: why is he alive and not dead like all the other plus-ones—Holee"—Perrin's tone raised an octave—"shit! There's more blood on the pavement than inside Loki! I swear to Lilith, if he croaks before removing these magic-choking manacles …"

His chest riddled with bullet holes, his fur matted with his gore, Loki weakly smiled before dipping his hand in his blood and drawing a crude shape of a key in the air.

Pepper caught Loki before he collapsed to the flagstone and cradled him in her arms. Honestly, Pepper couldn't muster up a single thought that didn't involve saving Loki or staunching the blood gushing from his multiple bullet wounds. She knew she hated Kimball, but the why, his actions that led her to feel that way, were cloudy at the moment.

Perrin plucked the key from midair, curiosity blazing in her eyes, and unlocked her handcuffs before liberating Pepper from hers. As the magic-chokers sizzled out of existence, Pepper's magic returned with a zing and with it a boost of adrenaline.

The survivors ran like the blazes to the moored boat. Perrin fired it up and began idling through the Port Royal canal that dumped them into Naples Bay and asked anxiously, "Where're we going?"

"Backwaters of Keewaydin Island. Your twelve o'clock," Pepper replied over her shoulder as she morphed into triage mode. When Perrin hit the throttle, Pepper added, "Just keep going straight!"

Hidden in Loki's satchel were blood-staunching firebush roots and its medicinal paste packed in poultices. Before Pepper began the doctoring, Loki extracted a vial, bit off the cork, and gulped down the golden concoction. A beat later, he convulsed, foam spewing out of his mouth, yelps of agonizing pain escaping from his throat. After the last cry, a supernatural force ejected every bullet lodged in his tiny body, the metal casings *pinging* off the fiberglass floor.

Perrin sneaked a peek at Loki's battle wounds; though she remained mum, her rage-stricken eyes betrayed her otherwise unruffled demeanor. Pepper had not been completely honest with Perrin about Loki's real identity, and the Lolly'ka was catching a whiff of that betrayal.

Loki nodded for Pepper to start the ministrations. Sizzling sounded the moment the firebush touched Loki's wounds. Once the blood stopped gushing, Pepper applied poultices and dramatically exhaled when Loki's wounds began healing in real time.

No longer engaged in busywork, Pepper found herself besieged by shock. By betrayal. Hopelessness. Untold fear. Her skin, down to her very soul, felt clammy. Her wobbly legs gave out, and she slid to the ground, her back resting against the cabin's entrance.

"It's all my fault. Jaylyn escaped Jhi, and like an idiot, I led him right to her, or close enough. The Syndicate has her because of me, and they're gonna torture her unless I return something I don't even remember stealing. Twelve years ago, my sister nearly died protecting me, and now she's right back where she started. But I believed Jhi. I thought … He knows things." The existence of Agents of Karma, but she didn't dare breathe a word of that. "Things I should never have entrusted him with. I'm so stupid."

Kimball chimed in. "I heard you had a sister. News to me she's alive. Her name came up briefly at Evil Headquarters, but they only spoke about her in the past tense, and they referred to her as Kassendra, not Jaylyn, for whatever that's worth."

Sea spray showered Kimball, pooling in his wounds, and he yelped from the boat's starboard. Fang marks were visible on his neck, the skin ragged and raw, but Pepper didn't care, nor would she spare a firebush poultice. He could doctor himself up. Should he bleed out—not likely, unfortunately—she'd simply push him overboard. At least the sea scavengers would find some use for him.

"Dear Lilith, *enough* with the moaning already. It's gonna take a fuh'karing miracle for you to de-whimpify, isn't it?"

"Who the hell are you?" Kimball barked back.

"She who saved your pathetic ass. Listen up, lowlie. That big, ratty mouth of yours has gravely inconvenienced *my* life *and* criminal enterprise. I'm a wanted Lolly'ka in Hell and on Earth because of you! So, until we whip up a plan of action to obliterate those fuh'karing scumbags that need to die *a lot*, you best shut the fuh'kar up and do everything I say. If not, that paper cut will be nothing compared to the torturous fun I have in store for you." Perrin flicked her yo-yo; the gore-encrusted string sliced Kimball's cheek. "Oh, and in the future, when referring to me, you will do so using the honorific Mistress."

A wicked storm was brewing off the coast, fomenting the

waters. The boat jumped over heavy swells, and more saltwater crashed onto the passengers. Perrin's dainty fingers slipped from the wheel, and she lost control of the vessel.

Kimball's elbow slammed into a side storage compartment, and an empty vodka bottle escaped. It rolled port side, and a wild-eyed Kimball crabbed after it as if it were water, and he'd been parched and stranded at sea for days on end. He grabbed it before it smashed into the side, then tried to smother it with a towel but failed.

Pepper, Perrin, and Loki had already hazarded a glance at the unmistakable vaporous substance trapped within. Unlike multi-hued magic in reliquaries, this matter was nearly invisible, like fumes seen when filling up a gasoline tank. Pepper had seen the same matter in Hell. And she was looking at it now—a soul.

Lost in a mangrove-dense preserve, tucked away and out of sight, Perrin shut off the ignition and snatched the vodka bottle right from Kimball's hands, dregs of liquor swishing about. Pepper picked herself up from off the floor and inspected the compartment. Inside was a duffel bag stuffed with clothes, cash, food, a passport—all the essentials needed for fleeing.

"My father always had a warped sense of humor. Thought it would be funny to store Mom in what she liked the most."

That's when the truth came out of hiding and walloped Pepper. "You lied! To my face! It was a setup from the get-go, wasn't it?" A life for a life. Bunny in exchange for Pepper. And after the ball, he was planning on escaping indefinitely.

"When lying, a sprinkling of the truth always makes a story more palatable," Kimball said.

Pepper wanted to punch that smug look right off Kimball's face.

"And you're a goddamn hypocrite, Pepper, if you dare say you wouldn't've done the same thing if in my shoes. That you wouldn't've done the same for your *dad*." When he uttered the word "dad," his eyes darted to the right, then down. "My father needed a way to move up the Syndicate's ladder, and I needed

Mom's soul back. With that, a symbiotic relationship was born. Loyalty is shown in action, not platitudes. All I had to do was convince you to attend the ball, which took zero effort on my part, and when the time was right, I'd point out your location to Shelly, knowing full well you'd be shadow-cloaked."

"Why'd you do it?" Pepper asked through numb lips.

"For my mom's soul, and I got to live another day."

And judging from his reserved tone and stony eyes, he'd do it again, no second thoughts. Pepper swallowed back bile and fought off the welling tears.

"As far as the Firebird and her cohorts were concerned, you had vanished. They had a search party out for you in Hell; the Hounds *were* surrounding your home. That part wasn't a lie. The plan was to keep your attendance at the ball hush-hush until after the resurrection ceremony when the mother lode of all surprises would be unveiled by my father. By that action alone, Shelly would prove to Cazzian how only he wrangled the white stag, not the Firebird, nor the vampire High King, but my father."

"Did Jhi put you up to this? He in on it?" Pepper pressed.

"No. That news was a shocker. Can't imagine how *stupid* you must feel. Then again, you've never had much luck with the opposite sex." Kimball possessed not even a quark of shame.

Perrin held the bottle over the edge and threatened to christen the boat. "Who is Cazzian holding hostage?"

Kimball beseeched Perrin to stop, to hand over his mother, his voice gravelly, choking for breath.

"Last chance. I have no qualms about uncorking your mommy's soul, and once I do, then buh-bye forever. Who. Is. Cazzian's. Hostage?"

A sputtering mess, Kimball wouldn't spill.

"I'm done. Time for a burial at sea." Perrin unscrewed the bottle and placed her hand over the lip.

"Pepper's dad!" Kimball lunged Perrin's way. "Larry! He's the hostage! Miles ambushed him on the cruise ship. Now hand her over." Kimball swiped the bottle out of Perrin's grasp and cradled it, his mom, in his arms. He continued speaking, refusing to make eye contact with Pepper. "When you disappeared in Hell, my father came up with a contingency plan. He figured capturing Larry would be the one thing that would smoke you out of hiding." He retrieved a cell phone from his go-bag and handed it to Pepper. "Here. Take it. I have no use for it anymore."

A string of texts between Larry and Pepper—scratch that, from Kimball pretending to be Larry to Pepper—filled the screen.

The world went dark. Pepper didn't recall how she reached Kimball or how she knocked him to the ground. Or pinned him in place with her thighs. Or how many times she had pounded his head into the fiberglass and rained down punches, her knuckles raw, his face a map of bruises and blood. Nor did she recall when she had wrapped her hands around his throat and began squeezing the life out of him.

"You were the only one who knew my father's whereabouts. So when Pops called you looking for me, that's when you screwed him over!" Her hands squeezed harder; his legs flailed. "You're worthless"—his face reddening, eyes bulging as she pressed tighter and tighter—"useless. A waste of oxygen."

His pain brought a modicum of delight to Pepper. As did the fact that she was in control. His life in her hands. Only she decided if he lived or died. The power … it felt euphoric, like returning home after a long journey. A smile touched the corners of her lips. But she must have more. She wanted him to choke out his last breath. She wanted to watch him die.

A force hurled Pepper backward. As she bang-crashed into the bench seats port side, her entire body smarted. Loki held his quarterstaff in defense mode, a warning that he would do far worse if Pepper dared move a muscle and then stationed himself between her and rat Kimball, who was gasping for breath.

Hands shaking uncontrollably, body following suit, Pepper drew her knees to her chest, hugged them tightly, and rocked. The one person who mattered most to her in this world was in danger because of her.

She cried silently. Nothing else mattered. Not the cold-blooded killing machine Pepper had tapped into. Not turncoat Jhi, who shattered her heart. Or Cazzian or Goddess Karma. Nor her missing sister. Not even the world as she knew it ending. Because life meant nothing without her pops in it.

Larry was her world—her everything—and living without him wasn't a possibility. What would that life be like anyway but endless nothingness. No joy, no purpose … just dread. She'd be a stranger in a strange land, out of place, walking about aimlessly. One foot here, the other firmly planted in that snapshot of time where she experienced such unconditional love from her dad.

For this only child and single parent, the bond between Pepper and Larry was insane and unbreakable. The two of them against the world. Best friends till the end.

Pepper felt a furry finger mop away her tears. She wanted to say thank you but couldn't speak, let alone breathe properly. So resting her head on Loki's bony shoulder would have to suffice.

The murky water began churning, waves angrily splashing, rocking the vessel back and forth. Standing at the bow, Perrin tore her eyes away from gazing out at the moonlit bay, her black lace dress twirling in the rain-cooled winds, her ebony locks whipping about, and returned her attention to her fellow passengers, specifically Pepper.

"My life is in peril." The Lolly'ka's calm tone belied the tempest brewing within her. "Loki isn't just your garden-variety demon hybrid, is he? His quarterstaff. Summoning fuh'karing shadows. The way he single-handedly took on Vlad's cabal of Hounds. But the biggest giveaway is his proficiency in sigil magic, which means he can speak and comprehend Tun-fendin'ga." Her anger mushroomed with each word spoken. "I nearly died tonight, and if not for Loki, I would have eaten lead."

The fin of a bull shark broke the surface of the water and circled around the boat, the predator agitating for a fight.

"Earlier, you mentioned Jhi knows things. Things you should never have entrusted him with." Perrin's face twisted into a look born of pure evil and rage. "I thought I made myself abundantly clear back in Pandæmonia that there were to be no secrets." Her icy tone chilled Pepper to her core. "And what would happen should you break that covenant. Seeing as how you're not with me. You are now my enemy!"

The veins in Perrin's neck bulged as indigo-hued ichor rushed through her blood vessels. A network of purple-black veins spidered over her glossy lips, around her nose, and on the whites of her eyes, her baby blue irises bled out like watercolor on canvas. As her arms raised, so too did her slight frame until she was hovering above the slowly sinking boat.

As if in tune with Perrin, the waves mimicked their master, rising to a crescendo and then crashing onto the vessel and its inhabitants, nearly tossing them into the murky, predator-infested water. "YOU LIED TO ME!"

The bull shark snapped at the side of the boat, inches away from Pepper's arm.

"I WILL NOT BE KEPT IN THE DARK!" The waves crashed anew. "I HAVE RISKED LIFE AND LIMB, ONLY TO BE DISRE-SPECTED!" Her voice dropped an octave. "Mother Lilith, hear my prayers—"

"Perrin! Stop! PLEASE!" Pepper cried out, her voice breaking, as she held on for dear life, her body half in the boat, half out, the shark targeting her like a laser, its fin racing toward her.

Loki grabbed Pepper in the nick of time and tossed her back into the boat. "I'm sorry! You're right! I should have been upfront! I should have told you about Loki, but I thought that was his story to share!" Her throat felt raw from screaming.

"And how the hell would Loki do that, Pepper? I don't speak chittering!"

Just like that, the boat stopped its tilting and righted, and the waves instantly calmed down. Right as Perrin's Mary Jane's touched the floor, the girls simultaneously let out a weak chuckle at Perrin's retort, which broke the ice—somewhat—and whatever else Perrin was planning to do to her "enemies" was shelved, for the time being.

Blame it on the abject fear, pure exhaustion, sleep deprivation, the over-it-all-ness, and if anything, Perrin was owed the naked truth, so Pepper laid it all out on the table. "It" being Loki's true identity, Agents of Karma, and her invitation to join the sisterhood, and how Agents as a whole made up Karma's Achilles heel. It no longer mattered if Kimball heard the whole truth. Here on out, he was their prisoner. Besides, Kimball needed Pepper and her allies if he had any hope of saving Bunny.

"Being an Agent of Karma is in my blood, apparently. And Cazzian is picking off my kind, one by one. How many Agents are left is anyone's guess," Pepper said, her voice lifeless. "They're all probably dead except for Sawyer. Or so said Jhi—No, she is an Agent, I think—I don't know what to believe anymore. Still, Agents of Karma are the goddess and Earth's last line of defense. It's they who keep evil at bay. With them out of the picture, Karma isn't long for this world, and now that Mephistopheles is MIA … Well, once both creators and signers of the Hell and Earth peace treaty are wiped off the map, the treaty and all it stands for is rendered null and void, and evil reigns supreme."

"Actually, the girls aren't all dead," Kimball added meekly. "Not yet. Someone compiled a list of active Agents and Initiates."

"What d'ya know about Agents?" Pepper drilled Kimball, her tone implying that there'd be hell to pay if he didn't supply answers.

"Nada! Just figured Agents of Karma was a girl gang or something. Makes sense you'd be a member, Bell. You *are* prone to violence …" When Pepper's eyes bore into Kimball, communicating something like, "I want to kill you," he got back on point. "What I'm trying to say is that it's news to me that Bell's an Agent, I swear. And I don't think anyone else knows either. Besides, I didn't see Bell's name on the list. Not that I pored over it extensively. Just sneaked a peek, is all. But still."

"And you came by this intel *how*?" Perrin asked skeptically.

"I happened upon the list in my father's office while on the hunt for my mom's soul. The Firebird recruited Miles, y'know, my father's guy Friday, to head Operation: Kill Karma. Seeing as how he fancies himself a stalker-enthusiast slash murder specialist. Dude waxes psychotic about that thrill that goes up his leg whenever he's on the hunt for humans. Now add mages into the mix. Anyway, most names have been crossed off—only a few Agents left. I saw Sawyer's name, though. Not sure Sawyer knows she's on the list or that she's a dead Agent walking."

"So Cazzian doesn't know Pepper's an Agent." A devilish smirk ignited on Perrin's bee-stung lips, a prelude to her huffing out air through her nose.

"But *Jhi* knows." Speaking itself exhausted Pepper. "Which means Cazzian will know shortly. And I guarantee Jhi is helping with the 'Agent of Karma' list compiling!"

"Not necessarily," Perrin said. "Don't get me wrong. Jhi's a traitor and deserves a painful death, but not before we figure out his angle. If I were Jhi, I'd keep that game-changing knowledge of what you are, Pepper, to myself, for the time being. It's the perfect blackmail material against you. But what's fuh'karing pissing me off is that I can't figure out what skin Jhi has in the game? And it's not you, Pepper, because let's face it, he had you right where he wanted you. Still, if what Kimball said is true, and Cazzian doesn't know your sister's alive, it's only a matter of time until he does."

"I know." The dagger of betrayal in Pepper's heart would have hurt tenfold with Perrin's revelation if not for the despair suffocating her.

"If there's any good news out of this entire mess, it's that Jaylyn's still in hiding, which means she's safe," Perrin added.

"True. But to answer your question about what Jhi wants. He's hell-bent on finding my sister, like it's his life mission or something, and he's not gonna stop hunting her. It makes me sick that we helped that son of a bitch. We practically signed Jaylyn's death warrant." Hate a few rungs higher than despair—too bad Pepper couldn't make the climb. "I can't believe that all this time we've been working with the Ven-ad'tsay, feeding him intel. Is he even a soul broker?"

"Is that he told you?" Perrin shot Pepper a withering look.

"Jhi reeled me in, made me feel important until I was no longer valuable. Then he discarded me. All he ever really cared about was finding Jaylyn. I guess that's one thing he didn't lie about. My sister escapes the Hunter. So the enterprising Jhi follows a lead in the form of Sawyer and runs right into me. Talk about a mother-effing stroke of luck. I guess Seren doesn't discriminate when it comes to her damned blessings."

"I think Jhi discovered your true identity at the same time we all did," Perrin reassured, and Loki seconded with a chitter.

"From the get-go, he led me to believe Jaylyn was his coworker who had disappeared suspiciously, and while sleuthing the missing person case, he just happened to land at my doorstep. I suppose there are nuggets of truth in his story. I'll give him that. He really laid it on thick, too, with this Seren delivered him to me bullshit. Warned that there was a contract out on my life and scared me senseless—Liar!"

Anger and sadness were engaged in a brutal tug of war within Pepper. She took a moment to catch her breath.

"I mean, there is one now, but still. 'Trust me,' that backstabbing prick said, 'I can keep you safe.' Oh yeah, you really did a bang-up job there, Jhi! And yet, I bought what he was selling and couldn't get enough of it and wanted more."

Pangs of humiliation were written all over Pepper's features, so she smothered them with her hands. "Even after you warned me, Perrin." Her words were muffled. "I'm so stupid."

"Love in any form can turn even the strongest into a fool." Perrin looked off wistfully at the moonlight shimmering on the murky water as if recalling some past pain, then shook it off and switched to slow speak, tailor-made for the thick, each word given special care.

Pepper lowered her hands. "But his story was so believable.

Not even Loki sensed danger when Jhi was around." Loki nodded assent, which gave Pepper some solace. "I hate him!"

"You were nothing but a mark to Jhi. He read you and found a weakness, then exploited it to get closer. And those moon eyes of yours eclipsed the telltales of deception. Sure, he's dangerously handsome and a skilled liar to boot. Hell, he even played the part of a human with aplomb. So, I can't blame you entirely. It's happened to the best of us. Fool me once, though! You don't get do-overs in life, so lesson learned never to be repeated again! Remove that chink that is falling hard and fast for silver-tongued boys from your armor. Your father's life depends on it. As does yours."

"Wha-huh? Played the part of human?"

"Oh, sweetling. Jhi's about as human as that driftwood over there. The scintillating green of his eyes, while arresting, was not of your world, or mine. Still, it wasn't his eyes that gave him away. No, it was his quarterstaff, the shadow-summoner he wields." Loki chittered in agreement.

"So does Loki."

"Uh—yeah, because Loki's a demigod. The shadow-summoner is a legend in the criminal circuit, and for good reason. It's forged from Nitherian, an alloy of unknown elements mined in a dimension thought to be inhabited by gods. Only those with *divine blood* can wield such a formidable weapon."

"Uh—" Pepper's lips felt numb, her skull tingling, her addled heart forgetting how to do its one job, bile rising in her throat. Slowly and with great effort, Pepper wrangled her thoughts. "Wow! He sure played me like a fool." She felt the need to defend herself. "I was scared to death and nearly died the night we met. Jhi swore he could help me if I helped him in return. A quid pro quo. It's not like I could chaosnaut to Hell on my own or summon a rukba—Whatever. He preyed on my desperation to find my magic and memories. Anyone would have done the same thing if in my shoe—"

"You entered into a devil's covenant with Jhi?" Perrin's tone begged for a "no."

Pepper's cringed expression only served as a colossal letdown.

"Was it written, verbal?" When Pepper nodded her head at the latter, Perrin snapped. "What the fuh'karing fuh'kar? How fuh'karing stupid can you be? Jhi owns you! He'll always be able to find you! You might as well have a LoJack shoved up your ass! If, in fact, he's after the Li sisters like Cazzian, then your whereabouts are already known, so all that remains is Jaylyn."

"Why change to Team Evil at the last minute, though?" Kimball inquired.

"I don't think he switched teams at the last minute," Pepper replied bitterly. "He was always with them. Right after we first met, Jhi had to leave unexpectedly for business in Hell. Said he'd return shortly. Shortly turned into a month. His excuse was that he was in another dimension, a place where time moves differently. He only learned about Bhi'gow's island time difference when I did. So it was somewhere else."

"A place like Tartarus? Where Cazzian was imprisoned? You think he visited Cazzian and struck a deal?" In response to Perrin's question, Pepper nodded. "Yeah, but he didn't have a Firebird tattoo, just the dragon. Ember, Sawyer, and Cazzian were completely blindsided with Jhi being outed as an ally."

"Not Vlad, though," Pepper said. "And Cazzian quickly came around. He was in contact with someone, something. Like he was receiving communication from them. The way he cocked his head as if receiving whispered messages from an invisible someone. Whoever it was gave Cazzian an order to accept Jhi on the spot. I just know it."

"Hm, another player calling the shots. A kingmaker? Like shadow governments on Earth," Perrin mused.

"Or a godmaker," Kimball added.

"Perhaps that's who Jhi answers to," Perrin surmised. "It's all a web of confusion and speculation until we get hard facts. Well, it's officially become a race. The first to find Jaylyn wins. As it is, your sister's mysterious ally in Georgia is our only lead."

"Jhi's got a head start. Yet again, I've endangered my sister. My dad's life is hanging in the balance. I nearly got Bhi'gow killed. I'm cursed. I must be, by that evil Shi'rue, goddess of death, despair, and misery." Pepper felt trapped in a box with walls that climbed to infinity, no windows, and one door, and at it, Death was knocking.

"Probably are cursed." Perrin, in full-on war strategizing, ignored Pepper's doom-and-gloom fugue. "Bright side, Cazzian can't negotiate over a corpse, so while your dad'll endure torture, at least he'll be kept alive."

Rat Kimball set his sights on Pepper. "I won't apologize for what I did," judging from his tone, he meant it, "but I'd want to know the truth if I were in your shoes. Cazzian blew smoke up your ass. He's going to kill your father, Bell. And soon. At some ritual, a vampire shindig or something."

Time on her side had brought Pepper a modicum of solace. She held on to the hope that until she returned with her missing memories, her dad would be kept alive. But that wasn't the case. No, his death warrant had already been signed and sealed.

The thought of not being able to see him again, to talk to him, to bring him to safety, hear him say, "I love you to the moon, to the stars, and to infinite galaxies and back, kiddo," whipped her into a hair-pulling, heart-pounding, breath-stifling, going-out-of-her-mind frenzy. Her dad's murder was imminent, and the Syndicate would rip him away from his daughter, their lives destroyed. No more talking, laughing, hugging, living, loving, dancing …

Like a flick of a light switch, Pepper snapped. At first, an ember of fire roared within her belly, her eyes a blazing inferno. Then, suddenly and swiftly, like a bolt of thunder in the clear night sky, she shot to her feet with the aid of some unknown force.

A burst of flames born of vengeance and fueled by rage chased across her neck, arms, torso, legs until they licked her whole being, until vengeance itself devoured her and cocooned her within a fiery chrysalis. Once the two became one, the chrysalis collapsed into a pile of crackling embers and was carried away by the salt-laced air. Gone was the whimpering Pepper of old.

Standing before them now was an assassin of Lady Justice.

An Agent of Karma.

"I will rescue my father. And I will destroy anyone who gets in my way." Pepper meant every spoken word, leaving no room for doubt.

In the middle of the boat, winking into existence, then fading from view, only to struggle back into sight, gaining traction, was a woman or a hologram thereof.

At first, the woman was of Asian descent. Then Far East Indian and so on. Then an amalgamation thereof. She represented a slice of everyone and of no one. An olive-skinned beauty swathed in a skintight red suit, pants that fit like a glove, a blazer sans top underneath that plunged dangerously low, the sides of her breasts peeking out. The raven-haired beauty with striking features was tall, sylphlike. Licked by flames, her long, iron-straight locks were perfectly parted down the middle, firelight flickering within her eyes.

She was a goddess.

Lady Justice.

She was Karma.

Perrin curtsied in reverence, Loki nodded in deference, and Pepper genuflected by instinct alone.

"My child, I was forbidden to contact you until you underwent your Awakening. And now you have." Though her tenor was regal and authoritative, it carried a hint of feebleness. "Karma Academy has been besieged by the Syndicate. The Nine are missing. My Agents are few in number. Initiates have been wiped out. And I am dying. A spell born of darkness thwarts me from contacting my girls, who I pray to Seren have gone to ground. But not you, by the grace of Goddess Seren, not you, Pepper. You must defeat Cazzian."

"I can't! Not on my own! He nearly killed Loki, a demigod!"

Karma inspected Pepper up and down, reading her. "You are not ready"—disappointment coated her words—"for what is coming."

"R-r-ready for what?"

"Armageddon." Her voice dropped an octave. "There isn't much time left. And you must train."

A lump formed in Pepper's throat. "M-m-my sister, though, she can help." Panic-stricken, the words were getting stuck on her lips. "She's outmaneuvered Cazzian once before. Please tell me where she is." If anyone knew, it would be a goddess.

Goddess Karma looked to the aether and shuttered her eyelids as if trying to pick up Jaylyn's energy, then returned her gaze to Pepper. "Kassendra is neither here nor there, but somewhere in between."

"Witherwhere?" Perrin asked politely.

"Perhaps." Her answer carried much uncertainty. "No. No, someone far more powerful than even I is cloaking her from sight …" Her eyes crackled with intimate knowledge. "Beatrice. Find her and warn her before Cazzian's men seek her out and end her young life and answers die with her."

"I can't. My father, he comes first." Pepper crossed her arms in a gesture of stubborn defiance.

"NO!" That response felt like a slap to Pepper's face; in fact, blood pooled on her cheek. "You are untamed. Reckless. A danger to those around you. Unless and until you calm the mind and control your magic, what happened in the past will repeat. I was lenient once and showed you mercy. Don't test my patience, child! Find Beatrice! Train! Focus! And get your magic and emotions under control! That is an order! Need I remind you, Pepper Li. You started this. Your actions were a catalyst to Armageddon, and so you must end it!" She whipped her head to the side like a rabbit picking up the scent of nearby prey, then whipped it back just as quickly. "We'll meet again when you're ready."

And then Karma was gone. Tomb-like silence pervaded.

"Holy shit!" Kimball so eloquently muttered in response.

"And here I thought nothing would out-trip shrooming." The only time he shut his jaw was when he bit down on a cigarette before lighting it with his quivering hands. After taking a few deep inhales, the smoke tumbling off his lips, Kimball added, "Beatrice. That was the other name on that list, the Agents of Karma list, right under Sawyer's. I think Beatrice is their next target."

Pepper produced the letter written by Jaylyn from inside her satchel. "Chances are that whoever Jaylyn was warning, whoever lives on Peachy-keen Lane in Dillard, Georgia, knows Beatrice or can at least point us in her direction. It's the only clue we've got."

"I agree," Perrin said. "So I say we dock this boat, draw us a chaosgate, use the Georgia address as the destination, and find out the identity of this mysterious ally."

The hell Pepper would put off rescuing her father for a total stranger. "I'm not going anywhere until my father is safe and sound. End of discussion!"

"This is fuh'karing fantastic." Annoyed, Perrin spewed a fusillade of more curse words before schooling her features into an expression of serenity. "Cazzian explicitly stated that you must return to him with your memories intact. And return what you stole from him. So do that, we will."

"About that. I was a toddler at the time, for God's sake. What could I have possibly done to provoke him to wrath? What did I steal, his rattle? Even so, I don't have time to embark on an impossible quest in the name of getting back my memories. Not when my dad's life is hanging in the balance. Besides, my memories are gone. Bhi'gow admitted he didn't remove them. Childhood amnesia, remember? And not even the almighty Cazzian could find them when he violated my mind. So what am I to do, hire a hypnotist?"

"Sweetling"—Perrin swallowed a nasty lump of a biting remark, her patience visibly threadbare—"Cazzian is *not* referring to present-day memories. Dear Lilith, give me strength. He is referring to memories of a past life. He most likely has centuries of built-up, seething hatred for you. Now multiply that by the number of years spent tortured in the Pits, plotting and planning your demise, and now, apparently, Armageddon. I mean, he didn't exactly paint you in the best light. He made it sound like you were a sociopathic wicked mage who kicked babies and skinned puppies alive before eating them.

"That brings me to a point my sister made in the letter that at the time I found odd and still do. She specifically instructed her contact to not approach me and that it would be too risky to give me my magic."

"I'm not sure who would be at risk, you or those around you. An aside, I'm so ready to make you a Lolly'ka on the spot. But back on track. Whatever you did to Cazzian, it happened in another life, and he has not forgotten it and is moving Hell and Earth to exact revenge. As for your sister, who isn't too keen on you reuniting with your magic—Oopsy. Too late for that. So, yeah, we need to find Jaylyn stat. She is the only one who knows what happened between you and Cazzian and how to stop him."

Pepper's jaw set, her mind made up. Her dad was priority number one. Nothing else mattered.

Perrin sighed. "Listen up, Pepper two point oh. Whatever the fuh'kar happened to you, that fireworks spectacle when you burst into flames, you're still a fledgling mage. In your state, what're you gonna do, kill all your enemies, one being an invincible douchemage, with a ball of hellfire? Good luck with that."

Pepper wouldn't budge, her resolve as steely as ever. And crossed her arms over her chest for added emphasis.

"Oh really? Then consider your pops already dead."

That reply got the rise out of Pepper Perrin clearly had wanted, because when Pepper's arms collapsed and her hands balled into fists, Perrin smirked.

"This Beatrice seems to be your saving grace. She can get you ready and trained for whatever Goddess Karma has planned for you; at least, that was my takeaway. Slight problem, Beatrice, one of the last remaining Agents of Karma, is marked for death. So, the first order of business, we visit Jaylyn's mysterious ally, seek her, or his, help in warning this Beatrice. And on the way, we formulate a plan to stop Armageddon. So what say you, Pepper, Loki"—huffing, Perrin rolled her eyes at Kimball—"Twinkle Dick?"

Everyone not-Pepper nodded in agreement.

Perrin shot daggers at Pepper. "I swear to Lilith! Nobody said we're giving up on your dad! Am I speaking in Laramaic or something?"

When Loki shook his head, Perrin took in quite a few measured breaths, then quaffed some Grissel's ale.

"We're already on the losing side of this war, Pepper. Beatrice is a day away at the most from being killed. Let me repeat." Perrin spoke slowly. "We have hours. At the most. Not days. But hours to find Beatrice before Team Evil does. Before Jhi. That's not the case for your father. Larry has more time on his side, from what Kimball said. So, once Beatrice is safe, we'll have another Agent of Karma on our side to help rescue your dad. And we need all the help we can get."

We need all the help ... Pepper harkened back to her sister's letter, specifically when she spoke of a contact in the Ministry and the code phrase: *Only if it's infused with pomegranate.* Why was that so famil—

"That's it! 'Only if it's infused with pomegranate.' I knew I had heard that somewhere but couldn't remember where until now." Pepper relayed the odd exchange she had with Sala'dee, Mephistopheles' assistant. "I bet she's the contact. If I'm right, then we have someone on the inside." A frisson of hope-laced excitement surged within her. "Okay. I'm back in the game. But on one condition. We rescue my father no matter what!"

Perrin and Loki gave Pepper their word, relief shining on their faces.

"Good. We're all in agreement. First order of business. Have Tavi retrieve the memory of when Kimball viewed the Agents of Karma list. We need to be one step ahead of Miles and Jhi."

Pepper focused her attention on Kimball, a devilish grin tugging on the corners of her lips. "The memory retrieval won't hurt a bit, Kimball, I swear."

With that, an army of misfits was born.

Perrin white-knuckled the wheel and pushed the throttle to its breaking point. The hull crashed over the tempestuous waves.

While standing at the stern of the boat, canopied by a starless nightscape, clouds scudding over the engorged moon, wind stabbed at Pepper's cheeks; the pinprick discomfort felt refreshing. This wasn't like a birthday where turning a year older felt no different than the day before. No, she felt alive, awakened, driven, wrathful. So much wrath. And woe to those who harmed her father, for they would pay dearly with their lives.

As for you, Jhi, lesson learned; a fool no more, she thought. *Next time we cross paths, I'll show you no mercy as I give you a kiss from Karma.*

They docked the boat at Tin City marina and made their way to an out-of-sight wall, the briny Naples Bay feet away. When Pepper put the finishing touches on the way-sign—a random address on Peachy-keen Lane in Dillard, Georgiathe chaosgate knob popped into existence. Kimball barreled over the threshold first with the help of Perrin's foot, then Perrin, followed by Loki.

Pepper paused, her hand covering the Cocytus-cold knob, her heart heavy with the knowledge that the chaosgate served as her event horizon, the unknown waiting for her on the other side. There would be no going back. She feared reuniting with memories past, memories that echoed of evil belonging to a version of her she found utterly terrifying. But she had no other choice, saving her dad, the driving force.

Though she could barely cast a spell, didn't know one magic gem from the next, couldn't fight on her own to save her life, she vowed to heed Goddess Karma's advice, to train, to focus, to learn, and the hell she'd let Cazzian win, or Jhi.

She squared her shoulders and took comfort in the fact that wherever the chaosgate led, she wouldn't be alone; Perrin and

Loki would be by her side, as too would her dad: *Remember, Pepper, I'm always with you, heart and soul, so use that certainty as a beacon to banish the darkness and find your way back to me. We are each other's light.*

"Hang on, Pops. I will rescue you, and soon," Pepper said solemnly, right as the door to the chaosgate snicked shut behind her.

THE END OF
Book One in the
AGENTS OF KARMA SERIES

ABOUT THE AUTHOR

Kelly L. Marsh is the author of the award-winning novel *Kill Karma*. Before she started writing fantasy, she earned a B.S. degree in chemistry from the University of Miami in Coral Gables. After that, she embarked on a career in forensics. By day, Kelly is an EFT-Tapping master practitioner. By night, she dives into fantasy worlds of her own creation. She lives in Naples, Florida, with her family, where she was born and raised.

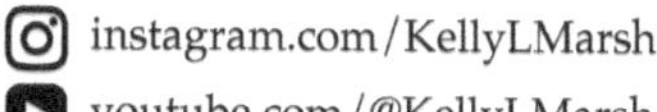
instagram.com/KellyLMarsh
youtube.com/@KellyLMarsh

www.ingramcontent.com/pod-product-compliance
Lightning Source LLC
Chambersburg PA
CBHW030105310726

48970CB00004B/1157